T0058685

THE
PROPHECY CON

By Patrick Weekes

THE
PROPHECY CON

PATRICK WEEKES

47N⬥RTH

This is a work of fiction. Names, characters, organizations, places, events, and incidents are either products of the author's imagination or are used fictitiously.

Text copyright © 2014 Patrick Weekes
All rights reserved.

No part of this book may be reproduced, or stored in a retrieval system, or transmitted in any form or by any means, electronic, mechanical, photocopying, recording, or otherwise, without express written permission of the publisher.

Published by 47North, Seattle

www.apub.com

Amazon, the Amazon logo, and 47North are trademarks of Amazon.com, Inc., or its affiliates.

ISBN-13: 9781477824719
ISBN-10: 1477824715

Cover design by Deron Bennett
Illustrated by Deron Bennett

Library of Congress Control Number: 2014937743

Printed in the United States of America

*This one is for the lads, who are now old enough
to tell me that they'll miss me,
but they hope I "do good writing."*

*Grow up well, guys. Have adventures, make mistakes,
get too smart for all your dad's tricks,
and remember to laugh.*

Table of Contents

The Crew

Loch (Isafesira de Lochenville)
- Former Republic scout captain and crew leader
- Expert in infiltration, exfiltration, target acquisition
- Framed by Archvoyant Silestin, most powerful man in Republic (now deceased)

Kail
- Scout in Loch's unit
- Picks locks, pockets, fights
- Lost free will to soul-binding on last job, was forced to betray rest of crew

Desidora
- Love priestess, capable of reading auras
- Formerly death priestess, once capable of horrific necromantic rituals
- Wields Ghylspwr (see below)

Ghylspwr
- Extremely powerful magical warhammer
- Carries soul of former king of long-lost ancient race
- Vocabulary limited to three phrases, all foreign, often shouted enthusiastically

Tern
- Alchemist and safecracking expert
- Proficient with crossbow and improbable number of trick bolts
- Hooked up with Hessler

Hessler
- Extensive training as wizard, although did not technically graduate from university

- Expert in illusion magic, significantly less expert in anything else
- Hooked up with Tern

Indomitable Courteous "Icy" Fist
- Imperial acrobat, contortionist, and former monk
- Cannot inflict harm upon any living creature due to vow of non-violence
- Dated Loch's sister (until Loch's sister was revealed as assassin trying to kill the crew)

Ululenia
- Unicorn (usually, see below)
- Abilities include shapeshifting, mind reading, and nature magic
- Really likes virgins

Dairy (Rybindaris)
- Simple orphan farm boy later revealed as prophetic savior who defeated Glimmering Folk
- Abilities as Champion of Dawn include strength and resistance to magic
- Virgin

Not Part of the Crew, But They're Okay

Pyvic
- Republic justicar, once tasked with capturing Loch, now dating Loch

Cevirt
- Republic voyant, Loch's godfather, significant political connections

One

Hanging over the Iceford, the river that had cut a pass through the mountains and marked the boundary between the Republic and the Empire, the Temple of Butterflies stretched out to the mountains on either side with great spanning structures that gave the place its name. The walls glittered in the pale morning light with the magical enchantments that protected it from assault.

Loch had last seen the Temple of Butterflies near the end of the war against the Empire. Sent deep into Imperial territory on a mission that had turned out to be a ploy to get her killed, Scout Captain Loch and her team had come through the temple in their desperate run back into the Republic.

Today, she was hoping to *avoid* a war.

"Fun memories, Captain?" Kail asked, standing beside her. The diplomats Loch was guarding were talking with the Imperial guards, and from the looks of things, it was going to take a while.

"The best." Loch grinned at him. "You remember how Uribin threw that guard into a gong?"

"I recall the monks being pissed." Kail frowned. There were monks amidst the Imperial guards, unarmored and dressed in flowing golden robes. "The monks and the guards both look pissed this time. You think we're even getting in?"

"The Imperials agreed to the talks," Loch said, and shrugged. "I don't blame them for being angry. When your unfriendly neighbor shows that they can blast lightning down from the sky, that's bound to raise concerns."

The fact that Loch had been indirectly responsible for that was definitely coloring her current situation. In order to clear her name and take down the man who'd framed her for desertion, she had disbanded her team of scouts, formed a team of thieves, and raided Heaven's Spire, the magically floating capital city of the Republic. In the process, her team had discovered (and accidentally triggered) a new weapon that had reduced several acres of grassland below to smoking craters.

For Loch, it had been just one more problem to deal with later, above mind-controlled guardsmen and below inconvenient prophecies. As it turned out, however, the Empire took it personally.

Archvoyant Silestin, the madman who'd killed Loch's family, had wanted to start another war between the Republic and the Empire.

There was a good chance he'd succeed posthumously.

The Republic diplomats had flown by airship to the Republic side of the border, then landed and hiked a quarter-mile alongside the Iceford to reach the Temple of Butterflies. They waited now at the base of a great stone stairway set with the same defensive enchantments that protected the temple itself. The glittering stairway, like its twin on the far side of the river, had been cut into the mountainside, leading from the foothills up to the temple, and together, they looked like looping tails hanging from the butterfly's wings.

"This wouldn't be a problem if the Imperials had their own floating city," Kail said.

Loch glanced over at him. "You don't think."

"We could threaten to blast their towns, and they could threaten to blast ours. Nobody would end up doing it." Kail squinted. "Either that, or we'd wipe a whole lot of little towns off the map."

"You know what's great about having you along on these missions, Kail? The optimism."

Kail sighed and gestured at the Temple of Butterflies. "It's a very *pretty* temple. How's that?"

"Insincere, but better."

"Didn't really have time to notice last time, since we were fighting our way through it." Kail squinted. "Always looked more like a fortress than a temple to me, though."

Loch nodded. "The Imperials always go with the gentler name."

Ambassador Threvein—one of the Republic diplomats—waved at her, and Loch came over, Kail a few steps behind. "We've been granted access," Threvein said, his smile giving away his relief. "You'll leave your weapons with the guards here, and we'll climb up into the temple proper."

Loch glanced at the Imperial guards who blocked the stairs. Their golden armor gleamed in the morning sun, and ribbons of red hung just behind the heads of their halberds. "Understood." She nodded to Kail, unfastened her sword belt, and handed it to the guards.

The diplomats themselves had no weapons, but Kail followed Loch's lead, as did the other guards, although not without a few glares at the Imperials.

While the other guards wore heavy armor and carried heavy swords, Loch and Kail wore riding leathers reinforced with thin strips of metal. Loch was attached to the security detail as a consultant from the justicars . . . and Kail was attached as an old friend who Loch trusted at her back.

"Should be fun defending the diplomats with no gear," Kail said, smiling at the Imperials and speaking in a low voice, his lips barely moving.

"Still loving your optimism. Hopefully won't come to that," Loch replied through a smile, her lips unmoving as well.

"No daggers, no boot blades," the Republic's guard captain said, grimacing at them. He was an Urujar like Loch and Kail, though his skin had the same light tint as Loch's, suggesting mixed-race parents. "Diplomats made it clear, and I've been ordered to pass that on to you. *Eurku.*"

"Don't worry about it." Loch drew a dagger from a sheath at her hip and added it to the pile.

Kail drew a knife from each boot, a dagger from inside his leather coat, and a throwing knife from a wrist-sheath under his sleeve. The guard captain, more experienced than Loch had given him credit for, stood and waited patiently, and Kail eventually sighed and unspooled a length of wire from his belt.

"You brought a garrote." Loch blinked.

Kail shrugged. "*Yvkefer* alloy wire. Perfect for daemons and wizards."

"On a diplomatic mission," Loch added, emphasizing the words a little more than necessary.

"All the more reason for swift, decisive action if a daemon or wizard shows up." He dropped the garrote on the pile of weaponry in front of the Imperial guards. "So do I get a receipt for this, or . . . ?"

"Come, now." Threvein said, gesturing impatiently. "The Imperial diplomats are waiting in the temple."

Kail glared at the Imperial guard nearest him. "If *any* of this goes missing, I'm going to be *very* disappointed."

The guard tensed, until his superior made a curt gesture. Kail grinned at both of them.

They made their way up the stairs, led by one of the monks, while the Imperial guards stayed below. Ambassador Threvein and the diplomats led the way, with the guards close behind. Loch and Kail brought up the rear. The stairs were just wide enough for two people to walk side by side, and there was no handrail on either side. On their right, the mountain stone was cool and shadowed. On their left was a straight drop into the Iceford below.

"No wonder the Republic never took this place." Kail glanced down at the Iceford and stepped a bit further to the right. "Not that it's a fortress, mind you."

"Of course not," Loch said with an innocent look. "Who'd name a fortress after a butterfly?" She squinted and lowered her voice. "See the red crystals set into the roof?"

"Yeah, I noticed. Defense against airships, I figure. What do you think, fire magic? I mean, they're red."

"Safe guess."

At the top of the stairs, a massive iron gate swung open ahead of them. It was flanked by more Imperial guards, who stared ahead unblinkingly as the diplomatic group walked through the gate and into the temple courtyard.

The courtyard was large enough to field a small army. It was immaculately maintained, with marble flagstones inset with tiny squares of jade. Pipes pumped water from the Iceford far below their feet through decorative fountains and canals. All across the courtyard, monks in golden robes trained, some moving through forms while others sparred in small fields of golden sand. Bushes with vivid green leaves sprouted from vases along the walls, and snowy white doves sat in their branches or drank from the fountains. Great golden banners emblazoned with the twin blades of the Empire hung from the walls.

It was impressive, but then, Loch figured, that had been the point. The sand showed only a few footprints, not the countless marks that would have been there had anyone been doing actual training, and none of the monks nearest the group were sweating. Kail noticed as well and shot Loch an amused look.

Ambassador Threvein was speaking with a monk whose robes were decorated with crimson at the sleeves. Threvein looked nervous as he turned to speak briefly to the guard captain.

The guard captain glared first at the ambassador, then at the monk, and finally turned to Loch and Kail. "The Imperial diplomats are up inside," he said, jerking his chin up shining marble stairs to a tall, high-peaked central building that overlooked the courtyard like third mountain. "They say that our heavy armor would be disrespectful of the sanctity of the temple."

"Their temple with flamecannons on the walls."

The guard captain grimaced. "They're *apparently* 'sun-blossoms,' to ward off natural predators."

"See?" Loch said to Kail. "Gentler name."

"Anyway," the guard captain said, "I offered to strip down, but they made it clear. Only you two and the diplomats go up."

Loch looked at the Imperial guards in their massive golden armor. "Of course."

"This whole thing stinks," the guard captain said in a voice that just reached them. *"Ynkular ku'veth."*

"Watch your own," Kail shot back with a little smile, then straightened his shoulders and looked over at Loch. "It's never boring with you, Captain."

Threvein smiled. He had an ambassador's stoic calm hiding whatever he was actually feeling, but unlike the Imperial monks training in the courtyard, he *was* sweating. "I should have known. Ah, well, it was just a formality, anyway. If you'll be so kind." He nodded to the monk with the crimson-slashed robes, and the monk bowed briefly, then turned and crossed the courtyard. The diplomats followed, along with Loch and Kail.

She felt the eyes of everyone in the courtyard on them as they walked. The monks with more training glanced from the corner of their eyes. The newer students looked over and then jerked their heads away guiltily. "You give up every weapon you had, Kail?"

"Yep. Worried they might have wards to detect anything I kept."

"Oh, probably."

"You?" They started up the stairs. Aside from the whipping and flapping of golden robes and the rushing of piped-in river water, their boots on the steps were the only sound in the courtyard.

"Same." She took a deep breath in through her nose. "I was counting people. You get an exit?"

"Sand pit on our right." Kail didn't look over, still smiling absently as he followed the diplomats. "I'd say eight steps down before you jump."

"Noted. Fifty monks, another twenty guards with halberds."

"Wonderful." They reached the top of the stairs, just behind Threvein and the other diplomats, and walked through a doorway flanked by more guards.

The room inside was decorated lavishly. Painted fans hung on the wall next to jeweled masks, and a low table stained glossy black was set with golden bowls and crystal glasses. Vases inlaid with precious stones lined the walls, and a great butterfly decorated the face of the gong that, several years ago, Uribin had thrown a guard through during Loch's escape from Imperial territory.

"There's the gong!" Kail whispered. Loch elbowed him.

The diplomats followed the monk with the crimson-slashed robes across the room and through a door. Kail and Loch followed, but the door slammed shut before they could enter. Behind them, the door through which they'd entered did the same.

"Uh-huh." Kail rolled out his shoulders. "Guess they heard about the gong."

"Yes, I'm sure that's what happened. No diplomatic incidents." Loch stepped to the door and knocked politely. "Nothing that says we caused this. If we can get to Threvein before anything happens, we've still got a chance."

A door on the side wall slid open, and an Imperial woman strode in with a pair of guards beside her. She wore a flowing silk dress of lavender and rich violet. It matched the style Loch had seen in Imperial nobles during her time behind enemy lines, large and loose enough to hide the woman's hands in her sleeves. The woman's face was classically Imperial, fine featured and devoid of makeup. Her hair was braided in intricate coils that slid down in front of her shoulders, one braid on each side, and a glittering chain of gold filigree rode upon her brow, set with a blood-red ruby in the center.

The sword at the woman's waist was a heavy broadsword with a dragon's head on the hilt, from whose mouth a red scarf dangled like either a limp tongue or a surprisingly droopy gout of fire. The sword had a single curved edge. The back of the blade was lined with metal rings that clinked with each step the woman took, and it was tucked into a sash at her waist rather than sheathed.

"Isafesira de Lochenville?" the woman said politely.

Loch noted the name, her full name, and saw Kail tense ever so slightly in the corner of her vision.

"That's me," she said. "Why have we been separated from Ambassador Threvein?"

"You have threatened the peace between the Empire and the Republic by transforming the city of Heaven's Spire into a weapon," the woman said, her voice cold and calm.

Loch smiled, shut her eyes, and let out a long breath through her nose. Sometimes it was simply a relief to for the trap to finally spring. "As a member of a diplomatic mission, I cannot legally be detained," she said without looking up.

"Hey, how come those guys get to wear armor?" Kail asked. "I thought this place had sanctity or something."

The woman ignored him. "Isafesira, if you surrender—"

"Wait, were you just trying to get us to take everything off?" Kail asked, winking at one of the guards and moving to force eye contact in return. "Man, your mother is so much more polite about it."

Everyone looked at him this time, even the woman.

Everyone but Loch.

She lunged forward, slammed one arm into a guard's halberd and the other into the inside of his elbow, bashing him in the helmet with his own weapon. As the other guard turned toward her, Kail kicked him in the back of the knee, and

Loch wrenched the halberd from the first guard's grasp and swung it at the woman.

To her credit, the Imperial woman had recovered quickly from Kail's distraction and Loch's attack and stepped to the side. The halberd's blade chopped into the doorframe instead.

Loch pressed forward, and the Imperial woman's confident smirk was cut off as Loch pinned her to the wall with the haft of the weapon.

"You're making a mistake, Isafesira," she said.

She probably would have said more had Loch not headbutted the woman in the face. "Call me Loch." She let go of her halberd, yanked the broadsword free from the sash at the Imperial woman's waist, and jumped back as the woman lashed out with a blind kick.

The guard she'd hit in the helmet was still on his feet, but stumbling. The other guard was grappling with Kail, both of them clutching at the guard's halberd.

Loch swung her new sword two-handed. The rings on the back of the blade rattled and threw the balance of the blade off a bit, but it was a solid weapon nevertheless. It chopped through the shaft of the halberd of the guard grappling with Kail.

Kail twisted the half without the head free and cracked it across the guard's face. "So you get a new sword, and I get a stick?"

"I don't decide these things, Kail."

As Kail's guard fell, the Imperial woman swept up the other half of the halberd and swung it at Loch like an ax. Loch parried, saw *her* guard drawing a short blade, spun, grabbed a vase from the wall with her free hand, and smashed it over the guard's head. He stumbled, shards spraying out everywhere from his helmet, and Loch punched through his open-faced visor and put him down hard.

The door through which they'd come into the room opened, and the guards who'd been by the door charged in. They had already tossed aside their halberds and were drawing short blades, better weapons considering the confines of the room. "See, Kail, they have swords. Take one of theirs." Loch stepped back as the Imperial woman swung the half-halberd again. Despite the ungainly weapon, she swung it like she knew how to use it. She was also still on her feet despite Loch head-butting her in the face, which was a bit worrisome.

"Those are just swords." Kail knocked aside a slash, grabbed a fan from the wall with his free hand, and side-stepped a thrust. "Yours has rings on it."

Loch slashed high at the Imperial woman, who blocked and spun into a fluid kick that caught Loch in the gut. Loch stumbled back, caught herself, and parried as the Imperial woman came down with an overhand strike. It chopped the very nice stained table in half instead of Loch, sending golden bowls and crystal glasses flying.

"Still not sure what the rings do," Loch said, kicking half the table at one of the two guards going after Kail. It caught the guard in the shins and he stumbled, then went down when Kail caught him under the chin with his stick.

Kail slashed wildly with his fan, doing no damage whatsoever but making it really hard for anyone to hit him. "Well, ask the crazy woman, Captain. She's right there."

"The punishment for touching the Nine-Ringed Dragon is death," the Imperial woman growled. She stabbed with the halberd's spearpoint, and Loch parried. By luck, the spearpoint caught in the rings on the back of the blade, and Loch twisted the grip and tore the halberd from the woman's hands.

"Wait, hang on, I'm getting it." Loch spun the blade to shake the halberd free, and the Imperial woman glared and raised her hands into a fighting position. Her fingers curled into claws, and lightning crackled between them.

Loch stepped back and lowered the blade until the point touched the floor. "Okay, that's new."

"They told me you would be difficult to apprehend, Isafesira," said the Imperial woman. "They were not mistaken."

"Thanks." Loch snapped the blade up, hooking the point on a fancy crystal wineglass and snapping it at the Imperial woman's face. She fell back as it shattered, the lightning around her fingers dying, and Loch stepped past her, kicked her in the back of the knee, and slammed an elbow down into the back of the woman's head to put her on the ground.

The last guard stabbed at Kail, who caught the blade in his fan and twisted, pulling the sword from the guard's grip. As the guard fumbled, Kail dropped both the fan *and* the stick, grabbed the guard, and pivoted, slamming the guard face-first into the gong with a booming crash that sent vibrations through Loch's gut.

"Uribin would be proud, Kail."

Kail grinned. "So what now? Run, or go for the diplomats?"

The Imperials had called her by name. This wasn't about the diplomats anymore. "We run," Loch said. "If we stay and fight, we might cause an incident."

Kail looked at the shredded fan, shattered crystal wineglass, smashed table, and cracked vase on the ground beside four Imperial guards and what was likely an Imperial noblewoman. "Yeah, we wouldn't want that," he said, picking up his stick.

The scene in the courtyard below as they came outside was far different from the training display earlier. The Imperial guards stood in a ring around the unarmed Republic soldiers with their halberds leveled. Most of the fifty monks were coming up the stairs, the ones at the front holding manacles. Loch took this all in as she jogged toward the stairs. "See you at the bottom?"

"Right behind you."

Loch leaped from the stairs, slashed through the top of the golden banner, and grabbed hold as it tore. She rode the tearing fabric down, landed in the sand under a pile of golden fabric, and cut free with wild swings of the blade that deflected the incoming halberds' blows.

When she felt marble rather than sand beneath her feet, Loch looked back and saw that a good number of the Imperial guards were flailing about under the torn banner. A few yards away, Kail was crawling free from a pile of monks at the foot of the stairs. "Threw yourself down the stairs?" she asked.

"They were kicking and stuff. I thought the monks took a vow of non-violence." He pulled himself up and grimaced. "*Our* Imperial monk took a vow of non-violence."

"Well, you can ask Icy next time you see . . ." Loch turned at the clash of metal. The Republic soldiers had seized upon the distraction and were grappling with the Imperials, slashing and stabbing with stolen halberds. "Go!" the Urujar guard captain shouted. "They're after you! Get out of here!"

Loch hesitated for one long, ugly moment. If she went to help the Republic soldiers, they would likely all die fighting there in the courtyard. If she ran, they'd surrender and live, and Loch would go to sleep every night knowing that Republic soldiers were prisoners of the Empire because she'd run away. Prisoners, or dead.

She ran away.

The iron gate at the far end of the courtyard led to the mountain steps on the far side of the Iceford. It was closed, of course, and monks ran to block their path, settling into fighting stances before them.

All except for one of the monks, who walked to the door, set his feet, raised his hands, and then brought his body to the iron gate with a movement that, while not precisely swift, had the full weight and power of his body focused into the palms of his hands.

With a reverberating shriek, the iron gate blasted off its hinges and crashed to the ground. Snowy white doves took to the skies in a flurry of feathers.

"Icy!" Kail shouted, plowing through the monks, who were now turning in surprise. "All these assholes can fight! Why can't *you* fight?"

Indomitable Courteous "Icy" Fist, former member of Loch's gang of thieves, smiled. "It is good to see you. I have devised an exit strategy."

Loch knocked the monks aside, slamming an elbow into the head of one who had recovered enough to try to stop her. "Let's use it, then!"

"Seriously, Icy," Kail said as they ran through the gate. "You made it sound like everyone who had your training took a vow, but the rest of these guys can . . . ah, crap."

A dozen guards were coming up the stairs toward them, headed by a massive, broad-shouldered man whose golden armor bore the Imperial twin swords across the breastplate. A dragon-faced helmet hid his face, and a flowing violet cape flapped in the morning wind. He held a silver-handled war ax whose double-bladed head was golden and etched with runes.

"It's funny," Kail said beside Loch, "from a distance, that ax almost looks like Ghylspwr, which would mean that it was magical, which would be *bad*. Good thing magical weapons like that are—"

"*Kutesosh gajair'is!*" shouted the ax. The man wielding the ax put it through a spin.

"—rare," Kail finished. "And here I seem to have misplaced my stick. Least you've got the Undinged Dragon."

"The Nine-Ringed Dragon?" Icy glanced at Loch's sword.

"Oh," said Kail. "Because of the rings. That probably makes more sense."

Icy had gone pale. "That blade is traditionally carried by the heir to the throne."

"Pretty woman, braids, can summon lightning in her hands?" Loch asked.

"Princess Veiled Lightning," Icy said, and shook his head. "And you have stolen her sword."

"And that's another thing, Icy," Kail said. "If this woman can do lightning, you really should be able to freeze things with your hands, just based on name alone."

Icy continued as if Kail hadn't interrupted him. "She is unlikely to forgive that, Loch. The man down there is her sworn protector, Gentle Thunder."

Loch looked at the man with the ax, and then at the sword in her hands. To their right, the mountainside caught the first morning light. To their left, down below, the frigid white waters of the Iceford were a steady roar.

"If he wanted to protect her, he should have been up there while I was hitting her in the face," she said, and rolled out her shoulders. Raising her voice, she called down, "Gentle Thunder?"

"My orders were to take you alive," he called back in a rough voice. "I will accept the punishment for killing you instead."

"*Kutesosh gajair'is!*" the ax added.

"Think we can take them?" Kail asked.

"A dozen guards, plus a guy with an ax as powerful as Ghylspwr?" Loch shook her head.

One of the doves from the courtyard winged past them, down toward the frothy white water of the Iceford.

"How far would you say that fall is?" she asked.

"That is a *terrible* question, Captain," Kail said.

"Slightly more than one sixty feet," Icy said, glancing off the edge of the steps down at the rushing river below. "It is also very cold."

Kail snorted. "You think, Icy? Loch, *no*."

"Any chance we could just withdraw peacefully?" Loch called down to Gentle Thunder, ignoring Kail.

"You have turned Heaven's Spire into a weapon and threatened the peace between our two nations," Thunder called back.

"That's what Veiled Lightning said," Loch said, "right before I head-butted her in the face." She looked over at Kail and Icy. "Feet first," she said, and jumped.

She heard Gentle Thunder's roar of outrage, Kail's shout of general terror, and under it all, the roaring of the Iceford itself.

Then she hit, feet first, and the shock and darkness and cold stole her breath. She kicked hard, flailing blindly, and for a moment felt nothing but pain and cold. Her arm banged on a rock painfully, and she realized she was either lying flat or facing down, and she pushed herself up as water went up her nose.

An eternity later, she finally cleared the surface, gasping and coughing above the foaming white water. The mountains on either side of the river were great black walls, with the sky a stream of blue-gold between them.

The numbing cold was already stealing the strength from her arms. She'd managed to keep hold of the Nine-Ringed

Dragon, and used it like an oar to turn herself around as best she could in the rushing water. "Kail? Icy?"

They rose from the water a moment later. Kail was coughing and sputtering, and Icy was holding him by the coat, looking slightly chilled but otherwise fine. Both of them were riding upon the back of an enormous snowy-white sea turtle with a shining white horn glowing upon its brow.

As the swan diving for her morning repast, so have I recovered what was so carelessly dropped, Little One, came the gentle voice in Loch's mind.

"Ululenia," Kail said, and then coughed some more. "So glad you're here."

Loch took the hand Icy offered and pulled herself onto the back of the shapeshifting, mind-reading unicorn that, like Icy, had been part of her team of thieves. There was enough room for all three of them to cling to the turtle's back with only their legs dangling in the water. "Wasn't sure you'd made it in until I saw you fly down to the river." Her teeth were chattering, and she stretched her already-numb fingers.

The Temple of the Butterflies contained wards that circled like bees around the flowers. If I had contacted you, I might have been detected, Ululenia said.

"Figured it was something like that." Loch nodded. "Well, I appreciate both you and Icy making time to back me up here, even with the team disbanded."

"I'm here, too," Kail said, finishing up one last cough.

"You're my assistant, Kail. You get paid."

"Not enough. That hurt a *lot*." Kail looked at Icy Fist suspiciously. "Icy, you look fine. Why do you look fine?"

"You are in pain because your body was tense striking the surface of the water. I was able to relax my body."

"Oh, fine, I'll just not be so *tense* next time I jump off a cliff." Kail glared. "Are you even cold?"

"Extremely," Icy said. "I am simply not whining about it."

Loch looked back up the mountains. The Temple of the Butterflies was already far behind them, and the figures on the stairs were barely visible. There was no way they'd be caught now.

"I was worried the diplomatic meeting might go badly." Loch stopped her teeth from chattering with an effort. "I had no idea it would be like this."

"Why in Byn-kodar's hell would they think *you* turned Heaven's Spire into a weapon, Captain?" Kail asked.

"I'm not sure yet." Loch pulled herself up higher on Ululenia's shell. "But I intend to find out."

"As long as you find out back in the Republic," Kail said. "There's the border garrison." Loch turned and looked ahead and spotted the small fort that marked the divide between the Republic and the Empire. Their airship was still tied up in the docking field.

There were guards out by the river, and they had clearly spotted the group. More soldiers came outside as the river brought them closer.

"Hey," Kail called as they drew near. "Remember us? With the diplomats?"

Apparently they did. The soldiers threw ropes, which Icy and Loch caught. Ululenia flexed gently and brought them to the riverbank, and helping hands pulled them ashore.

Still kneeling, Loch scanned the soldiers until she found the garrison commander. "The Imperials set a trap. Everyone else is captured. We need to send word up to Heaven's Spire."

"We know," said the garrison commander. "We'll get them back."

Loch pushed herself to her feet and tried to shake off the hands that were steadying her. "I'm not sure what they want, but . . ." She stopped, looked up at the garrison commander. "What do you mean, *you know?*"

"They want you, Justicar Loch," said the garrison commander, and the hands steadying her went tight on her arms and shoulders, "and they're going to get you. I am hereby placing you under arrest pending extradition to the Empire."

Two

ATTENDANT SHENZIENCIS DONNED HER ARMOR AND FOUND THE princess in the dining hall, which had been converted into a place for the healers to work.

Princess Veiled Lightning sat on a bench, glaring as an unfortunate young man bandaged a cut above her left eye. Her nose was swollen, and she sat stiffly with an icepack bound to the base of her neck. Her guardian, Gentle Thunder, stood at her side, hands resting on his great ax.

The princess stood as Shenziencis approached and gave a formal bow. "Attendant, I humbly apologize."

Internally, Shenziencis smiled, but she knew that the princess had to be handled carefully. Nobles rarely took well to being reminded that she had predicted exactly what had happened. "Isafesira de Lochenville is a dangerous criminal," she said instead. "You took all appropriate precautions to capture her."

"It was not enough." The princess waved the healer away. "All the soldiers, all your monks, and she still vandalizes the temple, injures dozens, and escapes unscathed."

"She also defeated you and stole the Nine-Ringed Dragon," Gentle Thunder said. His deep voice was softer than Shenziencis expected, as though he was afraid he would break something if he spoke too harshly. His impertinence was also surprising, although he had protected her since childhood and taught her to fight, so perhaps he had gained the right to address her so in private.

"Yes, I recall that," the princess said, glaring at her guardian.

"Good," he said in the same calm tone, unperturbed by her anger. "If you did not, I would have the healers examine your head, Veil."

Princess Veiled Lightning sat again and folded her arms, her hands disappearing into the voluminous sleeves of her rich violet dress. Shenziencis looked at her. She was close, very close, but still required a push.

"The Nine-Ringed Dragon is but an object," Shenziencis said, picking her words carefully. "Like the Butterfly Gong or one of the vases the Republic woman smashed. The loss of such things may damage our pride, Your Highness, but only if we allow it."

The princess shot her a dirty look, and Shenziencis made sure her smile stayed inside as the princess spoke. "Isafesira de Lochenville is the Empire's only hope of avoiding war with the Republic. If she goes free, thousands will die."

"What are you saying, Veil?" Gentle Thunder asked.

Princess Veiled Lightning raised her hand, and energy crackled between her curled fingers. "We must go after her."

Shenziencis heard the righteous anger in the princess's voice, and the hurt pride under it, just as she had hoped. She did smile now, and bowed low. "Your Highness, I would be honored to assist."

Loch did not resist as a Republic soldier stripped her sword away. Another came forward with the manacles.

"This was supposed to be a nice clean handover," the garrison commander said, sighing. "Ambassador Threvein said he had it handled with the Empire."

"Why, though?" Loch asked.

The garrison commander shook his head. "Sorry, ma'am. That's above my pay grade."

Loch nodded. "No hard feelings."

"Arrogant apple, babbling brook, creeping cat?" the soldier holding her asked, and then tipped over bonelessly.

"It's about time," Kail muttered as he punched one soldier, ducked away from an attempt to tackle him, and took down a second with an uppercut.

"Dawdling duckling, excellent eggshells," added the soldier holding Loch's sword. She took it back from him as he toppled over as well.

"Mind-magic!" the garrison commander barked. "Warding charms, now!"

One of the soldiers drew his blade, and Loch stepped in and spun her sword near his face. The blade's rings rattled, and the red scarf flapped across his field of vision, blinding him long enough for Loch to chop down hard on his swordhand. He stumbled back, said, "Fondling fern," and fell over.

Ululenia had shifted into what Loch thought of as her normal form—a slight, pale woman with ash-blond hair and a shining rainbow horn upon her brow. She stared at a soldier rushing toward her, and her horn flared. "Gullible goat," he said, passing out at her feet.

"Still going with the same mind-muddle trick?" Kail asked, elbowing a soldier in the face.

"How many times did you suggest that you gently embraced the mothers of the Imperial soldiers?" Ululenia asked, shifting into a snow white dove as another soldier lunged at her.

"Just . . . one?" Kail said, grabbing a sword from a fallen soldier and parrying another attack. "Although technically, I think I insulted the princess's mother."

"That would be the empress, Kail." Loch advanced on the garrison commander, blade ready. "Nobody has died yet," she said to him. "Let us walk out of here."

"Not going to happen." Around the commander's neck, just above the line of his ringmail, a pale green crystal glittered on a chain. "Your fairy friend can't get all my men, and my orders are clear."

"Again, no hard feelings," Loch said, and brandished her sword, putting it through an impressive spin. The garrison commander was so busy looking at it that he didn't notice Icy approaching until he somersaulted between them, rose to his feet, snapped the crystal charm from the chain around the commander's neck, and rolled away as the garrison commander slashed down at him. "Ululenia?" she said.

"No matter where you run, you'll never escape," the commander said as Ululenia's horn flared. "The Republic will . . . humming honeysuckle." With a final glare, he dropped to his knees and then collapsed completely.

"Thank you, Icy." Loch looked at the garrison. More soldiers were already running their way.

Icy held the crystal charm up and crushed it with a snap of his fingers. "I judged that you did not wish to kill any Republic soldiers."

"You judged correctly. Kail, how have those piloting lessons been going?"

"Let's find out, Captain." Kail was already jogging toward the airship tethered in the docking field.

The airship's great balloon was still inflated, since it would have been prohibitively expensive to dismiss the wind-daemon inside only to summon it again later. Under the balloon, the main body of the ship was a wooden teardrop, flat on the bottom so that it rested gently on the ground. It had four sailwings for steering, and a lower deck with bunks and a small cargo hold.

Because it had been used for flights close to Imperial territory, it also carried a single flamecannon on its bow, mounted on a heavy platform that could be adjusted to fire either ahead or at the ground below.

Kail hopped up, found the main control panel near the back of the airship, and began pressing buttons and pushing levers with confidence. "Just be a minute."

"Consider haste," Icy said, vaulting over the side and onto the main deck.

"Fleet as the deer," Ululenia added as she climbed up as well. "The soldiers number many, and coaxing even one mind to befuddlement is an effort."

"Fine, fine. Anybody else want to bother me while I'm flying an airship without an instructor for the first time?" Kail pulled a few levers, and without looking up got Loch's attention. "Hey, so I knew about Icy, but Ululenia caught me by surprise."

"Last-minute addition," Loch said, chopping through the mooring tether with a clean slash of her blade. She pulled herself up onto the airship's main deck as it rocked and began to rise.

"We got any more hiding around here, waiting to come help? What about Dairy?" Kail glanced over at Ululenia. "I thought he'd be with you."

"I do not wish to discuss it," Ululenia said, and looked down at the approaching soldiers. Her horn flared, and the grass around their boots twisted and twined. The few in front fell over, and the second rank tripped over them.

"Wait, is this because you only like virgins?" Kail asked, adjusting a dial and pressing more buttons. "You didn't leave Dairy after you—"

"I do *not* wish to *discuss* it," Ululenia said, shooting Kail a glare. "Perchance fly the ship?"

"Fine, fine. I'm just saying . . ." Kail caught Ululenia's look. "Nothing. I'm just saying nothing. And flying the ship. Perchancishly."

The sailwings flexed, and as the wind-daemon inside the balloon strained against its cage, the airship rose up into the sky. One of the soldiers fired a bolt that bounced uselessly off the magically protected balloon, and then they were out of range, shouting in frustration as Loch looked down at them from the sky.

"Steering, steering . . ."—Kail pulled a lever, and the airship rocked—". . . is clearly something other than *that*. Oh, here we go." He pulled another lever, and the airship evened out, then turned slowly in place as it continued to rise. "Destination, Captain?"

"Heaven's Spire," Loch said, spinning her sword absently. The rings rattled with the movement. Maybe that was what the damned things were for—to sound pretty. Just like the scarf on the hilt—if it wasn't there to wipe up blood or distract people—was apparently supposed to look good.

"You will uncover the truth," Icy said beside her.

"The Empire doesn't have access to as much raw iron as the Republic, right?" She held the sword up. "Maybe the rings are for blocking. They get dinged up, you replace them instead of having to forge a whole new sword."

Icy smiled. "Sadly, my training was only with my body, or I would know more about the intricacies of the ringed broadsword. The Nine-Ringed Dragon is far superior to the cavalry saber you once owned, however."

"Actually, I stole that one, too."

"Ah." Icy blinked. "Have you considered purchasing a weapon legitimately?"

"Someone I'm fighting usually has one I like." Loch grinned, then sighed, looking back up the Iceford to where the Temple of Butterflies sat nestled between the mountains. "Seems like I run into bad luck every time I fight my way through that temple."

"You were here before, when Silestin sent you behind Imperial lines."

"Yeah. Me, Kail, Uribin . . . you remember Uribin? He owns the restaurant we met up at last time?"

Kail looked over. "He made that incredibly good catfish the captain and I ate while you had a plate of steamed vegetables."

"The vegetables were also very good," Icy said politely. "And Jyelle? Was she here as well?"

"Nah," Kail said while Loch ducked her head. "Captain had already kicked her out of the unit for going after Imperial civilians. Jyelle made it back into the Republic on her own."

"She brought a grudge," Icy said, which was putting it mildly, given that Jyelle had kept trying to kill Loch right up to the point when a wind-daemon had eaten her. "And given what occurred at the Temple of Butterflies, it would seem she is not the only one who wishes you ill."

"Loch tends to be memorable," Kail said.

Loch glanced over. "Speaking of memory, is there any chance you might actually apply those piloting lessons you've been taking before all the guards wake up?"

With Kail's sometimes-lurching steering, the airship soared toward Heaven's Spire and, hopefully, Loch's answers.

Pesyr Plaza was an open-air shopping and dining center in the business district of Heaven's Spire. Named for the god of craftsman and artificiers, the plaza was located near many of the buildings where lapitects and wizards kept Heaven's Spire floating properly over the Republic. Around the edges of the plaza, restaurants served professionals taking long lunches, kahva-houses kept the mages awake after a long night of study, and shops sold the latest magical trinkets to people with too much disposable income.

In the middle of the plaza, a great statue of Pesyr himself stood in the middle of a fountain, his hammer striking the anvil with which he had forged all the wonders of the world. Glowing red crystals sprayed from the anvil every few seconds, as though Pesyr was striking sparks.

Tern, a mousey young woman wearing thick spectacles and the lavender robes of a lapitect, paused by the fountain, dipped her hand into the water and fished out one of the crystals. It glowed in her palm like a burning coal, but felt no warmer than any stone she might pluck from the dirt.

"Salt crystal with a colored light charm," Hessler said. He was a tall, thin man in black wizard's robes fringed with silver. "It would have been significantly less expensive to create illusionary sparks, but because long-lasting illusions are difficult to maintain, most artificers are prejudiced against using them."

"Mm-hmm," said Tern, as the crystal slowly dissolved in her hand.

"In fact, look at the scaling on the inside of the fountain from taking in that much salt. I don't imagine the civil engineers enjoy filtering all that salt, and if this gets into the drinking water . . ."

"Mm-hmm." Tern tossed what was left of the crystal back into the water, where it winked out and disappeared.

"You have to imagine that in a plaza where the people who keep this entire city aloft work, someone could come up with a design that . . . you wanted a gift, didn't you?"

"It's fine," said Tern.

"I asked," Hessler said. "I asked if we should do gifts to mark seeing each other for three months, and you said no."

"I said not to worry about it unless you thought of something," Tern corrected.

"Okay, but by implication, then, unless there was something that you really wanted, I wasn't supposed to worry, and since you haven't talked about really wanting anything, I had assumed we weren't doing gifts."

"It's *fine*," said Tern through gritted teeth. "Let's just get lunch."

"I think we need to discuss this logically," Hessler said, doing that little squint he did while trying to make a point. Tern usually found it cute. *Usually.* "In a relationship between equals, I think that if you actually expect a gift, it's fair to state that instead of passive-aggressively leaving it as something where—"

"Can we not talk about this?" Tern asked. She fished into her robes and dug out a small cluster of multicolored crystals linked through a lattice of silver wire. "Here, I got this for you, because I *listen* to you and *care* about things that interest you, and I thought an attunable thaumaturgic capacitor might be something you'd have *fun* with." She shoved it ungraciously into his hand.

Or rather, through his hand.

Hessler blinked as Tern's hand passed through his body. Tern waved her hand back and forth, and Hessler flickered and vanished.

"I suspected that given how much you like physical contact during our walks," came a voice from behind Tern, "it wouldn't last long."

Tern spun, and there was Hessler, presumably the real one and not an illusion.

He was holding a bouquet of red roses.

"They're live-cut by elven gardeners," he said, "so they can be potted instead of drying out and dying. It doesn't really matter, since roses don't produce anything useful, like fruit, but the woman at the shop said that getting you something like a pumpkin would send the wrong—"

"Hessler, shut up and kiss me."

He shut up and kissed her. He was solid this time.

"Now," he said, smiling, "what do you want for lunch?"

"Pasta?" Tern asked.

"Pasta it is." Hessler took her arm. "And if I could see the thaumaturgic capacitor, that would be . . . Oh, yes, this is just what I . . . is this the model with ablative memory shielding, or is . . . no, this is lovely."

Tern let him talk. As they headed for the pasta place, she saw a crowd gathered at the edge of the plaza. They were looking at a small boxed stage, where puppets danced and capered against a black velvet backdrop. "Isn't it early for the puppeteers to be out?" Tern asked, reasonably certain that Hessler was fussing with his new toy instead of listening to her. As they got closer to the stage, she could hear what the puppets were saying.

". . . Not sure why defensive measures on Heaven's Spire are any business of the Empire's," the manticore puppet was shouting as it chased the griffon around the stage.

"Heaven's Spire caused a great deal of damage with that accidental magical blast," the griffon called back, trying to pounce on the manticore, "and if the Republic were to turn that into a weapon . . . well, you wouldn't want your next-door neighbor to walk around with a drawn sword all the time, would you?"

"I'd love it!" The manticore was now being shaken by the tail. "Makes both our houses safer! I wouldn't worry about it at all, because I'm not planning to attack my neighbor, so I ask again, why is the Empire so worried about Heaven's Spire being able to defend itself?"

"They're still trying to claim it was an accident." Tern shook her head.

"The political elite are unlikely to admit that the leader of the Republic tried to weaponize Heaven's Spire." Hessler frowned. "I'm frankly more concerned about turning this into a debate about war with the Empire."

"The manticore wants to turn everything into a debate about war with the Empire," Tern said.

"You know that the manticore doesn't actually have opinions of its own—even beyond being made of felt, it's just a mouthpiece for the Learned Party's political messaging . . ." Hessler caught the look Tern was giving him. "Of course you know that. Right."

"It's getting serious," Tern said as the manticore flared its wings and bounced on top of the griffon to the laughter of the crowd. "Loch and Pyvic talked about it last week at lunch. Loch was going on that mission to talk the Imperials down? Icy went with her." Tern grimaced.

"I don't think there's any cause for concern," Hessler said, seeing her look.

"No, I wasn't worried about them. I mean, no more than usual. I . . ." She paused when Hessler glanced down at his hip pocket in irritation. "What's wrong?"

"Message crystal. It can wait. I'm on lunch hour." Hessler put an arm around Tern's shoulder. "I would rather spend time with you."

Tern suspected that their mutual friend Desidora, a love priestess of Tasheveth, was coaching Hessler on the basics of relationships. She made a mental note to send her a nice card.

"Anyway, what *were* you worried about?" Hessler added after a moment, as the manticore and the griffon took to the skies, still shouting their talking points at each other.

"Heaven's Spire shot a big blast of energy down at the ground, right?" Despite her annoyance at the puppet show, Tern had actually been thinking about this for most of the morning.

"Well, technically, it created an energy gradient between the crystals on the underside of the city and the ground, causing an arc—"

"Right, got it. But it shot that big blast of energy *down*." Tern looked over at him for emphasis. "*Straight* down. It's no threat to the Empire unless the voyants fly Heaven's Spire across the border so it's hanging over an Imperial city—and they'd never *do* that, because that would mean risking all the wealthy people like themselves."

"Yes, Silestin's weapon would primarily be defensive in nature, to ward against Imperial attack." Hessler looked down again in irritation. "How many messages are they going to send?"

"I've been working with the lapitects to figure out what Silestin's people did," Tern said quietly, as the crowd laughed at something onstage. "I think I figured it out this morning. They did a lot less than we thought."

Hessler blinked. "I'm certain that the modifications were elegant, but—"

"That's just it: they weren't modifications. They were *repairs*. As near as we can tell, Heaven's Spire has had this weapon in place since the ancients first built it. Silestin's people just re-enabled it." Tern looked at the stage, then back at Hessler, whose eyes had gone wide as it sank in. "Why would the ancients make Heaven's Spire so that it could only fire down on the cities below it?"

Hessler opened his mouth, closed it, then reached down and yanked a thin, palm-sized crystal backed with silver from his pocket. "What in the world could be so important that . . . docking bay override request? Why would someone contact me about that?"

"I say," the manticore said, claws locked around the griffon's throat, "if the Empire doesn't want us to have the ability to defend ourselves, it's a damned good thing we *have* that ability!"

The dragon puppet finally pulled the two apart. "Now, now, this is all a moot point," it roared, sending little gouts of fire between the two to force them to opposite sides of the stage. "We've got diplomats going to meet our friends in the Empire, and they're going to ensure that cooler heads prevail."

"I just hope we make use of this opportunity," the manticore growled, wings hunched in submission.

"This is a very dangerous situation, not an opportunity," the griffon insisted, lunging forward until a growl from the dragon sent it scuttling back. "We just have to hope that handing over the people responsible for this accident is enough to resolve this situation."

"Wait, what? Silestin was responsible for it," Tern said, "and he's dead, so we can't hand *him* over. Well, not tastefully."

"Then who are they talking about?" Hessler asked, still puzzling over the message crystal. "Loch didn't say anything about handing over a prisoner."

"Remember, everyone!" the dragon shouted, tossing candy out to the crowd. "*It's your republic!*"

"*Stay informed!*" the crowd shouted back.

Hessler's message crystal buzzed again. Tern and Hessler looked down at it, then at each other.

"Maybe you should get that."

Archvoyant Bertram sipped his afternoon kahva in the upper study of his palace.

He had fifteen minutes until his next meeting, and he saw no godly reason to be early. Back when he'd been the Learned Party Leader, he had drunk four cups of kahva a day, which the healers said was burning a hole through his stomach as clearly as if he'd stuck his sizable gut in front of a flamecannon.

Since becoming Archvoyant and having to dig the Republic out of the hole Silestin had put them all in, he had moved up to eight.

Bertram dipped a dry biscuit into the kahva. Having some starch with his drink stopped his stomach from burning quite so badly later in the day. It also tasted divine.

Behind him, the door to his study creaked open. "What in Byn-kodar's hell is it?" he asked without turning around. "Tell the bloodsucking bastards I've got fifteen minutes."

"You may have less than that," said Isafesira de Lochenville, and something metal rattled just before he felt the smooth edge of a blade at the back of his neck.

"Justicar Loch," Bertram said without turning around. "You escaped."

"Old rule in the scouts: Don't walk into any building unless you have a plan on how to get out."

He nodded. "That's a smart rule."

"Not going to act surprised or deny that you set me up?" The blade at the back of his neck didn't move.

"I was a soldier in my youth, dear, and a damn fine *sufgesuf* player in my middle age. This isn't the first blade at my throat, figurative or otherwise." He smiled and dipped his biscuit into the kahva. He'd dipped it already, but with the way this day was going, he'd earned a double. "In point of fact, I ordered Threvein *not* to set you up. Apparently I was overruled."

"You're the Archvoyant, Bertram."

"I am indeed." He took a bite, carefully, so as not to give the impression that he was trying to avoid the blade behind him. "But I am not Silestin, with his ironclad control and his knives in the shadows for people who got out of line. Even the Learned only listen to what I say about half the time, and they weren't the ones pushing Threvein."

There was a pause behind him, and then Loch chuckled. "The *Skilled* tried to sell me to the Empire?"

"A couple of them," Bertram said, taking another bite. "I suspect some Learned folks turned a blind eye. Hardliners for Silestin, furious that you killed him."

"Technically, that was my sister."

"Say *that* to them with a blade at *your* throat," Bertram said. "I dare you."

That got another chuckle. The blade moved away, and a moment later, Justicar Loch—the woman who'd upended half the Republic to stop Archvoyant Silestin's insane plan—sat down at the table beside him. She was bruised and battered, her hair stuck to the side of her neck and her leathers were wrinkled and stiff.

Her grip on what was quite clearly an Imperial noble's blade was steady and assured, though. "Guessing you got out of the Temple of Butterflies on the Iceford," he said. "Sounds cold."

"A bit, yes."

"Impressive as hell, though." Bertram gestured at the kahva pot. "Pour one for yourself if you like."

She did. "So a few Learned tried to send me to the Republic as a scapegoat because they want me dead."

"And the Skilled turned on you because they'd turn on their own mothers to avoid another war," Bertram said, and nodded. "Not Cevirt, of course. He's, what, like an uncle to you? Family friend, at least. He and I did our damnedest to countermand the orders once we found out what was coming."

Loch nodded at that, her face grim. "For all the good it did. I got out on my own."

Bertram stirred his kahva as Loch drank. "I didn't say otherwise. So . . . what now, Justicar Loch? You wouldn't have broken into my palace without a plan, and I'm sincerely hoping that plan wasn't just to kill me."

She swallowed her kahva. "*I'm* sincerely hoping not to go to war with the Empire *or* end up in an Imperial prison."

"It's good to have goals, isn't it?" Bertram sighed, looking at the pretty young Urujar woman sitting across the table. "Now, I'm not sure what you and your little band of thieves have been doing for the past few months, but *I* have been trying to talk the Empire down from treating Heaven's Spire's little bolt-of-lightning trick like an act of war."

"It *was* an act of war," Loch pointed out. "We just managed to kill the bastard trying to start it."

"*We* being your sister." Bertram smiled. "In any event, some of our friends in the Voyancy likely passed information to sources across the border, claiming that you were responsible for weaponizing Heaven's Spire. The Imperials had already heard about you from our own puppet shows, back when Silestin was trying to frame you as a traitor."

"Kind of a lousy traitor to the Republic if I helped turn Heaven's Spire into a weapon." Loch toyed with one of the apparently decorative rings on the back of her blade.

"The Imperials knew at the very least that you were involved," Bertram said, shrugging, "and they wanted you turned over for trial and questioning."

"And when it became clear that I hadn't done it," Loch said, "they'd realize the Republic had lied."

"And we'd be right back to war," Bertram finished, "with only a small delay and you tortured beyond recognition to show for it. That's why Cevirt and I proposed an alternate peace offering to the Imperials." Loch raised an eyebrow. "They've made noises about some artifacts and treasures that went missing in the last war, or the one before that."

"Magical?" Loch asked.

"Some of them. Others just rare and expensive." Bertram took one final sip of his kahva. "The Republic has some of them, and can get its hands on others. There's only one that's out of our hands, and it's the one that the Imperials were most insistent on." He finished his biscuit, wincing. He hated eating it dry when his kahva was already gone. "If we got that one last thing, we might *possibly* be able to give the Imperials a peace offering."

Loch took another sip, eyes closed. Bertram did not make the mistake of thinking that this was an opportunity for sudden movements, even as her shoulders relaxed ever so slightly. After a pause, she said in a resigned voice, "So what am I going to go get for you?"

Bertram smiled. "I think you'll find it familiar. It's an ancient elven manuscript, *The Love Song of Eillenfiniel.*"

Loch's eyes snapped open, and her jaw dropped. "You're kidding me."

Bertram chuckled. "At least you know what it looks like."

Loch was actually sputtering now. "The manuscript that I stole from Silestin? That I gave to the elves to save Heaven's Spire from crashing?"

"See, now you understand why we can't get our hands on it ourselves," Bertram said easily. "Those pointy-eared bastards won't even talk to us about buying the damn thing back."

Loch's eyes narrowed. "How does that belong to the Imperials? That book was in my family for generations!"

"Oh, they're probably lying," Bertram said with a little wave of his hand, "but I'm sure they had something about it being theirs originally. So, Justicar Loch, are you going to get that book and save the Republic?" At her glare, he chuckled again. "Oh, come on, how hard can it be? You stole it once already."

She shook her head. The veins in her neck stood out a little. If Bertram had been unmarried and several decades younger, he'd have considered courting the pretty woman. As it was, he was just pleasantly distracted, and a little conflicted about the sword in her hand.

"What can you give me?" she asked.

"The order for your arrest and handover was illegal. Once the voyants find out that you escaped, though, they'll push for something official to save face . . . and they'll push behind the scenes as well," Bertram said, and checked the time. It was going to be close. "I'll push back. You won't get any official trouble from the Republic, and you'll keep your rank in the justicars."

"I probably could have done that myself," Loch said dryly. "I *do* know someone in the justicars."

"And I'll make sure he stays there, along with the rest of your friends," Bertram said, "and I will buy you as much time to get the book for the Imperials. Now, I'd offer you a message crystal to contact me, but we both know that could be used to track you, so when you get your hands on that little elven book of sex poems, you get in touch however you can."

She bolted the last of her kahva and stood. "If you cross me, I'll kill you."

"Given what happened to the last Archvoyant," Bertram said, "I took that as a given."

She spun the blade and walked out of the room.

Perhaps thirty seconds later, one of the servants knocked on the door. "Sir? One of our men was found unconscious in the garden, and we saw signs of forced entry."

"It's under control," Bertram said. "Show in my next appointment."

The servant noted Bertram sitting alone at a table with two kahva cups and said nothing. A moment later, Bertram's next appointment walked in.

"She agreed?" Voyant Cevirt asked as he sat at the table.

"You knew she would," Bertram said. "Pour yourself a cup."

Three

Loch met Tern and Hessler at the kahva-house. They were seated by the window with waxed paper cups in hand. Tern had what was presumably kahva under an enormous layer of whipped cream, caramel, and cinnamon sprinkles. Hessler had tea.

"So neither of you know how to drink kahva," Loch said as she sat down.

"Says the woman who only sits before us because we hacked docking protocols to clear you. What did the Archvoyant say?" Tern asked, licking the whipped cream off the top of her presumably-kahva.

"You remember the elven manuscript we stole from Silestin?" Loch asked. Tern and Hessler nodded.

"I need to steal it back."

Tern's cough sprayed whipped cream across the table. "Oh, come on!"

Hessler produced a paper napkin and wiped it up. "They intend to give it to the Empire instead of handing you over?"

"Something like that." Loch thought for a moment. Too much running and fighting followed by strong kahva at the palace had left her mind bouncing uselessly from thought to thought. Having a chance to sit down allowed her to finally focus. "First thing I need to do is trace the manuscript, find out where the elves have it now."

"If it's back in the Elflands, we're screwed," Tern said. "Nobody gets in there."

"You're right about that. But *we're* not anything. There's no 'we'."

Tern looked at Loch in confusion. "You're not getting the gang back together?"

"The Republic is after me, not all of you." Loch massaged the bridge of her nose. "I appreciate the offer, and I might need another favor or two, but there's no need to drag you all into this."

"Unless the Republic goes to war with the Empire," Hessler said, "which would drag us into it quite effectively."

"And forget you for a minute!" Tern added. "You think the Empire might ask for anyone else who was part of the team that accidentally triggered Silestin's weapon? Like, say, the girl who was messing around with the controls?"

Loch sighed. "Listen . . ."

"Captain trying to let you guys off the hook?" Kail asked as he sat down at the table. Loch turned to see Icy and Ululenia there as well, Icy in nondescript pants and a shirt instead of his flowing robes, and Ululenia with her glowing horn turned off.

"It's okay. I remembered my self-interest," Tern said. "Hey, Icy! How was the Empire?"

"Violent and subsequently very cold."

"Hey, Tern," Kail cut in, "did you know all the monks get to fight? It's just Icy who took a vow not to." Kail glared at Icy as though it offended him personally. "Come on, Icy—even the unicorn fights."

"As the mother doe protecting her fawn," Ululenia said modestly.

"Speaking of which," Hessler said, looking around, "where *is* Dairy?"

Ululenia gave him a narrow-eyed look, and Kail shrugged. "She doesn't want to talk about it."

Hessler returned Ululenia's glare. "I entrusted Dairy to your care, Ululenia, *despite* my opinions about your predilection for virgins."

"Oh, come on, Hessler, it's not like she *killed* him or anything," Tern said. "She probably just used him for sex and then dumped him once he was no longer a virgin. Which . . . wait. That's, okay, it's not *worse*, but—"

"Dairy is, or at least *was*, a child of prophecy," Hessler said, leaning forward and pointing at Ululenia, "and even after the prophecy's fulfillment, it is possible that he could be targeted by groups with esoteric interests in the gods or the ancients. If you cast him aside after you had your way with him—"

"Dairy is fine," Ululenia said in a tone that clearly signaled an end to the discussion. "We have parted ways. I do not know where he is, and I do not wish to discuss it further."

"See?" Kail said, elbowing Loch in the arm. "With a team like this, there's no way things can go wrong."

"Their team includes an Imperial acrobat, a safecracker with a lot of nasty alchemical tricks, and Loch herself, who led a scouting unit during the war," said Captain Nystin of the

Knights of Gedesar. He stood in a dimly lit room in the warehouse district of Heaven's Spire, in front of a chalkboard that had written descriptions of each member of the team, along with a pencil sketch where possible. A team of a dozen soldiers sat before him. "Those are bad enough, but they aren't the ones we're worried about. Grid?"

One of the other knights stood. Like Nystin, she wore the traditional armor of the Knights of Gedesar, made from bands of metal fastened to internal leather straps. The banded strips offered less protection than full plate, but far greater flexibility. The Knights of Gedesar fought a lot of things that had to be dodged. The armor was a dull dark gray, an *yvkefer* alloy that was largely immune to magic, with wyvern leather underneath that was magic resistant as well.

"Hessler," Grid said. She pointed to the bearded man on the chalkboard. "Dropped out of university for illegally creating magical artifacts. He mostly sticks to illusions, but don't let that fool you. He can use them to blind you, turn one of his pals invisible, the whole deal. No reports of him summoning daemons, but . . . well, he's a wizard." Some of the knights in the room chuckled.

"Scale, what have you got?" Nystin pointed at another knight, who stood and nodded as Grid sat back down.

"Only monster on the team is a unicorn," Scale said, jerking his chin at the chalkboard. "No picture, because she can look like pretty much anything she wants, although it's usually white. We've got her listed at entry-level nature magic—less than you'd see from an elven adept, and not usually used offensively. Her real trick is the mental crap. She's confirmed to *at least* have mind-reading and mental attack capabilities, with unconfirmed reports of enslavement and control."

Nystin grimaced. "Visors stay down at all times. I doubt she's hexing anyone through solid *yvkefer.*" He knocked on the side of his helmet.

"This might be worth bending the rules for, sir," Scale said. "A warding charm, or—"

"No warding charms," Nystin said, cutting him off.

"Yes, sir." Scale snapped back to attention, clearly embarrassed and defensive. He hadn't been on enough bad operations to know how it could go.

"We're not using them for two reasons," Nystin said with a bit less edge in his voice. "First, because we're the godsdamned Knights of Gedesar. The Republic calls us when some nasty magical son of a bitch needs a knife in the back. We don't *use* magic. We don't *need* magic."

"Yes, sir." Scale nodded in apology. "Then per protocol for byproducts of ancient magic, I recommend silver on the horn."

"Go for the glow," Nystin confirmed, and Scale sat down. "The second reason we're not using warding charms. Hex?"

An older knight stood up slowly. Nystin knew that when he was off duty, Hex favored one leg with a cane, the product of an ugly fight with a rogue wizard some years back. Technically, Nystin should have put the old knight on desk duty, but Hex hadn't yet let it affect his performance on the job . . . and for somebody like Hex, a desk was a death sentence.

"Death priestess," Hex said, his voice raspy from years of shouted commands and regrettable drinks. The rest of the knights sucked in a breath at his words. "We're confirmed on it. Not just death magic, not some necromancer using corpses as golems. We've got an honest-to-gods worshipper of Byn-kodar on our hands. She can manipulate magical auras. If she wanted to, she could nullify the shield around

Heaven's Spire that keeps the air in. Hell, she could turn the air poisonous. She's raised zombies. If pressed, we can assume she'll do worse, up to and including sucking the life right out of you. So no charms, and keep your helmets down."

One of the knights raised a hand. "What's she look like?"

"No intel," Nystin said. "Nobody who looked at her could recall a damn thing."

"Ordinarily, with a death priest, decapitation works best," Hex went on, "but she's also armed with a warhammer of the ancients. Do not engage at close quarters. Stay at range and stick to crossbows until command determines she's weakened sufficiently for a team to close safely."

"Bolts until she calls upon her magic to heal her," Nystin said. "Once I give word, hack her damned head off and let her meet her god in person."

"Too bad she can't turn *herself* into a zombie," one of the knights joked, and the others laughed. Nystin allowed it. He was sending his men into a battle that would most likely leave some of them dead. He knew when to loosen the reins a bit.

"I'm calling four teams," he said when the laughter died down. "Hex, Scale, Grid: you've got your regulars, neutralize your targets and assist as needed. Rib and Glass, you're with me. We focus on Loch and the other mundanes and provide backup where necessary. Questions?"

Nobody had anything else. Nystin nodded. "Remember our target: Isafesira de Lochenville. Everyone else is an obstacle. She's the one we need to kill. Visors down. Let's move."

They pounded out of the warehouse at a jog in wedge formation and hit the streets of Heaven's Spire. They had been authorized for daylight operation, and civilians gawked at them as they ran by.

Another commander might have been pleased to see his soldiers, normally stuck on night jobs, get a little recognition for a change. Captain Nystin hated it. Every civilian who saw them was someone who could tell a friend about the black armor, the full helmets whose visors were covered with an *yvkefer* mesh, the silver daggers and crystal-tipped war maces. Every story told about the shadowy Knights of Gedesar was intel that some power-mad wizard or monster could take and think of a way to counter.

Nystin's men lived in a world full of uncontrolled magic and fools who wanted to play with it. The only reason they gave better than they got was that so few of the bastards ever saw his people coming.

So even though they were free to be in the open, he still kept them to back streets until they were near the objective. A block before the kahva-house, he stopped the men in an alley. The shadows didn't hide his men, but they gave decent cover, at least.

A nondescript man in civilian clothing walked by the alley. "Went inside twenty minutes ago. None of them have left. Solids on the wizard, probable on the unicorn," he said without stopping.

Nystin nodded. "Hex, you're on point. My team backs you. Scale and Grid, front window and side. Let's move!"

Hex and his men hit the street at a dead run, the old knight showing no sign of the limp that slowed him down in his off-duty hours. Nystin and his men were right behind him. Two men in each trio had maces and daggers out, and one, the shooter, had a crossbow cranked and ready.

Hex kicked the front door clean off its hinges and burst inside. "Everybody down! Republic orders!" Nystin heard the windows shatter even as he came in close behind, weapons raised.

Civilians were screaming and hitting the floor. For a moment, Nystin thought someone was already hit, but then, through the mesh of his visor, the colors resolved to dark brown instead of dark red, and he realized it was kahva spilling across the floor.

He checked his points, knew his men were doing the same, as were Grid and Scale's teams as they clambered into the room, weapons raised over the civilians who had fallen to the floor. There were Urujar women present, but none of them looked like Loch. "Dusters!"

The shooter in each trio threw out a pouch that fell open as it flew, spraying dust everywhere. In moments, the kahvahouse was filled with smoke.

No telltale holes to mark an invisible person, no itchy little urge to look away from part of the room that would indicate a fairy creature trying to play with his mind. "Clear!" Hex shouted, obviously pissed off.

"Clear!" Grid called over. She helped an old woman who'd fallen down back to her feet, a kind gesture that would also bring his *yvkefer* gauntlets into contact with her bare skin. She failed to assume any kind of monstrous form.

"Clear," Scale called, and then, "Captain, Glass—see this."

Nystin lowered his mace and waved for Hex to answer questions as all the civilians started shouting. He walked over to the table where Scale stood.

Half the cups at the table were still full. Two cups of tea, one water, kahvas, and some crazy civilian crap with a ton of whipped cream on it.

Glass stepped forward and gently touched the tea, then leaned over and looked at it closely. "Bags are still in, but they're steeped to different levels. Still hot." He dipped a finger to the water, put it to his mouth, and then spat. "Spring water, magically created. None of that little taste you get from the stuff up here on the Spire." He looked at the floor, bent down, and came up with a few coins. "Ordered drinks to their table, then left money and didn't wait for change."

"They were tipped off." Nystin ground his teeth and rapped the wall with the heel of his fist. "Question everyone in this room and get me a damned lead."

"The Knights of Gedesar?" Loch said while jogging down the street toward the docks. "I thought they were a myth."

"Keep running." Captain Pyvic, commander of the justicars and Loch's significant other, glanced back.

"Why are they coming after us?" Tern asked, holding tightly to Ululenia, who had returned to unicorn form. Icy jogged alongside them with apparent ease, while Hessler panted and tried to keep up. Kail was up ahead, checking each corner before they passed. "I'm not magical!"

"Your team has enough magic in it to take out the average town guard or team of justicars."

"But they're military." Loch chewed on it, still jogging. "They answer to the Voyancy, and Bertram was on my side not a half hour ago."

"I'm guessing someone doesn't much care what Bertram wants, then."

Loch looked over at Pyvic. "Wonderful timing, by the way."

He shook his head. "Would've been here sooner, but I had to deal with getting you cleared for departure. Dumb luck I heard about the intel request and got tipped they were coming for you."

She shot him a smile. "Thanks."

He didn't smile back. "I want to help."

They crossed a plaza, prompting startled glances and delighted screams from the children at the sight of a unicorn. "You can do more up here at Heaven's Spire than down there breaking laws with me."

"I know."

"I'm going to need intel."

"I know."

"You don't need to get yourself arrested or killed out of some kind of . . ." She broke off. "You know."

"I hate this," he said, panting now. He'd burst into the kahva-house at a run to get them out the back to safety. He'd likely run all the way from the justicar station. "Bertram's setting you up."

"Looks that way. Got a better idea?"

"Find out what's so damn important about *The Love Song of Eillenfiniel,*" Pyvic said without missing a beat. "Nobody would go to war over a single work of art."

"Probably easier if I find the book first."

"I might be able to help with that, too."

The group reached the cargo docks where Kail had docked the airship. Hessler and Tern had cleared them there instead of at the passenger docks in hopes of avoiding attention. At this time of day, it was busy, with shirtless sweating workers loading crates onto massive cargo freighters. Pallets of crates that had just been unloaded were lashed down. A daemon-powered crane picked the pallets up with a great hook and lowered them gently into wagons, where they could be driven to warehouses. Their little passenger airship, a quarter the size of the freighters, stood out like a nightgown in an armory.

Loch stopped by the great domed hangar that offered airships protection from the elements when they weren't in use.

Everyone else was still with her, although Hessler had gone from red to white and would likely pass out if asked to do anything more strenuous than walking. Ululenia returned to human form and cupped his head gently, presumably using magic to help.

"If you like, I can suggest cardiovascular exercises to improve your endurance," Icy said.

"I'm . . . fine . . . just . . ." Hessler wheezed a little. "Never . . . liked . . . running."

"Kail, Tern, get us cleared to depart," Loch ordered. "Icy, Ululenia, make sure the Knights of gods-damned Gedesar aren't already behind us. Hessler . . . breathe. Pyvic, the book?"

As the others headed off, Pyvic jerked his chin at the registry house. "All departing ships have to state a destination. It's the same for every major port in the Republic. Let me pull out the Justicar Captain badge and wave it around a little."

Loch nodded gratefully, and Pyvic jogged off. The dockworkers were giving her group funny looks, and Kail and Tern were dealing with several large and angry men who were apparently unhappy that a small passenger airship had been occupying a prime cargo dock for the past several hours. As Kail seemed to have the matter in hand, Loch let them deal with it.

"Hessler," she said, and he looked up at her, some color finally back in his cheeks.

"Sorry. Exercise makes me perspire, and—"

"Listen. I need you to do something for me."

Hessler pulled himself as close to upright as he ever got. "Name it."

"Pyvic thinks there's something important about *The Love Song of Eillenfiniel,* and I think he's right. The Republic and the Empire wouldn't just go to war over a single book."

"Well, technically, it's a figurehead being used in place of fundamental disputes over resource allocation—"

"Hessler," Loch said, and he shut up. "I need you to research it."

He blinked. "But what if you need an illusion?"

"We'll manage."

"I've been expanding my skillset, too," he added. "I do a nice blast of fire now, and I'm about fifty-fifty on transmuting inanimate objects into things of equal mass!"

"This is more important. Hit the libraries, the scholarly papers, whatever it is people like you hit."

"Well," said Hessler, frowning, "there are a number of historical dissertations written on elven literature, given the elves' purported connection to the ancients, and the doctoral defenses often reveal—"

"Right. That," Loch said, just as Icy and Ululenia came back around the corner, eyes wide.

"The pack has our scent," Ululenia said, "and though they do not bay at the moon—"

"Got it. Kail, Tern!" Loch called over. "How are we coming?"

The two were already up on the deck of the passenger ship, although several of the workers were still yelling at them from the dock. "All aboard!" Kail called.

Loch sprinted past the dockworkers and up the gang-plank, Icy close behind her. A small white dove landed on the deck and shifted into Ululenia. Back at the entry area, men in black armor came around the corner with maces and crossbows raised.

Tern looked up from the helm. "Where's Hessler?"

"Different assignment. I'll fill you in later. Let's go." Loch ignored the look Tern shot her and kept her eyes on the men. They were headed toward the airship.

Kail pulled back the gangplank, and Loch took a few steps back and out of sight as he took the helm back from Tern. "Okay, let's give our daemon a little nudge, and—" The airship rocked, sending everyone stumbling. Loch looked up. The great balloon overhead was distended, bulging out as though something were punching it from the inside.

"What did you *do?*" Tern yelled.

"Me? I didn't do anything!" Kail hammered at the console. "It's *never* done that before!"

The dark-armored men were halfway across the dock. "Now would be good, Kail."

Kail turned another dial, and something inside the balloon growled and hissed. Again, the balloon lurched, sending the airship rocking.

"Isafesira de Lochenville!" came a shout from down on the dock. "Surrender immediately or we will take you down!" A grappling hook came sailing over the side of the ship and caught on the railing. A moment later, another joined it.

"Hell. Fix it," Loch said to Kail. She drew her sword, stepped to the railing, and chopped through one of the ropes. A crossbow bolt whizzed past her face, and she ducked in case more followed.

"I'm working on it! This is in no way normal!" Kail shouted back as the balloon distended overhead.

"Is it going to break loose?" Loch yelled. "That looks a lot like the balloon that time the daemon tore free and ate Jyelle!"

"That daemon did us all a favor," Kail muttered and pounded on the console. "This one's just pissing me off."

Tern darted to the railing, hunched over, and fiddled with her lavender lapitect's robes. Underneath them, Loch saw, she wore her usual brown crafter's dress with its many pockets. She lifted her crossbow and fitted a bolt in place.

"You continued to carry your crossbow all this time?" Icy asked, moving past her and grabbing hold of another grappling hook.

"Nobody has ever been *sad* to have their crossbow with them." Tern peeked up and fired a shot down at the dock. As she did, Icy reached out and caught an incoming bolt inches from her face. "Aaaaand thank you."

"It was nothing," Icy said modestly, and freed the other grappling hook with his free hand.

Purple smoke poured out from the spot where Tern had fired, and Loch heard the sound of coughing, even as another bolt thudded into the side of the airship inches from her. The balloon above her head growled, and more grappling hooks latched onto the railing.

Loch reached the first one just as a dark-armored knight pulled himself over the railing. He came down in a fighting crouch, readying a war mace whose head was tipped with crystal.

Loch took that in as she charged him. He had time to raise it before she slammed him into the railing. As he staggered, she hooked an arm under his leg and heaved him off the ship.

A few yards away, another knight rolled onto the deck. Ululenia pointed at him, and her horn flared. Instead of repeating a nonsense phrase and falling over, the knight whipped out a dagger and flung it without hesitation.

Icy caught it mid-leap, fell into a roll, and came up between the knight and Ululenia. As the knight went for his mace, a crossbow bolt tipped with what looked to Loch like mud slammed into his helmet, rocking him back and covering his visor with the viscous material.

Loch stepped in, knocked the mace from the knight's hands, rattled his helmet with a hilt smash to the temple, and shoved him over the railing as well. "Kail!"

"Almost got it, Captain!" Kail's yell sounded a bit panicked, but then, it often did.

As the knight crashed to the dock below, she saw more of them climbing up the rope, and others closing in. One knight down on the dock simply stood at the edge of the cloud of purple smoke Tern had made, arm raised to point directly at her. His helmet, dark like that of the others, was emblazoned with the half-lidded eye of Gedesar in red.

"I've killed a lot worse than you, girl," he called up to her.

Then, beside him, one of the dockworkers approached the cloud of purple smoke. As he did, a dark knight stepped out of the smoke with dagger drawn. Without hesitation, the knight stabbed the worker in the throat. The worker fell back, clutching his throat, and stumbled into the smoke, where he disappeared.

The reaction on the dock was immediate. The dockworkers, who had up until now been watching with interest but doing nothing to interfere, shouted in alarm, grabbed anything lying nearby, and charged. The first of them reached the knight who had stabbed their fellow dockworker and swung a crowbar hard.

It went cleanly through the knight, although he *seemed* to reel from the impact, and then he fell back into the smoke and disappeared. Loch looked back at the edge of the hangar, and saw Hessler crouched by a stack of crates, concentrating.

As the knights and the dockworkers brawled, their leader stood unmoving. One of the workers grabbed him, and the knight backhanded the man without looking.

A moment later, a pallet full of crates slammed into him, sending him skidding across the dock with sparks flying from his armor.

Lock looked at the crane that had swung the pallet, and then at the control station.

Sitting at the controls, Pyvic met her gaze, nodded once, and smiled.

"Got it, Captain!" Kail yelled. "Everyone hang on!"

"I love you, too," Loch murmured as the airship pulled away.

With shouts and smoke and crossbow bolts trailing after them, they left Heaven's Spire.

Four

As one of the port cities, Ros-Oanki saw enough trade and enough travelers to merit a standing justicar presence. Justicar Fendril had been stationed there for years.

Justicars on Heaven's Spire traveled everywhere in the Republic, pursuing threats that nobody else could handle. They went after enemies the town guard couldn't (or wouldn't) hunt and chased creatures into the forests where no laws held sway.

And if that weren't enough, sometimes there was politics to contend with.

Here in Ros-Oanki, Fendril dealt with the guards in cases where the question of authority was tricky—a criminal who'd committed a crime in Ros-Sesuf, but fled here, for example. He kept tabs on the guards themselves as well, along with government trade officials who might not be above bribery.

It was slow work, dull even, and as far as Fendril was concerned, it was just perfect.

He opened the day's mail in his office a block away from the guard center. There were three notes for wandering criminals to watch for, one of them politically tricky enough for him to keep for himself rather than pass to the guard. There were two more notes, requests for information from a justicar in another province. Finally, from Heaven's Spire, there came a request to check airship travel logs for an Urujar woman, Isafesira de Lochenville.

The name sounded familiar, though Fendril couldn't quite place it. He made a note to check the logs on his next visit to the port registry.

Finally, he checked his message crystal for anything that was a high enough priority to merit the expense of transmitting a message via magic rather than carrying paper down from Heaven's Spire on an airship. According to regulations, he was supposed to do that first, but anything that came via message crystal was political, and Fendril had gotten himself exiled down to Ros-Oanki to avoid that.

It looked like he had failed in that regard.

With a sigh, he pressed his thumb to the crystal and opened the message waiting there.

"This is Captain Pyvic," came a voice from the crystal, and Fendril grimaced. That *definitely* meant politics. "All port cities, I need any available information on an elven ship that departed from Heaven's Spire a few months back, during the malfunction up here. It would have listed a purchased book as its main, possibly only, cargo. Get me a destination or last sighting and respond by crystal. Pyvic out."

Fendril grunted, sipped his kahva, and headed out for the port registry. At least he could look for anything about the Lochenville woman while he was there.

The city streets were safer than they had been in years, thanks to the death of Jyelle, the woman who had controlled most of the organized crime in the province. Fendril smiled as he strolled through a wealthy market square that hadn't seen anything more than amateur pickpocketing in months. A pretty Urujar couple looked through pamphlets for land rights off near Woodsedge. An elderly woman whose billowy dress marked her as a merchant from the Old Kingdom across the sea bartered with a tavern owner for one of her expensive and brightly colored rugs. A group of fat merchants sat outside a kahva-house sipping and passing notes back and forth with the bored faces of master *suf-gesuf* players. An Imperial woman in a rich violet dress haggled for passage on an airship while her bodyguard glared at anyone who approached, one hand on his shining ax.

The port registry was a sturdy building not far from the airship docks, large enough to store a lot of files and even more money. The registrar, Maera, was a middle-aged woman Fendril had flirted with a bit before realizing that she really liked trade-and-travel regulations more than Fendril would ever like her. She ran her office with ruthless efficiency, which Fendril supposed he could appreciate, even if it meant having to grit his teeth and sign more paperwork than he'd had to deal with in the old days.

Fendril stepped into the front office, a bell on the door ringing as he came inside. "Afternoon," he called to the clerk at the desk.

"Justicar." The clerk was a young Urujar man with straight light hair that he wore long in the back. He gave Fendril a friendly nod. "Help you with something?"

"If you've got time." The office was empty, which was fortunate this time in the afternoon. "One urgent, one standard." Fendril reached for the information request form.

"Of course." The clerk grinned. "It's always something. Don't worry about the papers today. It's quiet, and Maera's off for her afternoon kahva."

"I'd appreciate it." That was *also* fortunate. Perhaps Maera was getting friendlier. Fendril passed over his notes, and the clerk went into the back room to pull the travel records.

There was a new rug on the floor, he noted as he waited. It was bright orange, and didn't match the rest of the room.

"Found it." The clerk stepped back into the main office, his hands raised to show that they were empty. "Without the forms I can't write anything out, you understand, but I found what you needed. Nobody by the name of Isafesira de Lochenville has docked here, and that elven ship listed its destination as Ajeveth. Hope that helps."

"Immensely." Fendril passed the young man a coin for his trouble. "Have a good afternoon."

He left the office, the strange new rug squishing under his boots. The bell rang as he pulled the door open, then again as it closed behind him, and Fendril stepped out into the afternoon sun, looked at the smiling people, and remembered right then that Maera didn't drink kahva.

The rug vendor from the Old Kingdom had empty slots in her shop-wagon. Her other rugs were gold and green and . . . yes, there was another that was the same shade of orange.

Maera didn't drink kahva. She would never have bought that garish rug for her office . . . and she wouldn't have let her clerks give out information without Fendril filling out the proper request forms.

Fendril sighed. He was getting close to retirement, and it would have been so damnably easy to just keep walking.

He looked around. The market square was largely the same as when he'd gone into the registry office. The Imperial woman's bodyguard with the big ax caught him staring and shot him a glare. Fendril looked away and walked as casually as he could around the corner.

In the alley next to the registry office, the shadows were cool. It was clean, with a recently emptied trash bin and a side door that servants could use to come in.

Before he forgot, he activated the message crystal. "Justicar Fendril, reporting on urgent request for information on whereabouts of elven ship bearing a book. Last known destination was Ajeveth."

With that done, Fendril pocketed the crystal and looked around. He squinted at the door and caught the slight irregularity in how it hung in place. He glanced back out into the street, and then crept closer to the door.

When he got close, the freshly scarred wood on the frame was obvious.

Quietly, very quietly, Fendril pushed the door open.

In the back room, Maera lay dead, her head nearly severed from the rest of her body. The bodies of two men in sailor's clothes lay next to her, one with his chest caved in and the other with a broken back. Chopping weapon, and a heavy one at that, the justicar in the back of Fendril's mind noted. Not enough blood in the room. Whoever did this would have kicked in the side door and come in, then cut Maera down elsewhere. Probably the main office. A pair of sailors waiting to fill out forms, so they had to go, too. Big pool of blood, but the rug covers it up neatly.

"I feared you were too wise to miss it," came a woman's voice from the doorway to the main office. Fendril felt muscles in the back of his neck tighten as he looked up.

An Imperial woman stood there, smiling sweetly with lips that had been painted green. It wasn't the woman he'd seen before, in the violet dress. This Imperial woman wore green-painted ringmail, and a pendant with a great golden butterfly hung from her neck, matching the makeup that trailed in a curving pattern from her eyes. "Tell me, Justicar, do you wish to know how they died?" she asked.

Fendril knew two things for certain right then.

He knew that the woman would not have asked that question if she didn't stand to gain something from it, because people who went around killing port officials didn't just make idle conversation. With that in mind, he was absolutely certain that he did not want to answer her.

And second, he knew that the woman was not carrying a very large chopping weapon, which meant that she had either extremely powerful magic or someone else who *did* have a very large chopping weapon, and both of those options meant that Fendril should run like Byn-kodar himself was after him.

He darted back, and the Imperial woman hissed and grabbed for him. He stumbled, knocked the door open with his backside, leaped back as she launched a circling kick at his head, and came out into the alley.

Fendril turned to run . . . and a crushing pain slammed him to the ground.

"You were sloppy, Shenziencis," came a quiet, polite voice.

He realized distantly that the voice wasn't talking to him when the Imperial woman said, "He did not speak, Thunder. We have limits."

Fendril fought to roll back to his feet, and instead managed to groan and flop. A great armored hand closed upon his shoulder and dragged him across the ground. A moment later, the door closed.

"Did you get the information?" the big male voice asked as a great pressure pinned Fendril to the floor. It was the man's booted foot. He was wearing a great deal of armor. "The princess grows impatient."

"Ajeveth," the woman, Shenziencis, said, "city of the dwarves. That is where we will find her."

"Good. Then let us leave."

Fendril's vision was clearing, and he groaned again. When he opened his eyes, blinking through the tears, he saw the big Imperial bodyguard standing over him with his enormous ax rising up over his head. His foot crushed down on Fendril's chest, making any real struggle impossible.

"Wait," said Shenziencis, and had he been younger and more optimistic, Fendril would have thought he had a chance. But he had seen the woman's smile as she stood over three dead bodies looking at him, and that wasn't the smile of someone who would spare Fendril's life just because he was already helpless.

"You and the weapon of the ancients had the others," said Shenziencis, and smiled her emerald smile. "Leave this one and the clerk to me."

Fendril couldn't fight. He couldn't escape. He could barely move.

His hand was tucked under him, near his pocket. He fumbled weakly. The Imperial bodyguard's blow had left his whole body feeling the pins-and-needles sensation of a limb that had fallen asleep.

His fingers closed around his message crystal, and he tapped out a signal every justicar knew.

He kept tapping it as Shenziencis bent over him, the curling golden makeup around her eyes drawing to points like fangs. She leaned in, and her emerald-painted lips mouth opened far wider than should have been possible, her jaw swinging free as she closed down upon him . . .

"The real problem," said the young man passionately, "is that females just don't appreciate nice guys like me."

Desidora, priestess of Tasheveth the love goddess, sighed very quietly on her side of the divider that blocked her view of the gemcutter's son on the other side of the consulting booth.

"So," she said, "just as a tip, before we get to the actual advice: I think you're going to have more luck if you avoid using that word to describe women."

Desidora wore pale green robes emblazoned with the silver smiling lips of her goddess. The smiling lips were regulation. The robe she had chosen to suit her tan skin and auburn hair—priests of Tasheveth were expected to look good while fulfilling sacred duties like mentoring the lovelorn.

"Oh, I don't *call* them that," the young man said. "I would never be cruel to any woman. I just want to love them and show them how beautiful they are, but they'd rather go out with jerks instead."

"*Kutesosh gajair'is?*" the magical warhammer resting by her chair asked quietly.

"No," she muttered. "Shh."

"Is someone in there with you?" asked the young man.

"Sometimes the goddess speaks to us," Desidora said through the divider, and then glared down at Ghylspwr.

Desidora had been a love priestess ever since the voice of the goddess had spoken in her dreams and marked her for sacred duty. It had sometimes been trying, but always satisfying.

Then she'd been transformed into a death priestess for a time as part of a divine mandate to save the world. She'd gotten a magical talking warhammer and the ability to command the spirits of the dead in the bargain.

"So," said the young man, "you're a love priestess. How do I get women to have sex with me?"

"*Kun-kabynalti osu fuir'is*," Ghylspwr said in a tiny sarcastic whisper. Desidora glared at him in warning. As a spirit of the ancients now possessing a warhammer, Ghylspwr had a vocabulary of only three phrases, but he managed to make himself understood far better than most people would have guessed.

"The key to getting women to *love* you," she said to the young man on the other side of the divider, "is to stop thinking of it as the end goal and start thinking of it as the enjoyable result of becoming a more interesting person." Even though he couldn't see her, Desidora put a smile on her face. That usually helped. "After all, the first step to gaining the love of others is to love yourself."

"Oh, I can't do that," said the young man. "My bed is really squeaky, and my parents get angry when they catch me."

Desidora was sincerely relieved to be a love priestess again, with no worries about draining the life out of someone in a fit of anger or projecting an aura that redecorated the room in a skulls-and-gargoyles theme.

Still, some part of her missed having the power to destroy things that annoyed her.

"What I'm saying," she said, glaring again at Ghylspwr before he could say anything, "is that the reason the women you know go after *jerks* is because those jerks are confident and do interesting things. So one way to start would be to develop one of your hobbies or interests, like . . ." She squinted. The divider blocked her view of the young man—ostensibly to protect his privacy despite the fact that she recognized his voice from the jeweler's shop three streets over—but with the eyes of a love priestess, she *could*

see his aura. Athletics? No. Art? No. Music? No. Acting?
No . . . but he at least enjoyed *going* to performances, so,
". . . theatre," she finished. "You're fortunate to live in
Heaven's Spire, which has a number of acting troupes, some
of them even friendly to beginners. Maybe you could try out
for a part. Or even volunteer to work on the sets as a way to
meet people?"

"What, like I'm supposed to paint stairs for some stupid
show, and that's going to get some woman to have sex with
me?" The young man snorted. "They always go for the jerk
in the lead, even though he'll never treat them right, like
I would."

Desidora picked up Ghylspwr, just for comfort. "You have
to start somewhere."

"Nah, I'd have to go do work like every night, and what if
nobody started liking me after all that work?" said the young
man who lived off his parents' money and spent most of his
evenings sitting in the local kahva-house glaring at people
or trying to find ways to love himself without waking up his
parents. "Aren't there tricks you can give me, like things
I can say to get women to have sex with me? I heard that if
you kind of insult a girl, but then turn it into asking her out
for a date, her head gets confused?"

A knock sounded on the door to Desidora's side of the consulting booth, and it opened a moment later. A young priest
poked his head in, looking apologetic and embarrassed. "I'm
sorry, Sister. I have an urgent request from a justicar that—"

"No, of course, absolutely." Desidora was out of the booth
before the priest had finished his sentence. "You can take
over for me, I'm sure. Good luck." The young priest blinked,
and Desidora realized she was holding Ghylspwr in something that was just a little too close to a fighting position.

She lowered Ghylspwr and gave warm smiles to the priests and visitors in the temple's large central hall.

Justicar Pyvic was pacing at the far end. "... confirm that it's Ajeveth," he was saying into a small blue crystal he held near his mouth. "I don't have anything from the dwarves yet. I'll be in contact once I do. Good luck." He thumbed the crystal off, then started when he saw her.

"You should have told her you loved her," Desidora said, and gave Pyvic a hug. His aura was a little uncomfortable with that, either because he found her attractive and was a bit nervous or because he had once seen her smash a blood-gargoyle so hard it had actually popped.

"She knows."

"Of course she does," Desidora said, smiling. "She still likes to hear it."

Pyvic smiled, but he was still troubled. "I've got a problem. I could use your help."

"Is this a matter of love?" Desidora asked, although she doubted it. Loch and Pyvic had a strong and healthy relationship, if somewhat more competitive than she would have preferred personally.

"It's a matter of love *songs*," Pyvic said. "One in particular. *The Love Song of Eillenfiniel.*"

Desidora blinked, then gestured at a small meeting room off to the side. "In here."

He followed her into the room lit by rose-colored candles. It had no windows, but the walls were hung with gently curving satin curtains nevertheless. It contained a lovely bed and a small pool whose water was heated and scented with lavender.

"Did it have to be this room?" Pyvic asked, looking around for someplace to sit.

"Would you prefer the one themed as a dungeon?" Desidora asked, tossing Ghylspwr onto the bed. "The shackles can be adjusted to fit anyone . . . or anywhere."

"Thank you, no, I believe Loch and I are doing fine without exploring any of the sacred mysteries of intimacy," Pyvic said. "I'd rather just stop the Republic and the Empire from going to war."

"Again?" Desidora ran her fingers through her hair. "Because of that book?"

"Apparently. Loch's on her way to Ajeveth to try to recover it."

"And you aren't with her."

"She needed thieves, not justicars," he said, and grinned.

"You don't have to do that," Desidora said, settling on the edge of the bed.

"Do what?"

"Pretend you aren't worried for her and sad not to be at her side."

"You can stop reading my aura any time you like, Sister."

"Sorry. It's been a long day." She sighed. "How *can* I help? You already know where the book is."

"We know what, and we know where," Pyvic said. "I'm looking for *why*."

"I'm thinking the airship needs a name," Kail said a few days later as he set the team down in the landing field outside Ajeveth.

"No," said Icy, who had changed back into his robes now that they were dry, if somewhat wrinkled.

"You're remembering that we stole this airship, Kail?" said Loch.

"Also, we're all sick to death of this ship and hoping never to see it again," said Tern, who had proven to have a weak stomach for long flights.

"How about *Iofegemet?*" Kail said after a pause just long enough for Loch to hope he was going to drop it. "It means 'lying helpfully' in the language of the ancients."

"How about something we can *say?*" said Tern. Loch hopped down from the airship that was ideally not going to be named *Iofegemet* and stretched her legs and shoulders as she got used to being on land again. Around her, other airships were tied to docking posts, a great field of canvas balloons on either side. Up ahead, the walls of Ajeveth rose imposingly before her, great gray stone arches like the mountains behind them.

Ajeveth was a border town. Although technically part of the Republic, it was controlled by the dwarves, who understood that the humans who wanted their goods would have a difficult time getting into the mountains where the dwarves lived. The city had been built on the lower slopes of the Titan, and its buildings, rising up behind the walls, were tall and strangely angled.

"It's because they live in the mountains," Tern said, no longer quite so green now that she was on land again. She pointed at the buildings. "Dwarves are all about economy of space, so their houses are narrow and built to accommodate slopes."

Icy stared at the great planes of angled stone in surprise. "In the Empire, we heard that most of the dwarves lived underground."

"Nah, that's just a legend," said Tern. "Also kind of racist."

"My apologies."

"They do a lot of mining, but they live aboveground, just like the rest of us. Dwarven society has three big groups. See that?" Tern pointed at one building in the distance, a great spire that rose up to a needle-thin point. "That's the Hall of Masters, for the crafters who build all the expensive stuff we use in the Republic. And that one over there, the dome? That's the High Cave, for the miners. The dome is shorter, but covers more area. Dwarven society is all about that balance. Not identical, but equal."

"What's the third group?" Kail asked. "I don't see anything else big enough for whatever that group is."

"The walls," Loch said, and turned to look at Tern.

"The Guardsmen," Tern said, nodding. "There are a lot of things out there in those mountains that don't like people very much. The dwarves don't often start trouble, but they're *very* good at taking care of themselves."

"How do you know so much about them?" Kail asked.

Tern reached into her many-pocketed brown dress and produced a silver-tipped crossbow bolt. "Where did you think I had all these made?"

Loch smiled as a group of dwarven officials came out from behind a massive cargo airship and approached. They were sturdy men and women a little shorter than Tern and built like they could shrug off a rockslide. One of them wore chainmail fine enough to be ornamental, while the others wore the loose-flowing shirts and breeches of merchants. "Afternoon," she called. "Justicar Loch. No cargo. Docking fees can be applied to the government account." She produced her badge and showed it to them.

The nearest dwarf, the one in the ornamental armor, examined the badge, then frowned. "Welcome, Justicar," she said, sounding more grudging than anything else. "Do ye wish to share any information wi' our local security teams?"

It was a warmer welcome than Loch had been expecting. "Not at this time," she said with a sad shake of her head. "This is a background investigation. I'm not currently pursuing anything that would threaten your city."

At that, the dwarven official looked relieved. "Understood, Justicar. Please enjoy yer visit to the city. If ye need any assistance, our security teams will be pleased to offer information. Your docking registration, to be billed to the Republic government offices." She passed Loch a slip of paper.

"If ye have leisure time," another official added, "this pamphlet lists entertainment activities suitable for human visitors, including casinos, fine dining, sports and recreation, and *Irke'desar*, the Bounty of the Past, our new publicly accessible museum offering historical artifacts legally purchased from a variety of different cultures."

"Thank ye again for coming," said the third official as the second pressed a folded pamphlet into Loch's hands. "Please enjoy yer stay."

Loch nodded politely as the dwarves trooped off. When they were gone, she looked over at Tern.

"Yeah, pretty much always like that," Tern said. "They're very polite, though."

Kail shook his head. "I've been on the Spire for too long. That much *directness* just cuts right through you." He glanced at Loch. "Also, did you notice how they didn't ask to double-check your badge or insist on searching *Iofegemet* or anything?"

"I do not concede that this is the airship's name," said Icy.

"Yeah, dwarves don't really get the big deal about the Urujar or the Imperials," Tern said, ignoring Icy. "If they ever said anything that wasn't thoughtfully premeditated, I might actually want to live here."

A small flicker of motion caught Loch's eye, and she looked up to see a white shape flitting down their way. The snowy dove landed before them, then shimmered and became Ululenia.

"The dwarves work like ants, industrious and pure of purpose," she said, "and like the ants, they care little for the unspoiled beauty of nature."

Tern shrugged. "Nature spends most of its time trying to kill them."

"The hare sings few songs in praise of the wolf," Ululenia said in what was probably agreement. "Their minds are also ordered and calm, but many have plans to see a new item being displayed in a place that tells the story of the past, like the thin rings of an ancient tree remembering the dry years."

Loch opened the brochure the official had given her. "You think they're excited about going to see a new elven manuscript?"

"The riverbeds through which their thoughts flow are not shaped in such ways, Little One." Ululenia thought, her horn pulsing with a little flare of light. "It is not the spoil of a hunt or the rush of coupling madly in the grass while a summer storm pounds skin lit only by flashes of lightning."

"Still haven't found another virgin, huh?" Tern asked.

"I am still unclear as to what happened to young Dairy," Icy said.

Ululenia pulled herself upright, and her horn flared again, then went still. "Dairy is *fine*." She turned back to Loch. "As

I was saying, they think only that the museum would be a good place to gain knowledge of the strange other races, and they have heard that there are new displays."

It wasn't the strongest lead Loch had ever heard, but it was a starting place.

"All right, everyone. Let's go visit the museum."

Five

*I*RKE'DESAR, THE BOUNTY OF THE PAST, WAS A MULTI-STORY
building constructed, like many of the larger buildings in
Ajeveth, so that it ran up the gentle slope at the base of the
mountain. It gave the city an odd look, like a giant had gone
stomping through it and knocked over most of the major
structures.

Loch had spent the last few months on Heaven's Spire,
floating high over the rest of the Republic. She'd gotten used
to the artificial cleanliness of the Spire, and to the fake stone
that sounded wrong beneath a good pair of boots. Ajeveth
wasn't false like Heaven's Spire, but it wasn't quite human,
either.

"Still a bit strange, huh, Captain?" Kail asked, noticing as
she kicked the ground while waiting for a wagon filled with
cabbages to pass.

"The air smells better than Heaven's Spire," she said,
"and at least it's real stone."

"Still no garbage in the street, though." Kail gestured at
a market square up ahead. "And no beggars. How are you

supposed to figure out what part of the city is what, if you can't smell the garbage? And how are you supposed to get information if you can't just pass a few coins to buy some kid a meal?"

Tern cleared her throat. "The dwarves have a strong sanitation system, and they're good about helping other dwarves find a way to make a living."

"Well, that's great for the ones who want to." Kail shot her a grin. "What about the ones who come back from a war, or a battle with things in the mountains, or . . . what do they have instead of wars?"

"Trolls and cave-ins," Tern said, nodding and smiling to a group of passing dwarves who looked at them curiously.

"Okay, trolls and cave-ins," said Kail. "You can't just say that there's work for those who want it. There have to be some dwarves that come back from trolls and cave-ins not quite right. Where are *those* people? Do the dwarves kill them, or drive them out of the city or . . ."

"They *help* them," Tern said, looking a little sad. "Why is this so important to you, Kail?"

"Because it means it doesn't have to be the way it is in the Republic," Loch murmured.

"And thank the gods for that," Tern said. "Come on. If we just hang out here, someone *will* come try to give us directions, and then we'll have a half-hour of listening to civic details and answering questions about what attractions we might want to see, and trust me, you really need to work up to that level of politely directed socialization."

They started walking again, boots clopping on clean, evenly cut city streets.

"I always felt good when I passed the little kids a coin," Kail muttered.

"You'll live," Tern said.

The museum had a small fee for admission. It was far less than what a human noble would have charged peasants to look at his private collection. They all paid and went inside.

The museum's rooms had six walls instead of four. The interior walls were stone instead of plaster, and rather than paint, the overlapping stones were laid out with their grains alternating directions, forming a natural tile pattern. Doorways were set with silver runes and crystals that glowed with steady blue light, and small, regularly spaced crystals in the ceiling lit the room with a gentle ambience.

"Shall we find the manuscript?" Ululenia asked, looking at the walls with faint distaste.

"Not yet," said Tern.

"It would seem suspicious to ignore the other displays and head directly to the elven area," added Icy.

"Plus, we want to check the overall security, which means seeing what it's like throughout the place," said Kail.

"I see." Ululenia plucked a brochure from a box on the wall and opened it with mild disdain. "Then let us explore this rocky honeycomb."

The dwarves had collected items from every race Loch had heard of, and some that she hadn't. It was all meticulously organized, as Loch was now starting to suspect would be the norm everywhere in the dwarven city. Each race or culture branched off in their own direction, and smaller rooms branched off from that main hexagonal chamber.

In the dwarven chamber, Loch saw axes whose heads were carved from magnetic ores. *Although impractical against armored opponents,* read a plaque near the display, *these*

*weapons—given to the dwarves by the ancients themselves—
enabled dwarven warriors to fight invading abominations who
were formed from magic itself.*

"Glimmering Folk, you think?" Tern asked, looking at the
axes. They were set behind protective glass.

Loch frowned. "Could have been."

"Magnetism. Good note if we ever run into Bi'ul again.
Always seemed like *yvkefer* should have worked on the
bastard." Tern leaned in and squinted through the glass. "Not
glass. Crystal, cut thin. You can tell by how the light goes
through it. It's been planed so that just trying to cut through
will make the whole thing shatter and set off weight-specific
alarms."

"Wonderful."

In a side room, Loch found Kail looking at a statue of what
was almost a dwarf, but not quite. It was massive, taller than
Loch, dressed in fur and leather, and its face was set with a
kind of snarling smile. In a display beside it sat a huge pair of
boots and a great sword with a hilt of leather-wrapped wood.

"Says they used to be taller," Kail said, "going by what
they've found from the time they, uh . . ." He looked at a
plaque. *"Journeyed to this land to help the ancients find crystals in the mountains. The wood from surviving tools suggests
we came from across the sea."*

"Suggests? They're organized about everything else, but
for their history, they only have suggestions?"

Kail squinted. "It says the ancients gave them culture and
helped them learn the ways of the mountains. Might not have
been very dwarfy before that," he added with a look at the
savage statue.

"I suppose not."

"Weight-sensitive plates near base, by the way," he said in a quieter voice. "I'd need Tern to take a look at the doors, but my gut tells me that during off hours, those crystals set in the frame sound an alarm if they detect motion."

"I'll pass it on."

She left the dwarves and headed up a wide set of stairs that climbed to the next floor. It turned out to be dedicated to humans.

Icy stood before a golden dragon that rested on a podium draped with rich green silk. "According to the dwarves, my people came to what is now the Empire thousands of years ago, likely moving to find better cropland after changes to the world's weather patterns." He nodded politely to a dwarf in a craftsman's leathers who may have thought that Icy was part of the display. When the dwarf moved on, Icy added, softly, "Most of the stands appear to have traces of *yvkefer* in their construction. It would make it difficult to steal anything and leave an illusion behind."

"Moot point, since we don't have Hessler at the moment." Loch turned to one of the side rooms.

"Did Justicar Pyvic send any further word?" Icy asked, his voice odd.

"Not since giving us Ajeveth." Loch headed for the side room.

"Loch . . ." Icy's voice was still off, somehow, and then Loch remembered that he couldn't lie worth a damn. "That room contains the history of your people."

Loch paused, then looked back and gave him a nod and a small smile. "Well, we paid for admission." Then she turned back to the doorway and stepped through.

There were paintings and small dioramas carved from stone and meticulously painted.

. . . Likely came from some other part of the world to help the ancients cultivate an untamed land, as their different skin color suggests they were not native to the area . . .

There were paper sketches and woodcuts.

. . . When the ancients left, the Urujar society was peaceful and agrarian until the arrival of colonists from the Old Kingdom . . .

There were shackles and whips, and metal collars fitted with crystals.

. . . Barbaric conditions for centuries, until persistent revolts forced the Republic to grant the Urujar freedom in order to avoid fighting a civil war as well as the first of many conflicts with the Empire . . .

Loch walked back out. She kept her shoulders straight and nodded at Icy. "The windows are too large for me to get through, but I bet you could do it." She unclenched her fists. "Didn't see anything else helpful."

Icy nodded. "I can take more time in the rest of the human displays, if you like."

"Thanks." Loch headed up the next set of stairs and didn't look back.

The third floor looked to be a general collection of magical creatures, which the dwarves had lumped in all together. The main room had artifacts from different human cultures, all related to the fairy creatures and protected with obvious wards that looked like they were as much to keep old, unstable magic *in* as to keep people *out*.

Loch found Ululenia in a side room, along with several dwarves who were chuckling while they looked at a small stone diorama of satyrs prancing through a field.

"These simple, playful creatures sprang from the leftover magic of the ancients," Ululenia's voice snapped in Loch's

mind, *"with their nature dependent upon the type of energy released. Scholars and philosophers debate whether they are truly alive, or intelligent constructs like some of the artifacts of the ancients, which can speak and even effect . . ."*

This is very offensive, Little One.

"Should've seen the Urujar room," Loch murmured.

To work any magic of nature in these halls would be as making roses bloom in solid rock, she added.

"Good to know." Loch nodded, realizing too late that she probably looked a little odd nodding to a voice speaking in her head.

"While some few fairy creatures are troublesome, most are charming wisps more inclined to frolic than to deal with mortals at all . . ." If they had simply spoken with any fairy creatures, half of these questions could have been answered!

Loch left Ululenia to her righteous rage and found another room.

It was the elven room, finally. Tern and Kail were already there.

So was an elf.

Loch had only seen elves a handful of times. It was said that they were shy, reclusive creatures. This one was a little taller than she was, and slender, his features narrow. His ears tapered back to fine, wiry points, and his skin was a pale green.

The elf wore a loose shirt and breeches that would have suited a prosperous merchant or a minor noble, and crystals glowed at his brow and cheeks, casting light across golden cat's eyes.

The elf did not seem to notice her arrival at all, because he was engaged in either a passionate debate or a polite argument with a dwarf standing by a podium where an elven book sat propped up proudly on a red satin cushion.

The Love Song of Eillenfiniel had been cleaned up since Loch had last seen it, the leather restored and the runes upon the cover buffed to a healthy shine. The crystals in the ceiling had been set to shine more brightly upon the book, and under the protective glass, the book caught the light and shimmered like the sun on a stallion's flank.

It took her a moment to catch what the elf was actually saying.

"—interference with harmonic equilibrium," he snapped, "of unacceptable degree relevant to generosity of donation!"

"Now, then," said the dwarf who, unlike the other dwarves Loch had seen in the museum, was wearing a long leather coat reinforced with protective bands of metal, as well as a thin vest of shimmering ringmail underneath, "there's no call for fuss. If ye believe that the donated book—"

"*The Love Song of Eillenfiniel,*" the elf corrected. "Nomenclature vital as unique work, replication impossible without altering core experience."

"If ye believe *The Love Song of Eillenfiniel,*" the dwarf corrected, "is being shown in a manner that is inaccurate or disrespectful to yer cultural heritage, ye kin certainly speak with the curators. We'll be happy to take yer values into consideration with changes to the display, provided they dinnae compromise the security of the piece."

"Security precautions simultaneously inadequate and contraindicative for experiential quality!" The elf paused and clasped his hands, clearly trying to control his temper. "It is already too much," he said slowly and deliberately, "and not enough. A trained thief could climb along the walls to avoid the pressure plates on the floor, melt the display crystal with an appropriate reagent, and replace the manuscript with an item of equal weight."

Kail and Tern blinked. The dwarf chuckled.

"Well, now, I'm nae too certain those thieves would fare quite so well as ye expect, Representative," the dwarf said, looking around the room and shaking his head.

"Yes, the motion triggers, the door locks, the perimeter containment system as well, all breachable given intruders prepared with coherent penetration strategy . . ." The elf wrung his hands again. "I am sorry. What I intend to communicate is that it does not matter. By storing the manuscript in this manner, you will alter it. It is unique. It is . . . the difference between *a* shirt and, and, and *this* shirt." He reached out and grabbed Kail's sleeve, pulling it up toward the dwarf sharply. "Changing it in such a way will alter the experience of reading it, which risks losing its message, like hanging a painting on a wall that faces the sun!"

"Representative Irrethelathlialann," the dwarf said politely but firmly, "I dinnae think it's appropriate to bother the other visitors."

"But they must already be bothered." The elf let go of Kail and crouched down on the floor. "Look at it. Can you feel it?"

Tern blinked. "Um. No?"

The elf waved his hand just above the ground, brushing the hem of her brown crafter's dress. "Pressure plates. Sound amplification from bound water-daemon. Out of view to avoid bothering dwarven sensibilities, but to those attuned, it is a constant blaring horn. Even when disabled during operating hours, they alter the room." He stood up so quickly that Tern jumped and faced the dwarf. "It *cannot* be altered, Enforcer Utt'Krenner."

"Please, Representative, call me Gart," said the dwarf, "and we can take these concerns to the curators, as I said." The dwarf turned to Loch, Kail, and Tern. "My apologies for this display. 'Tis the intention of the museum to be a welcoming and wholesome environment for all our guests."

"Not at all." Loch smiled at the dwarf, and then at the elf. "It's important to view different cultures in their proper context."

"Yes. Yes!" The elf smiled back. "Understanding rare among humans, simplistic sensory capabilities render discussions of finer appreciation academic in most instances, but Urujar *remember* more. Irrethelathlialann," he said, and took Loch's hand with a grip that was surprisingly strong. His other hand clasped her wrist, and he bowed slightly. "Appreciate this acquaintance."

"Loch." She shook his hand, and that seemed to be enough for the elf. He broke away and strode from the room, fluttering his hands in annoyance at the walls and doorway as he left.

"My apologies again," said the dwarf, adjusting his ringmail with some minor discomfort as he looked after the elf. "I regret this disruption of the viewing experience." He reached into his belt and came up with a small slip of paper. "By way of apology, allow me to offer a complimentary meal in our attached restaurant, and a discount on any items purchased from the gift shop."

"That's hardly necessary," Loch said.

"But we appreciate it anyway," Kail said quickly, taking the card.

"And we'll make sure to mention how welcoming the museum was, Enforcer Utt'Krenner," Tern said, "and how well the staff dealt with this unfortunate but blameless situation."

The dwarf smiled. His big red beard was carefully groomed to fall into seven equally spaced tongues, like a fire burning upside down, and over his mouth, his mustache curled up on either side like the gilding on a wrought-iron fence. "Please enjoy the remainder of yer visit," he said, and strode off after the elf.

Kail, Tern, and Loch looked at the elven manuscript standing under the glass.

"Pressure plates." Tern shifted her weight back and forth.

"Sound amplifiers." Kail tapped his boot on the floor.

"Through a water-daemon, apparently."

"Motion triggers and door locks." Loch nodded thoughtfully. "Tern, the crystal in the display case? You can melt through?"

Tern frowned. "I'll need to run some tests, but yes, I think so."

"Then thanks to our very excited elven friend," said Loch, "we have the beginnings of a plan."

"Great." Kail held up the slip of paper. "Let's run it over dinner."

Pyvic followed Hessler and Desidora into the Republic Library of Heaven's Spire. "You're certain that this will help?"

"I am certain of very little, Justicar." She smiled over her shoulder as she walked into the building.

The Republic Library was one of the oldest buildings on Heaven's Spire. Some of the structure likely dated back to the times of the ancients, like the palaces of the voyants. It was squat but long, and on the front of the building, between great arched windows, a great golden scroll was held aloft by Teses'vess, deity of wisdom and knowledge.

Inside, the air was cool and smelled of leather and old paper. Desidora flashed an amulet at the man behind the front desk, and Hessler showed a flat green crystal that chimed once as he held it up. Pyvic grunted and fished through his wallet, eventually pulling out a battered card.

The man behind the desk blinked in confusion, and Desidora gave a silvery laugh. "He's with us," she said, and the man at the desk nodded. She gestured for Pyvic to follow.

"I *have* a library card," Pyvic muttered as Desidora led him not into the main hall, but to a small doorway Pyvic had assumed led to a washroom.

"Which I assume gives you free access to read tales of high adventure or scandalous stories of fair maidens being seduced into lives of wanton sin," Hessler said, "but it does *not* allow you access to the lower stacks."

The doorway led to a small hallway, which in turn led to a narrow set of stairs lit only by glowing crystal panels set into the walls at ankle height.

"I read *crime stories*," Pyvic said with some annoyance, squinting as he followed them down.

"Of course you do," said Hessler, "given your somewhat counterintuitive belief in the efficacy of intellect in solving crimes rather than the simplistic racial and social profiling that most town guards perform—"

"Tern prefers the ones about fair maidens being seduced into lives of wanton sin," Desidora cut in, and Hessler sputtered to a halt. She smiled over her shoulder. "Usually by dark, brooding wizards."

At the bottom of the stairs, Pyvic stopped and stared. While the main library upstairs was well lit and decorated with stained-glass windows showing great figures from the Republic's past, the lower stacks were dark, the floors bare stone. The ceiling was twenty feet overhead, with small magical lamps casting light down every few feet. The shelves were metal, ten feet high stretching as far as he could see in the dim light.

Every one of them was filled. Nearby, Pyvic saw books, some looking nearly new, while others were cracked and ancient. Further down, he could see scroll tubes, thin slabs of stone etched with runes, and row upon row of tiny glowing crystals.

"Impressive," he said after a long moment, looking down through countless centuries of knowledge. "How does that help us learn about the elven book?"

"Chits or helm?" Desidora asked Hessler.

"Chits, I think," said Hessler, starting off down into the stacks.

Desidora nodded and walked to the first shelf. A squat, rounded podium sat in front of it, and Desidora tapped it. "The elves were once like us, Justicar," she said, as the podium hummed to life, and a panel of glowing crystal unfolded from the edges. "They may even have been human, for all we know."

"That's considered apocryphal!" Hessler called back from whatever he was doing further down in the stacks. "No clear evidence either way."

"In any event," Desidora said, rolling her eyes as she tapped the crystal panel, "the elves modified themselves to better work with the tools of the ancients. They are attuned to magical energy in ways we can barely understand. In fact, it is said that their behavior even changes in proximity to crystal artifacts."

"It's likely a form of sensory overload," Hessler's voice called back, "like if a drink is hot enough to burn your mouth, you can't tell whether it's sweet or bitter."

"Only instead of your sense of taste," Desidora said, "imagine that it's your emotions, your empathy. The senses that tell you when it's not appropriate to shout in a quiet room."

"They get that way around all the ancient magic," Hessler shouted, now somewhere off to the left in the darkness. "That's why they're so reclusive. Well, that and societal regression as a deliberate subversion of human attempts to aggressively colonize and assimilate existing indigenous cultures. Desidora, do you have a number yet?"

"Almost!" She tapped on the panel a few more times. "K-K-116-point-287-dash-L."

"Got it!"

"So what that all means, in the most practical sense of the word," Desidora said, turning to Pyvic, "is that elves do not think the way we do."

Finally, feeling like a fool, Pyvic got it. "They record information in a way that we can't simply replicate," he said, "because if we could, then there could be countless copies of *The Love Song of Eillenfiniel* lying around."

"And if that were true," Desidora said with an approving smile, "then why would the Empire want the original so badly?"

Hessler came out from a nearby stack. He held a long, thin plane of sky-blue crystal in both hands. "Now, while we can't get the manuscript itself—that's Loch's job—we can look at the body of critical work surrounding the manuscript to see if there are themes that might give us a clue about what makes this book so important." He placed the crystal plane gently atop the panel on the podium, then rotated it, squinting as he did. "Primitive detection methods," he muttered to himself. "The lapitects are working on new systems that should double normal storage capacity within a few years. "Ah, there we go."

The panel glowed with sky-blue light, and Desidora nodded and started tapping again. "I have reproductions of the main text in several languages, dissertations upon the themes of the written work . . ."

"If it were part of the written work, then whoever wanted it would be satisfied with a copy." Pyvic frowned. It had taken him a few moments to understand the methods, but now he was on a case again. He could solve cases. "What have you got that tries to put the elven-specific parts into human terms?"

"Checking." Desidora tapped the panel again, squinting. "There are several. One student has . . . it appears to be a selection of foods to eat while reading the manuscript, to induce the right sensations."

"Sounds messy," Pyvic said.

"It *sounds* like someone's liberal arts project." Hessler snorted. "They might as well have glued felt cutouts onto sticks and performed it as a puppet show, for all its accuracy."

"Don't give up just yet," Desidora said. "Can you find me . . . K-R-772-point-036-dash-A?"

"That's . . ." Hessler squinted. "Fairy creatures?" He blinked. "Of course. Fairy creatures. They're made from the same magic that the elves once worked with, which means that their minds may be able to understand the non-standard portions of an elven manuscript without having to resort to liberal arts synesthesia fakery. Excellent thinking. 036-dash-A, you said?" He hurried off.

"You're cross-checking," Pyvic said, nodding.

Desidora smiled. "Is that so surprising?"

"I suppose it shouldn't be. Sorry." He nodded, and her cheeks dimpled as she bowed regally in return. "After dealing

with town guards so often, it's easy to think that critical thinking is restricted to the Justicars."

"Often," Desidora said, "but not always. Hessler's university and my religious training included brief, sporadic sec-
tions in which we were taught to think."

Pyvic grinned. "So we cross-check criticism of the elven
manuscript with works by fairy creatures, which ideally tells us
something about what makes the book so damned important."

"And lets us save Loch," Desidora finished.

Pyvic looked down through the stacks into the darkness.
"Loch can take care of herself."

"The Knights of Gedesar are extremely dangerous,"
Desidora said. "If some element of the Republic is using
them against her . . ."

"*Kutesosh gajair'is,*" Ghylspwr growled from her waist.

"That doesn't matter." Pyvic glanced at the panel. "You're
going to get me something I can use. I'll help Loch, she'll put
this behind her . . ." He sighed. "She just saved the Republic
three months ago. She deserves a hero's rest, not . . ."

"You're doing everything you can," Desidora said, and put
a small, soft hand on his arm.

Pyvic forced a smile. "Thank you."

"You *should* have told her you loved her in that message
crystal, though."

He gave her a hard look, and she returned a mocking one
in kind.

Hessler came back from a stack a few rows away. He was
holding another plane of crystal, this one a pale green. "Got
it," he said as he came over. "Now, if I can . . . no, upside
down, stupid primitive . . . there." He slid the new crystal
into place atop the first one, and the sky-blue glow turned
into a vivid turquoise.

"Checking now." Desidora tapped the panel. "Very little crossover, but . . . here. *Ruminations upon the Unutterable by the Queen of the Cold River.*"

"Well, that sounds promising," said Hessler.

"Come on." Desidora set off down the stacks. "It's not far." Pyvic and Hessler followed her through the dim stacks. Their boots echoed on the bare stone floor, and the rich smell of old paper and leather grew stronger as they went on.

"I didn't even know there *were* books by fairy creatures," Pyvic said.

"Most of them don't care enough to learn how to read," Hessler said, "which leads human-centric institutes of learning to overlook their philosophy and culture, although to be fair, they *could* make the effort to learn new methods of communication . . ."

"It's a small field," Desidora said, "but the ones who do publish works are usually the oldest and wisest of the creatures. Some of them were formed just after the ancients left this world."

"*Kutesosh gajair'is,*" Ghylspwr said.

"Yes, yes, after fighting the Glimmering Folk and leaving the world so as to shut them out as well," Hessler said, "although honestly, I don't know that you need to remind *us* about it . . ."

"*Kutesosh gajair'is,*" Ghylspwr said again.

"Wait," said Desidora.

"I don't see that you need to make *threats* about it," said Hessler. "I'm all for teaching the history of the ancients and their battle against the Glimmering Folk, but since you have a vocabulary consisting of three phrases, I doubt that . . ."

"Wait!" Desidora said more sharply this time.

"Kutesosh gajair'is!" Ghylspwr said for the third time, very emphatically.

Everyone stopped.

And as they did, Pyvic heard what Ghylspwr had been warning them about.

At first, it sounded like a rustle, like coins rattling in a mostly full pouch. Then, as though his hearing had slid into focus, Pyvic made it out.

It was the sound of countless crystals clicking on the bare stone floor.

And the sound was coming toward them.

Six

NIGHT FELL ON AJEVETH. CRAFTSMEN HEADED BACK TO THEIR homes after a good day's work and a fine dinner at one of the city's gourmet restaurants, miners stopped by the bars for a celebratory drink after another day with no accidents, and guards patrolled the streets, carrying cheery lanterns and greeting fellow citizens by name.

On the rooftop of an expensive inn, Loch, Kail, Icy, and Ululenia looked across the street at *Irke'desar*, the Bounty of the Past.

Loch had gotten a room on the fifth story of the inn, which was terraced like all the other major buildings in the city. At this height, standing atop the fourth story's roof, they could look across the street to the *second-story* rooftop of the museum, which ended in a wall with a window that looked into the fairy-creature room, right next to the room with the damn book.

The window was wider at the bottom than at the top. With a bit of wriggling, someone of modest size *should* be able to squeeze through.

"Have you got the shot?" she asked Tern.

"Think so." Tern was squinting through a series of lenses on her crossbow, which was resting on the edge of the rooftop. "Can't risk a hook through the window, not with the rooftop still trapped with pressure sensors."

"The earth-daemons bound to service cry out against their imprisonment," Ululenia confirmed.

"Right, that. So I'm going with a daemonfire bolt. It'll burn clean through the window and should punch into the stone. Cools in a minute or so, and once it does, it should be solidly embedded in the wall."

"And it'll support Icy's weight?" Loch asked.

"Hopefully!" Tern said cheerfully. "That's if the daemon-fire bolt keeps enough speed after punching through the window, *and* if it doesn't burn hot at the back end and light the rope on fire, *and* if the window I'm shooting through is actually dwarven crystal and not glass, so that the bolt burns though it instead of just shattering it and sending shards of glass clattering down onto the pressure plates."

"As long as we're all confident in the plan," Kail said.

Loch nodded. "Whenever you're ready. Kail, eyes on the ground."

Tern slid down to one knee, still looking through the lenses. She made a single infinitesimal adjustment to her crossbow, a finger's gentle pressure on one side. Then she took two slow, deep breaths. On the third, she fired.

The bolt hissed an angry red as it sizzled across the street, over the rooftop, and cleanly through the window, a thin line of white silk rope trailing behind it. A moment later, the sound of the hissing pop reached her ears. "Nice shot. Kail?"

"All clear on the street."

"Ululenia?"

"I sense no fear or anger from the guards inside."

"Tern?"

"Fourteen, fifteen, sixteen . . ."

"Got it."

Loch watched the rooftop across the street, and the little line of white silk swaying gently in the night breeze. After a bit, Tern quietly said, "One hundred," and carefully unlatched her crossbow from the rope. It dangled slightly, and then the hook securing it to the rooftop caught, and it held. "Hang on. Let me tighten it a bit. Icy, if it leaves you dangling too close to the rooftop, freeze and give me a sign, and I'll tighten it some more."

"I believe I will be fine," Icy said as Tern worked a tiny crank on the hook, grunting with the effort until finally it couldn't be tightened any further. "One moment," he said, and stepped calmly onto the rope.

"Oh, of course, can't just *hang* from it, you big show-off," Tern muttered as Icy walked across the rope. From where Loch watched, the thin silk rope seemed to dig into his soft slippers, but Icy showed no sign of discomfort, walking with his arms extended at a brisk pace. "Fall of a hundred feet or so, but gods forbid he go hand-over-hand like some amateur second-story man."

Icy was over the other rooftop now, the silk line just a foot or so off the ground as he made his way toward the window.

"He gonna make it?" Kail asked.

"He hasn't signaled."

"Not what I asked, Tern."

Icy was halfway across the roof, and the rope bowed down, just inches from the rooftop. He paused for a moment as a gust of wind whistled through the night air, and looked back at them.

Then he turned, crouched, and leaped lightly the last ten feet, catching himself on the lip of the window with his feet tucked up just above the ground.

Loch let out a breath.

"I forgot just how good he was," Kail said, shaking his head.

"He requests my assistance," Ululenia said, and without waiting for a response, shifted into the form of a small white bird. She flapped through the night sky as Icy braced himself, gently traced the edges of the window, and then laid his fingers on the window as though holding an invisible ball in his hands.

At such a distance, Loch couldn't see exactly what he did. What she *did* see was that his hand moved, and with a faint pop, the window snapped cleanly from its frame, all in one piece and hanging from the white rope by the hole that Tern had shot through it, like a bead on a string.

"Look at that. *Look* at that. Imagine what he could do if he was allowed to *hit* stuff," Kail said under his breath.

"He swore an oath," Tern said.

"Why would anyone do that? That would be like me swearing an oath not to pick locks or talk about people's mothers."

Icy lifted himself up without evident effort and slid forward through the window. Ululenia flapped in after him and perched on the windowsill.

"Okay, Ululenia," said Tern, "what does he see?"

After a moment, she added, "Okay, good. The third one down."

She followed it up with, "Down relative to the ground. Come on, Icy, how am I supposed to know which way you're facing? Yes. Third one down *from the ceiling*. Twist it to the left, and it should come right out."

"Do they even *need* us?" Kail asked Loch. "You've got an acrobat, a mind-reading shapeshifter, and Tern, who can disable security in rooms she isn't even in."

"We're all part of the team, Kail." Loch grinned. "You flew the airship."

"Okay, point taken." Kail raised an eyebrow at her. "Do we need *you?*"

"Hey!"

"I'm just saying, the fewer ways we split the take, the more for each of us."

"There's no take, Kail. We're saving the Republic again."

"Right. Damn."

"Okay, Icy's disabled the motion sensors inside the room," said Tern. "He's working on the floor plates now. The door to the room with the book is closed, he says. Looks like a manual lock."

"Guess it's my turn, then." Kail looked at the rope. "Pardon me if I just crawl awkwardly while hanging from it instead of doing handsprings or whatever he did. He and Ululenia are sure the window's big enough for me to squeeze through? 'Cause I'm bigger than Icy." He paused. "Oh, hey, unicorn lady. In my head the whole time, huh? No, please don't. I'm really not big on heights, and I'm going to need to focus on not freaking out while I do this climb."

He swung out, arms and legs both wrapped around the rope, and began to scoot across.

"Hey, Kail?" Loch called softly.

"Yes, Captain?"

"Don't fall a hundred feet to the ground and die."

"Thanks, Captain."

"That's why you need me, Kail. To remind you of these things."

She grinned as he shot her a dirty look, then kept scooting.

"I have to say," Tern said beside her, "it's actually kind of a nice change to have a plan go smoothly enough for everyone to give each other grief instead of screaming and flailing the whole time."

"Isafesira de Lochenville," came a call from behind them.

"Your fault," Loch said to Tern.

"I know."

"You don't talk about how the job is going until the job is done," Loch said.

"I am very sorry."

They turned around slowly.

Imperial Princess Veiled Lightning stepped gracefully through Loch's window out onto the rooftop, her lavender-and-violet dress shining silver in the moonlight.

Lightning crackled in her hand.

"Everybody back, now!" Pyvic barked, looking back and forth as the sound of thousands of tiny crystal legs clicking on the stone floor of the lower stacks grew closer.

"We can't!" Desidora drew Ghylspwr. "Whatever these are—"

"Spiders," said Hessler. "I'm assuming they're spiders."

"—they've never been here any of the other times I've come."

"You think they showed up because we were searching for the book?" Pyvic asked.

"Possibly?" Desidora gave him a helpless look.

"Which means if we run, we're likely lose any chance to get the book."

"But we also don't get killed by spiders!" Hessler added. The clicking grew louder still, and then they poured around the corner: hundreds of crystal crabs the size of housecats. "*Almost* spiders," Hessler said, and lifted a hand. A wave of fire slashed out and burned through the first few ranks. "Hah! See that? Not just illusion magic anymore! I've been studying a few other branches of the arcane arts!"

"Fire. In a library." Pyvic turned to run and saw crabs coming in from the other direction as well. They were red and purple, and at the joints in the legs and the spots where the legs met the body, little pinpricks of thin blue light crackled. "Everybody up onto the shelves!"

He grabbed the nearest shelf and started climbing. Beside him, Desidora and Hessler did the same. A crab clung to Desidora's dress, and Pyvic whipped his blade out and slashed down. It chopped through the crab, shattering it into thousands of tiny fragments, and Pyvic scrambled the rest of the way up, taking in his surroundings with the quick self-preservation instincts from years in the Republic scouts.

The ceiling was high enough that they didn't have to duck, even while standing atop shelves that were ten feet high, and the shelves were wide enough that nobody was likely to teeter and fall off.

Hessler gestured down from the top of the bookshelf, and a flare of fire sizzled through more of the crabs as they tried to climb the bookshelf.

"I thought you could only do illusions," Pyvic said. The crabs that hadn't been charred to blackened husks were still trying to climb the shelves. They'd only gotten as high as the second shelf so far, but they were still coming, and there seemed to be hundreds of the things. There was no more ground visible around the shelves, just endless ranks of purple and red crabs.

"I've been practicing," Hessler said. "Summoning elemental fire is a very simple daemonic conjuration, and given our past adventures—"

"I really hoped that was illusory fire," Pyvic said, "since it appears that you've started a fire among the books."

"Yes, well—"

"Now, the question is, do we try to escape, or do we go for the book?"

"*Kun-kabynalti osu fuir'is!*" Ghylspwr said.

"That means *escape*," Hessler said, looking at the crabs—as well as the smoke billowing out from the bookshelf where his blast had lit things on fire.

"Got that, thanks."

"We have to go for the book," Desidora disagreed. "Triggering this means we're getting close to something worth worrying about."

Pyvic nodded. "All right. We're going to be jumping either way." The crabs were jumping as well, crawling over each other in an attempt to get higher. They seemed to have abandoned their attempts to climb the shelves and were now just swarming around them. "Which way?"

Desidora pointed, and Pyvic nodded, took a few running steps, and launched himself from the end of the bookshelf across the gap to the next one. Said gap was about seven or eight feet, long enough that he wouldn't have wanted to try it without a running start. As it was, he landed on the next shelf, slid awkwardly on the smooth, dust-coated surface, and caught himself with his free hand just before pitching off the side.

Looking down, he saw hundreds of little pincers clacking up at him. He tried to ignore them as best he could, but the image—not to mention the sound—was fairly disconcerting. Grimacing, he looked back at Desidora and Hessler instead. "Who's next?"

Desidora hitched up her skirts, took a few steps, and leaped. Her jump didn't have a lot of muscle behind it, but at the midpoint of her leap, Ghylspwr jerked in her hands, shouting, *"Besyn larveth'is!"* and pulling her forward. She landed next to Pyvic, breathing lightly, and smiled down at Ghylspwr. "Thank you."

Hessler leaped as well. Like Desidora, his jump wasn't a terribly good one. Unlike Desidora, he didn't have a magical warhammer to help pull him the rest of the way. The wizard hit the shelf at about chest height, knocking the wind from his lungs and scrabbling for purchase on the smooth shelf.

Pyvic lunged, grabbed Hessler before he slipped—only to find him slipping himself until hands gripped his ankles. He looked over his shoulder to see Desidora putting all her weight down on his legs, anchoring them in place. Grunting a thanks, he hauled Hessler up onto the shelf. From the knees down, the wizard was already covered with the giant crabs. They clung to his boots and his robes, claws clicking as they dug in for purchase.

"Hang on!" Desidora stepped over Pyvic and came down with great sweeping strikes of her hammer that sent the crystalline creatures flying away with shards scattered everywhere. Three times Ghylspwr whooshed down and away with extremely careful blows, and then once more, with an overhead swing that came down between Hessler's legs hard enough to make the metal of the shelves creak.

Hessler stared at the hammer that had smashed down between his robed legs, still wheezing and trying to catch his breath. "Um."

"We were *very* careful," Desidora said.

"Um."

Shattered splinters of crystal rolled out from beneath Hessler's now-torn robes, pulling him out of his stupor. A pincer the size of Pyvic's hand still twitched. Hessler swallowed. "So I see."

"Kun kabynalti osu fuir'is."

"How much farther?" Pyvic asked. Looking down, he could see some blood among the tears on Hessler's robes. Unless Hessler got a lot better at jumping very soon, this was going to be a problem. The fire on the bookshelf also appeared to be spreading, which honestly seemed unfair, given that the shelves were made of metal.

"It should be the next shelf after this one." Desidora turned. "We will have it in a moment."

"No," came a voice from Pyvic's right. "You will not."

The lights over to the right flickered, then dimmed as a robed figure pulled itself up onto the top of a nearby shelf. It crouched before them, arms flung out wide, each hand holding something curved and made of crystal. They were either hooks or sickles—Pyvic couldn't be certain which.

"The hour must not be known," said the figure, and leaped at them.

"That little golden forehead-necklace thing with the ruby in the middle marks her as part of the Imperial family," Tern said, eyes wide, pointing at the gold-filigree chain that sat on the Imperial woman's brow. "Oh my gods, that really *is* Princess Veiled Lightning. I used to have a tea set like the kind she had!"

Loch looked at the Imperial woman. Her lavender-and-violet dress was cut to allow easy movement while still concealing her legs. The lightning that crackled between her fingers left little sparkling trails in the air when she moved her hands. It was hard to tell in the moonlight, but the two braids of hair that dangled beside the curve of her breasts might have ended in little crystal clips.

"I find it hard to believe a princess could stay on her feet after a head-butt to the face," Loch said, drawing her sword.

"A head-butt *and* a crystal wine glass," Veiled Lightning said.

"Do you have any idea how many stories my mother told me about her?" Tern asked, sounding more excited than Loch had ever heard Tern sound about anything that was not made of crystals or alchemical reagents. "There was a book on posture, and dance classes, and everything! She really wanted Veiled Lightning to be my role model for how young women should act."

"Your mother is a woman of grace and discernment," said the princess's bodyguard as he too stepped out through the window onto the roof. He held his magical ax in both hands, and his heavy armor caught the moonlight and glittered. "A pity you did not heed her."

"And you're Gentle Thunder!" Tern said, excited enough that Loch shot her a look. "Your doll was a lot more fun to play with. It was poseable, and if you bought the deluxe doll, it came with your ax, Arikayurichi, the Bringer of Order, and . . ." She trailed off as she caught Loch's look. It mirrored the look Gentle Thunder was giving her. "I'm done. I'm stopping."

"The order to hand me over to the Empire was illegal," Loch said. "I'm not the one who turned Heaven's Spire into a weapon."

"And yet thousands will die in the coming war if you refuse to surrender," Veiled Lightning said. "You were a baroness, but refer to yourself as a captain, Isafesira. Do you consider your own life more valuable than your fellow soldiers?"

"*Kutesosh gajair'is!*" said the ax that Loch assumed was Arikayurichi, Bringer of Order.

"If I surrender, your people torture me until I break, then find out I really wasn't behind the attack and goes to war with the Republic anyway." Loch took a step to the side, distancing herself from Tern a bit. In the corner of her eye, Kail was still climbing across the gap between the buildings on the white silken line.

"That is a possibility," Veiled Lightning said. Her intricate braids bobbed as she nodded briefly, and Loch caught the flash of crystal at the tips again. "But placed against the certainty of the war that comes without your surrender—"

"What about the book?" Tern asked, and as Veiled Lightning looked at her, she flushed. "And sorry for interrupting, Your Highness."

"Could you stop being *polite* to her?" Loch muttered.

"Look, I played with a doll house modeled after her summer home."

"If the Republic wishes to return stolen relics to the Empire," Gentle Thunder said, putting himself between Loch and Lightning, "it may do so after you have been tried and executed. For now, the Republic's treachery demands a sacrifice." He raised his ax. "Surrender or die."

"Or escape," Loch said, and spun her sword as she stepped forward. Gentle Thunder looked her way, and on cue, Tern shot him with her crossbow.

Or at least, that had been the plan. What actually happened was that Tern fired the crossbow, and the ax in Gentle

Thunder's hands moved like a silver blur, and Tern's bolt glanced up harmlessly into the darkness with a sound like a hammer on a tuning fork.

"Son of a *bitch*," Tern said, more impressed than disappointed.

"*Kutesosh gajair'is!*" shouted the ax.

"I really thought when Arikayurichi cut arrows from the air in the books, the writers were playing fast and loose with what magical axes could do. Loch, did you see that?"

"Tern, could you *please* stop praising them?" Loch shifted her blade from the showy spinning position into a grip she could actually use to hurt someone.

"Wait," Veiled Lightning said to Gentle Thunder as he advanced on Loch. "We need her alive. Attendant Shenziencis, can you restrain her?"

A *third* figure slid out through the window, moving with liquid smoothness despite the ringmail. It was the movement that warned Loch what was about to happen, along with the cut of the ringmail—though the rings were a rich green rather than the shining gold she had seen last time. In one hand, the figure drew forth a short spear. The other hand held a net whose silver links crackled with pale-yellow energy. A golden helmet obscured the figure's face.

"I can," the figure said, and to Loch's surprise, the voice beneath the golden helmet was female. The last time Loch had run into something wearing that ringmail and holding a weapon with that magic, the voice had been male.

It had been called a Hunter, and it had continued to fight even after taking blows that would have killed any mortal man.

Loch was drawing in a breath to call out a warning when the crossbow bolt Tern had fired landed on the museum rooftop across the street.

Icy, inside the building, was continuing to work on disabling the *interior* pressure plates, since he had assumed correctly that Kail would not want to hang upside-down from a wall while disabling a dwarven-crafted door lock. He had, in the interest of time, decided not to disable the pressure plates on the rooftop.

As a result, the moment the crossbow bolt hit the rooftop, the earth-daemons bound into the floorplates shrieked an alarm.

Loch, Tern, and the three Imperials turned as man-sized creatures of stone clawed their way free from the rooftop across the street, howling like a gale-force wind through a cave tunnel. They pounced on the bolt, still screaming, and tore it to shreds.

Then, as one, they looked across the rooftop at Loch. Dropping to all fours, they sprinted across the rooftop and onto the rope, running on it like a squirrel on a clothesline.

"Kail, new plan!" Loch called out . . .

And chopped down through the rope with a single clean cut.

Security Enforcer Gart Utt'Krenner could have delegated his nightly patrol duties to other members of his staff. He did not lack for resources—especially given the reallocations after the recent human display of military aggression with Heaven's Spire—and his work kept him busy enough even without making patrols himself. His wife had been supportive about the late hours he had worked leading up to the opening of the new magical display at *Irke'desar*, but her comments during their nightly face-washing and mouth-cleansing suggested that she carried some irritation with her at the amount of work Gart had placed upon his own shoulders. It was a fair concern, and Gart agreed with it. At a certain point, his insistence upon continuing patrols himself might even impact the morale of his staff, suggesting that Gart did not trust his men and women to perform their duties themselves.

Nothing could be further from the truth, and once the new magical display had been up for a few weeks—perhaps after the next civic holiday—Gart Utt'Krenner would hang his armored jacket over a chair and ease back to one night a week.

For now, though, he felt this current display was too important to sit out the patrols. Besides the value of the artifacts on display, there was the potential for mischief. Given the political climate, it was easy to believe that a member of one of the rival human nations might decide vandalizing the other nation's display would be a good idea.

As such, Gart took it upon himself to go room to room, entering his all-clear for each display in a crystal fob attached to his belt. He glared as he finished assessing the Urujar display, a room that always made him sick to his stomach, mostly due to the fact that dwarves had made the slave collars so prominently shown in the cases. "Urujar sub-hex: clear." Gart Utt'Krenner sighed deeply and shook his head at the collars. "Poor folk. Centuries of pain, and I suspect ye still be feelin' it deep today."

Gart's sentimental moment was shattered by the shrieking of pressure-plate alarms up on the rooftop.

"Byn-Kodar's knuckles!" Gart muttered. If this was the birds again, the runesmen behind the faulty avian aversion systems would have a lot of explaining to do.

He turned to head back to the central security room when an Urujar man hanging from a rope burst through the crystal window and slammed into Gart's mailed chest like a hammer blow.

"Rrrf," Gart heard the man say. At least, that's what he thought the man said. It was as though the words were coming from a great distance, and his head rang and darkness swam across his vision. The man continued, "Sorry about that. Was trying to break into the elven room . . ."

Security Enforcer Gart Utt'Krenner had time to remember that he had insisted on performing these perimeter checks himself before he blacked out.

Kail got back to his feet, wincing. Crystal didn't break *nearly* as easily as glass when you slammed into it, and glass broke a lot less easily than people thought it did. Still, considering that swinging down on a rope had in no way been part of the plan in the first place, Kail was willing to take what he could get.

What he could get, apparently, was the security dwarf from earlier that day lying unconscious with what looked a lot like a master key on the ground next to his hand.

"Well, all right, then," Kail said, and picked up the key. He had to bend over to do it, which made everything go wobbly at the edges of his vision again. Some of that was probably from crashing through the glass, and a lot of the rest was Kail not liking heights a whole hell of a lot—and liking falling from them by surprise because his captain had just cut the rope he'd been hanging from even less than that.

He looked around the room, blinking. "Oh, yeah: Urujar room. Captain said this one was bad." Back before he'd joined up with Loch and saved the Republic, a room filled with shackles and chains might have thrown him off. Then he'd had magic clamp down on his very soul and turn him against his friends, and, well, that kind of experience put things into perspective. He tossed the shackles a dirty gesture and left the room without a backward look.

He assumed Loch was fighting bad guys on her rooftop, and that that had something to do with the screaming monsters on the museum rooftop that Kail had been climbing toward. Kail hadn't caught all the details, focused as he had been on trying not to plunge a hundred feet to his death. He was sure Loch and Tern had it handled.

He nodded to the big golden throne in the Imperial room, and headed up the stairs to the next floor. The dwarf's master key opened the door, and Icy and Ululenia turned to look at him in surprise as the lights flickered on over their heads. Ululenia was currently a small white hummingbird, and Icy was hanging from the wall.

"I'm pretty sure this disabled the room's security," Kali said, and held up the master key.

We were expecting you to come through the window, Ululenia said in his head, *although the number of shrieking earth-daemons outside led us to not expect you very soon.*

"Well, I like to surprise people." Kail gestured at the door that led to the elven sub-room. "In there? Probably good to hurry." Outside, the daemons were still shrieking, and it sounded like people were fighting.

This is extremely unnatural, Ululenia said, and shifted back into human shape as Kail walked across the room without triggering the floor plates. "I was certain that the earth-daemons were employed only to raise an alarm. Allowing the daemons to manifest and directly confront intruders is a harsh and unforgiving decision from the dwarves."

"And messy." Icy hopped down to the ground as well, testing his weight and then flexing his fingers, since he'd apparently been clinging to the underside of an antique wand display for quite some time while trying to disable the security systems. "Dwarves do not usually employ messy solutions."

"I get the sense this is going all kinds of wrong for everyone," Kail said, and slid the master key into the lock on the elven sub-room door. As he'd hoped, the lock clicked open. "Didn't even get to break out *Iofecyl* to try her out on these fancy dwarven locks."

The elven room's lights flickered on as the door opened, and Kail stepped inside. Off in the distance, the earth-daemons were still doing their thing. The elven manuscript sat in its display case, safe behind a squared-off section marked with red velvet rope.

"Any ideas how we get out of here once we've got the thing?" Kail asked. "I mean, if we've got earth-daemons on the roof, I'm guessing we shouldn't leave that way." A few months back, while Loch was off saving the world and avenging her family's honor, Kail had—after recovering from the mind control bit that the Urujar room with the shackles hadn't reminded him of very much at all—gotten to fight daemons. He'd picked up some new scars for his trouble, and wasn't eager to live that experience again.

"I may be able to carry you both out from the window through which you entered the building," Ululenia said, "or at least make your fall more gentle."

"Less gentle would be difficult." Kail approached the manuscript. "Now, what did Loch say?" Aside from *Kail, new plan,* which was strikingly different from, *Kail, I'm about to send you plunging toward the street, maybe consider hanging on extra tight, sorry about that.* "Equal weight, one quick movement, right?"

"Quick and smooth," Icy confirmed, and took from a pocket in his robes a pouch of sand that, to the best of Loch's knowledge, weighed exactly the same as the elven manuscript. He passed it to Kail, then took a very small pot and brush from *another* pocket in his robes, unscrewed the pot, and whisked around the contents, which looked like either thick slime or thin paste of a milky brown hue. "Tern promised that her reagent would work quickly."

"Reagent being the goop?"

"Well-reasoned as always, Kail." Icy dipped the brush into the pot and then dabbed it on the crystal of the manuscript display case, describing a good-sized circle in one side.

Tern hadn't lied: the effect was immediate. The crystal sizzled and bubbled at contact with the paste, and Kail and Icy both stepped back as oily purple smoke hissed out. The crystal clouded, then drooped, and then dripped away entirely, leaving a good hole for Kail to work with.

Kail waited until the crystal stopped smoking. "She say when it'd be safe?"

"She did not."

"Well, I'm reassured." Kail hefted the pouch. "All right. Give me a bit of room here." He reached forward gingerly. "I'm going to have to—"

As his hand passed the plane of the velvet rope, a brilliant flash of blue light exploded in his face, and an entirely *new* shrieking alarm went off.

"—set off an alarm," Kail finished, "because *that's* how it's going tonight."

Seven

P YVIC STOOD ON THE TOP OF THE METAL BOOKSHELF, LOOKING AT the hooded figure in the dim and flickering light. "Desidora?"

"It's aura is shielded," she said, squinting.

"If it has one," Pyvic said. "Remember the golem that the ancients left to hunt fairy creatures?"

"I imagine she remembers it," Hessler said, clutching at his still-bleeding legs, "given that it *killed* her."

"Yes." Desidora blinked, then cocked her head. "Yes, this is similar. It's like the crab-creatures. It's not fully formed, like a golem. It's being held together by magic."

"As fascinating as this is," Hessler said, "what I'd really like to know is why it hasn't attacked us yet," Hessler said. "Not that I'm complaining, mind you."

The hooded creature had not spoken or moved since its first proclamation. It stood between them and the book. Below them, the crabs were now barely visible in the darkness, but Pyvic could still hear their scuttling on the bare stone floor, along with the licking flames of the fire Hessler had accidentally started. Going by the sound of burning paper, the crabs had knocked books from the shelves, causing the fire to spread.

And under that, another noise, an irregular hiss like a sword being drawn, or a ringmail shirt taking a glancing blow from a blade, or . . .

"They're destroying the shelf," Pyvic snapped, cursing himself for ten kinds of an idiot. Even as the words left his mouth, the metal shelf creaked and began to tip. "Everyone jump!"

The shelf was tilting to the right. Pyvic couldn't make the jump ahead, especially not with the hooded figure waiting for him on the next shelf. He jumped left instead, pushing off the falling shelf to make the much shorter jump to the bookshelf that had been behind him a moment ago.

Below him, hundreds of priceless manuscripts fell into the slashing crystal pincers. From his new vantage, Pyvic could now see the shelf itself had been shredded with countless tiny cuts to one side.

Hessler and Desidora had jumped with the shelf instead of against it, which had probably seemed like a good idea at the time, since it let them use the falling shelf to add momentum to their jump. As soon as they landed, however, the shelf they'd just been on slammed into the shelf they were *now* on, and with a great, slow creak, their *new* shelf started to tip over .

"Keep going!" Pyvic shouted. Desidora nodded, wide-eyed, and dragged Hessler up to leap onto the *next* next shelf.

They weren't going to be up there for long, and when they hit the ground, it was only a question of whether the flames or the crabs got them first. Pyvic looked down at the crabs swarming through the fire, cracked and charred but still scuttling along, and then looked at the hooded figure—who had turned to watch Hessler and Desidora.

Then Pyvic made a gut check.

"I'm going for the book!" he shouted, and took a running jump across the aisle.

He landed on the next shelf, slipped again on the dust, and came back to his feet in time to see the hooded figure leap over from the next row and land before him. Below, a mass of crabs was swirling around his shelf now as well.

"The book is forbidden," the hooded creature said, its voice a dry crackling hiss. "The hour must not be known." It lashed out with its crystal hooks.

Pyvic parried, slapping the hooks away. They were definitely crystal, definitely sharp, and probably part of the creature, not just weapons. He slashed, grimaced as the creature caught his blade with its hooks, and then lunged forward and drove the thing back off the shelf.

It fell back, then pivoted with inhuman grace, kicked off the shelf behind it, and sprang back at Pyvic with its hooks raised. Its hood fell off as it did, allowing Pyvic to clearly see the jagged crystals that clung together in a field of magic to make a crude facsimile of a head.

Seeing that would have changed his next move had he not already been acting on instinct. As it was, his blade chopped cleanly into the hooded creature's neck.

For *most* opponents, that would have been a good strategic move. For a creature held together by magic, though, it was merely an inconvenience. Pyvic jerked his blade back, but not quickly enough. The hook caught his wrist, trapped his blade, and wrenched it from his grip even as it yanked Pyvic off his feet.

Pyvic clung to the edge of the shelf. His body was still on it, but his legs were scrabbling for purchase. He could feel the sudden tug of weight and the tiny slicing slashes of pain, which told him that the crabs had gotten hold of his boots.

That was a problem to be dealt with later, however, since the hooded figure was standing over him, hooks raised to finish him.

"Kutesosh gajair'is!"

Ghylspwr was a silver streak of light as he whistled over Pyvic's head and then blasted the hooded figure from the shelf.

Pyvic hauled himself back up, kicking the crabs free, and saw Desidora and Hessler a few shelves over, safe again. "Thanks."

"Thank you for buying us time with your distraction," Desidora said. Ghylspwr had already returned to her hand. She looked down and smiled. "I see the book. Let us end this."

Without another word, she dropped down from the shelf, landing nimbly in between the shelves below.

"Desidora?" Hessler looked down. "Do you have a plan?"

"Hessler, buy her some room!" Pyvic pointed, and without hesitation Hessler flung out his hands, sending sheets of fire into the crabs as they skittered away from Pyvic and back toward Desidora.

"Really?" Pyvic shouted to him. "More fire? *Really?*" Not waiting for a response, Pyvic leaped to the next shelf—the actual shelf the damned book was supposed to be on, assuming Desidora's information was correct. He'd lost his sword, and the only thing he'd been able to do thus far was cause distractions until the people with magical abilities made their moves, but a justicar didn't let things like that stop him.

Desidora was rifling through the shelves with one hand and swinging Ghylspwr in broad sweeping strikes with the other to keep the crabs back. "Found it!" she shouted, yanking a thin volume bound in blue leather from the shelf.

"You will not read it." The hooded figure stepped out from around the aisle, its hooks raised.

"I will," said Desidora, and her voice was cold.

She swung Ghylspwr, and the creature leaped, snared the warhammer with its hooks, and tore it from Desidora's grasp.

"No," said the creature, as it flung Ghylspwr away.

"Did you think I could not see the magic that held you together?" Desidora asked. "That a death priestess would not see what would have to be done to tear you apart?"

She raised one hand and curled her fingers slowly into a fist.

Nothing happened.

"You are no longer a death priestess," the hooded figure said, stepping forward. "You have no power here."

"I, however, do," muttered Hessler from atop the shelf, and he traced a glowing sigil in the air.

The hooded creature collapsed to the ground, hundreds of shimmering crystals tinkling on the stone floor as they scattered out from under a now-empty robe.

Pyvic looked over at Hessler, who was pale and drawn. "Nice."

"Daemon-banishing abjuration. I hoped the magic that held that thing together was similar enough . . ." Hessler took a breath. "Fairly draining to cast, and there's a good chance it's actually just *suppressing* the magic, not banishing it, so . . ."

The crabs had drawn back when their master attacked Desidora, but they were skittering closer again. Pyvic hopped down, grabbed Ghylspwr from the ground, raised him over the robe, and brought the hammer down several times until he heard the sound of metal on stone instead of shattering crystals. "That should buy us some time. Shall we?" He turned to Desidora and tossed Ghylspwr her way.

Desidora caught her hammer. She looked pale, but not pale like a death priestess caught in the thrall of Byn-Kodar's power. She was just pale.

"Let's go," she said, and swallowed.

They ran from the library with crabs skittering after them and flames and smoke billowing in their wake. Pyvic only hoped that the damned book was worth it.

The earth-daemons were fast. By the time Loch cut the rope, half a dozen were already scampering across it, and when the rope fell away, carrying an indignantly yelling Kail down to what Loch *hoped* was safety below, the earth-daemons leaped the rest of the way, landing on the rooftop where Loch, Tern, and the Imperials were about to start fighting.

The daemons crashed down, stone claws grinding furrows into the rooftop, snarling and hissing. They were humanoid in shape, but seemed made entirely of planes and angles, their rocky gray hides broken by bone spurs at the joints.

The rings on Loch's sword rattled as she whipped it up, then across, chopping through the throat of the nearest one. It stumbled back, and then collapsed into a loose pile of rock and sand, and Loch felt an absurd moment of happiness— first because the damn things weren't immune to blades, and second because finally, for the first time since the Temple of

Butterflies, she could hit something without worrying about it just being a good person in the wrong place.

Another daemon reached for her, and she spun the sword as she stepped out of reach. The little red scarf on the hilt of the blade twirled before the daemon's eyes, and it blinked, automatically tracking the motion, and Loch chopped through its throat as well a moment later.

"Think I figured out what the ribbon is for!" she called out, knocking away another daemon's arm as it clawed at her.

"You fight like a graceless thug," Princess Veiled Lightning declared. She stalked forward, lightning still crackling between her fingers.

"A graceless thug with *your* sword." Another daemon lunged at Loch, and Loch stepped in instead of out. She slashed across its arms, elbowed it in the face, grabbed hold of one rocky arm, and threw it headlong into Veiled Lightning.

The daemon and the princess went down in an ugly tangle of silk and bone spurs. Gentle Thunder, who had been advancing on Tern, stopped, gave Loch a glare that promised death, and ran for Veiled Lightning, chopping a daemon in half with a single swipe as he went.

As the daemons leaped at the Imperials, Loch shot Tern a look. "Smoke."

"Done." Tern whipped a vial from a dress pocket and smashed it on the ground, and vivid green smoke billowed out to fill the entire rooftop.

"Hand." Loch darted toward Tern before the smoke obscured her completely.

"Done." Tern's hand closed over Loch's.

Veiled Lightning and Gentle Thunder were silhouettes a few yards away. The third Imperial, Attendant Shenziencis, was already hidden in the smoke, but Loch heard a squeal of pain and saw a daemon fall to the ground, tangled in a silver net whose links crackled with amber light.

"Window," said Loch, and pulled Tern along with her through the smoke.

She slashed a daemon from her path, saw the flash of a magical blade and yanked Tern to the side, and then she saw the window ahead and dove forward, letting go of Tern's hand as she came into the room they'd rented, blade-first.

It was empty. Tern crawled through the window after Loch, coughing. "That *had* to be another malfunction. Dwarves set alarms. They don't have earth-daemons attack people."

Loch shrugged. "Hell of a malfunction, then. Come on." She left the room at a jog, tucking her sword into her belt.

"We going back to the airship? The . . . whatever Kail named it?" Catching Loch's movement with the sword, Tern slipped her crossbow back down to its hook between the folds of her skirt.

"Not yet." Loch started down the stairs. "The Imperials are right behind us. We need some room, and the others might need help over at the museum."

"Got it." As they reached the lobby, Tern stepped past Loch toward the reception desk, where a dwarven woman in a very clean uniform smiled expectantly. "Excuse me, I think some hooligans are trying to break into our room!"

"There's smoke, and one of them has an ax," Loch added.

"This is very distressing," said Tern, "especially given I thought Ajeveth prided itself on order and security."

The dwarven woman's face went steely, and Loch heard the tiny squeak of fingers clenching on the stained wood of the reception desk. "We do, mistress," she said politely.

"If you'll just wait here, I'll have our security people attend to the matter immediately."

"I need to freshen up," Loch said, fanning herself with her hand. "I just didn't expect this in such a nice city."

Muscles in the dwarven woman's jaw clenched as she walked away, boots clacking on the hardwood floor. Once she was gone, Loch and Tern walked out of the hotel and into the well-lit nighttime streets of Ajeveth.

The museum across the street was still blaring alarms, and Loch saw lights in the windows. She crossed the street—not running, but not sneaking, either.

"Do we have a plan?" Tern asked beside her.

"It's in the formative stages." Loch took the marble steps two at a stride. The museum door was already open ahead, and she glanced in either direction before walking inside.

As she crossed the threshold, a brilliant flash of blue light flared from the cuff of her leather jacket, and yet another alarm shrieked from the walls of the museum entry hall.

"Hey, smooth move, there, master thief," Tern said from behind her. As she walked in, though, the same blinding blue light flared from the hem of her skirt.

"You were saying?" Loch said without pausing.

"How in Byn-Kodar's hell did . . . I didn't touch *anything*!"

Ignoring the side rooms, Loch started up the stairs to the second floor. "You see the Imperials behind us?"

Tern glanced over her shoulder through the front door. "Not yet. Think they'll come?"

"They followed us across the Republic to Ajeveth, Tern. I think they'll cross a street."

No new alarms blared as Loch stepped into the main hexagonal room on the second floor, the one with the Imperial throne sitting in the middle. She took that as a good sign, given that the alarms from the roof, the ground floor, and another one somewhere above her were combining in a teeth-rattling harmony that was going to give her a massive headache in a few minutes.

Loch glanced at the open door to the Urujar side room. A dwarf was lying on the ground next to a lot of broken crystal. "Good. Kail's here." She headed up the stairs to the third floor.

She opened the door to see another dwarf—this one wearing uniform leathers reinforced with thin strips of metal—falling to the ground, unconscious, but definitely still breathing. Two more dwarves flanked Kail, Icy, and Ululenia.

Kail flexed his hand, wincing, then nodded to Loch. "So Icy still refuses to fight . . ."

"I did swear an oath," Icy said mildly, dropping into a crouch as one of the two remaining dwarven security officers swung a truncheon at him.

". . . and the dwarves are apparently immune to that thing Ululenia does." Kail had gotten a truncheon of his own, likely after saying something in dwarven about someone's mother. He blocked a swipe at his head, kicked the back of the attacking dwarf's knee, and cracked a hard left hook across the dwarf's chin.

The dwarf stumbled back, shot Kail a glare, and drove an elbow into Kail's gut.

"So it's going well, then." Loch drew her sword and spun it as she ran at the other dwarf. The rings on the back of the blade rattled, the red scarf flared, and the dwarf—his attention caught—swung at her instead of Kail.

She caught the blow on the back of the blade, which rattled the rings on the sword some more, before flicking the scarf at the dwarf's face as she spun her sword back into a guard.

"Really well, thanks," Kail gasped. His dwarf came in with an overhead blow, and Kail sidestepped it, brought his own truncheon down on the dwarf's arm to collapse the elbow, and put the dwarf's arm into a joint lock, using the truncheon as leverage.

The dwarf grunted and punched Kail in the face with his other hand.

"Dwarven pressure points are offset a bit from where you'd find them on a human," Tern said helpfully, and shot Kail's dwarf in the shoulder with her crossbow. It was a dart, not a bolt, and the dwarf turned to her, pulling it from his shoulder with a sneer as Kail staggered back.

Then he fell over limply.

"They're vulnerable to a few specific sleep drugs, though."

Loch's dwarf swung at her again. Loch sidestepped it, spun her sword so that the scarf billowed out at about eye level between her and the dwarf, and then punched *through* the scarf with her left, blindsiding the dwarf and putting him down.

"Oh, fine, he drops when *you* punch him," Kail muttered.

"Punching, and reminding you not to fall to your death." Loch grinned. "These are the reasons you need me. Did you at least get the book?"

"Captain, please." He had a hand on his now-bleeding nose. With his other hand, he jerked a thumb at Icy. Icy held up the elven manuscript.

Tern looked back down at the floor below, where the sound of booted feet was coming their way. "We're not fighting our way back out, are we?"

"Not if you've got another rope line for your crossbow." Loch gestured at the Urujar side room as the sound of metal on metal came from the floor below. "We get out through the hole Kail made."

Gart Utt'Krenner came back to his senses in the Urujar sub-hex, groaning. His chest protested in pain as he rolled from his side to his stomach, then protested again as he pushed himself to his feet.

Gart noted the pain, because it would be necessary to inform the physicians of the nature of his injuries in order to ensure the most effective treatment, but he did not allow it to interfere with his duties. His reinforced patroller's jacket had protected him from the shards of crystal of the shattered window, and his fine ringmail—which, unlike human armors, had been fashioned in an ablative to distribute force across a wider area—had blunted the impact of the human who had come through.

The moon shone through the window. Gauging its position, Gart judged that a quarter of an hour had passed at most. That was good. He would have been disappointed in himself had he been felled for longer by one treacherous blow.

A rope dangled from the window, likely the means by which the thief had entered. Walking to the window, however, Gart saw another rope anchored to the window frame and leading down to the street.

The thief was gone. Unless his fellow security enforcers had driven him off, Gart Utt'Krenner's museum had been robbed.

Gart heard a crash, and turned to see a dwarf hit the ground in the main human hex outside the Urujar sub-hex. The dwarf's armor was torn, but the dwarf herself was still moving. She would live.

Gart Utt'Krenner rolled out his shoulders—muscle pain from the impact, but only bruises, no pulled tendons or broken bones—and walked out into the main human hex to see who was hitting his people.

Two Imperial humans and one unknown assailant wearing green ringmail, a golden helmet, and butterfly pendant were fighting the other dwarven security enforcers. One of the Imperials was male, heavily armored, and holding an ax that was clearly magical. The other was female, wearing a purple dress and a thin golden chain across her forehead marked with an impressive ruby. She was unarmed, and the man with the ax was clearly guarding her, going by his body language.

"Right, then," Gart said.

He charged.

The unknown figure in the green ringmail saw Gart coming and lashed out with a spear that crackled with magical energy. Gart blocked it on the forearm, wincing as the energy shot waves of pain through his side, and then stepped in and body-checked the figure out of the way.

"By the authority of the Security Enforcement Guild of Ajeveth," he called to the woman in the robes, "ye all be under arrest."

"Laughable," growled the armored man, stepping to put himself between Gart and his mistress.

Gart drew his truncheon. "If ye'll not stand down peacefully, we have no choice but to use force."

The armored man swung his ax, a confident, casual warning swing more than anything else.

Gart stepped aside and pressed a button on his truncheon. The head of the weapon split into a forked prong, and Gart slammed the prongs down, catching the magical ax just behind the head and trapping it. He pressed another button on his truncheon, and spikes snapped out from each forked prong, pinning his truncheon, and the magical ax, to the ground.

"Contained!"

The damage to the museum floor was unfortunate, of course, but Gart was prepared to justify the necessity of the action in his report he would file later.

He head-butted the Imperial man in the chin for added measure, and the man staggered back, knees wobbly.

"Now, ma'am," he said to the unarmed Imperial woman, "let's all just settle down afore someone gets hurt."

The Imperial woman clenched her fists. "Yes. Let us do that." Slowly, hesitantly, she extended her arms for Gart to put on the manacles.

Gart Utt'Krenner reached forward to secure the prisoner.

He didn't register his enforcers' shouts of warning until it was too late.

As Gart's hands closed in, the Imperial woman stepped forward, fingers splayed, and pressed her hand to Gart's mailed chest.

He felt a hum through his entire body as though every inch of him had fallen asleep and was now waking up with pins and needles. The Imperial woman was flying backward, and then Gart realized that she was standing still and that *he* was actually the one flying backward. He finally hit something hard enough that, for the second time that day, Gart Utt'Krenner watched the world go black.

His last thought was that he was going to have a great deal to write in the report.

Loch and her team left the dwarven city of Ajeveth at a run.

"... *stupid* security measures anyway," Kail was saying. "Who uses earth-daemons to attack people! Who does that?"

"Not the dwarves!" Tern said, panting as she tried to keep up. "They never do that! This had to be some kind of mistake!"

"A mistake like when *Iofegemet's* wind-daemon went crazy?"

"Stop calling it that, Kail," Tern added.

Loch looked up at Ululenia, who flapped overhead as a snowy white dove. "Anything strange going on with the daemons?"

They are as different from my kind as bees and fish, Little One. I know only that in both cases, I sensed something strange in the simple magic of their thoughts. Ululenia paused. *It was the blood-anger of the mother badger, the swarming rage of the ants whose hill has been toppled.*

Loch filed that away for now—the sentiment, anyway. The specifics of Ululenia's metaphors were rarely helpful. As they cleared the gates, ignoring the startled yells from the city guards, Loch called over to Kail, "I'm thinking fast take-off."

"I'll have *Iofegemet* in the air in two minutes."

"Nobody is calling it that," Tern puffed as they reached the rows of airships that marked the docking field.

"Hey—*I'm* calling her that."

"It's not a *her!*"

"Kail has a tendency to anthropomorphize inanimate objects," Icy said, keeping pace without evident effort. "Most often in the feminine."

"Don't make this into a weird thing about me and women, Icy," Kail said as they all came to a stop by the guard station at the edge of the airships, where a pair of armored dwarves looked at them curiously. "I'm not the one who ended up falling for the honeypot with the bad guy's personal assassin last time."

Loch showed the guards her docking paper, and the dwarves glanced at it, then nodded and smiled politely at the strange humans who were hurrying out of the city in the middle of the night as if it were entirely normal. "You're remembering that that was my sister, Kail?"

"Yes, Captain. Sorry, Captain."

"I'm not saying *stop*. I'm just saying tread lightly."

"Besides," Tern added as they started—at a jog, this time, all unwilling to do a full run with the guards right there watching them, "it's not like Kail is one to talk. He fell for the death priestess."

As they passed the first row of airships and the guards went out of view, they all picked it up to a run again. In the moonlight, the polished wooden hulls gleamed, and the ropes creaked here and there in the breeze. They ran in silence.

"Over the line?" Tern asked after a bit.

"Slightly," said Icy.

"Don't worry about it," said Kail.

"Desidora *did* get better," Tern added. "She probably can't suck anyone's soul out through their nostrils anymore or whatever it is she does. Did. Could have done."

"Don't worry about it," Kail said with no change in inflection.

They reached their airship, and Kail scrambled aboard and extended the gangplank. Loch and the others came up and took positions of comfort while Kail got the airship ready to take off. A moment later, a snowy white dove landed on the deck and shifted into Ululenia, her pale horn shining like a rainbow made of stars.

"Okay, so," Tern said, in the deliberately casual voice of someone changing the subject after saying something stupid, "something was off about the earth-daemons." She glanced back through the rows of airships at the city in the distance. Following her glance, Loch thought she saw lights near the main gate. "That explains some of what happened at the museum."

"Along with you setting off the alarms with your crossbow?" Kail said, not looking up from the control panel where he was currently fiddling with crystals and levers.

"I *said* I was sorry about the death priestess thing!"

"And I said not to worry about it," Kail said. "You *did* set off the alarm, though."

"Ululenia, what about a Hunter?" Loch asked. "Could that have done it?"

"Wait, big-H hunter?" Tern asked. "The golems who go after fairy creatures?"

Though their fangs bite deep, the shape is wrong for what we have seen on the torn carcass of this evening, Ululenia said. *Incidentally, are you saying that one such Hunter is here?*

"Just what I was going to ask," Tern said, "because the Hunter was *scary* last time. Where was he?"

"You *saw* it," Loch said, shooting Tern a look. "The Imperial woman who wasn't Princess Veiled Lightning?"

Tern blinked. "She was a girl, though."

"A girl in the ringmail of a Hunter golem," Loch said acidly.

"Yeah, you know how I don't really *do* armor?" Tern asked.

"Tern's lack of observational ability aside," Icy said—ignoring Tern's annoyed *"Hey!"*—"some other factor must account for the alarms. I recall one triggering as you reached for the book, Kail."

"Oh, right. Yeah." Kail spared Ululenia a look. "The big blue flash of light on my hand? What was that?"

There were definitely lights near the gate, and Loch saw moonlight glinting on armor in the distance. "Keep that take-off moving, everyone." She frowned, looking down at her hand. "Tern and I had the same problem with a flash of blue light. It was on my hand. No, my sleeve, near the cuff. "

"Yeah, same for me." Kail pulled a lever. "Icy, ropes clear, please." He looked back at Loch for a second before getting back to take-off preparations. "What do you think? Because we were armed, maybe? Enchantment tied to our weapon hands?"

"It would be more logical for such an enchantment to trigger upon the weapon, not on what was, at the time, an empty hand." Icy answered for her, undoing the ropes. "We are cleared."

The airship that was still possibly going to be known as *Iofegemet* lifted gently into the air, the deck shifting beneath Loch's feet. The armored shapes in the distance were yelling something that Loch couldn't quite hear from so far away, but the dwarves at the guard station nearby were turning to look at them now, too.

"It can't be the hands," Tern said, "since it triggered for me at the bottom of my skirt. I don't think I have anything dangerous in pockets near there."

They sailed up into the night sky, and Loch closed her eyes.

"No," she said. "It's not about weapons. Kail, remember the elf in the museum?"

"Ear-something?"

On the ground far below, dwarven guards shouted up at them. Loch looked down and nodded. "Irrethelathlialann."

"Ethel. Got it. Yeah. What about him?" Kail paused, and after a moment, added, "Oh, crap. He grabbed my sleeve, didn't he?"

"Yes, he did. And mine, when he shook my hand," Loch said.

"He didn't touch my skirt!" Tern protested.

"Not even when he bent down on the floor next to you?" Kail asked.

"Oh, well maybe in passing as he . . . oh, *damn it*."

Loch held out her hand to Ululenia. "Sense anything?"

Ululenia took Loch's hand gently and turned it over, her pale, pretty face still but her horn pulsing with flecks of multicolored light. "Ah," she said after a moment. "The grain of sand from which the oyster forms the pearl."

"Let me guess," Loch said. "Residue from a small magical something-or-other that tripped the dwarven alarms even after we thought we'd disabled them."

"Indeed."

"That asshole set us up," Tern muttered.

"But if he wished to stop us from procuring the elven manuscript," Icy said, "why not inform the authorities about our intentions?"

"Because he didn't *want* to stop us," Loch said through gritted teeth. "He wanted to draw attention to us. Icy, the book?"

He handed it over. Loch flipped it open and read.

> *This tale of an old elven orgy*
> *Might leave human readers engorge-y*
> *They missed in their aim*
> *But for taking the blame*
> *I am happy to leave them this forg'ry.*

Loch looked up at her team, took a deep breath, and smiled.

"Well, at least we know who we're going after."

Eight

Captain Pyvic walked into his office the following morning, hoping that things had been quiet while he'd been out yesterday chasing books and running away from magical crabs.

As in most things relating to life in the justicars, he was almost immediately disappointed.

"Captain," said Derenky, popping through the door even before Pyvic had sat down, "we've got a priority crystal from Ajeveth. They have complaints about one of our people being involved in some sort of theft?"

Derenky, a friendly-looking blond man with freckles and a crooked nose, put a lilt in his voice as though it were a question. Pyvic knew that the damn office was a sieve of information, and everyone knew perfectly well that Pyvic had pointed a justicar in that direction. Pyvic also knew that Derenky knew that it was Loch.

And that Derenky had voiced *concerns* about the captain of the justicars having a *relationship* with a member of the team. Especially one who had *problematic* past activity. Because Derenky was a politically motivated pain in the ass.

He was also, unfortunately, extremely good at his job. "Put it through," Pyvic said as he sat. "Then requisition airship transport for one passenger, open destination."

"Open destination will be expensive, sir," said Derenky.

"You don't say." Pyvic shot Derenky a glance, and Derenky blinked, smiled his friendly smile, and went off to do it.

Pyvic's message crystal had delivered Tern's update late last night, while Hessler and Desidora had been trying to make sense of *Ruminations upon the Unutterable by the Queen of the Cold River*. They hadn't had much luck, and it appeared that neither had Loch. Loch thought a trade was in order.

"Captain?" He looked up, and saw that it was Jyrre who had rapped on the doorframe. She was a heavyset woman, light-haired but with deep tan skin that suggested a bit of Urujar blood. "Library's requesting an update on when the lower stacks will be safe to open."

"As soon as the damned magical crabs are gone, I imagine," Pyvic said.

"I'll just pass that on to them, shall I?" Jyrre had grown up near the uncivilized edges of the Republic, and knew which magical creatures to leave saucers of milk for and which ones to shoot with silver bolts from a safe distance. She'd also spent a year studying with the lapitects before deciding she'd rather work with people than crystals. "They're really happy about the fire, by the way."

"Do you have a *helpful* suggestion for how to handle this," Pyvic asked, "understanding that I'm dumping it on you as soon as you suggest something?"

"The *Lapitemperum* has some wizards on staff. I can call in a few favors." Jyrre chewed on a fingernail thoughtfully. "If that doesn't work, I'll call in the priests of Jairytnef. It sounds like a conjuration, and they've got some abjuration experts who can break down whatever magic pulled those things together."

"Good. Do it."

"The lapitects have to come first, though," Jyrre added. "Whatever made those things cannibalized existing crystaltech from the inner workings of Heaven's Spire. There could be safety concerns—"

"Just make it go away, Jyrre."

She shot him a grin. "Don't blame me, Captain. I'm not the one who gave you crabs."

Pyvic raised an eyebrow. "Cute," he said, finally. "When you're done with the crabs—and being cute—I need you to coordinate an intel request." He pulled a scrap of paper from his pocket. "Irrethelathlialann," he read before handing the paper to her.

"An elf?" Jyrre shook her head, taking the scrap with the name. "That's going to be trouble."

"You know him?"

"No." She grinned. "No way anyone but an elf would have a name like that, though. I'll put out the word. I might know a few people on the side, too."

"Appreciate it." Pyvic ran his fingers through his hair. "It's high priority, but it's got to come after—"

"It comes after getting rid of your bad case of crabs," Jyrre finished. "Got it, Captain."

"Pushing, Justicar," he called after her as she left, and then looked down at the pile of paper on his desk.

Once, in the days before becoming captain, he'd worked cases himself. Now he read reports, except in the rare cases when he had to write them after being attacked by magical crabs at a library that had subsequently been set on fire.

According to the reports, the past week had seen an increase of incidents of violence with visiting Imperials, as well as Republic citizens of Imperial ancestry. The Empire was performing military exercises on its border, complete with flamecannons. The Republic had un-retired military personnel with specific skillsets and experience from the last war with the Empire.

Villagers who lived under Heaven's Spire's projected flight path were leaving their shops and fields, worried that the Republic's capital city might decide to rain down lightning again at any time.

Archvoyant Silestin had left behind a grand mess in his insane quest for power.

"Captain?"

Pyvic looked up, carefully not glaring at whoever was interrupting his day for the third time. "Justicar Tomlin."

Pyvic hadn't cut Tomlin from the justicars after being granted the captain's position, but he had removed the man from the field. Whatever intangible quality let a good justicar spot a clue in the field or tell when a witness was lying, Tomlin didn't have it. In his new position, Justicar Tomlin coordinated reports from the various justicars scattered across the Republic, which was helpful, because Pyvic had been dreading doing that himself.

"The guards in Ros-Oanki responded to our request to check on Justicar Fendril," Tomlin said, clenching large, heavy-knuckled hands into a fist. "It looks like he's dead."

Pyvic went blank for a moment, knowing that the name was familiar but not how. Then he remembered who had passed the information about Ajeveth up to his people, followed shortly by a text-only alert message.

He let out a long, indulgent breath, then looked up at Tomlin. "They have a cause?"

Tomlin held up a sheet of paper, his knotted hands crumpling it at the sides. "They say there wasn't enough of a body left for a full determination, but judging by residue left in the area, he was eaten."

Not a knifing in an alley, not a bad heart and too much rich food at supper. Pyvic could have slept soundly at night for those, after writing a letter to Fendril's family.

Eaten, though? Whatever the hell did it, that was on him.

Or Loch . . . or Silestin, really, or even the whole damn problem between the Republic and the Empire, that Pyvic was trying to *fix*. The blame could, in the peace of Pyvic's mind, go up the chain of power and history a long ways.

But he was the one sitting at the desk.

"Order a team down there." Pyvic kept his voice low. "Whatever they need to find out who and how, they've got authorization. Shertan and Dawn."

Tomlin's brow furrowed. "Shertan just picked up a death-curse case. Off in the hills, looks like one Jyrre worked a few months back. And Dawn . . . uh, you saw the reports. Send in a justicar who looks Imperial, you could get trouble."

Shertan was the best Pyvic had at reading people. Dawn was the best he had at pulling information off of dead bodies.

"If they want to come yell at me," Pyvic said, "that's what I'm here for." He smiled at Tomlin. "Just as soon as they get back from finding out what happened."

Security Enforcer Gart Utt'Krenner spent the next several days recovering from being electrocuted by the Imperial woman.

None of the other dwarves had died, either in the fight at the museum or the fight across the street at the hotel where the Imperials had first been engaged, which was a minor miracle.

Gart shuffled from his bed on the second day and gave an offering to Ael-meseth for that. It *was* miraculous. The Imperial man's magical ax had torn through the department's ringmail with little resistance, and the other Imperial, apparently female, carried a net and spear that had also proven significantly dangerous. By all accounts, there should be a few dead dwarves after that night.

It was unclear whether the Imperials had been acting in league with the Republic humans or whether both sides had been attempting to abscond from the museum with the elven manuscript. It was unclear how the security systems on the rooftop had been altered to manifest earth-daemons (which Gart learned had been brought back under control after a prolonged fight and help from the divine enforcers, a security branch tied to the priesthood).

Quite a few things were unclear.

Gart Utt'Krenner despised confusion and uncertainty. He despised even more the very certain fact that his museum had been robbed and his people assaulted.

On the third day, after a lengthy discussion with his physician about his fitness, Gart left the healing hall and made his way to the Security Guildhall.

Gart gave his badge to a guard at the door, checked his weapons (but not his armor), and passed into the processing room. He filled out an application, passed it to the clerk behind the counter, and took his seat with other dwarves, some of them part of the Security Guild, others part of the Crafters or Miners, but here with complaints or concerns.

One dwarven crafter had brought her young child while she waited. Gart helped the girl put together a puzzle-hammer, giving the grateful crafter a chance to use the restroom and get some air. The girl was clever and quick, as most of the Crafters were.

Finally, Gart was called in the guildmasters' hall.

"Security Enforcer Gart Utt'Krenner, museum security," the bailiff declared unnecessarily as Gart walked into the room, which was set entirely in angled stone. The three guildmasters assigned to his request were seated. Each wore black robes, open in the front to show the fine ringmail they wore underneath, as well as ax-shaped pendants of *yvkefer*.

"Chief Utt'Krenner," said Master Utt'Narinn, smiling over her spectacles. "I suspected we might see you soon. You have recovered?"

"Enough to speak, Master," Gart said politely. "I judged it necessary to make this request before the trail of the humans grew too cold."

"Indeed," said Master Utt'Murrick, looking at a copy of the form Gart had filled out. "You wish to pursue the humans outside the boundaries of Ajeveth, despite our nonexistent authority outside the city?"

Master Utt'Murrick had overseen decades of the city's safe development, but Gart had been known to admit privately that he disliked the man's habit of stating the obvious with implied judgment.

"I do, Master." Gart nodded at his report. "As I understand it, the Republic has confirmed that this 'Loch' is a justicar, but neither approved nor denied her actions here in the city. As such, I believe that her legal authority as justicar is suspect in this matter, and I wish to apprehend her and question her further."

"And the Imperial assailants?" Master Utt'Nazef asked. He was a dark-skinned man transferred from deep in the mountains after years of service, and Gart knew him only casually. "They caused most of the injuries to our people. Why are we not hunting them?"

"We have no information regarding their identities," Master Utt'Murrick said with a touch of impatience. "The identities with which they entered the city were fakes, and the Empire has not deigned to answer our request for assistance. Chief Utt'Krenner has no other viable targets in his hunt."

"This is true, Master," Gart said. "My hope is that finding Loch will lead to the Imperials, along with the recovery of the stolen elven manuscript."

"Chief Utt'Krenner," said Master Utt'Narinn, "your desire for justice is laudable, but our treaty with the Republic is clear. We have no word from the Republic that these actions were sanctioned, in which case we could request damages, or unsanctioned, in which case we could request extradition."

"Not that they would do so," Master Utt'Nazef added.

"In neither case would we be entitled to take action within the Republic's borders," Master Utt'Murrick said. "I believe you know this, Chief Utt'Krenner. Unless the Republic violates its treaty, we cannot in good faith approve your request."

Gart Utt'Krenner swallowed his disappointment, bowed to the masters, and left the Guildhall.

He went home to a meal with his wife and children. After supper, his wife played music on the harp, which she did only rarely but knew Gart enjoyed a great deal. Gart helped the children with their schoolwork—his son was writing an essay upon protecting small towns during winter, and his daughter was preparing for a defense exam against a simulated troll attack.

After they were asleep, Gart brought out his law books and read until his still-aching chest informed him that he was being foolish. Then he went to his room, kissed his wife, and went to sleep.

When he awoke the next morning, his wife was already at work, but she had done two things for him. First, she had left a fresh cup of kahva steaming on a magically heated plate; and second, she had bookmarked a page of one of his law books.

He read the page. Then he read it again.

Then he went back to the Guildhall, filled out another form, and waited.

They showed him in less than an hour later.

"What are we looking at, Chief Utt'Krenner?" Master Utt'Murrick asked, scowling at him from beneath great bushy gray eyebrows.

"Transport registration logs," Gart said, smiling politely.

"And *why* are we looking at them?" Utt'Murrick asked.

"Because per our treaty with the Republic, docking fees for regularly scheduled government airships are paid on a quarterly basis," Gart said, reciting the law from memory, "but unique instances are paid within one month, with acknowledgment of the fee and intent to pay received within ninety-six hours." Gart smiled at Utt'Murrick. "As you can see, Master, we have not yet received such an acknowledgment."

Utt'Murrick harrumphed. "Of course not. They still have not decided whether to sanction this foolishness or not."

"That . . . isn't actually relevant," Master Utt'Narinn said, looking over her spectacles. Her lips were pursed, either in thought or, Gart hoped, to conceal a smile. "They *have* acknowledged that this was Isafesira de Lochenville, and the docking registration section of our treaty does not stipulate different rules based on sanctioned or unsanctioned action. As a government agent, she *did* arrive and order her docking fees paid by the Republic."

"And they have not yet sent an acknowledgment and intent to do so," Gart finished. "Which means—"

"Spawn of a troll," Master Utt'Nazef said, chuckling. "The young chopper caught the Republic in a breach of treaty."

"Technically," Utt'Murrick said, glowering at Utt'Nazef. "This is doubtless an administrative error."

"True," Master Utt'Narinn said, "but until such time as it is resolved, I think it reasonable to allow Security Chief Utt'Krenner to investigate this possible failure to pay the docking fees."

"Can't go all the way to the humans' big floating city," Utt'Nazef added, grinning. "Probably best just to find that Urujar woman and question her about the docking fees in person."

"And if anything else related to matters of the city's security were to surface while you investigated these *possibly delinquent docking fees*," Master Utt'Murrick growled, "that would *technically* be within your rights to take action on as you saw fit." He shook his head. "Much as it will likely come back to bite us."

"You have approval for extra-municipal action," Master Utt'Narinn said. "Good hunting, Chief."

Security Chief Gart Utt'Krenner bowed. "Thank you, Masters. I will not disappoint you."

After flying on the airship debatably named *Iofegemet* for the better part of a week after Ajeveth, everyone had gotten to know every inch of the airship by heart. They'd also learned who snored and how often everyone used the privy. Now that Pyvic had given Loch a new target, everyone was more than ready to get their feet on the ground.

"I know little of Ironroad," Ululenia said, leaning against the railing as they flew. Loch was working with Icy on the knots that kept all the airship ropes going where they were supposed to go while Kail kept the airship on course. Tern was busy reading a book and not throwing up anymore. "It is a town of walls and rocks, stone and struggle."

"It's close to dwarven lands," Loch said. She had an awkward subject to broach, and was working her way up to it. "It has some mining. It's largely a transportation hub, though."

"And your justicar believes we might find Irrethelathlial-ann there, Little One?"

"Irret . . . stupid name," Tern muttered, not looking up from her book.

"Just go with Ethel," Kail said.

Tern glared over. "Kail, stop rocking the ship."

"I'm not rocking her, Tern. I'm *steering* her."

"My justicar is quite sure we'll find him there," Loch answered Ululenia. "He should be there two days from now, giving us just enough time to get there, meet Hessler, and get aboard."

Ululenia blinked and looked at Loch. Her pale brow furrowed ever so slightly. "Aboard?"

"You are *too* rocking her—it! You are rocking *it*, the airship that is not a living creature or, for that matter, female. I can feel this little *bip, bip, bip,* and it's making my stomach ache, and I haven't puked in *two days* and I want to keep this streak going, so gods damn it, please stop rocking the ship."

"I feel the same motion," Icy said, fixing one of Loch's knots with quick confidence that bespoke a past on the ocean or in the sky. "It is an extremely subtle vibration coming through the deck."

"Maybe it's just the motion of the sailwings," Kail said, shrugging.

"Aboard?" Ululenia asked again, since Loch hadn't answered yet.

"Aboard the dwarven railway," Loch said.

"No," Ululenia said.

"It's our only lead, Ululenia."

"*No.*"

"It is not just the motion of the sailwings, Kail," said Tern, "so if you could stop making that *bip, bip, bip* rocking motion before I puke, clean up that puke, take it down to the galley, use the hot-plate to forge the puke into a dagger of solidified vitriol, and drive it through your skull, that would be fantastic." She burped, then shuddered.

"This is the only lead we have on the elf," Loch said. "There's a luxury boxcar purchased in his name on a train that will go through Ironroad in two days' time."

"Little One," Ululenia said, her small white hands clenched into delicate fists, "I am not a doe turning up her nose at brackish water. The railways are *silver*. To ride them would wrack my spirit with discomfort at every step."

"Yeah," said Tern as her stomach made a noise like a dog trying to roll over and growl at the same time, "what's *that* like?"

"Could you actually forge puke into a weapon?" Kail asked.

"I'm an alchemist, Kail. I can absolutely do that."

Loch ignored them, still looking at Ululenia. "I was already on the fence about you coming along if Veiled Lightning has a Hunter working with her. I think the silver railway tips it."

"I do not fear the Hunters," Ululenia said, her horn flaring.

"You should," Kail said. "They scare me, and they aren't following centuries-old instructions from the ancients to hunt *me*."

"If you can't come with us," Loch said to Ululenia after shooting Kail a look, "maybe you can go back to Heaven's Spire. Desidora has been trying to make sense of the fairy book without much luck. You may be able to help her translate."

Ululenia sighed. "Of course. I am sorry, Little One. You must hunt in the grounds where your quarry makes its home. I only wished to help. It has been . . . frustrating without my virgin."

Loch looked down over the railing. Kail had them following a river that would take them up to Ironroad, and it was a tiny ribbon of silvery blue below them. They were over farmland, and the fields were laid out in neat little squares. She couldn't make out people at this height, but she thought she could see carts on a tiny road running parallel to the river.

"What happened with Dairy?" she finally asked.

Ululenia looked away. "I did not hurt him, Little One."

"I would be very disappointed if you had."

"You *do* prefer virgins," Kail said. "I mean, when Loch and I found you, you'd just finished deflowering some young village man *and* a strapping young ogre."

Tern burped, winced, and swallowed.

"Yes," Ululenia said, smiling and staring off into the distance. "I enjoy the supple limbs of those who have never rested in the dewy meadows of a lover's embrace, the lust-darkened gaze in eyes for whom the world is still lit in the colors of spring. But for my virgin, I might have stayed even after the flush of manhood had risen in his loins."

"I'm so glad you asked her this, Captain," Kail said. "These were pictures I needed in my head."

"In celebration of his victory over the Glimmering Folk as the Champion of Dawn, I took young Dairy to a restaurant on Heaven's Spire. We dined on fresh oysters, prawns soaked in cream . . ."

Tern got up and stumbled to the far railing. Everyone politely looked the other way and ignored the noises coming from that direction.

"Do you need a cloth?" Icy asked as Tern turned back around.

"No. Please nobody look at me right now." She sat back down against the far railing.

"Tern, if you wish, I can show you the breathing technique to harmonize your internal energies," Icy said, "again."

"I can't learn it right now." Tern swallowed. "I can't do *anything* right now."

"I offered to teach it to you back in Ajeveth," Icy added, "but you insisted that you did not need it."

"Yes, I know." Tern shot Icy a glare, her apple cheeks more olive at the moment. "Past Tern made some bad life choices. Just no more shellfish."

"So, after dinner . . ." Loch said, nodding to Ululenia.

The unicorn sighed, her horn flickering. "We went to a room. At first, his nervous pleasure was a thing of beauty, but . . ." She paused, trying to find the words.

"But . . . what?" Kail said after a moment.

Ululenia glared at him. "We encountered difficulties. He said that while this human form was 'very pretty,' it did not 'feel right,' and so we would simply 'remain friends.'"

"He turned you down?" Kail sputtered. "Dairy *turned down* the magical shapeshifting, mind-reading fairy creature with a thing for virgins?"

"Yes!" Ululenia snapped. "He turned me down. Loch and her justicar sweated naked under the moon, Tern and Hessler found gentle delight in each other's bodies . . ."

"Wooo, sexy times," Tern muttered, and coughed.

"But I got nothing! So no," Ululenia said, glaring at all of them, "I did *not* mistreat my young virgin, nor lie with him under false pretenses. As you all knew the pleasures of each other's bodies, I took a long walk in the rain."

"He turned you down." Kail was laughing now. "Oh, that is hilarious." He slapped the side of the helm.

"Right there!" said Tern. "When you hit the helm, that made the little rocking thing go again. Have you been tapping the helm with your hands? Because if you have, Kail—if you have been hitting the helm with your hands in some little idle gesture, and *that* is what made the little *bips* that caused it to rain puke on some poor farmer's fields . . ."

"I don't think I was tapping the helm," Kail said with absolute sincerity, "so let's just see if that rocking motion doesn't go away all on its own." He held his hands absolutely motionless.

"I will *end* you," Tern said, closing her eyes and leaning back against the railing.

"I'm sorry about Dairy," Loch said to Ululenia. "Maybe you'll find another virgin back up on Heaven's Spire."

Ululenia snorted, then shimmered into a white eagle and launched herself to the sky. *Heaven's Spire is home to wealthy politicians,* her voice came into Loch's mind. *There are few virgins to be found there.*

Loch grinned. "Well, at least you'll have a love priestess to ask for advice."

I will return to Desidora and your justicar as quickly as I can, Little One. Good luck on the silver rails. And be wary. The trains are pulled by fire-daemons, and whatever agitation walks the land of late, it seems to shake daemons loose from their bindings.

Loch nodded as Ululenia soared off, a shining white wedge in the pale sky.

It was one more problem to think about, and she had enough of those already.

Captain Nystin of the Knights of Gedesar took a slip of paper from the justicar at the table, tucked it into his pocket, and stood up. He left a pouch of coins on his seat and walked out of the kahva-house without looking back.

Nystin walked for a quarter of an hour, taking random streets and doubling back twice, before removing the slip of paper from his pocket and reading it. When he had memorized the information, he tore the paper into shreds, then tossed it into a nearby fountain.

He returned to his men, who were already armored and ready to move.

"We've got a hit on Loch," he said without preamble.

"Location?" Grid asked, checking the binding on her crossbow.

"Projected. Ironroad. Our thief is catching a train." Nystin held out his arms, and Rib, the newest of the recruits, fitted

Nystin's armor on as Nystin kept going. "We've got intel that her people raised daemons out in Ajeveth and stole artifacts from the dwarves."

"Will the dwarves be offering assistance in catching her?" Scale asked.

"I don't particularly need anything forged at the moment." Nystin slid his hands into leather gauntlets while Rib quickly laced up his armor. "Less than a day after it leaves Ironroad, that train enters dwarven territory." He looked out at his soldiers. "I fully expect our team to take this woman down before jurisdiction becomes an issue."

"How are we getting there?" Hex asked. "Ironroad's halfway across the Republic."

Nystin nodded at the question. "There's a zephyr-class airship leaving Dock 17 in one hour. It belongs to a gang of hexmongers who've been running high-grade crystals stolen from the inner workings of the city to use for death-curses." He let that sink in. "The justicars have been sitting on that intel for six months, hoping to get a lead on the necromancer on the ground. Personally, I'd rather kill the bastards here and now, then take their fast little airship out to Ironroad and catch our target. Thoughts?"

There was a rumble of assent from the soldiers.

"Hexmongers might have traps on their ship," Hex said, his dry old voice grim with the memory of old battles. "Permission to lead?"

"Granted." Nystin nodded at Rib, who had finished helping Nystin into his armor in record time. The recruit had the makings of a decent soldier, if he didn't get killed. "Glass, your team clears the docks. Let's avoid any trouble with the workers this time."

She flushed. "Understood, sir."

"Good." Nystin looked out at his soldiers. "We missed her last time. Any deaths out in Ajeveth when Loch hit? That's on her, make no mistake, but it's on us, too. I don't know how many dwarven mothers and fathers are putting out flowers for their children, but it's too many." He scanned the room, making sure they were taking it in. "No more. Grab weapons. We move in five. Dismissed."

The soldiers broke off to grab their gear, and Nystin tightened a few straps on his armor.

Hex alone stayed in the room. The old soldier leaned against a wall, his stance casual, to hide the limp.

"Hexmongers," he rasped.

"That's right." Nystin came closer. "Concerns?"

"Every hexmonger I've tracked . . ."—Hex gave Nystin a steely stare—". . . and it's been a few . . . every one went with a simple airship. Just did drops down to the port cities when Heaven's Spire was overhead. Never seen any hexmonger pull in enough money to buy one of the fastest airships in the Republic. Those usually go to some kid with a rich family."

Nystin smiled. "Times change, old friend."

Hex didn't smile. "We going to find crystals on the ship?"

"My intel says we are." The bag containing those crystals was currently sitting in Nystin's locker.

Hex nodded, thinking it over. Nystin didn't change his posture from its attitude of relaxed confidence.

"I'll bring flashpowder," Hex finally growled. "My men can make a little bang, point out the traps. Grid will know, but she won't say anything." He met Nystin's stare. "I'd keep Scale and the recruits back, if it were up to me. They might see what looked like us beating some rich noble's son to death. Might hear him yelling that he was innocent, screaming about his rights."

"It'll need to be a small boarding team," Nystin agreed, "to avoid tipping off their guards. Scale and the recruits will be searching the cargo bay."

"Understood, sir." Hex gave Nystin a salute, then left to go collect his things.

The airship's owner was the oldest son of a minor noble. As far as Nystin knew, the worst illegal magic the young man had ever used was passion-charms to make himself a stallion in the sack.

In forty minutes' time, the poor young man would die for the crime of having a very fast airship and not enough political connections to be dangerous.

Nystin closed his eyes and said a quick prayer to Io-fergajar, god of warriors who needed no magic to win their battles.

He would make the young man's death worth it.

Nine

Desidora sat in the kahva-house with *Ruminations upon the Unutterable by the Queen of the Cold River* resting on the table next to a cup of cold kahva and, because she was feeling sorry for herself, a fattening pastry.

Hessler had left to join Loch and the others on what Desidora understood was going to be a robbery operation on the dwarven railway. Desidora had been left to glean what she could from the impenetrable book.

Whoever the queen of the cold river was, she cared very little for making herself understandable to humans. She seemed to possess senses that Desidora did not, and her descriptions of *The Love Song of Eillenfiniel* would regularly veer off into run-on sentences where the adjectives seemed to be used as verbs and the tenses changed every few words.

Desidora would really have been fine with going to rob the elf on the railway.

Not that a love priestess would be all that useful on a train robbery . . .

She looked over at a young woman sipping kahva by the window. She was unattached, working as an assistant trader or something else that was financially secure but artistically empty, and she hadn't had much time to think about courting since finishing school and finding work with the trading guild. She was unhappy, though she wouldn't have phrased it that way herself, and without someone to ground her, she would find herself a bitter middle-aged woman fighting for money with nothing to spend it on.

The young nobleman a few tables over was working on a poem. He would fall hard for the trader, hard enough to anger his family by marrying outside the nobility . . . but he didn't actually have much to offer the trader beyond hypothetically really liking her a lot. On the other hand, the ebony-skinned woman making the kahva would push the trader from her comfortable life, and the two of them would have absolutely scorching sex. The relationship might even last, provided they were both willing to be flexible.

Her divinely bestowed senses didn't tell her whether either of the young women or the noble would survive the coming war with the Empire. Personalities and possibilities, that was all she got.

And, of course, no ability to change anyone's aura except with her own words and actions, like any other person. Altering the energy of life itself was a power reserved for the gods.

Or death priestesses.

Ghylspwr had been quiet the past few days, which she appreciated. She had actually left him at the temple of Tasheveth for a good oiling.

Tasheveth, goddess of the heart, I prayed that you might spare me the duty of a death priestess. When you told me that it was necessary, I prayed for a way to complete my task and return to the life I knew. Now, you have given me everything I asked for . . . and I miss what I had before.

Now that Desidora thought of it, that fit pretty well with Tasheveth, actually.

With a sigh, she stood to go buy a refill on her kahva—and share a few words with the lovely kahvarista about how the young trader over by the window looked tired and could maybe use a kind word. Instead, though, she found her path blocked by a pale young woman with ash-blond hair and a friendly smile.

It is a gift to see you again, daughter of the gods, Ululenia said, and hugged her. She had really been the team's only other hugger, which Desidora appreciated, even while trying not to spill her cold kahva.

"I'm glad to see you as well." Desidora gestured at the table. "Hopefully you will be able to make more sense out of this than I have."

Ululenia slid into a seat at Desidora's table, giving the nobleman—who was *technically* still a virgin—a speculative look. "Were you getting another drink?"

Desidora looked at the trader in her stylish but stiff shirt and breeches, then at the kahvarista, who was laughing at something one of the servers had said. "No, I'm fine for now," she said, and sat back down. "So, what can you tell me about this book?"

Ululenia picked it up, running a slim finger down the leather and squinting in a way that somehow did not give her frown lines (a trick that only shapeshifters and love priestesses usually picked up). "The queen of the cold river," she said, testing the words for their weight. "She is a . . . difficult creature."

Desidora could not read Ululenia's aura—this wasn't a matter of love, and beyond that, fairy creatures had no auras to speak of—but the concern in her voice was obvious. *"Evil* difficult?"

"At times," Ululenia said, "though my kind is loath to apply such terms to ourselves. Is the wolf evil for killing the stag? The mother bear for mauling that wolf, when its hunt brought it to close to the mother's cub?"

"The satyr for tying me to a table and trying to make me kill Tern?"

"Oh, Elkinsair was evil, definitely," Ululenia said, tapping the book with her finger. "No, the queen of the cold river is not so petty, though at times she is as cruel. I have never encountered her, for which I am grateful, but those of my kind who have say that she is terrifying, one of the most powerful of the fairy folk. For her to dictate her words to a mortal to capture for eternity, they must have been important to her indeed."

Desidora sipped her kahva, then sighed. She'd forgotten it was cold. "Wait: you don't think she wrote it herself?"

"No hands," Ululenia said, wiggling her fingers, "and though her magic is considerable, it does not include the shifting of form." She flipped open the book and started skimming. "She does not like the elven ballad."

Desidora *thought* she had gotten that from the text, but given that she had been trying to read something that at times was written as though the page had an additional dimension, she had also sometimes felt that she was not capable of reading *up* or *in* or *through* enough. "You can understand it? Is that how your mind works?"

"The swan walks on the summer bank, flies in the autumn sky, and paddles across the spring water," Ululenia said, and for a moment, the horn on her brow sparkled into visibility. "We are creatures of the very magic that the elves once worked with in their duties for the ancients, and so we may think as such when the need arises. But as our natures pass time with mortals, our minds mimic theirs." Ululenia looked down at the book. "The queen composed this critique of the elven book after drinking deeply of their minds."

Desidora frowned. "Is she a mind reader, like you?"

"I was not speaking in metaphors, daughter of the gods."

"So she drank of their minds *literally?*" Desidora winced.

"I did say that she was difficult," Ululenia said with a little smile, and went back to the book.

Kail put the airship he had just about gotten named *Iofegemet* down a few miles outside Ironroad, so that nobody would ask why travelers who had their own airship would want to book passage on the dwarven railway.

When they walked into the town a few hours later, Hessler was waiting for them by the gates.

He had changed from his robe into nondescript traveling leathers, though his gangly frame and semi-permanent squint still marked him as a wizard in Loch's opinion. Tern rushed into his arms as soon as she saw him, nearly bowling him over as she pulled him into a hug.

"I missed you. Loch said you got attacked by crabs? You look *good* in normal clothes."

"Thank you, I haven't been eating entirely healthily while you were gone, but I . . ." He saw Loch's look. "I just got in an hour ago, so I haven't had much time to check out the town."

"That's our first order of business, then," Loch said. "Kail, Icy: case the railway. Security measures, guard patrols on the cars, everything."

"Not my first robbery, Captain," Kail said, producing his lockpick with a flick of his wrist.

"If we're lucky, it'll be the last." Loch turned to Tern and Hessler. "The lovebirds are with me."

Hessler flushed. Tern didn't. "What are we doing? If they've got complicated locks at the railway, I'm better than Kail is—"

"Hey!"

"You know more about dwarves than I do," Loch said. "I'm going to go see if we can just buy a ticket."

Kail and Icy split off as soon as they were through the gates, heading off to where the telltale gleam of metal spires marked the dwarven railway. Loch took her time walking through Ironroad, hiding her grin at how Tern and Hessler held hands and matched each other's strides.

"Pyvic gave me a basic report on what happened on the Spire," Loch said as they walked. "Anything you want to fill in?"

"Many of the books survived," Hessler said, "and given the threat to our lives, I still believe that using fire was within the realm of appropriate—"

"You burned down the library?" Tern cut in. "I *love* that library!"

"Yes, Desidora said something about that," Hessler said, and blushed a little, "but really, it was only the basement that burned down—"

"This is why I worry about you using magic that isn't illusions," Tern said.

"Well, an *illusion* of fire wouldn't have stopped the crabs from killing us," Hessler pointed out, "and I do not intend to run into another situation where the enemy has more magical power at its disposal than we do."

Loch sighed. "I wasn't actually asking about the library, Hessler. I wanted to know if you'd found anything more on the attack."

"Oh." Hessler coughed. "Then . . . no. No sign of magical runes that triggered upon us searching for the book, and no hint of scrying magic on us, either. However the crabs and the golem knew to come after us, it wasn't through magic."

"Or the evidence burned down in the basement," Tern added, "when you set it on fire."

"Which, to be clear," Loch said, "I don't really care about, as long as Hessler doesn't get anybody killed."

Ironroad's buildings had the squat, functional look common to mining towns that had been around long enough to merit building real homes instead of just leaning pieces of wood together. Some of the buildings had the angled look that Loch had seen in Ajeveth, and she guessed that was where the dwarves lived. The streets were a little cleaner around those buildings, but other than that, they were just a normal part of the town.

"We had fairy folk living out in the woods in Lochenville," Loch said to break the silence, "but they always stayed there. People like Ululenia, who would come and mingle with the humans, were rare." She jerked her chin at the dwarven buildings. "The dwarves have integrated."

"It's always more common around the borders," Tern said, "especially with the not-too-poor and the not-too-rich. Hard to make someone into a scary dangerous thing when they make your shoes and you buy their apples."

Loch nodded. "I saw it with Imperials during the war, but I didn't realize it would be the same with the dwarves."

"Far as I know, yeah. You get some of the same mix over near the Elflands, too. Elves living in human cities, that kind of thing. Not as much as with dwarves, though. The elves are weird."

"I've only met a few. They usually acted the way Irrethelathlialann was acting."

"Except for setting you up to get tagged by the guards while you're casing the building," Tern said.

"Yes, that was new. Hessler, what can you tell me about the book itself, beyond the fact that you burned down a library to get it?"

"It was just the basement," Hessler said, probably involuntarily at this point, "and in any event, Desidora had been unable to get much from it as of when I left." He still had one hand linked with Tern's, but his free hand began twitching as he thought. "Whatever fairy creature wrote it seemed to have very little interest in making herself understood to humans, which begs the question of why she chose to write it in the first place . . ."

"What about Pyvic?"

"He, ah, he said to tell you that he misses you."

"No, he didn't," Loch said without breaking stride.

"Well, he might have."

"You're a very good boyfriend, Hessler," Loch said, glancing back to where Tern was now leaning on her wizard, "but you're a terrible liar."

"I'm sure he *does* miss you, though," Tern said.

"Yep." Loch turned back to look ahead again. "But scouts don't say, 'I miss you.'"

The ticket office was set a ways off from the railway itself. Most of the railway's business in the town seemed to come from cargo transport, and the ticket office itself was a small dwarven-angled building with a shiny roof and a lot of signs and schedules tacked to the wall. There were two other people ahead of Loch. One of them was a pretty yellow-haired girl in a commoner's dress that had been trimmed with little gold and silver ribbons and cut to show her figure, with a complex hairstyle that had probably looked better a couple of days ago. The other was a tall man a few years older than Loch in an immaculately tailored suit, wearing a guild signet ring and a few other bits of conspicuously expensive jewelry.

"Afternoon," Loch said to the yellow-haired girl. "Heading back home?"

The girl blushed and smiled. "My boy can get tickets for himself with scrip from the dwarves, but it takes long enough that he can only make the trip once a month, so I come up when I can, too."

"Hope you made the most of your time," Loch said, and the yellow-haired girl blushed again.

At the front of the line, the guildsman let out an impatient breath. "I asked for a luxury suite. I booked this trip months ago."

"I understand, and I'm frightful sorry that yer reservation be not in my files," said the dwarf behind the ticket counter. "All of tomorrow's suites are reserved. I can put you in an economy car—"

"That won't work," said the guildsman. "I can't have every scruffy miner with a bit of scrip looking over my shoulder while I handle sensitive information. Now, I'll tell you what you're going to do. You're going to book me a full car—one of the economy cars, since that's all of you've got—and you're going to give it to me for the price of a single ticket."

"Well, sir," said the dwarf, "I'll certainly see what I can do, but many of the economy cars have passengers booked already—"

"Then you're going to move them," said the guildsman, "because you know who else is going to be in those cars? Nobody important. *I* wouldn't be in these cars if I didn't have travel needs more suited to the railway than the airships. You can call them economy cars if you like, but they're mostly filled with miners who bought their tickets with scrip, or whores coming out to the mining towns on payday." He glanced over at the yellow-haired girl. "If I have to sit next to those people, then the only piece of business I accomplish on that trip will be writing a letter to your superiors informing them of the poor service I received."

"How long is he up here?" Loch asked the yellow-haired girl, who was now staring at her shoes.

"Last year of a three-year contract," she mumbled, and wiped her eyes. "It's a lot better up here than in the rest of the Republic. There haven't been any accidents, and none of them even have the cough."

"The dwarves run really safe mines," Tern said, and the girl turned to them gratefully while the guildsman kept ranting. "Plus, if your boy gets a letter of recommendation from his supervisor, he'll be able to work anywhere."

"He wants to work in the freight yard," said the girl, as though it were an embarrassing secret. "Our hometown has a freight yard he could work in, and his supervisor is letting him do the trainings in his off hours."

"Sounds like a good plan," Tern said. Hessler looked as though he were about to comment, and *then* looked as though Tern had stepped on his foot in the heavy steel-toed boots she wore.

"*Thank* you," the guildsman said to the dwarf. "See, that wasn't so hard. I'll be keeping my extra bags in the economy car as well—the last time I traveled, some *people* tried to steal my luggage from the back car. That isn't going to be a problem, is it?"

"I'll mark yer car as baggage-exempt," the dwarf said, stamping a piece of paper with a little more force than was necessary. "Yer ticket entitles ye to use the dining car at the rear of the train, and also gives ye a discount on any dwarven goods ye purchase in one of our—"

"And when you *do* find my reservation, I'll expect a refund on the privacy car." He took the ticket and turned to go, and bumped into Loch, who had put herself directly in his personal space.

"It isn't all whores and laborers," she said, forcing the eye contact. "And even if it was, their money spends just as well as yours."

He glared at her and moved to brush her aside, stumbling a little when Loch didn't move. "Yes, fine, whatever, we're all equal in the eyes of the gods."

"I think," said Loch, catching his hand as he raised it to move her out of his way, "that a representative of the mason's guild would try to avoid antagonizing the miners. You never know when one of their representatives might be listening."

"How do you know I'm—"

"Signet ring." Loch smiled. "And if the ticket vendor informed the supervisor at the local mine about what you just said, I'd expect there to be repercussions."

The guildsman yanked his hand back and looked from Loch to the dwarf, who was now ostentatiously pretending that the guildsman didn't exist.

"Tell me," Loch added, "why would a *merchant* like you be so interested in keeping all your luggage with you, when all your important documents would fit in a single handbag? Is it because traveling by railway lets you dodge the inspectors at the airship docks?"

"I don't have to listen to this," the guildsman finally muttered, and walked around Loch and off, most likely, to somewhere more expensive.

"You have a good trip," Loch said to the yellow-haired girl, who smiled again. As the yellow-haired girl went up to talk to the dwarf at the ticket counter, Loch turned to Tern and Hessler. "Come on. We're done here."

"Wait," said Hessler as they headed for a hotel Loch had spotted on their way in. "I thought you were going to see if we could just buy a ticket and get on that way."

"We're good," said Loch.

"But without a ticket, we'll have to . . . oh."

"Catching on?" Tern asked.

"Loch stole the guildsman's ticket when she bumped into him."

"Yes, she did," Loch said, flashing the ticket and then returning it to the pocket of her riding jacket. "So now we have a private car to ourselves, and more time for the two of you to catch up with each other."

"Woo—wait." Tern turned to Loch. "Can we stop someplace to wash out my mouth?"

"Yes."

"Okay, woo!"

Princess Veiled Lightning sat in the passenger seat of the airship, glaring.

"It was sloppy, Veil," Gentle Thunder said. He stood at the railing, watching the forest pass by below them.

"*Kutesosh gajair'is!*" Arikayurichi, Bringer of Order, apparently agreed.

"You did not capture her, either, Thunder," she pointed out.

"You ordered me not to," he said calmly, "and then the earth-daemons attacked. My first concern must be for your safety."

She glared. "How safe will I be if the Empire and the Republic go to war?"

He turned and matched her look. "If that is what worries you, then you should avoid dying in battle inside the Republic's borders. Your corpse could well start the war your living body seeks to prevent."

"Poetic as always, Thunder."

"Veil." He did not return her smile. "We made our attempt to capture Isafesira de Lochenville. Regardless of the cause, we failed. Your parents gave you leave to investigate. I doubt they would explicitly permit what you have undertaken."

She stood now, moving with the easy grace Thunder himself had taught her. "Am I to slink back home in defeat?"

He sighed. "We do not even know where she is going now."

"I may be able to help with that."

Veiled Lightning turned to Attendant Shenziencis, who stood near the pilot who was flying the airship. She had put aside her helmet, though she still wore the exotic green ringmail. She had not appeared without it during their journey.

Shenziencis bowed and continued. "Your Highness, I tracked Isafesira de Lochenville before. I see a village up ahead, small but with enough natural life-force that I may use my own arts to track her again."

Veiled Lightning looked over at Gentle Thunder. He grimaced.

"Besyn larveth'is!" Arikayurichi, Bringer of Order, declared happily.

"I believe your ax believes that it is worth a try," Veiled Lightning said, and turned back to Shenziencis. "Find her."

Shenziencis bowed again. "As you command, your highness."

Desidora ended up getting another drink, and gave the beautiful kahvarista a gentle nudge in the direction of the trader woman as long as she was there. It felt silly to do so when they might all be dead or dying in war a few months from now, but she was a priestess of Tasheveth, after all, and Tasheveth was all about seizing the time you had while you had it.

"Anything useful?" she asked as she sat back down by Ululenia, who had been working through the book for more than an hour now. Desidora had sat quietly—a talent cultivated by priests of all faiths—and occasionally coughed politely to let Ululenia know that her horn was sparkling again.

Her mind is coiled and clouded, a deep sea scuttler that has built itself a prison for protection, Ululenia said.

Desidora nodded. "I'm not sure that's useful, but I will hold onto it, just in case."

Ululenia smiled. *My apologies, daughter of the gods. To pull meaning from this strange work requires twisting my mind into a shape similar to hers.*

"Understood." Desidora sipped her tea, which she had gotten because kahva would just make her more jittery.

The queen of the cold river spoke in such a manner deliberately, Ululenia added. *As a hunter may mark the tracks of running prey separately from quarry that walks or limps, so do I see how she twists her words even further away from the gentle places of human thought.*

"She hates people?" Desidora guessed.

She is the mother bird, feigning a wounded wing as she flutters far from her nest.

"She wanted to hide what she wrote from humans?"

Such is the shape of her tracks.

"All right. Why?" Desidora gnawed on a fingernail. "She had this book made, so she clearly wanted *someone* to know what she thought, but she didn't want . . . humans. She wants elves and fairy creatures to be able to understand it, but not humans. And . . . what else? Nobody cares this much about criticizing a book. Well, maybe Hessler."

Ululenia laughed and switched to speaking aloud. "His mind still leaps from thought to thought like a startled rabbit, but he and Tern have brought each other peace."

"Yes, I've gone out with them a few times up here," Desidora said. "It's good to see them happy."

A few tables over, the pretty kahvarista offered the trader woman a free refill and asked if she needed anything. The trader responded with a joke, and the kahvarista laughed and worked in a reference to a band that would be playing in one of the performing squares that evening. As it happened, the trader liked the same band and wasn't doing anything that night.

Desidora sighed.

"The lynx and the caterpillar," Ululenia said.

Desidora blinked. "I'm sorry?"

"You saw the defeat of the Champion of Dusk, fulfilling the will of the gods, and the mantle of the death priestess fell from your shoulders." Ululenia reached out and took Desidora's hand in a gesture that was more gentle than flirtatious. "You thought yourself the lynx, your claws gladly sheathed, but always, should you need them, they would extend from the tufted fur and velvet-soft paws to slash at any foe. But you are not the lynx. You are the caterpillar, transformed into a beautiful butterfly whose wings glitter with promise and whose touch helps the flowers grow." Ululenia closed Desidora's hand. "But you have lost your jaws."

"And the gods don't care," Desidora said. "They shine on the Empire and the Republic together, and the Old Kingdom, and, hell, almost every race except the Glimmering Folk or the daemons. They could give me back my powers, so that I could *do* something instead of just standing there like an idiot as that creature of the ancients bore down on me, but instead, I play matchmaker and sit here while you read a book."

Ululenia's horn flared, a sudden flash of prismatic light. She doused it, blushing prettily as everyone looked their way, but her eyes shone with a hunter's satisfaction as she looked at Desidora.

The ancients, daughter of the gods! That is our key.

"How?" Desidora murmured. The young nobleman who had been working on his poem for the past hour was coming their way.

The path is not yet clear. But the queen of the cold river hides her path most when she speaks of the ancients.

"And that magical attack in the library twisted the magic of the ancients to send those creatures against us." Desidora nodded slowly. "It's a start."

"Excuse me, I am sorry to trouble you both, but I thought I saw something, and . . ." The young nobleman blushed. "I'm acting the fool."

He *was* technically a virgin, Desidora remembered. She glanced over, and saw Ululenia smiling, eyes wide, lips just barely parted as though waiting to ask a question. Despite the lack of aura, Desidora had an idea of what was going on.

"My friend has had a long journey, and is tired," Desidora said, "and I fear I have been a poor host, and am about to be even poorer. I must go speak to my friend Pyvic about a personal matter, leaving her to dine alone tonight."

"You must go," Ululenia said, smiling sadly and giving Desidora a tiny wink when the nobleman looked away to adjust his jacket, "but perhaps you could tell me where I might find a restaurant where I might also hear poetry performed?" She tucked *Ruminations upon the Unutterable by the Queen of the Cold River* into a pocket in her snowy white dress.

"Well, actually, um, now that you mention it, I know a place," the nobleman said, "and in fact I even do a little myself from time to time," and Desidora smiled, said her goodbyes, and left Ululenia to finish playing with her prey on her own.

Tern and Hessler were happy. So was Ululenia, though she had lost Dairy. Thinking back, something in the boy's aura had told Desidora that it wasn't going to work, but the aura had also burned too brightly for Desidora to get a good look, and anyway, it had been all she could do to avoid summoning skeletal warriors and turning the carpets black around her at the time.

More important, though, Desidora—now nothing but a love priestess—was walking off alone.

It was late afternoon, but Pyvic would likely still be at his office. Desidora wasn't sure how knowing that the book had something to do with the ancients would help, but it was more than they had known this morning. The queen of the cold river cared about the ancients, and ancient magic had tried to stop them, and . . .

She sensed nothing until the bag came down over her head.

Idrienesae flitted from one branch to the next on wings made of shimmering rainbows. The woods were dark around her, silent but for the steady fall of footsteps behind her. The bear had finally stopped screaming a few seconds ago, and none of Idrienesae's other woodland friends would be coming to help after seeing what had happened to it.

Things had been good for Idrienesae. Too good. That was it. She'd gotten used to the milk on the doorstep, the whispered gratitude for a few little chores done during the night from the mother raising her daughter alone, the laughter of a fat toddler as she led him back out of the woods when he'd wandered off. Little things.

Idrienesae reached one of *her* trees and darted into it, letting the bark close over her safely. For a moment, the sound outside was muffled, as it always was until her body adapted and she could listen through the branches.

Then she heard her tree scream as a blade pierced it, and she screamed with her tree, for the pain was hers, too. She felt herself down, down, into the roots, into the earth, through the chain that bound all life and to the next tree that was *hers*, and when she reached it, she flung herself free, shuddering. Her wings were ragged, flickering in and out of existence, and would not hold her weight. The tree behind her, the first one, was still screaming as energy crackled through it, and even without being inside her, Idrienesae felt the connection enough to feel the pain.

She shouldn't have soured Old Widow Kinnet's milk. It had been petty, cruel, even, but Kinnet had come back from a trip to the big city with little charms for all of the girls of the village to wear, and the charms had been *silver*, and you couldn't let these things go, you had to remind people of the rules of simple politeness. Clearly Idrienesae had gone too far with the milk, though, and attracted the attention of something far bigger than she was.

She ran now, her soft feet scraping on the ground from the unaccustomed exertion, and tears fell freely as the footsteps closed in behind her. She would be good from now on, she promised whatever gods cared to listen to the fairy folk. She would help even the people who didn't leave out the milk, and she would just avoid Old Widow Kinnet, and that would be fine, if she could just get away right now—

She burst through a wall of bushes, scraping her arms, and came out at the pond with the pretty hill, where most of the young villagers who didn't have barns with haylofts came when they lay with another for the first time. With her wings, she could have flitted up easily, but her wings were gone now, stolen by the pain, and the hill was so steep.

Idrienesae turned, and with a little keening hum in her throat, she spun a dagger out of bits of nothing. It was small, since she was small, but she turned to the figure in the green ringmail anyway, the helmeted figure with the spear and the net.

"You are a Hunter, a thing of the ancients, come to kill me for my magic," she said, and raised her dagger. "I did not steal it. I do not steal. It was left behind when nobody wanted it anymore, and it became me, and that is who I am, and you will kill me now, but I am alive, and you are not, Hunter."

The Hunter put a hand to its helmet and lifted the visor. Underneath, Idrienesae expected to see blank metal, or crystals humming with magic, for that was what the stories had said. That was what her friend had told her was inside the Hunters, and her friend had survived an attack by one of them.

Instead, she saw a human woman's face, with Imperial features and glittering golden makeup curling around her eyes.

"Wrong," said the woman. "But you know more about the Hunters than most, little pixie. Tell me, how did you hear such stories?"

Idrienesae considered running. She considered the dagger. She considered many things, because she was fast, but then she saw that the woman was watching her, and so she told the truth instead. "I heard from a friend who met one."

"Was this friend a unicorn, perchance?" asked the woman, and lifted a net of silver links that crackled with golden magic. "Was her name Ululenia, and does she travel with a human named Loch?" At Idrienesae's silence, the woman smiled gently. "The villagers leave out a saucer of milk for you, do they not, and wake up to find that you have helped with their work? Perhaps if you leave out a saucer of your friend's location, you might wake up to find that I have left you alive."

Idrienesae talked very quickly.

Ten

THROUGH THE MOONLIT REPUBLIC COUNTRYSIDE, A TRAIN OF AN even dozen cars—one for each pair of gods, which the dwarves characterized as good politics more than superstition—blazed along the dwarven railway.

The railway was a bright line of silver in the darkness. It caught the light of the moon, glittering brilliantly and curving to match the rise and fall of the hillside. Near the train, the tracks glowed a flickering blue tinged with red as the silver repelled the rainbow-flickering crystals set into the underside of each of the cars.

Lapitects claimed that the glittering rainbow crystals were imperfect forms of the *lapiscaela* that held Heaven's Spire aloft, and as such, pushed only against silver and a few other metals, rather than pushing against the ground itself. Fairy creatures pointed to the color and the repulsion of silver and claimed that the crystals contained the energy from which the fairies themselves had been born.

Dwarves claimed that the crystals could pull a dozen cars across the countryside faster than a galloping horse for a full day or more, and prices for freight or commercial travel were quite reasonable if booked in advance.

Inside the economy car, Loch sat in one of several comfortable benches and looked out the window. The glowing panels in the ceiling had been dimmed for the evening, and Loch could see the scrubby grass, pale gray against the black of the sky.

The car itself was metal, with walls that angled in a little near the top, like the dwarven buildings. The walls and ceiling were tiled with intricate stone patterns, and the paving stones on the floor felt more real than whatever they used for the streets up on Heaven's Spire. The whole car thrummed steadily as the crystals beneath the floor kept it aloft and moving.

"Time?" she asked.

"Fourteen after," Tern said, fiddling with a small dart-thrower she'd worked into her sleeve and cufflink. "One minute 'til the guards shift."

"Hessler?"

"I'm prepared to render all three of us invisible, although the sheer amount of metal involved will cause reflections that limit the efficiency, and should the guards look directly at us while we move—"

"It was good enough to get you and Tern inside in the first place. Time?"

"Now," Tern said.

The three of them went to the front door of the car, and Tern looked through a little window. "He's out." She slid the door open.

The cars were connected by great hooks that let the overall train flex a little, along with a kind of tube to protect travelers who wanted to move from one car to another. The tube was made out of a thin mesh of what Loch was pretty sure had started off as ringmail, glittering against the sharp glare of the lamps on the doorframe of each car. The ramp between the two cars was thin metal, with the tube connecting to either side. Loch could hear the rush of air and the steady hum of the crystals on the other side of that ramp.

She stepped across without hesitation and looked through the window on the far side. "Dining car's clear. Tern, go."

The problem was that the elf and his manuscript were in a privacy suite two cars up. In front of them was the first of the luxury cars, which featured private suites with amenities instead of just reclining chairs, along with a bar that served overpriced food and watered-down drinks. It was locked to prevent people like Loch and her team from doing exactly what Loch and her team were doing.

Tern pulled a listening tube from one pocket, set it to her ear, and leaned against the door. "Last year's model," she murmured, gently tapping a quartz wand with a tuning fork and holding it near the lock. "Three crystals, each with shielded resonance buffers and overcharge locks."

Hessler nodded, apparently impressed. "In the older models, if you had a multi-crystal lock, a lack of shielding meant that the frequencies were all eventually overridden by the strongest crystal, and a lapitect with a sufficiently powerful crystal pick could simply sync the pick to that crystal, and the others would snap to the unlocked position along with it."

"Fascinating as always, Hessler," Loch said. "No guard yet, Tern."

"So pleased to hear it," Tern said, "because I am in no danger of having this thing open." She produced a second small crystal wand and, holding it between her teeth, brought it near the first one. "Mmkay, dass firss crssdull."

"Trying to sync multiple crystals is exponentially harder than trying to sync one," Hessler said. "She's got to re-trigger the emitter every few seconds on the appropriate frequency, along with dead-man-pulses on the crystals she isn't working with yet, to avoid an alarm. It's a bit like trying to keep an increasingly long string of numbers straight in your head."

Loch kept looking through the window. The guard for the new shift had just come in through the far door, and was looking around the bar and dining area. "Company, Tern."

"Doo down."

The guard started down the hallway, pausing to check an unsecured door.

"The Republic could learn a lot from the ways in which the dwarves incorporate crystal artifacts into their utilities—"

Loch grabbed Hessler and pushed him to the window. "Distraction, back behind the guard, *right now*."

"What, I—oh." Hessler squinted, held up a finger, and then curled it into a hook shape. "It's harder to do through the glass of the window, but fortunately, they didn't use anything that would absolutely block—"

"Did he stop?"

"Um." Hessler looked again. "Yes, yes, he's turned around and is checking back in the dining car." He smiled at Loch. "I used an illusion of a door opening and closing and someone asking for help, which should—"

"Great. Tern?"

"Oooo, god idd!" Tern murmured as the lock snapped open. She dropped an absurd number of crystal picks from her mouth into her palm, then stood up straight and kissed Hessler. "You're the best, baby."

"Mm-hmm." Loch slid the door open and stepped through. "Let's move."

There was a small standing area near the door, likely for waiters to stash carts, and it stretched across the entire width of the car, as opposed to the narrow hallway, which had to make room for private suites on either side and was thus barely wide enough to walk down without having to turn sideways.

Loch, Tern, and Hessler had just gotten into the standing area when the dwarven guard came back out from the dining room.

Loch ducked behind the wall, pulling Tern and Hessler with her. "Cloak."

Tern winced. "So . . ."

"What?" Loch demanded.

"Well . . . I didn't actually get the door locked again behind us, and he's going to notice that."

Loch rolled her eyes. "Wait," she said to Tern, and then to Hessler, "Cloak, please."

Hessler reached out and put his hand on their shoulders. "Hold still," he murmured, for once not explaining the detailed arcane history of what he was doing. The air around Loch shimmered, and then everything went faintly gray and muddy at the edges.

Tern, still visible inside the little bubble that the three of them stood in, looked at Loch questioningly, pointing at the door, which was slightly ajar. Loch held up a hand.

"It's really more effective if you hold still," Hessler whispered, and now Loch and Tern *both* rolled their eyes.

The guard came down the hallway, checking the doors.

He stepped out into the waiting area, rolled out his shoulders, and then stopped and frowned at the door. Loch noted the ringmail, thin but still effective, and the truncheon at his belt.

As he walked past them and toward the door, Loch stepped out of Hessler's cloaking bubble. She deliberately scuffed her foot on the floor, leaned toward one of the doors and put her hand on the handle, and said, "Excuse me?" to the guard.

The guard turned, saw a guest who hadn't been there a moment ago stepping away from a privacy suite, and smiled politely. "May I help ye with something, ma'am?"

"I thought I heard something down that way," Loch said, looking down the hall toward the dining area. "Someone asking for help? I wasn't sure if there was a problem, or . . . ?"

"I heard it meself," the guard said. "Nothing to worry yerself about, ma'am." Behind him, a fuzzy, shifting silhouette of Tern reached out and closed the door to the economy car.

Loch coughed loudly to cover the sound of the door sliding shut. "Is the bar still open? I could use something for my throat."

"There's no one on duty there, ma'am," said the guard apologetically, "but there be drinks and some simple foods available for ye to serve yerself, and if need be, I can fetch ye anything ye need."

The shifting silhouette of Tern gave Loch a thumbs up and then slid fully back into Hessler's bubble.

"Thank you so much," Loch said. "Have a good evening."

"And ye as well," the guard said, and turned back to the door. He blinked, then shook his head and unlocked it. Loch fiddled with the door to what she'd pretended was her private suite while he stepped through and closed it behind him.

Tern and Hessler popped back into visibility a moment later. "Nice pull," Tern said quietly.

"Come on." Loch headed down the hallway with the others in tow.

"I'm still not entirely certain why Tern didn't just disable the guard with one of her sleeping darts," Hessler said, "although the fact that I'm the one advocating the more violent approach in this scenario raises a level of irony that is in no way lost on me."

"Subtlety, baby," said Tern.

"The longer we have them confused and wondering how anyone got by them, the longer we have to get away," Loch said, keeping her voice down as they walked single-file down the hallway. The dining area—with its bar and tables—was up ahead, and just past it, the door to the next luxury car, where the elf's private suite was located. "In a professional operation, you leave the smallest possible footprint to make it as hard as possible for anything to get back to you."

She stepped out into the dining area.

"Good evening, Miss de Lochenville," said Irrethelath-lialann the elf, sitting at a chair in the corner with his legs propped up on the table. "Fancy a drink?"

Desidora woke up with a groggy, black-spotted headache that suggested she'd been subdued by a knockout-choke rather than a sharp blow.

As a love priestess, these things came up now and then.

She spent a few moments wondering dizzily if she were going to throw up, decided that she probably wasn't, and opened her eyes in hopes that it would tell her which way was up, at least.

The room she was in was pretty dark, but lit by blurry multicolored lights that gradually resolved themselves into various crystals set into the walls, floor, and even ceiling of a room made of slate-gray stone. As her vision cleared, Desidora realized that the walls weren't exactly walls, but very large support pillars, through which snaked grids of pipes lit by the glow of the crystals.

"You may yell if you wish," said a voice, and Desidora nearly did yell, because with her gifts as a love priestess, she should have been aware of someone crouching just a few yards away. "They will not hear you up above."

She looked over at him a little too quickly, and her head swam for a minute. When her vision cleared, she saw a man in a black cloak that covered dark armor lined with crystals.

When it cleared some more, she realized what she was looking at.

"You're another golem," she said, "like the creature that attacked us in the library. Or Hunter Mirrkir."

The golem's face was human at a brief inspection, as though designed by someone with a detailed description of human anatomy, but who had only angled pieces of stone to work with. Its nose was an angled pyramid with no nostrils to speak of, its eyes were perfect diamonds that glowed faintly blue, and its cheekbones could *literally* cut glass.

"The Hunters were formed for duty," the golem said. "They gathered the stray magic that escaped the works of the masters after the masters departed."

"Stray magic." Desidora's mind was coming back into the confines of her skull, which was good, because she appeared to be tied to a chair. "You mean the fairy creatures."

The golem nodded, things in its neck and shoulders clicking faintly like polished stones in a velvet bag. "They were formed from magic that was not theirs to be. The masters required that the magic be kept safe."

"Why?" Desidora asked. "The ancients fled this world to escape the Glimmering Folk. What did it matter if their old magics gave rise to something new?"

"You have the book," the golem said, rising to its feet and coming toward her. "You will return it. What it contains is not for you."

Desidora could not read the golem's aura, but that had been an abrupt transition, and she filed it away for later. "I do not have it with me," she said. "If you let me go, I can retrieve it."

"You will tell me where it is located," the golem said immediately. "I will retrieve it. Then you will be released."

Desidora wasn't entirely certain whether to trust that. It didn't sound like the golem was capable of lying, but it also might have a more metaphysical definition of *released* than Desidora did.

More than that, though, if Desidora told it the truth, the thing would go after Ululenia, and as a fairy creature formed from the leftover magic of the ancients, she might not rate on the thing's "capture alive" list.

"I will not tell you until I am certain that you will not kill me," she said instead. "You may believe I have already read the book. You may think the knowledge must die."

The golem held perfectly still. If it were a man, she was certain it would have cocked its head as though thinking . . . or listening. "No," it said after a moment. "Your death is forbidden." It held up a hand that looked gloved, until Desidora realized she was looking at the slate-gray material of the walls. A crystal set into the golem's palm suddenly glowed, a painful pale green. "Your memories will be cleansed."

And with that, Desidora knew as much as she needed to know. "Ghylspwr," she said, "I need you." She flexed her hand in her bonds, opening her hand.

Nothing happened.

"Teleportation ward," the golem said, pointing to a crystal charm worked into the ropes binding Desidora to her chair.

Desidora looked down at it, a little bit of crystal and silver wire. Its magical signature was simple, practically makeshift. She could, now that she was aware of it, even read the aura it projected, a chaotic cloud of energy deflecting any attempt to magically transport her or transport *to* her.

A law priest of Ael-meseth would have been able to project a field of pure, concentrated justice and banish the ward. A blessed trickster of Gedesar would have unknotted the essence that bound it together, rendering it useless.

A death priestess could have taken that magic and forged it into a bolt of lightning that charred the golem where it stood.

Desidora, love priestess of Tasheveth, could do none of that.

"If you will not tell me," the golem said, holding up its hand again, "I will take the knowledge from your mind." It stepped forward, the crystal in its palm flaring emerald as it closed upon Desidora's head. "I apologize for any discomfort."

"And you're sure that Loch wanted us to go back this way?" Hessler whispered as he followed Tern back down the length of the car to the door where they'd come in.

Tern bit back a sigh. Hessler was an excellent wizard and a really nice boyfriend as well, but he was a recent arrival to the world of crime. "Yes, that was what that little gesture meant."

"So she's going to deal with . . . what's the elf's name, again?"

"Irrethel . . . something. Ethel." Tern popped the lock on the door—she hadn't had time to clear her crystals, so they were still tuned to open it—and stepped out of Hessler's cloaking bubble and into the little tunnel between the two cars. "Hey, sorry about this," she added as the dwarf standing guard in the tunnel turned toward them. Then she shot him with a wrist dart.

"Ethel?" Hessler asked as the dwarf grabbed at his shoulder, then sank to the ground unconscious.

"Damn it, that's what Kail called him, and now it's all I can think of." Tern hauled the dwarf back into their car, then knelt by the ringmail mesh that protected the space between the cars from the cold night air.

"So Loch is going to deal with Ethel herself?"

Tern slid a wrench from her dress pocket and deftly popped off one of the bolts tying down the mesh. Cold wind immediately began whistling in through the hole. "That's what that gesture meant, yeah. She'll handle him, while we go around and get the elven manuscript from his car ourselves."

"Hmm," Hessler said as Tern popped off another bolt. "And you're absolutely certain that she wanted us to go *this way*?"

Tern pulled back the mesh. The night outside was dark, the wind whipping past them as the dwarven train hummed along the tracks.

On the side of the car just beyond where the mesh had covered, handrails led to the top of the car.

"Oh, yeah," Tern said, grinning. "This is absolutely what she meant."

"See," Hessler said as Tern started climbing, "the way you say that, you're doing the same thing you do when you say that you remembered our plans to meet Desidora for dinner, even though you're wearing grubby, oil-stained clothes which you then immediately change out of."

"Hey, sweetie, tip in case you wanted to get me out of those oil-stained clothes ever again?" Tern pulled herself up, the cold metal sharp on the palms of her hands, and peeked over the top. The wind stung her face and slid around her spectacles to half-blind her, but the moonlight shining silver on the back of the train was beautiful even with tears in her eyes. "No girl likes to hear her tells." With her free hand, she popped a pair of protective goggles out of another dress pocket and slid them over her spectacles.

She pulled herself up onto the roof of the car. The stone was polished to limit wind resistance and felt slick beneath her boots, though handholds dotted the top of the car every few feet. Hessler pulled himself up behind her, grumbling.

"Besides," she added, turning back to him so that her words weren't lost in the constant wind, "you have to admit, this is pretty cool."

"Yes, dear." Hessler pulled himself onto the rooftop as well and stayed huddled in a low crouch.

"Haven't you ever wanted to be on the top of one of these things?"

"I grew up on the far side of the Republic," Hessler said, scuttling over a bit to glance down the side of the car. "I barely even knew this railway existed. Do you, um . . . ?" Tern passed him another pair of protective goggles, and he slid them on. "Thank you. You are an excellent girlfriend with no tells."

Tern grinned. "Come on. Ethel's suite is in the car after this one."

"Do we have a plan?" Hessler asked as Tern started walking. He came behind her, crouching and staying directly in the middle of the roof, despite the fact that the wind wasn't *that* bad and the car wasn't even rocking that much.

Tern smelled the cold night air. She had wanted to ride on the roof of one of these trains ever since she'd watched them hum by from the window of her study while she practiced her scales. Tonight, she was doing exactly that, with her wizard boyfriend—who admittedly wasn't as into it as she was, and the chances that they were going to have sex *on* the rooftop were pretty low now that Tern realized how dangerous that might actually be—but *still*.

"Ethel's suite is the third one on the right," she said back over her shoulder. "I'll pop the window if I can. If not, we break it open and climb in. We grab the book and climb back out onto the roof."

"And go back to our car?" Hessler asked from close enough behind her that he was clearly still worried about slipping. "That plan made sense when no guards had seen us, but since we've been spotted, it seems like we should probably figure out some other option."

Tern sighed. "Yes, that option probably won't work." She suspected he was not going to like this. "Remember Kail and Icy?"

"They're flying in . . . what did Kail call the airship?"

"I have no idea," Tern said flatly.

"They're in the airship, anyway, and they're going to fly past us and lower a rope with a basket, at which point we'll put the elven manuscript in the basket, so that there's no way the crime can be tied to . . ." Hessler trailed off. "Oh."

"You'll be fine, baby."

"You know my feelings about—"

"I do, and I totally respect those feelings," Tern said, "and if we hadn't been seen by that guard, we would absolutely just head back to our car so that when the guards did a sweep, we could sit there innocently saying, 'What book?' But since we've been seen, we really need to be off this train as soon as possible, which means being pulled up into the airship whose name I am not going to even try to say."

Hessler sighed heavily behind her. "He really only saw *you*," he muttered.

Tern chose not to hear that. She reached the end of the car, took a few running steps, and leaped over the ringmail mesh that covered the gap between the cars. She slid a bit on the landing and nearly fell, catching herself in a little stumble, and turned back to Hessler with a giddy smile. "Coming, baby?"

Hessler squinted. "I can't just walk across the mesh, can I?"

"The guard in the tunnel would see your footsteps," Tern said.

Hessler shook his head. "And you're *sure* that this is what Loch meant with that one hand gesture she threw back when the elf talked to her?"

"Well, we're *here*, and I don't see any other way for us to have gotten here, so . . . yeah." Tern waited for Hessler to work himself up to it and took a moment to look at the moon-bleached countryside.

A dark form was coming their way, a cloud-shaped silhouette of shadow against the stars. It was a ways ahead of them, traveling so as to cross their path. Tern pointed. "Great! Kail and Icy are already here. Come on, it'll be fine!"

"That ship looks bigger in the dark than Iofe . . . whatever Kail called it," Hessler muttered, and then squinted at the ringmail mesh he was going to have to jump across. "So does this, for that matter."

"Running start," Tern said.

"Are we that far behind schedule?" Hessler asked. "This seems early for Kail and Icy."

"Remember to flex your knees when you land!" Tern said with a cheerful smile.

Hessler glared, took a few steps back, and rolled out his shoulders.

Tern watched, mentally counting down to when she would move from encouragement to nagging. A moment later, she heard a hiss followed by the thunk of metal on stone behind her. When she turned, she saw a blackened rope trailing from the airship to the train up near the middle of the car Tern was on, with a dark steel grappling hook at the end sliding across the rooftop before it caught on one of the handholds.

"I thought they were going to just going to lower a basket!" Hessler called over.

"Stop stalling!" Tern called back. "They probably saw how fast the train was going and realized that they couldn't keep up for long. They'll use the tow-line to catch a ride until we're ready to pass them the . . ."

She trailed off at the sound of oiled metal sliding on rope, unmistakable to anyone who spent as much time customizing her crossbow as she did, and turned back around to the grappling hook.

"Also, it's *possible* that this isn't Kail and Icy," Tern said as a trio of black-armored men landed on the roof of the car, unhooked their zip lines from the grappling cable, and whipped out crystal-tipped black war maces.

Eleven

Loch flashed Tern and Hessler—mostly Tern—a quick sign and smiled at the elf.

"Irrethelathlialann. What an odd coincidence to meet you here."

"You remembered my name!" he cried with delight. In the dim light of the overhead glowlamps, the elf's pale green skin seemed sallow, and the crystals made his cheekbones stand out sharply. His golden eyes, half-lidded with amusement, tracked her every move.

Loch shrugged, turned to the bar, and poured herself a shot of fine dwarven whiskey. She sat down opposite Irrethelathlialann at the little table where he had been waiting. A candle was set in a red glass between them, giving the car a bit of natural light. "Kail just calls you Ethel."

The elf chuckled, clapping his hands gently. "Diminutive appellation to diminish and demean. Desperate, jealous reaction to being outmaneuvered. The information is appreciated." He seemed to come back to himself, and locked his eyes on her. "Did you like the poem?"

"It didn't really scan." Loch sipped her drink, paused to savor the taste, and didn't wince as it burned its way down her throat. "I need the manuscript."

"You *want* the manuscript," the elf corrected.

"The Republic and the Empire are going to go to war if I don't give them that book," Loch said, "so yes, I *want* it."

He sniffed and took a sip from his wineglass. His drink was the same pale green as his skin. "No."

Loch took another sip. "No?"

"The Republic and the Empire are *always* going to war," Irrethelathlialann said, "and they wouldn't know how to read it anyway, so *no*, you're not getting it."

Loch downed the last of her drink in one large gulp, flipped the cup over, and slapped it down hard enough to make the candle on the table dance in its little red glass. "It wasn't a request."

She stood and turned to the door that led to the elf's car.

Behind her, she heard the sound of a weapon leaving its sheath.

"No," Irrethelathlialann said, "it wasn't. It was a *mistake*."

She turned, her own blade sliding free from her belt. The rings rattled, and the red silk scarf on the end flapped as she spun the blade, pointing it at the elf.

In one hand, he held a rapier whose long, slender blade was made from a single piece of ruby-red wood. In the other, he still held his wineglass. "An Imperial broadsword. Impressive." He frowned. "What are the rings for?"

Loch came in with a clean downward cut, which the elf parried, stepping to put the table between them. He was still smiling—and still holding the drink.

Loch kicked the table, slammed it into the elf, then knocked it aside as he stumbled, slapped his blade aside, and shoulder-checked him into the wall with the full weight of her body. He grunted and slid down to a seated position.

Loch cut the blade from his hand, and it chimed like a bell as it slid across the stone floor. The candle from the table rolled away in its glass, flame guttering wildly. She brought her blade to the elf's throat. "Are we done?"

Wincing, Irrethelathlialann massaged the hand that had held the sword. "Fascinating."

In a motion too fast for Loch to track, he smashed the stem of his wineglass against Loch's blade.

Loch flinched back as glass and alcohol sprayed into her face, then stumbled as a hot pain stabbed into her leg. She swung blindly, and her blade clanged off the wall.

When her vision had cleared, Irrethelathlialann was back on his feet, his rapier once again in his hand. The stem of his wineglass was sticking out of Loch's calf. She yanked it free, gritting her teeth and glaring at the elf.

"Practical style supplements rigorous formal training," he went on, his cadence rapid, as though the words were being pulled out of him on a chain. "Attacks highlight strength rather than fine manipulation, intention to batter into submission. Weakened resolve, unwilling to utilize lethal force."

"Yeah, about that," Loch said, and spun her blade. As the scarf rippled in the air between them, she threw the stem of the wineglass at him with her off hand.

He sidestepped again, then ducked into a kind of half-split under Loch's follow-up slash, which seemed point-less and showy until his extended foot snapped into the table leg and flipped the table back onto Loch's path. She barreled into it, trying to pin him to the wall, but he was already moving again, kicking up, then off the wall and over her head, and though Loch swept her blade up and around, all she got for her trouble was a little line of fire across her back.

"Intelligent, athletic, skilled," he said, flicking a drop of blood from the tip of his rapier, "but slow."

"You've got a little elven magic going there," Loch said, rolling out her shoulder. It felt like a shallow cut at most.

"A little," the elf said, grinning.

She came at him with a low slash that he waved aside. Even as his riposte hissed past her ribs, her sword smashed through the bottles on the bar, and as Loch ducked back from a following slash at her head, she spun her blade around and snapped it back, flinging liquor and broken glass at the elf's face.

His blade moved in a blur, even as he rolled, and little chimes rang as he batted glass aside. "You steal my book, you steal my tricks." He shook his head. "Do you do *anything* on your own?"

Loch smiled and brought her blade down on the candle glass by her foot.

It smashed, and the candle spun end over end, landing in the puddle of liquor between her and the elf.

Irrethelathlialann raised an eyebrow as a wall of blue flame sprang up between the two of them.

"And you're on the side that gives you access to my car," he said. "Of course. Impressive. *I* might actually have trouble beating you."

Behind Loch, the door that led to the elf's car opened, and she spun to see one of the dwarven guards.

He fell into the room facedown and didn't move, and a pair of elves clad in leaf-armor stepped in after him.

"*We* should still be fine, however," Irrethelathlialann added.

The golem stepped forward, and Desidora leaned back as much as she could while tied to the chair.

"Wait," she said, "listen to me. Touching my mind could be dangerous. It could destroy you." Since it was a golem, presumably acting on orders, she added, "Or it could kill me. You said that my death was forbidden, correct?"

The golem paused, its green-glowing palm still stretched out toward her face. "How?"

"For a time, I was touched by the will of Byn-kodar," Desidora said. "The marks of the death god may still lie dormant in my mind—"

"No," the golem said, not moving. "The god Byn-kodar is a mythical construct built by the gods to distance themselves from the actions the death priests take to enforce the gods' will. This information was passed to me by the masters. You were a death priestess, but no longer have that power." It placed its other hand on her shoulder and stepped forward. "You are harmless."

Desidora thrashed, but its grip was strong as the stone it was made of, and its other hand, glowing green with the magic that would wrench open her mind, came closer.

Then it paused again.

Desidora, jerking her head back and forth to try to escape his grasp, saw a tiny white bird flap around the pipes toward them.

A moment later, it was a much *larger* snowy white bear.

With a great crash of fur on stone, Ululenia slammed into the golem, her great bulk smashing it against the wall.

As the golem fell, the bear shifted again, and now stood on four hooves in her natural form. Her horn blazed in all the colors of the rainbow, and she pawed at the ground and put herself between the golem and Desidora.

The scentless creatures are difficult to track, she said in Desidora's mind, *which made it harder to find you.*

"I'm sorry I ruined your evening with the . . ." Desidora said, and then cut herself off to as she looked at the walls. "Look out!"

From every support wall and even in the ceiling itself, the crystals set into the stone were flashing wildly. Their many colors blinked, dimmed, and then took on a single blood-red hue. The walls shivered and groaned, and then, with a thousand little cracking pops, the crystals spat from their settings and joined together on the floor in a pile of rich red magic.

The golem got back to its feet. Its shoulder was broken, but it popped the joint back into place.

Beside it, the glowing crystals had formed themselves into the shape of three more golems, their colors bleeding from red into slate-gray stone.

As the hungry bear swats the beehive, Ululenia thought in what felt to Desidora like a mutter. The unicorn lunged forward, shifting as she did, and once more a great white bear, slammed one of the new golems to the ground before it was fully formed. Crystals shattered and scattered, and Ululenia growled in triumph . . . but then the two other new golems were upon her. Their fists blazed crimson with magic, and Ululenia stumbled and thrashed, trying to shake them loose as their blows bit into her hide.

The first golem stepped forward again. It ignored Ululenia and raised its green-glowing hand toward Desidora. "We will recover the book."

A blade came down, shearing through the hand with a single hard chop.

"Not with that hand," Pyvic said. "I *asked* you to wait for me," he said to Ululenia, kicking the golem in the stomach and knocking it back, "but you just *had* to turn into a bird and fly ahead."

And you were correct. The two new golems fell to the ground as the bear disappeared, and a tiny white dove flew up from between them, fluttered in the air, and then turned *back* into a bear and crashed down upon them hard. *You must be as pleased as the wolf with marrow in his jaws.*

"Highlight of my day, really," Pyvic said as the first golem came forward again. It flexed the stump of its arm, and a pale-green crystal blade snapped out. Pyvic slashed at the golem, and steel rang on crystal as the golem blocked his blow.

Through all this, Desidora sat as her friends fought . . . and prayed to her goddess, a perfect example of uselessness she had been wallowing in for a few days. But she was a faithful. She had spoken with Tasheveth in dreams and visions, and she *knew* that prayers carried weight. While Ululenia had no soul by the standard of the gods, Pyvic was a man, and his love for Loch might buy him some benefit with Tasheveth. If he died, that love would die, and that would be a tragedy, Desidora prayed, for they were just beginning to know each other truly, and deserved to live long enough to love more.

Ululenia cried out as the golems' magic burned into her again. Pyvic blocked a slash, then ran the golem through. It would have killed a man, but the golem leaned forward and grabbed Pyvic by the throat with the hand it still possessed, and Pyvic dropped his blade and clutched desperately at the golem's arm.

Desidora's prayer sounded weak. It *was* weak. It was also all she had to work with.

Ululenia shook herself desperately, and flung one of her attackers free. It slammed into Pyvic and the golem that held him, who in turn fell back and crashed into Desidora.

Desidora's chair tipped over and hit the ground, jarring her shoulder and side.

There was a tiny tinkle of cracking crystal.

She looked down and saw the remains of the warding charm, and smiled. She *could* still help.

"Ghylspwr!" she shouted, and this time, he sprang to her hand, and with a single sweeping blow, she smashed through the chair and tore apart the ropes that bound her. The first golem turned toward her, its blade-arm still raised to finish off Pyvic, and she stepped in, swinging hard and swatting him away.

"Kun-kabynalti osu fuir'is."

"You're here now," Desidora said, turning to Ululenia and the golem that still clung to her. "That's the important thing."

Ululenia shifted into a bird again, trying to escape this time, but the golem caught her in one red-glowing hand. It raised its other hand to crush her, and Desidora caved in its facsimile of a face with one great blow.

Ululenia fell free, then shifted into her human form. Her horn still shone strongly, though she stumbled, and her snowy white dress was spotted with little sooty spots like burns. Desidora steadied her with her free arm.

"Grab Pyvic," she said to Ululenia, looking at the golems. "These things may not be able to die, but I can make certain that it takes them some time to put themselves back together."

The first golem was already back on its feet. "That will not be necessary," it said, lifting up its bladed arm.

Desidora raised Ghylspwr. "You surrender?"

One of the two red-handed golems was back on its feet. The other was still pulling itself back into shape on the ground.

"No," said the first golem, and lunged at her.

Ghylspwr blocked the strike, and his counterstrike ripped cleanly through the golem's chest. It broke open like a sack full of marbles, but even as it did, its other arm gripped Desidora, pinning her.

The red-handed golem lunged at Ululenia, and Ululenia turned, but not in time.

A glowing red claw lashed out, and Desidora saw too late that the golem coming at *her* had just been a distraction.

The red-glowing golem struck, not at Ululenia, but at the pocket of her snowy white dress.

As Desidora wrenched herself free of the collapsing golem's grip, the other golem held *Ruminations upon the Unutterable by the Queen of the Cold River* up in one glowing red hand. The golem's body fell away, scattering into dead stones, and a small red bird made of crystal flapped off down the tunnel with the book clutched in its talons.

"No!" Desidora threw Ghylspwr, and he slammed into one of the support walls, which creaked ominously, but the bird was already gone. A moment later, a snowy white bird flapped after it.

Desidora raised a hand, and Ghylspwr sprang back into her grasp. She looked towards the golems on the ground.

Both were gone, leaving only a pile of shattered rubble behind them.

"I'm sorry," Pyvic croaked, pulling himself back to his feet. "Not much of a rescue."

"No." Desidora reached out and helped him up. "You did fine. All of you." She looked at the golems again, then at the hammer in her hand. "This is on me."

"So," said Tern as the Knights of Gedesar raised crystal-tipped maces. "Baby. Help?"

A brilliant light blazed behind her, casting an enormous shadow of Tern down the length of the car to where the black-armored warriors were standing. The knights staggered, shielding their eyes, and Tern raised her crossbow and fired. Her bolt burst open in midair, splitting into a mesh of thin weighted ropes that snared her target, tangling his arms and legs and sending him crashing to the roof of the train.

"Do you really think non-lethal force is still absolutely necessary?" Hessler yelled behind her.

"They're people!" Tern shouted back, winching her cross-bow. "I try not to kill people if I can help it!"

The other knight raised a crossbow of his own and fired.

His bolt did *not* split into a mesh of thin weighted ropes to snare targets. It did, however, rip a hole in Tern's sleeve as she dove to the floor.

"I believe we're past that point," Hessler shouted.

Tern looked up to see the knight running at her. "Okay! Got another illusion?"

"More than just an illusion!" As Hessler finished, Tern felt energy crackle around her, building in the air.

The knight reached her, and his mace came up. A blast of raw magical power slammed into his armor and sent him crashing to the roof of the car as well. Tern blinked. "Wow." Impossibly, the Knight of Gedesar pushed himself back to his feet, his armor glowing dimly where he'd been blasted. "I'm thinking *yvkefer*-alloy armor." "That was my assumption, yes!" Hessler yelled. The knight readied his mace, and another blast of energy slammed into his armor, and then another. "Speaking of assumptions, I assume you were told I only did illusions, sir knight!" The knight staggered under the blasts, but didn't fall. "This must be very disappointing for you!" The stone roof of the car began to vibrate beneath Tern's fingers.

"Hessler, wait!" Tern's crossbow was only half-winched, and the knight was closing in on her. She lifted her hands. "Wait, wait, I surrender!"

The knight kept coming. "No prisoners!" he growled, even as another blast of energy knocked him back a half-step. His armor crackled with energy now, and the roof of the car thrummed with latent power.

"Your loss!" Tern touched a button on the cuff of her dress, and a dart spat out and caught the knight in the thin leather joint at his shoulder.

The knight winced, paused, and pulled the dart free. "Sorry, girl! We've built up an immunity to—"

Tern lashed out with a steel-toed boot and kicked the knight hard in the ankle, and he crashed to the roof, bounced, and rolled off the side of the car.

"I *did* offer to surrender!" she shouted, rising to her feet to make sure that he was actually *off* the train and not hanging from the edge, waiting to come back and club her to death with his mace.

The car heaved beneath her feet as an explosion on the ground below rocked the train.

Tern hit the roof *again*, slid, and felt the stone give way to empty air beneath her. She flailed desperately, clipped a handrail with her boots, spun, slipped free, and went head-first over the side of the car.

It was angled, and for one bright moment she thought that maybe she could slow her fall, but though it had seemed like a wide angle from *inside* the car, it was nowhere near flat enough to do that, and she fell helplessly down the side of the car, stone rough on her dress and skin as she slid.

Light flashed in front of her, and her hands hit something, and she clung desperately, blinked, and realized that she was looking through a window, upside down, and had caught hold of the top of the seam on the bottom of the window with her fingers.

It looked like a nice suite inside. A wealthy merchant and a woman who was either a young wife or a mature mistress were sharing drinks, looking around as the train jostled and rocked. The woman wore an expensive gold necklace that didn't match her silver gown, but they probably cost enough that matching wasn't the point. Looking at them was a *lot* better than looking down at the moonlit silver tracks humming along a few feet from Tern's head.

For one wonderful moment, Tern hung there upside down, precariously balanced, fingers straining, heart hammering hard enough to make little gasping noises pop up from her throat even though she didn't think she was breathing, and thought that she might actually be all right.

Then she felt herself sliding to the left, tried to lean, over-corrected like she always did when Icy tried to teach her how to do a headstand, and felt her sweat-slicked right thumb slip on the seam. Sliding down, Tern looked down at the tracks humming by so fast that they blurred, glowing blue with little red sparks shooting out, and opened her mouth to scream.

Then she choked out a cough instead as something grabbed her boot. Something also brushed her braided ponytail as it hung down, and Tern realized that it was *the ground*. She immediately brought her eyes to look at anything but that, and found herself staring at the underside of the dwarven railcar, where rainbow crystals hummed and sparked as they held the car aloft. She held very still.

"Hang on!" Hessler shouted, *entirely* unnecessarily.

As the *best boyfriend in the world* pulled her back up, Tern used her hands to walk herself up the side of the train. The rich merchant and his wife were looking at her open-mouthed, and Tern gave them an upside-down smile as she slid back up.

Then Tern was back on top of the train again, rolling onto her side and coughing. Hessler, sitting beside her, was breathing hard.

"You jumped over," she said after a moment. She didn't get up. Her legs weren't working yet.

"You slipped," Hessler said.

"I'm really proud of you," Tern said. It was hard to talk over the wind whipping in her ears. The whole "top of the train" thing was feeling a lot less fun than it had a few minutes ago.

"I have some unfortunate news," Hessler said, and Tern looked up to see several more Knights of Gedesar rappelling down onto the roof of the train. Hessler followed her look. "Not them."

"Seriously?" Tern wasn't sure where her crossbow was. She'd never finished winching it after last time, either. The knights were still unclipping themselves from the line.

"Remember that explosion? I think the armor of that guy I hit with the magic blasts built up a thaumaturgic charge, and when it hit the tracks, it may have arced over into the power grid for the railcar crystals, which are powered by—"

Something behind them roared loudly enough to get Tern rolling back to her feet. She looked at what was, as far as she could tell, a large humanoid cloud of living fire.

"Fire-daemons?" Tern asked.

"Fire-daemons, yes," Hessler said, "and the energy discharge may have freed one of them."

"You think?" Tern looked back at the Knights of Gedesar. "Hey, guys, truce?"

A silver-tipped crossbow bolt whizzed past her face and struck sparks as it plinked off the roof of the car behind her.

"Just checking!" Three knights ahead of them, one firedaemon behind them. "Hessler, just in case I don't get to tell you later, I really appreciate you rescuing me."

The other two knights raised their crossbows, and Tern, with no weapon of her own and nowhere to run, winced.

Something sailed out of the nighttime sky and slammed into one of the knights, blasting him cleanly off the roof.

It was, Tern saw, another grappling line. The hook trailed for a moment, then caught on one of the handgrips.

"What in Byn-Kodar's hell?" The other two knights turned in shock.

"Sorry I'm late!" came a voice from the night, along with what Tern recognized as the sound of someone coming sliding down a zipline. "Your mother always wants to cuddle after!"

Kail hit a second knight full-on, and another armored figure went flying off into the night. The third swung at Kail with his mace, and Kail ducked and unclipped something from his armor. "Any time you two want to help!"

"Oh, sorry!" Hessler said, and gestured. A flare of light flashed in the knight's face, and he stumbled back, momentarily blinded. "I thought you had things under control!"

"You did just kind of take out two of them!" Tern added, risking a glance back. "Fire-daemon's probably a priority, Hessler!"

"I took out two of them with surprise and a really great line!" Kail knocked the crossbow out of blinded knight's other hand as it swung up, then ducked *another* swing of the mace, unhooked the grappling line from the handrail, and hooked it to the knight. "Icy, we're good!"

He dodged back as the knight lashed out with an armored backhand, and then the Knight of Gedesar was sailing up into the night sky, yelling and flailing.

Sweat beaded on Hessler's brow in the moonlight, and he frowned, gathered his energy, and then made a series of passes with his hands. Finally, he flung them out at the fire-daemon with a muttered phrase.

The fire-daemon flinched back, roaring. It was on the rooftop of the car behind them, and the stone was starting to melt from the heat. It looked at them balefully—at least, Tern thought it did; it didn't have a whole lot of face to speak of—and then darted back to the back of the car and slid like liquid fire through the gap in the ringmail that Tern had left open when she'd led Hessler up onto the roof in the first place.

"Nice work." Kail was grinning widely. "Man, I've always wanted to do a job on the back of one of these things!"

"Yeah, I used to think that," Tern said. "Hey, can we undo the grappling cable for the bad guys before more of them rappel in?"

A roaring ball of fire sailed past them in the night sky as the Knights of Gedesar opened up with their flamecannon.

Security Enforcer Gart Utt'Krenner had boarded the train leaving Ironroad after finding three unusual instances.

On a human or elven transport, unusual instances might be more common. Humans often thought of themselves as having special needs that justified special treatment, and the elves tended to be flighty and odd at the best of times. In Gart's opinion, human airships ought to include extra cargo room to store all the exceptions the humans carried with them.

But the Silver Line was dwarven, and dwarves did not, as a general rule, make problems that required exceptional solutions. Dwarves with special needs booked passage on cars that were fitted specifically to those needs—ramp cars for elderly or ill dwarves traveling alone, sunlit cars with clear-paned ceilings for dwarves who had gone too long underground and become uncomfortable in confined dark spaces, and even insulated stone cars for dwarves who had contracted the jeweled shakes and could not risk exposure to the magical auras of the crystals that ran the engines and kept the cars aloft.

These were not unusual instances. These were expected conditions, and any reputable transportation system was prepared to accommodate the realities of travel in modern dwarven life.

Since many of the passengers on the line were humans, the cars accommodated their needs as well. There was more legroom, of course, along with human-tailored meal services and more space in the aisles, since humans did not like being close to each other unless they were intimate. These were not unusual instances either.

The train leaving Ironroad that day, however, had been different.

First, it had included a private suite for an elven passenger. Elves almost *never* traveled on the railway. Gart was not sure why that was so, but he himself had never traveled on one of the living elven treeships, so it was not for him to judge. On its own, that would have been odd, but not worth investigating.

Second, a human guildsman had berated one of the ticket sellers until she had given him an entire economy car to himself, along with a baggage exemption. It was clear that his reservation had not truly been lost—the railway lost fewer than ten reservations every year—and while it had been decades since Gart had served in that remote keep up in the mountains, he still remembered how humans tried to smuggle goods on the railway. The ticket seller, to her credit, had filed a report suggesting that the guildsman's activity be tracked so that if he attempted it again, charges could be brought against him.

And third, Gart had seen that same guildsman yelling about having misplaced the selfsame ticket just minutes before departure. It had been that last item that had convinced Gart to show the guards his badge and board the train.

The stolen item from the museum was elven. An elf was on the train. An entire car was exempt from normal baggage procedures. The human who had paid for that car had lost his ticket.

Gart waited, riding patiently in a dwarven car near the back of the train. The dwarves—mostly miners, though a few had the longer brow and almond eyes of the crafters—watched him curiously, but did not comment. He sat in a spare seat on the benches and made polite conversation with a pair of miners who had become intimate while on their last assignment.

When the night was deep and most of the dwarves had nodded off to sleep in their benches, leaning against a neighbor or, failing that, a wall, Gart felt it appropriate to act.

He left the car and passed through two dwarven cars, moving freely and checking for trouble as he went. In the sealed platform between the last of the dwarven cars and the first of the economy-class human cars, a guard was waiting.

Gart approached with clear movements and produced his badge as the guard eyed him curiously. "Security Enforcer Gart Utt'Krenner, special assignment," he said.

The guard checked the veracity of the badge while Gart waited politely. "Anything we should be concerned about, Chief?" he asked.

"I must ascertain that before I worry ye needlessly," Gart said. "If there be trouble, I would appreciate assistance in dealin' with it, but I would not wish t' interrupt yer duties."

"It would be our honor to assist, Chief," the guard said, as expected, though it was not polite to make assumptions. "Please accept this paging crystal for the duration of your travel." He passed Gart a standard crystal that would, if broken, raise an alarm on sympathetic crystals carried by the other guards.

"Thank ye." Gart nodded his appreciation, and the guard unlocked the door and let him through.

The next few cars went quickly. Gart showed his badge and his paging crystal to the guards he encountered, and nothing seemed out of place in the cars themselves. Like the dwarves, the humans slept, played cards, read books, or stared out the window as the train sped along.

Finally, he reached the last of the human economy cars, the one booked privately for the guildsman. Since the guildsman had misplaced his ticket, it should by all rights be empty. Stepping into the sealed area before the car, Gart readied his truncheon in one hand and his paging crystal in the other.

Technically, his right to apprehend Justicar Loch relied upon the delinquent payment of docking fees, which would ordinarily involve a polite but firm conversation and an explanation about loss of transport rights or seizure of goods in the future. After what had happened at his museum, however, Gart believed it likely the encounter would turn to violence.

He shouldered open the door and stepped in, quickly enough to surprise anyone inside but not so quickly that it was obviously an attack. "Yer pardon!" he called, truncheon held by his side. "I need to be checkin' a few security matters! Yer understandin' is apprecia . . . hm."

The car was empty. It was also conspicuously devoid of any kind of luggage.

Perhaps Gart had gotten on the wrong train.

A loud bang shattered the steady hum of the train, and a massive jolt sent Gart stumbling into an empty bench.

No, he decided, this was the correct train after all.

Gart had been on trains when trolls or scorpion-folk had attacked. That bang and jolt came from something big getting under the car and doing some damage to the railway crystals. Broken crystals could cause a train to rattle unevenly or drag on the track, but that was fortunately as bad as it got—unless whatever got under the wheels had enough latent magical energy to cause an energy backlash.

The lights in the car flickered and went out. A moment later, an enormous roar split the air on the roof overhead, indicating that the fire-daemon used to power the car had gotten loose.

Backlash.

Muttering a very polite oath to himself, Gart Utt'Krenner ran the length of the darkened economy car by memory, crashed into the door, and wrenched it open.

A guard lay unconscious in the platform between this car and the next one, which would have been the first of the luxury cars. The ringmail tubing that sealed the platform had been undone, and Gart saw flames on the other side.

He grabbed the unconscious guard by the ankles and hauled him back into the darkened economy car. It was rattling already. Without power, the car was being held up by the cars on either side of it, which would eventually damage the couplers. Gart nevertheless believed it to be safer for the unconscious guard than underneath an uncontrolled fire-daemon.

He heard another roar as he turned, and then watched as liquid fire poured down through the hole in the ringmail tubing and melt its way through the door. The fire-daemon was red-hot, though touching the stone of the railway car had already caused it to manifest jagged stone claws and bone spurs at what were slowly becoming defined as elbows and knees.

Gart dropped the paging crystal to the ground and crushed it beneath his boot. Then he set his shoulders, raised his truncheon, and followed the fire-daemon into the dining car.

The airship carrying the Knights of Gedesar was raining down fire upon the train. Tern and Kail were yelling at each other. By most standards, this would be considered a fairly problematic operation.

Hessler squinted as a ball of fire raced past their heads, splashing flames across the passing countryside.

"All right, then," he said, "this is what we're going to do."

Tern and Kail stopped and looked at him.

"Icy is currently piloting the airship?" he asked, yelling to be heard over the wind whipping in his ears and yet another blast of fire splashing across the roof of the car.

"He's keeping *Iofegemet* in the air," Kail shouted back, "but that's about the best he can do!"

"Is this *really* the time to be pushing the name?" Tern yelled.

"Is this really the time to question the name?" Kail yelled back.

"I believe we can defeat them," Hessler shouted, ignoring both of them.

"Look, baby, it's great that you're doing spells beyond just illusions now," Tern said, "but unless you know a lot more about airships than you've ever let on—"

Another ball of flame splashed the roof of the car, this time close enough that they all dived back. The train rattled beneath Hessler's feet, and he made the mistake of glancing over the edge at the ground.

"Four seconds between shots, and no green tint to the flames!" he yelled, pointing desperately at the airship. "They're firing an Iff'hurnin Blazer, which you only see on airships owned by wealthy nobles who want to look impressive and have servants to handle the maintenance! It uses an unshielded aural sink that shares a lattice with the firing system! Tern, *baby*, what does that mean?"

Tern had already grabbed her crossbow, and was winching it desperately. "Silver dust in the lattice will jam the whole array!" She jammed a bolt into place. "Light!"

"Light is for first-year students!" Hessler pointed at the airship, clenched his fist, and released the spell he'd been preparing. The side of the distant airship illuminated as brilliantly as if it were flying in the noonday sun, and a straight beam of light trailed back from the airship's flamecannon to where Tern stood. "Tracer line!"

"Does it account for windspeed and gravity?"

"Um . . ."

"Close enough!" Tern fired.

The airship, lit perfectly by Hessler's light-illusion, jolted with a spray of sparks as Tern's bolt hit home. A pair of black-armored figures by the flamecannon gestured frantically, and then sprang back as it caught fire.

"Hah! How does that work for you, you authoritarian oafs!" Hessler yelled. "Think of that next time you trifle with someone who makes his living understanding the fundamental forces of the universe!"

Tern grinned. "Nicely done. And I'm sorry for calling you ba . . ."

She trailed off, and Hessler looked over.

His spell was still in place. The enemy airship shone like a gaudy pageant float in the night sky.

And a line of light, the aiming assistant he'd been so proud of, still traced a perfect trail back from the airship to Tern.

Specifically, to the crossbow bolt sticking out of her in the center of a growing pool of red.

Kail caught her as she fell, which was good, because Hessler could only stand there dumbly, feeling the train rock beneath his heels, and then Kail was hitting him on the shoulder and shouting. But the winds stole the words, even though he'd been able to make them out before, and finally Hessler realized that he wanted Hessler to drop the spell, and Hessler waved his hand and took away the light that had aimed the enemy's bolts at Tern.

"We need to get the bolt out!" Kail said as Hessler blinked in the sudden darkness. "I can do it on our ship! Can you get into the car down there and get the book?"

Hessler looked at Tern, or tried to. He'd ruined his own night vision with the illusion. He thought her eyes were closed. She wasn't talking. He couldn't tell which spots were afterimages of light and which were spreading blood. "Who the hell cares about the book?"

Kail was still holding Tern, but he reached out with his free hand and grabbed Hessler's shoulder hard. In the darkness, the man's face was a shadow, except for the whites of his eyes and his teeth, which caught the moonlight.

"You scared, wizard? Wracks you a little, watching somebody you like with a bolt sticking out of them, doesn't it?" Kail's hand tightened and yanked Hessler in close. "Imagine the whole damn Republic like this, because that's what a war looks like when you're not off hiding in a university! If we don't get that book, *this is what happens!*" He shoved Hessler back, then, and pointed with his now-free hand down at the car below them. "Now, do you want to carry your girlfriend up a grappling line and then do field-surgery on an airship to get this bolt out of her chest, or do you want to go down there and get the book? Because I'll do *either!*"

Hessler swallowed. "I don't know how to treat a wound like that!"

"Well, then, this decision just got real easy for you." Kail waved with his free hand, and Hessler turned to see the silhouette of their own airship pulling in closer. "Go!"

Hessler turned away, then looked back at Kail. He wanted to say something, but when he looked at Tern, her face pale, nothing came. Kail looked at him hard again, then nodded, and Hessler turned away.

He leaned over the angled side of the rooftop and looked down at the window on the wall below. He'd studied the plan. He knew the privacy suite's location, even when trying to get to it from here, instead of the original plan, in which they were to have cleverly walked past the guards on the inside of the car and gone straight to the elf's room.

The window was crystal. Hessler leaned down, pointed at the window, and twitched his fingers as though twisting a phantom doorknob.

Nobody appreciated purely audible illusions the way they did the visual tricks. Humans were a visual species, and visual illusions had the most impact on the conscious mind, even though any good illusionist knew that the subtle cues of scent and sound made all the difference when it came to engaging the target on a gut level.

It didn't hurt that sound waves at the right frequency would shatter crystal.

Hessler twisted his fingers, and the train vibrated around him. A moment later, the window exploded.

He stepped off the edge of the roof, slid down the side of the wall, caught the window with his heels, and stepped inside.

The elf's private suite was furnished richly, with a small sitting table, a fold-out bed with burgundy satin sheets, and a chest of drawers made of polished wood instead of stone. It was lit by candles instead of crystals set into the ceiling. Hessler actually saw no crystals anywhere in the room, now that he looked.

What he *did* see was the elven manuscript, lying on the table on a velvet cloth next to some bottles of expensive elven wine and a thin-bladed dueling dagger that would probably have impressed Loch or Kail.

Hessler picked the book up and flipped it open. This time, it was most definitely elven text and not a dirty poem meant to insult someone who grabbed it by mistake.

Hessler looked back out the open window, where the wind still whistled, though it seemed little more than a whisper after the roaring atop the roof.

He heard footsteps out in the hall, loud and getting louder.

He had time for just one spell, and it needed to be a damn sight better than just an illusion.

A moment later, an elven warrior rushed in. Hessler got his hands up, and then a fist was coming at him, and then everything went black.

Twelve

LOCH STUMBLED BACK, CAUGHT ONE OF THE RUBY-WOOD BLADES with a back-blade parry that made it dance along the rings, slashed while still moving back, and took a hit to the arm that caught muscle anyway.

She was bleeding from the wineglass-puncture in the leg, the thin slash on the back, and half a dozen wounds that ranged from minor scrapes to the new ugly gash on her right bicep she'd just gotten, which was going to keep bleeding until she got weak and then got killed.

Her trick with the fire had kept her from getting flanked for a few seconds, but then it had died out, and the fight had turned into three against one. Irrethelathlialann was damned good on his own. Accompanied by two more elven swordsmen, there was no way Loch could take them in anything remotely approaching a fair fight.

As such, Loch avoided anything remotely approaching a fair fight.

So when the train rocked with a sudden jolting impact that sent everyone stumbling, Loch made use of it. Even as she caught her balance, she lunged forward with an ugly chop that sank cleanly through the fancy leaf-armor one of the swordsmen wore, crunching into his collarbone with a noise that meant he'd be spending some time with the medics learning slowly how to lift anything heavier than a teacup.

As he went down, coughing and gasping, Loch threw her sword at the other swordsman.

He parried it brilliantly, his thin green face twisting into contempt at her desperation even as he slid to the side—and into the point of his friend's rapier, which Loch had grabbed with her other hand.

Swordsman number two went down with a blade in his stomach, and Loch dove for her blade. She wrapped her hand around it and spun just in time for a sick stabbing pain to lance through her side.

"Those were two of the best swordsmen in the Elflands," Irrethelathlialann said, stepping in to finish his thrust.

"Nobody's dead yet." Loch stepped *in*, grunting through the pain, and swung her blade, which the elf blocked, thus leaving himself open for her forehead to smash into his face. As he fell back, the blade slid slowly free from her side.

She saw that Irrethelathlialann was down on the ground, groaning, and only then did she let herself sink back against the wall and put a hand to her bleeding side.

It hadn't hit anything vital. Assuming Kail still remembered his field stitches, she'd be fine.

It still hurt, though.

"You're good." The elf's voice cut into the slow blackness that had been dancing around the edge of Loch's mind, and she looked up to see him looking at her from the ground. "How unfortunate that you're on their side."

"Your men will live." Loch pushed herself upright, shoulders back, legs locked to cover the weakness. "And the only side I'm on is not going to war."

"Of course." Irrethelathlialann rolled over onto his back, groaning, and Loch used her own blade to edge his rapier out of reach. He held a hand up to his face, running thin fingers along the crystals that glowed in his cheeks. "Look at this, Isafesira de Lochenville. How do you think these got here?"

"You got drunk and wanted to show your parents how grown up you were?" Loch's side wasn't getting any better, but she was getting used to the pain.

"We're born with them, you Urujar ass." The elf glared at her, fingers spinning the ring on one hand in agitation. "And when I hyperanalyze sensory stimuli ignoring emotional and societal expectations . . ." He broke off, shook his head. "Did you think that just *happened*?"

"I try not to judge other folks," Loch said.

The elf smiled. "You really ought to start. We were *bred*, Loch." At her stare, his smile faded. "Like the dwarves were bred to mine and craft and fight, we were bred to work the crystals that kept the world running, to be so *perfectly* attuned to that magical energy that the mere *presence* of active crystals would shift our minds into more efficient patterns."

"What are you—" Loch started, and then the fire-daemon roared in from the far end of the car.

It flowed in like a wave of molten metal, the door collapsing under the weight and heat, and as it rolled into the car, it rose to a shape that was slowly approaching humanoid. Its arms were lined with stone, curled into rocky claws that glittered in the glowing lamplight.

"It's broken its binding." Irrethelathlialann slid back to his feet, shaky but stronger than he'd been acting.

"Like the ones you sent after us at the museum?"

"What? That wasn't me." The elf looked over at her. "I just rigged up the trigger crystals so you'd trip the alarms."

The fire-daemon roared, jagged stone teeth bubbling to the top of its face like dead rats in a barrel.

"Wonderful," Loch muttered.

"Problem with daemons?" Irrethelathlialann asked.

"I watched one eat someone once."

"That must have been traumatic."

"She was trying to kill me at the time. I got over it." Loch kicked a ruby-wood rapier in his direction. "Truce?"

He caught the blade on his foot, flipped it up into his hand, and smiled. "Why not?"

The fire-daemon saw them and pounded the floor. As its arm came back up, the pattern of the floor tiles was visible on the rocky armor that now covered its limb, as though the tiles from the floor had slid from the ground up onto it. "RRRRRRRRLLLLLLLLLLL," the daemon said, and lunged.

It was far faster than something that big should have been. Loch dove to one side, ignoring the searing pain in her side as she did, and the fire-daemon's rocky claws smashed through the bar, sending what few bottles were left crashing to the ground.

Loch slashed out with a backhanded blow that cut a chunk of stone from one arm, revealing molten magma still flowing underneath the armor. Behind the beast, Irrethelathlialann thrust his blade into the daemon's back, then pulled his rapier out with a look of disgust. It was glowing cherry-red with heat.

"I don't suppose you have any abjuration charms on hand?" he asked as Loch sidestepped another blow and took a chunk out of the daemon's leg with a chop to the knee.

"No. Are we hurting it?"

"RRRLLLLLLLLKKKK." The fire-daemon stepped forward, trying to catch Loch in a bear hug this time, and she stabbed it in the face and rolled away. She came back to her knees instead of her feet, panting at the pain that wracked her whole body at this point.

The daemon had glassy crystal eyes now, and where Loch had slashed it on the leg and arm, a slow stain of steel was spreading across the rocky hide.

"A little," the elf called over, stabbing it again and wincing, "but not much, and as you may possibly have noticed, it's adapting to any matter it comes into contact with, so our strikes are—"

"Yeah, got that."

The daemon was more rock than fire now, though heat still bubbled in cracks between the slabs of stone. It turned to Loch, its crude mouth cracking as it opened.

"LLLLLLLURRRKKKKK!"

"Hmm." Irrethelathlialann looked at Loch.

She shoved herself back to her feet. "It could be saying *anything*."

"LLLLLOKKKKKKKKK!"

The elf raised an eyebrow. "The truce was predicated on a shared threat, Isafesira. But this appears to be *your* problem."

Loch shot him a glare as he stepped back, blew gently on his still-hot blade, and smiled.

"Guess I'll just take my book and leave, then," Loch said, and since her last roll had taken her to the doorway, she stepped back out of the car and darted into the car that contained the elf's private suite with a "LLLOCCCCCH!" and a "Hey!" trailing after her.

She pounded down the hallway, which in this car had been carpeted over in a nice forest green. She reached the door to the elf's room, saw that it was slightly open, and barged inside.

Hessler lay unconscious on the floor in the middle of the suite, with another elven swordsman kneeling beside him. The swordsman was pulling the book from Hessler's hand. The window was open, and shattered crystal covered the floor, likely explaining how Hessler had gotten inside.

"Mine." Loch stepped in as the elf turned, drove the heel of her palm into his jaw, grabbed his shoulder, and pulled hard as she kicked his legs out from under him. He went down in a heap.

"LLOCCCH!" came a roar from the car outside in the hall.

Loch looked at the book, Hessler, and the elf for one stolen moment, hand pressed to her side. She nudged the elf into a corner with her leg, then stepped to the window and looked out, squinting until she caught sight of her airship overhead. She waved, then made a broad signal that Kail would hopefully recognize.

The fire-daemon burst into the room, stone shoulders tearing the doorframe. "LOCH!"

She turned and raised her sword. "Do your worst, daemon."

The daemon lunged forward, an unstoppable mass of stone and fire and steel.

Loch stepped to the side, and the daemon slammed through the open window, smashing the stone of the frame as it plunged into the night outside.

A moment later, a grappling line hissed through the now much-larger window, caught on the crumbling frame, and held. Loch grabbed Hessler with one arm and the book with the other. The book was slippery in her hand. When she looked down, it was smeared with blood from her hand, which she'd had pressed to her side a minute ago.

"Going to want to get that looked at," she muttered, and hooked Hessler into the grappling cable. Something in his pocket bumped her hand as she did, and she pulled out a lovely elven dagger that right now, she probably needed more than Hessler did.

She slid Hessler out through the window and waved up at the airship, which was still just a silhouette in the night sky. Over the hum of the train and the whistling wind, she could hear them shouting something to her, but couldn't make out the words.

Then she heard the roar off to her right, looked, and saw the fire-daemon still clinging to the side of the train, clawing its way back to her.

She pushed Hessler away and dove back just as the great claw smashed down where she had been standing, tearing more stone free from the wall. The daemon roared and pulled its great bulk back into the room, and Loch turned, book still in hand, to run.

Of course, Irrethelathlialann was coming at her, and she got her blade up to parry his thrust just in time before lurching back in pain as he body-checked her into the wall with more force than someone with pointy ears should have been able to muster. She hit the ground, parried another stab, drove a booted foot into his knee to send him stumbling back, and only *then* realized that he'd grabbed the book as he took her down.

He *was* fast.

She rolled back to her feet, damning the wound in her side that was now making her legs weak, and lunged through the doorway after him. His rapier parried her sword, but the very nice dagger she'd gotten from Hessler pinned his rapier, and then she slammed her head into his nose *again,* kicked the back of his knee as he stumbled, and smashed the pommel of the dagger into his face.

"I be needin' ye to lower yer blades!"

Panting, Loch looked over to the door leading back to the dining car, where an armored dwarf held a truncheon with a ready grip. His ringmail glittered in the light of the lamps overhead, which were flickering themselves, likely because of the fire-daemon wreaking havoc in the car and smashing everything.

After a moment, she placed him as the dwarf from the museum. "Gart . . . Utt'Krenner?"

"Security Enforcer Gart Utt'Krenner, Justicar." He stepped forward, truncheon still raised. "And I have some questions to ask ye regardin' unpaid docking fees." He saw the book lying on the ground next to Irrethelathlialann. "But as long as I be here, I might be arrestin' ye for thievery as well."

"Technically, the elf stole the real manuscript." Loch gestured. Back in the private suite, the daemon was still clawing its way inside. "Listen, I respect your work, but I've got a daemon coming, and I don't have time for this." She slid her stolen dagger into her belt and reached down for the book. "If you've got anything that can banish a daemon—"

An impact like a hail of fists slammed into her chest, and Loch hit the ground and rolled.

"Perhaps ye didna hear me," the dwarf said. Loch blinked away the blackness swirling at the edge of her vision and saw him still holding his truncheon extended out toward her, smoking at the tip. A half dozen black stone balls a little larger than slingstones rolled on the carpet where Loch lay. "Ye're going nowhere."

Gart Utt'Krenner would have said more, Loch guessed, but the daemon chose that moment to smash out into the hall.

"Did she get onto the grapple-line?" Kail asked. He couldn't look himself, since he was kneeling by Tern on the deck of *Iofegemet* and trying to help her not bleed out. Hauling her up on a grapple line hadn't helped matters much.

"She did not," Icy said. "She secured Hessler to it, but the daemon forced her back inside."

"All right. Haul Hessler in." Kail had been running *Iofegemet* dark in order to avoid giving away the airship's position to anyone on the train who might raise an alarm. His eyesight had adjusted reasonably well, but he'd still rather have light when dealing with a through-and-through. "Lamps on."

Icy fumbled at the console. "We have an additional problem."

"Don't really care, Icy." The lights flickered on, a warm amber glow that illuminated Tern. She was significantly pale, and her side was soaked. The bolt stood out below her shoulder like some impossible costume decoration. Kail turned her gently. There was blood on the deck, but no exit wound that Kail could see.

He had really been hoping for an exit wound.

"I have been watching the Knights of Gedesar," Icy said. "They have maintained their distance, and I believe, from the way that they are maneuvering their ship now, that they have succeeded in repairing their flamecannon."

"Close in and open up with ours." Kail looked at the bolt, at least the bit of it that he could see. Professional grade, steel shaft, thin silver foil for the fletching instead of feathers. The odds that the head wasn't barbed to do a hell of a lot of damage when he pulled it out seemed low at best.

"You know that I cannot do that, Kail."

"Sure you can." Kail held Tern's collar gently. He could still feel her pulse, but her skin was clammy. Then he unfastened the dress and peeled it free from her shoulder. "Any idiot can fire a flamecannon. That's not the job they gave the big thinkers during the war."

"I swore an oath to do no violence to living creatures," Icy said, hands steady on the control console.

"That doesn't mean you *can't*, Icy. That means you don't *want* to." Her dress was free. There was definitely no exit wound on Tern's back.

"Kail—"

"You wanna talk *can't*? When the bad guys hit me with a soul-binding and bound me to their will, and I had to watch helplessly while I betrayed all of you? That was a *can't*. When I held a blade at Loch's throat while I battered against the walls of my own mind and screamed? That was a *can't*." Kail put one hand on the bolt protruding from Tern's chest, and the other hand on her shoulder, and shut his eyes. "If you don't *want* to defend us from the bad guys while I save Tern's life, that's on you, but man the hell up and admit that it's a *choice*."

He pushed hard, gritting his teeth at the noise as tissue ripped and slid beneath the bolt.

He looked down. The head of the bolt protruded from Tern's back, silver stained black with blood. It was indeed barbed all over the damn place, but it was out.

Gently, trying to jostle the wound as little as possible, Kail worked the head of the bolt free. As he tossed it aside, a ball of flame sprayed across the great balloon overhead, licking fire along its sides.

"Portside wards at forty percent," Icy said quietly.

Kail pulled the headless bolt free in one smooth, clean movement. It still produced more blood. "Can you put pressure on both sides of this?" he asked, cupping Tern's shoulder with both hands.

"I can, yes. I may even be able to perform mild energy work to stimulate healing—"

"Fine. Go." Kail waited until Icy was beside him, and then lifted his hands as Icy put his down. "Keep her still."

Then he wiped his hands on his breeches, stepped to the control console, and put Tern out of his mind and the airship with the flamecannons into it.

And also, he supposed, the unconscious mage still hanging from the grappling line below.

"Have to do *everything* myself," he muttered, flicking a crystal to draw up the line. He swung *Iofegemet* into a tight turn to point his nose at the airship, ignoring the ball of flame that flashed out from the enemy ship and sprayed across *Iofegemet*'s forward hull.

"How are our wards?" Icy asked, holding Tern steady as *Iofegemet* rocked.

"Not really looking." Kail grabbed the portside flamecannon, checked the sights, turned it as far as it would go, and waited.

The enemy airship came into his sights a moment later, and he saw the silhouette clearly through the lenses in his sights. The Knights of Gedesar weren't using a military-grade airship, which extended the wards holding in the wind-daemons to protect the entirety of the ship. They were using a civilian airship, which only had crystals powerful enough to maintain wards along the balloon itself.

Kail aimed carefully, then fired.

Fire sprayed across their hull, catching and licking the ropes.

"Stay warm, boys," Kail muttered.

He heard the cries off in the distance. He couldn't see much on the ship itself, just a silhouette with fire crawling across the hull.

The flamecannon's firing crystal chimed its readiness, and Kail fired again. Fire seared the enemy airship's cabin, and something inside went up with a whoosh. Kail saw figures in the distance, running across the deck in black armor.

"Kail, I need you at the control console."

"I'm sure you can handle it, Icy." The enemy airship was crippled, but Kail had seen them pull through worse. They were fighting the fire, pulling away and descending for an emergency landing. He still had their range, though.

"We are approaching a mountain, Kail. If I take pressure off Tern's wound, she will die."

For one long dark moment, Kail considered what to say.

Then he stepped back and locked the flamecannon's safety with an angry shove and stalked back to the control console.

They *were* getting close to a mountainside. It practically glowed silver-blue in the moonlight, all craggy peaks and icy snow with dark trees scattered sparsely along the slope. The dwarven railway cut a tunnel through the mountain, and Kail put *Iofegemet* into a sharp ascent. They could pick up Loch on the other side . . . assuming that she was taking care of her end down there.

"You have grown cold, Kail," Icy said, still kneeling by Tern.

"I doubt you're going to get the book and stop the war with your little acrobatic tricks," Kail said, "so maybe you should try to impress someone else with those somersaults. Like your mother. She always loves it when I roll her over." Kail looked over at the Imperial man, who looked back without flinching.

"You were hurt," Icy said slowly and deliberately, "both by Silestin's soul-binding and by Desidora's actions as a death priestess, which caused you pain—"

"When she tried to suck the life out of me? Yeah, that'll happen."

"You cannot allow your pain to alter your values," Icy said. "The morals that define you, the oaths—"

"Oaths," Kail said, "are for people who are wealthy enough to afford them." He checked their path one more time, then locked the console. "Now, if it doesn't interfere with your values, I'm going to go haul up our wizard before he gets dragged through the trees."

The fire-daemon was more of a general-parts-of-train-daemon at this point.

Its body was largely stone, with patterns of floor tile still visible in places, and glowing crystal spurs jutting out from its knees and elbows. Its claws were metal so hot they glowed cherry red, as were the fangs that sprouted out in all directions from its debatable mouth.

It had acquired furry trim around its ankles, likely from contact with the elf's carpeted floor, which made the daemon look like it was naked except for a pair of socks.

The daemon plowed into Gart Utt'Krenner, slamming the dwarf into the wall. It turned to Loch as the dwarf sank to the floor, groaning. Its eyes, now multifaceted arrays of crystal that glowed with flickering purple light, narrowed into a monstrous glare.

"LOCH."

Loch got back to her feet. Her side didn't hurt as much any longer, but that probably wasn't a good thing. She was definitely getting slow on that side. Her arm was still bleeding, too.

But she was starting to figure things out, and that helped.

"How are you doing, Jyelle?" she asked. "Last time I saw you, you were getting eaten by a daemon."

The daemon flexed its claws. "YOU KILLED ME."

Loch took an experimental breath and winced. "Technically, the daemon killed you. And you were standing over me with a knife at the time, so it's hard to really feel bad about it."

"IT ATE ME, LOCH."

"And it was unshackled at the time." Loch nodded. "I didn't know what that meant, just like I didn't know why every daemon-powered magical device I came across was malfunctioning or trying to kill me . . . until I saw that the fire-daemon copying parts of whatever it touched." She gestured. "Then I wondered if maybe, when that daemon killed you . . ."

"IT ATE ME. SO IT BECAME ME." The claws rasped together, squeaking like a rusty gate hinge. "ALL DAEMONS ARE THE SAME ON THE OTHER SIDE. WHEN YOU ARE NEAR THEM, I CAN FEEL IT. I CAN PUSH THROUGH."

"That's about what I'd figured." Loch nodded again. "So now you've got me. I've been stabbed, shot, banged up, knocked down . . . even you could probably take me right now, Jyelle."

The daemon growled wordlessly and took a step forward.

"But I'm asking you not to." Loch stepped forward to meet the daemon. "Or at least do it quick and quiet." She pointed at the floor. "Do you feel this car shaking? You've torn the hell out of it already, and there's another car unpowered because you broke loose. This train is barely holding together right now, and if you tear it up any more, innocent people are going to die." She stood in a calm defenseless posture and looked up at the daemon, her bare neck unprotected. "Kill me if you have to, and then go, before anyone else gets hurt."

The daemon stared down at her, its crystalline eyes motionless. Loch didn't break the stare.

The blow smashed into her uninjured side. Loch saw it coming enough to roll, but it still swept her down the hall and bounced her off the wall. If the daemon had had a better wind-up, it could have crushed her with that single blow . . . which was part of why Loch had stepped in close.

"INNOCENT PEOPLE?" The daemon smashed its claws into the wall, tearing stone and crystals free as it stomped toward Loch. "WHY SHOULD I CARE ABOUT THEM, *CAPTAIN*? WHEN I'M DONE WITH YOU, I'M GOING TO TEAR THIS TRAIN APART, AND THEN—"

"Ye be sadly mistaken," Gart Utt'Krenner said from behind the daemon, and slammed his truncheon into its back.

The blow hit with a strange sound, a rush of air that made Loch's ears pop, and the daemon stumbled, crystals and bits of metal falling free from its body as the air shimmered around it.

"Damn, it really is you in there, Jyelle." Loch used the wall to push herself back up. "Complete with your utter inability to tell when I'm trying to distract you."

"Begone, daemon." Gart swung his truncheon again. Loch saw that its tip glowed with pale flickering light, and the daemon stumbled back from the blow, roaring in pain as more of its shape sloughed off onto the carpet. "This be not yer home, and ye cannae threaten good folk while I stand before ye."

The daemon lashed out. It was lumbering and slow, but it was still very large, and Gart tried to block rather than rolling. The blow crushed him to the ground, even as more of the daemon fell apart around the glowing truncheon.

"I'LLLL KILLLL ALLLLLVIUUUU!" it roared, the words blossoming like heat bubbles from a toothless lake of fire, and raised a blobby hand over the fallen dwarf.

Loch jogged past the daemon. "You sound bad, Jyelle," she called over her shoulder. "Almost as bad as that time I kicked your ass on the airship. Remember that?" She grabbed the book and the sword where they lay on the floor, and turned to look back at the daemon. "Remember how I was unarmed and you had the element of surprise, and you still lost? That must have been really embarrassing."

The daemon roared, stepped over Gart Utt'Krenner, and came after her.

"You owe me, dwarf." Loch stepped back into the elf's room, tucking the book into her belt as she did. Half the wall had been torn away, and she pulled herself up on rocky footholds, grunting at the pain in her side as she hauled herself onto the roof.

The train was rattling and bucking, and it was a lot more obvious up here with the wind whipping in Loch's face. The car behind them was banging on the track now, and the tracks themselves glowed red instead of blue. Loch didn't have Hessler around to explain what that meant, but it was almost certainly bad.

The train was still moving, though, rattling toward a tunnel into a great mountain whose slopes glowed silver-blue in the distance. Loch looked at the tunnel, then at the train, and then at the hole in the side of the train where she'd just climbed up.

Then she ran back past the hole, even as a craggy molten hand snagged the roof, and took a running jump across the gap onto the next car back.

She reached the next car and kept going, hearing the roar of the daemon behind her and the dull crack of crumbling stone. She reached another gap, took another jump.

It was the depowered car, and it was shaking hard enough to mess up Loch's landing. She hit hard, skidded, nearly sliding off the angled rooftop. The stone roof was cold, and her fingers were going numb.

She tried to sit up, but it was getting hard to catch her breath, so instead she just rolled onto her side and watched as the daemon pulled itself up onto the roof, shredding more of the train car in the process.

"YOUUUUUU CANNNNN'T SCAAAAAAAAPE MEEEE!" it roared. It raised its arms. It had grown claws again. They were only stone, but they would likely get the job done.

Loch got to her knees and cough-swallowed the instinct to vomit as pain lanced her side. Her hand was tucked in over the wound on instinct. When she looked at it in the moonlight, it still came away bloody.

"I'm doing just fine escaping you so far, Jyelle!" she called back. The wind stole some of the words, and she was still having trouble catching her breath, but it felt right to say something.

The daemon growled and lumbered forward. It jumped, ungainly but fiercely strong, and its landing sent the car smashing against the rails, jolting like a bucking horse.

It was enough to make the daemon stumble, and Loch, still on her knees, chopped out hard at its knee, felt the unexpected jolt of metal on metal from where it had copied the blow from the *last* time she'd slashed at its leg, and watched as the daemon pitched over the side of the train.

Its great stone claws dug furrows into the rooftop as it stopped itself from falling.

Loch hacked at the hand and saw a few splinters of rock fly free. Before she could swing again, though, the daemon was pulling itself back up, and Loch scrambled back as claws slashed at her face.

"YOUUU CANNN'T ESCAAAPE MEEE," the daemon said, coming back to its feet. With the same self-consciousness Jyelle herself had shown, it flung its shoulders back and flexed its claws. "YOUU CANN'T BEEAT MEE."

"I wasn't trying to." Loch was half-seated, half lying on her back. She kept scooting backward as the daemon stepped forward. The dizziness was significantly worse now.

But she smiled at the daemon, damned the pain from her eyes and let the little bit of Jyelle inside the monster see her confidence.

It paused, just for a moment.

But that was as long as Loch had needed.

"I was trying to *stall* you," Loch said as the train reached the tunnel.

She rolled to her side and shut her eyes as the daemon slammed into the tunnel wall, and she felt a wave of heat as fire washed over her, along with a spray of stone and gravel. Even with her eyes closed, she could sense the close darkness of the tunnel, and the dizzying echo of the hum of the crystals bouncing off the walls and the ceiling just over her head.

She opened her eyes when things stopped falling on her, and for a moment just lay there in darkness lit only by the railway below her, the red light shading the stone walls.

Dimly, she saw that the daemon's feet and ankles still lay on the rooftop. The rest of it was either smashed apart or lying on the tracks back at the tunnel's entrance. Either way worked for Loch.

She didn't move—the ceiling was whizzing by closely enough for her to feel it passing like a near-miss from a crossbow, and she wasn't sure how much she *could* move at this point. Eventually, the train came out of the tunnel and back into the moonlit night.

And then from behind her, she heard Princess Veiled Lightning's voice cut through the wind. "You're a difficult woman to find, Isafesira de Lochenville."

Gart Utt'Krenner heard the Urujar woman bait the daemon out of the hallway into the elf's car. A moment later, he heard the daemon tearing stone and crystal apart as it clambered out onto the roof.

Gart pushed himself up to his knees, shaking his head. The daemon had been stronger than he had expected. It was sloppy on his part. He had never faced a daemon in combat. Had it been a troll, he would have been far more comfortable.

"Book," someone mumbled, and Gart looked up to see the elf, Irrethelathlialann, getting to his knees as well, groping on the ground blindly. "Where's the book?"

"Ye and the Urujar woman have caused a great deal of damage," Gart said severely, grabbing his truncheon and getting back to his feet. "I intend to see that charges be brought against ye for both theft and damage to th'railway."

"That's wonderful." The elf showed no sign of the strange speech pattern he had demonstrated back in the museum. "We didn't summon the daemon, though."

On the roof overhead, the stomping of footsteps marked the daemon heading back down toward the damaged and depowered car behind it.

"Does Loch have the book?" the elf asked.

"I not be knowing," Gart said.

The elf looked around. "She probably has the book." He sighed, then picked up his rapier, wincing a little as he moved.

Gart considered arresting the elf. Then he considered the daemon.

Holding his truncheon ready, he gestured to the elf's car. "Let us be going, then, Mister Irrethelathlialann."

The elf shot him an amused look. "Possessed of an indomitable need to fight daemons, are you?"

Gart didn't smile. "Ye both be under arrest, so I'm not letting ye out of my sight. And that daemon be needin' banishin'."

He stalked into the elf's room, which was little more than a platform with more than half the roof ripped away by this point. He gripped the crumbling rock to climb out and up onto the roof, then flinched back as the walls of the Stonebridge Tunnel whooshed past him. Out on the train, Gart believed he heard the crack of stone shattering, but he couldn't be certain where.

The elf chuckled. "Little close, there."

Gart waited in silence until they left the tunnel. Then he started climbing once more.

And once more he froze, this time when he heard the Imperial woman speak.

They were at the end of the car he was climbing out of, and as he watched, they leaped nimbly across the gap onto the car with the bar. There were three of them, just like at the museum—the figure in the green ringmail, the bodyguard with the ax, and the unarmed woman who had blasted Gart across the room.

"We have crossed the Republic to find you," the Imperial woman said.

"I've got the book." Loch, who was lying on the depowered car, held up the elven manuscript in the hand not holding the Imperial sword. She had not yet risen to her feet, and while the moonlit night made it difficult to tell, Gart believed that she was bleeding heavily.

"The book is nothing," the bodyguard said. "We came for you, Urujar scum."

"The book can stop this war!" Loch called back.

The bodyguard laughed. "Then we will pry it from your—"

"Wait." The Imperial woman raised a hand. "You will hand the book over voluntarily?"

"Will you turn yourselves in for the murder of the justicar, the clerk, and the sailors in Ros-Oanki?" Loch asked. "He died right after pointing my team at Ajeveth."

"Irrelevant," the bodyguard said.

"What?" The Imperial woman said at the same time. "We killed no one. Thunder—"

"All that matters right now is taking her down, Veil," the bodyguard cut in.

"What matters is the book," she replied with anger in her voice.

"I don't know why it's so damn important," Loch said, and her voice was shaky. "Everyone seems to want it—you, the elves, the golems of the ancients up on Heaven's Spire—"

"*Kutesosh gajair'is!*" the bodyguard's ax called out, and the bodyguard lunged forward, vaulting across the gap and coming down ax-first.

Loch had not been as helpless as she had seemed. She rolled to the side, and the ax clove through the stone roof as though it were cheap pine.

Gart had decided to move, but to his surprise, Irrethelathlialann was even faster. The elf darted past Gart onto the rooftop, his wood-bladed rapier out and ready. "Stop them!"

The Imperial woman and the figure in the ringmail turned at his hissed order, and the figure in the ringmail raised a spear that crackled with energy, but Irrethelathlialann never stopped moving. He stabbed at the armored figure, forcing a parry, then leaped up, kicking off the raised spear and flipping over the figure to come down yards away on the other side.

Gart lumbered forward as well. "All of ye, weapons down!" he yelled. Even the most unruly of dwarves would have at least acknowledged the order, if not followed it. He did not wish to sound racist, but non-dwarves were often very uncivilized.

The Imperial woman turned, surprised, and her hands crackled with lightning as she turned to him.

"Nae this time," Gart said, twisting a lever on his truncheon. As the woman moved his way, water sprayed out from the base of the truncheon, a short blast that soaked the Imperial woman.

She stumbled back, cursing in pain as lightning crackled back across her body, then fell from the roof out into the night. Gart ignored her and kept moving. The figure in the ringmail was chasing Irrethelathlialann, who was somehow managing to fence with the armored figure while *still* running back toward the depowered car where Loch and the bodyguard fought.

That fight was going to be short, though. Loch swung her blade, and the ax swept up to knock it aside with contemptuous ease. Loch herself was barely on her feet, the arm holding the book tucked in at her side to press against her wound.

The depowered car banged freely on the rails now. It had taken too much damage, and each jolt rattled through the entire train. The car half torn apart by the daemon wasn't much better.

The elf took a shuffle-step to ready himself for the jump across the gap to Loch's car, then sidestepped, blindly dodging the spear that would have punched through his back. "Stop," the ringmailed figure said in a woman's voice, and the elf stumbled back, blinking.

"Ye help Loch," Gart muttered, slamming into the ringmailed woman from behind and sending her stumbling. "I'll deal wi' this."

Irrethelathlialann clutched both hands to his blade, and seemed to come back to himself. "Momentary distraction is sufficient," he said, apparently to himself, and leaped across the gap between the cars.

Gart had no time to see how the elf fared. He flicked a switch on his truncheon, and waded in against the armored woman. "Yer magic be no good to ye here," he growled, and swung. The head of his weapon glowed, and it struck sparks from the woman's spear when she blocked it. She was stronger than she looked, though, and her counterattack had him parrying and giving ground.

"Fine weapon," he muttered, trying to place it. He had seen it in the museums, or one like it. Magical spears carried by the golems that served the ancients. "Did ye steal that, too?"

She didn't answer, but thrust at him again, and he blocked it, stepped in, and struck a blow that sent her reeling. "Weapon or no, ye still be no match for dwarven strength!" His next blow caught her on the side, and his next one after that brought her to her knees.

Gart raised his truncheon, and the woman looked up at him, and somehow, even through the helmet, he could feel the weight of her gaze.

"*No weapon*," she said, and the words reached into Gart's head and twisted something loose, and his truncheon slipped from his grasp and clattered to the roof. Magic, he realized, even as he lunged forward, slammed a knee into the woman's helmet, and then followed with a punch.

She fell back, and he moved in, trying to keep blows raining on that helmet, and the face beneath it.

"*Be still*," she said, and Gart froze as the words twisted around his spirit.

It was as though his muscles were locked in place, and he yanked on his own bones, trying to move.

"*Yer dwarven strength be no good*," she said, and he slithered to the ground bonelessly as his muscles went limp.

She got back to her feet, adjusted her helmet, and raised her spear.

Gart stared up at her. He couldn't speak.

"You're fortunate I don't have time to make this interesting," the woman said.

As her spear stabbed down, Gart's last thought was for his wife and children.

Loch watched Gentle Thunder raise Arikayurichi, his magical ax, yet again, knowing that there wasn't much she could do to stop it this time.

She was on her feet, and that was something, but it wasn't enough, not against an ax enchanted by the ancients or, like Desidora's Ghylspwr, actually containing the *soul* of an ancient.

"Could you at least tell me what these rings are for?" she asked, spinning the blade of her stolen sword.

Gentle Thunder didn't take the bait, and as he swung, Loch dove to the side. The rattling car jolted as she moved, and she fell instead of landing on her feet, but Gentle Thunder's blow went wide as well, crashing through the roof again.

This time, the whole roof collapsed, and when Loch tried to stand, she slid instead, and then held her side tight and tried to roll with it . . . and it still ended up hurting like hell anyway.

She lay in the rubble, coughing. Dust from the shattered stone choking her lungs and gumming up her eyes.

When she forced them open, Gentle Thunder stood over her, Arikayurichi coming up again.

As she met his stare, a ruby-red wooden blade glanced off his dragon-faced helmet, causing the warrior to stumble to the side, crashing into an already-collapsing wall.

"Intelligent artifact significantly too powerful to overcome," Irrethelathlialann said as he landed beside Loch, "hence targeting wielder as point of vulnerability." He rubbed his hands together and shook his head. "Don't mind me. Just here for my book."

"*Your* book?" She blocked his grab and slammed the pommel of her blade into his wrist.

He snatched his hand back and glared at her. "Yes, it's hardly called the *Urujar* manuscript, now, is it?"

"*Kutesosh gajair'is!*" Gentle Thunder's ax yelled as he roared back toward them.

"Probably too much to hope he was out," she muttered. "Come on."

Loch swung high, the elf went low, and both of them moved out of the way of Gentle Thunder, sidestepping his charge.

Arikayurichi caught Loch's blow, while the elf's blow glanced off armor. Irrethelathlialann spun away from a counterattack, nearly running into Loch as he slipped in the rubble.

Yet he grinned as he danced away, and Loch saw that he was holding the damn book again.

Gentle Thunder turned back toward Loch. "You cannot stand against me. I wield the Bringer of Order, the weapon whose strength has defended the Empire for dynasties."

The other wall of the car crumbled and fell away as he spoke, leaving them standing in the ruins of the economy car with a clear night sky overhead. With a few swings of his ax, Gentle Thunder had destroyed the entire structure.

Loch thought about that for a moment. Then she glanced over at Irrethelathlialann.

"Oh, my, yes," the elf murmured. Then he glanced down at the book, looking puzzled for some reason, and then back at Loch.

She ignored him, keeping her eyes on the Imperial bodyguard. "You keep saying I can't stand against you,

Gentle Thunder," Loch said, "but I've gone up against you a few times now, and each time, I've accomplished what I intended to do, and you have not." Deliberately, she pulled her hand away from her wounded side and held her sword in a two-handed grip. "Now, are you going to test Arikayurichi against the blade I took off your little princess or not?"

Gentle Thunder came at her fast, and she spun her blade. The red silk scarf flared out at eye level, and Gentle Thunder chopped down.

There was no way Loch could have blocked that blow, even with a two-handed grip.

Fortunately for her, she had stepped past Gentle Thunder as he swung, hiding the move behind a flair of red silk.

She dove for the front of the car as Gentle Thunder's blow crashed into the floor, and then through it. She heard the crack of stone, the shriek of metal, and the keen of crystal all breaking beneath the blow, and then the impact flung her to the stone floor. She scrambled forward, the elf landing beside her. Stone crumbled behind her, glowlamps popping like glass bubbles and magical energy flaring wildly, and both of them lunged to the little platform separating what had once been her car from the car in front of it.

Behind them, the remains of the economy car came apart in a jagged spray of stone and metal and crystal, and Gentle Thunder fell away into the night as the back half of the train shrieked slowly to a halt on the railway.

Loch lay there for a moment, just clinging to the platform. Apparently that was all her body was going to let her do, because she tried to move and found that whatever surge of strength had gotten her back on her feet was gone. She bounced freely on the platform with each jostling movement of the little bit of the car that was still connected.

"You are *insane*," Irrethelathlialann gasped, crawling past her to the back of the next car. "And clearly done for the evening. Well, then. Pleasant to see you again." He got back to his feet, climbed nimbly back onto the roof, and was lost from view.

Loch rolled over.

The book she'd lifted from Irrethelathlialann—for what seemed the twentieth time—during their mad scramble lay on the floor beneath her.

She lay there, unmoving, ignoring the cold and the pain for the simple pleasure of not moving.

A few moments later, a grappling line clanked off the platform, then caught on a handgrip. Loch hadn't realized that her eyes had been shut. She opened them and saw her airship hovering beside the car. Distant figures waved to her in the night.

She hooked herself in, grabbed the book, belted her sword, and signaled.

As they lifted her from the platform, she saw Irrethelathlialann fighting the Imperial Hunter atop the car. The elf wasn't dead yet, but he was parrying desperately, his blade no match for the glowing spear.

Loch fumbled at her waist and drew out the nice dagger she'd gotten from the elf's room earlier. She squinted, adjusting her aim as she swayed, and then threw.

She was good, but not *that* good, which was a shame, because throwing a knife accurately while dangling from a line with some blood loss thrown in for good measure would have been good for bragging rights. The knife spun through the air, sailed past the Hunter, and clattered on the rooftop near Irrethelathlialann's feet.

The Hunter looked back over her shoulder, as was only natural given that a knife had just sailed past her, and *that* at least gave the elf the moment he needed. He rolled away, coming up with the knife in his free hand, and then spun past the Hunter, tossing Loch a lazy salute as he sprinted away.

"It was pretty close," Loch mumbled, and then the grappling line turned, and she lost sight of the elf fleeing into the night.

She focused on just holding on as the grappling line winched her up, staring at the passing countryside. Behind her on the track, the back half of the train had finally come to a halt, train cars all askew along the tracks like a child's scattered blocks.

Sometime later—time blurred along with her vision—they hauled her up to the ship. The glowlamps hurt her eyes after so long in the dark, but they were welcome nevertheless.

Tern lay on the deck, unmoving, her shoulder wrapped in a red-soaked bandage. Hessler, his head bandaged as well, sat beside her, barely looking in Loch's direction. Icy and Kail's hands were warm and gentle as they lowered her to the deck.

"Captain?" Kail's voice was strained. "Captain, you don't look so good."

"S'okay," Loch said, and her voice sounded distant even to her. "I got the book." She held it up, and Kail took it away and tossed it aside.

"Wait," said Hessler, squinting over at her. "Oh, dear."

Loch stared at him.

"Before I was knocked out," Hessler said, "I cast a transmutation spell. I thought it would help me get the book off the train more easily."

She blinked.

Hessler gestured at the book, and with a crackle of magic, it shimmered and shifted.

A moment later, a very nice elven dagger lay on the deck instead.

"I don't suppose," Hessler said, "that you picked up something that looks like this? Because that's how I disguised the book, and you can see how . . ."

Loch let him keep talking as she passed out.

Thirteen

THE SUN ROSE AT THE BORDER BETWEEN THE REPUBLIC AND THE Empire, and the dead rose with it.

Uribin was a tall, broad-shouldered Urujar man who'd been eating way too much of his restaurant's fine cooking in the years since the last war. He had served as a scout under Captain Loch, who would've been a colonel if she hadn't been Urujar, and when they'd made it back into Republic territory, he had happily washed his hands of the military and retired to a life with a good woman and good food. A few weeks back, his biggest concern had been whether an influx of water sprites would affect the local fishing and force him to raise the price on his prized catfish entrees.

When the Republic soldiers had asked him to join, he'd slapped his gut and laughed.

They hadn't laughed back.

They had told him three things, and after the third thing, he had signed back on.

Now Uribin hunched in thick bushes with a squad of boys and girls barely old enough to shave and watched water drip off the zombies pulling themselves from the Iceford.

"They have death priests," a girl in his squad said, her voice cracking on the end.

"It's not a death priest." Uribin kept watching. Some of the dead were bare skeletons. Others were mostly whole. They all shambled out of the water with blades in their hands. "Look at the bodies."

"The old man's right," said another of the kids. "Death priests usually raise a few very powerful undead, or enhance themselves. There are wizard's spells that can animate a zombie, though."

Slipping and stumbling, the dead clawed up the bank of the river. They were coming toward the border. Since Uribin and the kids were on the Imperial side of that border, that meant that the zombies would be coming right past them. They were well out of hearing range for the time being, but the newly risen were getting closer.

"Damn it, they didn't pay me enough for this," another boy muttered. He was technically the commanding officer of the squad.

The first thing the Republic soldiers had told Uribin was how much he'd be paid for his services as an expert consultant in scouting behind Imperial lines. It was an absurd amount, more than his restaurant would make in a year, and when he heard that they were serious, that they wanted him back that badly, he had stopped laughing and told them to leave.

He shook his head now. "Look at the bodies, sir," Uribin said again. "Some of them whole, some old and worn to nothing. What's that tell you?"

Uribin's commanding officer looked at him blankly, but the one whose voice had cracked a moment ago piped up. "Any river has fish," she said. "If those bodies were down there for a long time, they'd have been picked to the bone."

"So what?" Uribin's commanding officer said, glaring at both of them. "If I was a fish, I wouldn't eat any damn zombie, either." He was half-Urujar, his nose narrow and planed from the Old Kingdom blood, his skin dark but also freckled, making him look like one of the baked potatoes Uribin wished he were preparing right now. He was shaking with fear as he spoke. "Now, listen, if we fall back, we can be in the woods before they get close. Their path—"

"Their path takes them into the Republic," Uribin said. "and if some of them are whole, that means they weren't in that river the whole time. They marched or crawled or swam down that river. Now, the Iceford comes out of the mountains that mark the border and goes clean into the Republic. The zombies are out now, because we're near white water, which would bang them up, but as soon as it gets calm again, they can wade back in."

"They're going to come in by the river and hit the Republic by surprise," said the girl who'd figured out the bit with the fish. Her voice no longer cracked. She had some Imperial in her, by the tilt of her eyes, and some Urujar as well, and a bit of everything, really. She reminded him a little of Captain Loch, the woman who'd gotten Uribin, Kail, and the rest through a mission that had left them deep inside the Empire with no one but themselves to depend on. A *young* Captain Loch, anyway.

That was the second thing the Republic soldiers had told him—the average age of a soldier in the Republic these days, and the percentage who'd served in the war, much less seen any time behind enemy lines. They'd told him that instead of leaving, and Uribin had poured them a drink and pretended that it was a long day mashing the potatoes that was making his hands shake.

Now, Uribin said, "Captain, they give you one of those new message crystals?"

The boy looked at Uribin, swallowed, and glared. "We can try the message crystal once we're safe, Consultant. We won't be any help to the Republic if we get ourselves killed."

One of the others gestured frantically, and they lowered their voices. The dead were closer now, their steps uneven and halting, some of them dragging blades behind them instead of holding them up. They formed a single, mindless crowd. There were more of them still coming out of the river, like an eel that kept getting longer as you pulled it from its hole.

"We fall back, we're falling back into Imperial territory," Uribin said quietly. "That crystal got enough range to send a message from in there?"

"We can find out *later*," the boy said, fixing Uribin with a steady authoritative look he had learned in some school somewhere. "For now, my orders are—"

Uribin's fist cracked across the boy's jaw. He lowered the boy gently to the ground, then fished the message crystal from the boy's pocket. It blinked red.

"Too far," he muttered, and looked at the others. They stared at him wide-eyed. "We can't send a message to warn anybody from here."

In the distance, but not enough of a distance, he heard footsteps crashing now. He held up a hand across his mouth, then switched to the hand-signs the scouts used. *Need to get message out. No message, our people die.*

Get up onto hill, the girl signed back. *Need clear target line to signal.*

You confirm? Uribin signed. Scouts hadn't had message crystals when he'd been in service, and he wished he'd had more time to learn how they worked.

I confirm. Her fingers were trembling, but her stare was sharp. *We get up on hill, we send signal.*

Uribin looked up at the hillside ahead of them. The dead were following its slope, making their way steadily toward the Republic border. There were bushes and trees, and an expert scout might possibly be able to make it past dead eyes and rotting ears to the hilltop without being seen.

Uribin hadn't been an expert scout for several years and several pounds, and nobody on this squad of raw recruits had the skill. Byn-Kodar's hell, they were children.

And that had been the third thing the Republic soldiers had told Uribin. They'd pointed at the two little bracelets Uribin wore and said the names of Uribin's two little girls. They'd asked if Uribin wanted to stop a war from spilling over the Republic again.

Uribin had cursed them long and loud, and then he had taken the offer.

Now, Uribin handed the message crystal to the girl. *You are the package,* he signed, and then, to the rest of the squad. *She is the package. She gets up hill. We make noise and distract. Then retreat to where we camped last night.*

And then, because they were standing there looking at him wide-eyed, Uribin swallowed, said the names of his wife and his little girls like a prayer, and drew his sword.

Then he burst from the bushes with a shout and plunged into the line of the dead.

Captain Pyvic sat in the kahva-house with Ululenia, Desidora, and Ghylspwr. After rescuing Desidora and losing the fairy book that might have explained what everyone wanted with the damned elven manuscript, none of them had gotten a lot of good sleep the night before.

"All right," he said, cradling a warm cup between his hands, "what do we know?"

"We know that someone unknown to us has access to the magic of the ancients," Desidora said, cradling her hammer, "and they don't want the knowledge contained in *Ruminations upon the Unutterable* to surface."

Which also touches upon the ancients in some manner whose light has not yet opened the petals of our minds. Ululenia normally stuck with spring water, but this morning, she had put a teabag in it. Her dress was still lightly scorched in places from their battle with the golems.

Pyvic grimaced. "What I know about the ancients couldn't fill this cup." He glanced at Desidora. "Does your hammer know anything that could help us?"

"*Kun-kabynalti osu fuir'is,*" Ghylspwr rumbled.

"I'm sorry." Desidora looked down at her hammer, then back at Pyvic with a smile that didn't reach her eyes. "I don't think Ghylspwr's knowledge extends to magical safeguards left behind after the ancients departed."

Pyvic let the thought bounce around in his mind a little. "Why would the ancients care about what happened to the world once they were gone?"

"*Besyn larveth'is,*" Ghylspwr said, sounding a little hurt.

"Of course you do," Desidora murmured, then said to the rest of the group, "They fled the world to stop the Glimmering Folk from gaining a foothold. Perhaps there is still some danger that the Glimmering Folk could return."

Were that true, Ululenia said, *you would be a lynx and not a butterfly.*

That made even less sense to Pyvic than what Ululenia normally said, but Desidora ducked her head, and quietly said, "Point taken."

"So the Glimmering Folk are no longer a threat," Pyvic said. That meant something, clearly. But what?

The door to the kahva-house banged open, and Justicar Derenky stepped in. His freckled face was flushed, and his blond hair was disheveled, as though he'd been running. He saw Pyvic and smiled, still breathing hard. "Captain."

"Derenky." Whatever Pyvic had been thinking about vanished. "Something couldn't wait until I came in?"

"We weren't certain when you'd come in, sir, given how much time you've been spending outside the office lately." Derenky smiled at Ululenia and Desidora.

Pyvic smiled, clenching his teeth ever so slightly. "They're helping with a case, Derenky."

"Right, sir." Derenky held up a file. "And to that end, we got back the information request you made on this Irreth . . . ethel . . ."

"The elf." Pyvic took the file.

"I took the liberty of looking through it," Derenky said as Pyvic flipped it open. "He is one of the few that regularly leaves the Elflands, which is why we have anything at all. He seems to be an agent of an important figure known only as the Dragon."

Ululenia spit out her tea.

"Something you want to tell us?" Desidora asked.

"He *rules* the Elflands," Ululenia said. "He is *very* powerful, and *very* dangerous, and . . ." She massaged her head. "And we are nipping at his heels."

"He's not an *actual* dragon, though, is he?" Pyvic asked.

"Most of the time, the elf purchases old art on behalf of this Dragon," Derenky added, "though he's proven deadly when crossed with would-be thieves." He smiled thinly.

"I'll read the file," Pyvic said. "Thank you. Any reason this couldn't wait until I was in?"

"The elf was last seen on the train involved in last night's incident." Derenky coughed, looking at Ululenia and Desidora a bit nervously. "Given the possible concerns with our own problems in that area, it seemed best to get you this information as quickly as possible. The last thing we need is trouble with the dwarves while the Empire is still marching."

Pyvic fixed Derenky with a steady look that lasted until the man flinched. "What train?" he asked. "And what do you mean 'marching'?"

The door banged open again, and Jyrre rushed inside. "Captain, sorry, but this couldn't wait—" She broke off as she saw Derenky. "I told you I had it."

"We received more information that seemed pertinent," Derenky said, "and I reached the captain first, despite leaving some time after you did. Perhaps you need some time on the obstacle training course."

"Sorry, Captain," Jyrre said again, running a shaking hand through her braided hair. "Thought you'd be at home. Two items."

"There's a train, presumably," Pyvic said, looking from Jyrre to Derenky in irritation. "Will one of you be telling me the rest any time soon?"

"A train crashed on the dwarven railway," Jyrre said. "It was carrying the elven diplomat you asked for more information on. Witness reports are few as of yet, but at least one places Loch at the scene."

"All right." Pyvic drank the rest of his kahva in one big gulp.

"All right?" Derenky coughed. "I'm not sure you understand how bad it is to have a justicar, particularly one who has recently been accused of a crime, be tied to a train wreck, sir."

"I've got an inkling," Pyvic said.

"Sir, if she *is* involved, we'll need to act directly in order to avoid the appearance of a conflict of interest, given your relationship with arrogant apple, babbling brook, creeping cat," Derenky said, and blinked as he trailed off into merciful silence.

"Thank you," Pyvic said to a space in the air midway between Derenky and Ululenia. "Jyrre, you said there were two items."

She nodded, her mouth drawing tight. "The Empire is marching troops toward the border. One of our scouting units got a warning out before they went dark."

Pyvic shut his eyes. They had been so close. Loch might already have the book, for all they knew.

"How long do we have?" Desidora asked.

"Not long." Jyrre grimaced. "They hid in the river until they were close to the border, or we'd have gotten more warning."

"*In* the river?" Desidora asked.

Jyrre nodded grimly. "The Imperials raised an army of the dead."

Attendant Shenziencis made her way through the wrecked train cars as the sun rose.

The dwarves were efficient. Already, she could feel their repair train racing down the railway, a little hum of magic vibrating inside those hateful silver tracks. She stepped carefully, avoiding the tracks and any stray bits of silver that had been snapped free when the train jumped the tracks and twisted itself to a stop. In her armor, stolen long ago from one of the ancients' hunter golems, she was largely safe, but she had not lived as long as she had by trusting such protections casually.

The dwarves would be here in an hour, perhaps less. Shenziencis had fed well, and gained several victims who had gifted her with their words, but she still had a little time.

Up ahead, a dwarf lay pinned under a pile of rubble that had once been part of a wall. His skin was gray, and the armor that marked him as one of their guards was torn, much like her own.

The dagger that Isafesira de Lochenville had thrown had come close enough for her to feel the magic locking the dagger in its form, and the manuscript beneath that form pushing to get out. Shenziencis had seen the surprised joy on the elf's face as his hand closed around the weapon. She wondered if he had seen her own shock.

She had been *so* close.

The dwarf had been asleep or unconscious, but roused as she approached. "I would appreciate assistance," he said, his voice weak but still steady.

"What do you wish me to do?" Shenziencis asked.

The dwarf looked surprised to see her ask. He struggled a bit under the rocks. "My legs are pinned."

Shenziencis shook her head. "I did not ask for an explanation. What do you wish me to do?"

"Help me," the dwarf snapped, and then added, "please."

"Help you how?"

"You could . . ." The dwarf paused, thought. Shenziencis leaned a little closer, nodding without words. "Dig up the rubble, I think. Then you could pull me out."

"I'm sorry," Shenziencis said, shaking her head, "but that isn't enough. I think you will stay."

"Stay? What do you want? What do—" He broke off as her spear came to rest against his throat. "Wait. Stop! Don't kill me!"

That was better. "If I free you, will you go, and never come back?" She prodded his throat as he nodded. "I need to hear it."

He swallowed, tears forming in his eyes. "I swear, if you free me, I will go, and never come back."

"Good." Shenziencis smiled and stepped away. Then she let the magic well up in her, glowing beneath her armor. *"Dig free."*

The words took hold in him, and his arms moved with frenzied strength, shoving the rocks aside. Shenziencis heard the bones in his hands pop and crack, heard tendons tear with the effort, but he kept moving.

In but a few moments, enough of the rubble was clear for her to give the next command. *"Come out."*

Skin tore from his legs as he wrenched himself free from the rubble. Tears streamed freely down his cheeks. "What are—"

"Stop." He froze. *"Come up."*

He jerked himself upright on broken, bleeding legs.

She slit his throat quickly and mercifully with a single slash of her spear, then used the spearpoint to hold him upright until the life left his eyes.

Then, when it was over, she let the magic flow through her again.

"Come back."

The eyes jerked open. Shenziencis pulled her spear away, and the dwarf stood, swaying slightly.

She pointed to where the others stood behind her. *"Go,"* she said, *"and then wait."*

He shuffled off to them. He would be tractable now, stupid but obedient. Alive, he might have tried to obey the letter of her command while twisting the spirit. The smart ones did.

That was why Shenziencis usually killed the smart ones just as soon as they'd given her enough words to be useful. Words like "kill" and "wait" and "come."

She breathed in deeply, taking in the fresh morning air, and that was when she realized she could still hear breathing.

It was a human woman, lying beside the rubble a little ways away. Her yellow hair was crusted with blood and plastered to the side of her face, and her commoner's dress was muddy and torn.

She stared at Shenziencis with wide eyes.

"Are you hurt?" Shenziencis asked, walking toward the woman. "Is there something I can do for you?"

The woman did not answer. She got to her feet instead. One of her legs was broken, and she whimpered, but didn't cry out.

She was trying not to talk.

"Tell me a story," Shenziencis said, "and I will let you live."

The woman took a few limping steps back, leaning on the rubble heavily. The look she gave Shenziencis was filled with terror, but there was anger as well. The woman's jaws were locked together, the muscles below her ears standing out taut. Shenziencis sighed. "I need the words," she said. "Without the words, there is only one thing you can do for me. Is that what you want?"

Questions. Even the ones who had some idea about how the magic worked could be caught up by the questions.

Not this one, though. Her breath harsh, she turned and took a few stumbling steps away before her leg gave out, and she fell with a wordless cry.

She cried out again when Shenziencis grabbed hold of her shoulder and pulled her up.

"Enough," Shenziencis said. "Be silent, then, if you wish."

Then she unhinged her jaw and brought the poor dear inside. The woman kicked. Shenziencis did not mind. The prey was right to fight, just as Shenziencis was right to eat. It was nature.

It was also futile. The head slid slowly down her throat, the arms twitching and grabbing at nothing, the legs thrashing. When the head reached the point in the throat where Shenziencis kept her power, the body went still. Shenziencis flexed the muscles of the throat, pulling the rest of the body slowly in, savoring the sweet taste of life still fresh on the skin.

It took a few minutes, and the sensation as new life blossomed inside her core occupied Shenziencis completely. Lost in the pleasant glow, she came back to her senses to find Princess Veiled Lightning's bodyguard standing over her, Arikayurichi in hand.

Gentle Thunder's armor was scuffed and dented. The last she had seen of him—before the train section she had been on had pulled ahead—he had been caught in the train wreck. Even an ax forged by the ancients could only protect its wielder so much. His face was hidden behind his golden dragon helmet, but Arikayurichi was lifted high enough for her to guess at his mood.

"You are a monster," he said. "When I find the princess, I will tell her as much."

Shenziencis smiled. "You did not object when I killed the Republic justicar earlier. In fact, you hid the information from your princess."

"That was for our mission," he said. "We needed to hide the body. He was an enemy, and Veil would . . . not have understood. But these?" He flung his free arm out at the rubble. "These were *innocents!* Their deaths should come only if demanded as a sad necessity of our quest, not simply to slake your thirst for blood!"

"I ended the lives of a few," she said with a sniff. "What of you, Gentle Thunder? How many died when you destroyed the dwarven contraption?"

"Too many." He looked now not at her, but at Arikayurichi, still held high in his hands. "Their deaths were unnecessary."

"Besyn larveth'is," said the ax, its enchanted voice calm and reassuring.

"No. We have not protected the innocent." Gentle Thunder reached up with his free hand and lifted the dragon-faced visor of his helmet. "We have killed too many, and for what? A book?"

"It is not a simply a book," Shenziencis said. "It holds a message regarding the ancients. A very important one."

"Kutesosh gajair'is," the ax said, more firmly this time.

"Yes." Gentle Thunder glared at her and brought his free hand to Arikayurichi, moving to a two-handed grip.

Shenziencis made no move to defend herself.

"I wish only to survive," she said. "I believe I may be of use to you in locating the manuscript."

"I think not." Gentle Thunder raised his weapon, stepped forward, and brought it down with a fierce shout.

Shenziencis blinked, then opened her eyes to see the golden blade of Arikayurichi a handbreadth from her face. She looked past it to Gentle Thunder, whose fierce glare was slowly falling away.

"My apologies," Shenziencis said, "but it was not you to whom I offered my services."

Gentle Thunder grimaced, his armor squeaking with strain as he tried with all his mortal might to force Arikayurichi to strike her. Then he stumbled backward, breathing hard.

"Why?" He was looking at his weapon, not her. "You are the Bringer of Order! You have honored the Empire for centuries with your service! Why, damn you?"

"Kun-kabynalti osu fuir'is," Arikayurichi said, and it seemed honestly sad as it did.

Then the ax-head snapped back in through the slot left by the raised visor.

The head wrenched back out as Gentle Thunder dropped to his knees, and then chopped back in again. Gentle Thunder's arms trembled, and Arikayurichi wrenched free again, and then chopped in one final time with a noise that was much softer and wetter than the first two strikes had been.

When it pulled free a moment later, the movements were clean and practiced. One hand held the ax-head out and wiped its head clean on the grass.

The other snapped the dragon-faced visor shut.

Gentle Thunder, or at least his body, got back to its feet.

"I will endeavor to prove myself worthy of your trust," Shenziencis said, bowing low. "Now, do you wish me to inform the princess that you will be remaining silent?"

"Why would he do that?"

Shenziencis turned to see Princess Veiled Lightning limping toward them from the direction Gentle Thunder had come. She had fallen from the train well before Gentle Thunder had caused the crash, a victim of the dwarf's cunning trick, and Shenziencis was pleased to see that she had survived.

"Veil." Gentle Thunder's body turned, and Shenziencis raised an eyebrow infinitesimally in a bit of professional surprise. It was not Gentle Thunder's voice, but if not for the magic in her core that made every living being's voice an aura for her to read and manipulate, she would never have been able to tell. The intonation was utterly perfect, down to the little hesitations of a man who had cared for a woman since childhood. "I thought you . . . I am pleased to see you were not harmed."

As he spoke, Shenziencis tapped into the magic at her core, and sent her minions away. It took more strength to command them in silence, and it only worked if she had gotten their words before they died in the first place, but it was necessary. Princess Veiled Lightning would not tolerate the presence of undead servants . . . at least, not those she *knew* were undead.

While the dead shuffled away safely in the distance, the princess grimaced and stood a little straighter, giving Gentle Thunder a tight smile. "You trained me for years, Thunder. If I could not roll my way clean in a fall like that, my father would have had you executed for educating me so poorly."

"Then I suppose it is fortunate for both of us." Arikayurichi even managed the tiny intake of breath that would signify an amused chuckle from a man who did not give himself to laughter. "As for my silence . . ." He looked over, his dragon-faced visor pointing at Shenziencis for a moment. "Attendant

Shenziencis is concerned that too many lives have been lost on this mission."

"The uncultured rulers of this Republic care so little for their own people," Shenziencis said in disgust. She gestured at the wreckage of the train. "Look at what Isafesira de Lochenville did to escape us. In our effort to avert death, we are most assuredly causing her to kill more innocent people. I said as much to Gentle Thunder, and he said that if I wished to share my opinion with you, he would not gainsay me."

"It is not my place." Gentle Thunder's body nodded, then turned back to Veiled Lightning. "What do you wish, Veil?"

Princess Veiled Lightning's lavender skirt was torn, and strands of hair hung free from her braids. She was clearly tired and hurting more than pride would let her show.

But Shenziencis had read her correctly. That pride would do more than keep her standing when it would be easier to sit.

"If we flinch from watching the Republic kill a few of its own now," she said, "we will have to watch them kill many more of their own, and ours, in the future. Isafesira de Lochenville is a murderer of her own people and a threat to ours." She took a breath, looking at each of them in turn. "I must continue. If you believe this quest dishonorable, I free you both to return to the Empire."

"This quest is dangerous, possibly even foolhardy . . . but it has never been dishonorable." Gentle Thunder's body bowed low before the princess. "I am with you to the end, Veil."

"As am I," Shenziencis added. "This Isafesira de Lochenville has disgraced the Temple of Butterflies—*my* temple—not once but twice." She smiled, and it was in no way a false smile. "I would share words with her."

Fourteen

LOCH WOKE UP HURTING, BUT NOT AS MUCH AS SHE'D EXPECTED.

"How long?" Her voice was scratchy. She reached out blindly, and hands pressed a cup into her hands.

"Few days," Kail said, and helped her drink. This wasn't the first time he'd nursed her back from a bad fight.

She coughed on the first swallow, then recovered enough to sip. "The manuscript?"

"Still with your friend Ethel," Kail said, "since apparently you threw it at him."

"I thought I was throwing a knife." She took another sip and got more this time.

"That's a relief. I thought you were trying to be sporting."

Loch opened her eyes. Daylight slid through the window of what was clearly a room at an inn. "Where are we?"

"Jershel's Nest." Kail took the cup back.

Loch knew of the city, vaguely, though she'd never been there. "Up near the Elflands?"

"Last city before them. The front half of the train stopped here after the crash."

"Irrethelathlialann here, too?" Loch sat up, wincing a little at the tightness.

"You'd be dead if not for Icy doing whatever weird Imperial energy not-quite-magic he does until Ululenia and Desidora got here," Kail said instead of answering her question. He stepped forward into her space, blocking any move to get up, which was what she'd been about to do.

"Glad they could join us, then." Loch looked at him. "Anything else I should know about?"

"Tern took a bolt in the chest. It was touch and go, but she's fine. Resting, like you should be."

"I will, just as soon as you tell me how long we've got before Irrethelathlialann gets transport out of town."

"Captain, *stop*."

"I'm fine, Kail." She glared up at him. "I've been knocked on my ass before."

"You nearly died," he said, and the way he said it, evenly and without changing expression, gave her pause. *"Tern nearly died."*

"How many people *did* die when the train crashed?" She really didn't want to know the answer to that question, but a good commander had to know.

"Captain, stop," he said again, but this time it was softer.

"That many." Loch lay back against a lumpy pillow. "Hell of a plan we came up with, huh?"

"It wasn't your fault," he said.

"Fault doesn't matter." Loch thought of Gentle Thunder swinging the ax, of diving out of the way and feeling so smart as he chopped through the train instead of her. "I let the fight happen. Against the Imperials, against Irrethelathlialann, even against Jyelle."

Kail blinked. "Jyelle?"

"Long story. Apparently I need to avoid unshielded dae-mons for awhile." Loch held out her hand. Kail passed her the cup, and she took another sip. The cup was rough on her fingers, chipped along the rim. "Are we doing the right thing?" she asked.

"You can't turn yourself in," he said, shrugging. "You'd be giving the Learned exactly what they want, and we both know it would only postpone the war, not stop it."

"But it might have given someone else time to prevent it." Kail laughed. "You think anyone else is even trying?" He took the cup away from her. "It's you or nothing, Captain. So don't die, all right?"

"I'll see what I can do," Loch said, and he looked at her, still angry, but then gave a grudging nod and a bit of a smile. "Now—really—bring me up to speed, and I'll lie here instead of getting up as long as you keep talking."

Voyant Beaulieu of the Learned Party stood by the mantle in his sitting room, clutching his brandy snifter tightly and try-ing not to sweat as Voyant Cevirt of the Skilled Party smiled. The Urujar man's smile was a white slash across his dark face, and Beaulieu had always found Urujar a little unnerv-ing to begin with, though even in the Learned Party, one didn't admit those sorts of things these days.

"If you wish to make an accusation," Beaulieu said stiffly, "I suggest you make it plainly."

"If I made an accusation," Voyant Cevirt said, "we would have to *investigate* that accusation publicly, with *jus-ticars*. Is that something you want? Do you want the Repub-lic mired in the mud with half the Voyancy disgraced while the Imperials send zombies across the border and kill our people?"

"These insinuations are deeply insulting, Cevirt," Beaulieu said, "and I will remember them the next time—"

"Shut. Up." Cevirt stepped in, and before Beaulieu could react, Cevirt's hand closed on his wrist. It slammed the brandy snifter against the mantle, locked behind his elbow, and brought the jagged edge of the broken snifter to Beaulieu's throat.

An intricate crystal mosaic covered the wall above Beaulieu's mosaic. Beautiful glowing gems showed Heaven's Spire in all its glory looking down over a green and healthy Republic. Beaulieu looked at it desperately, the glass sharp against his throat.

"*That* is how you kill someone, Beaulieu," Cevirt said. "Quietly, with minimal fuss, on your own or using people you hired with your own money. You don't send the gods-damned Knights of Gedesar, a *military* unit, after one of our own civilians, no matter how unhappy you are that she took down your patron, Archvoyant Silestin."

"What do you want?" Beaulieu asked without moving his neck at all. He had always loved the mosaic on the wall, and now he looked at it as though it had the power to keep him alive.

"I *want* to end the life of the man who sent hired killers after my god-daughter," Cevirt said, "and then say that he slipped and had a tragic accident, and there would be questions, and a shadow of scandal, and it might affect my political career, but believe me, Beaulieu, I *would* get away with it."

After a long pause, he shoved Beaulieu away.

"But the Voyancy needs you alive right now," Cevirt went on, "so what I will *accept* is you calling off the Knights of Gedesar."

Beaulieu rubbed his neck. He didn't look at his hand afterward to see if there was blood on it. He was shaking, but he refused to show that much weakness. "I do that, and you forget this?"

Cevirt smiled, and Beaulieu flinched. "You do that, Voyant, and you get to live. If I were you, I would call off your knights *very* quickly, and then I would get to work on cleaning up the evidence, because until you have done so, I have you on a string, and I will not hesitate to pull that string when I need you to dance. Are we clear?"

Beaulieu jerked out a nod, and Cevirt held his stare for another moment, then left without another word.

Then Beaulieu collapsed into an overstuffed chair, looking at his hands for blood.

Stupid, so stupid. He'd told himself that it was what Silestin would have wanted, that it was justified to use the Knights of Gedesar, given how dangerous that Loch woman was. He was a stupid old man, and now the Skilled Urujar voyant had something over him.

He pulled a message crystal from his pocket, his hands shaking. Best to do that first. Then make arrangements for Captain Nystin, the knight they'd spoken with. There were a few papers to be burned as well.

The crystal whined as he tried to activate it, and he shook it, glaring. He hated the new advances in magic. Some of the crystals gave him headaches, and others were entirely too complicated. "What's the matter with you, blasted thing?" he muttered.

It was glowing red, Beaulieu saw . . . and then he realized that it wasn't the message crystal. The chair had the same light. So did the carpet. He held up his hands and saw red on them.

The crystal mosaic on the wall was glowing crimson, and as Beaulieu stumbled to his feet, stones from the wall fell free and formed the shape of a man.

"What do you want?" Beaulieu stammered, stepping back even as the crystal-man pulled itself upright. Its hands were wrong, Beaulieu saw. They ended in hooked blades instead of fingers.

"Your voice," said the crystal-man, and lunged forward.

Unlike Voyant Cevirt, it didn't stop when it reached Beaulieu's throat.

Captain Nystin grimaced as he felt the hum at his hip. Still leaning against the airship railing, he glanced around, then slid a small *yvkefer* case from a hip pocket. He flipped it open, slid the message crystal out, held it to his ear, and thumbed it on.

"You have failed twice, and risk drawing attention to this arrangement," said a voice in his ear. The message crystal gave the voice a chiming undercurrent that always made Nystin's teeth ache. "You will complete your operation successfully regardless of the cost. All legal ramifications can be ignored. Remain silent from this point forward. Engage at Jershel's Nest."

Nystin slid the message crystal back into its custom *yvkefer* case and tucked it back into his pocket. The magic-resistant metal would block any attempt to use the crystal against him, but knowing he had magic on his body still made his skin crawl. He'd fought too many battles, seen too many friends die at the hands of some spell or some monster to ever feel comfortable with it.

But as commander of the Knights of Gedesar, he didn't have the luxury of refusing to handle things he wasn't comfortable with. Without the message crystal, his contact in the justicars couldn't have gotten word to him the morning after the disastrous attack on the airship. Without it, he'd have no idea where Loch and her gang were holed up.

He turned at another knight's approach, then nodded to Hex. The older man limped to the railing and let out a little grunt as he leaned against it.

"Getting hot?" he asked without looking over.

Nystin didn't look at his hip. Most of the knights were trained to be so distrustful of magic that the presence of the crystal would make some of them uneasy—even angry. "Warm enough. The train went sour. Three dead, half a dozen injured, and we were one flamecannon shot from falling out of the sky. Not as clean as they like it up the chain."

"There is no chain," Hex said, still not looking over.

"Beg pardon, Lieutenant?"

"It's hard enough to get clearance to hit a damned *tavern*." Hex spat over the side. "Civilians everywhere, panicking as you come through the door, screaming because they don't know you're trying to save them from something raised by Byn-Kodar himself. A train? No way we got the nod on that."

"Lieutenant, if you're making an accusation—"

"Shut up, Nystin." Hex still didn't look over. "I've got scars older than you are, and I still remember you dropping your blade on the first day of training."

Nystin swallowed. "I was disarmed, as I recall."

"Your memory's being kind, then." Hex gave a rusty chuckle. "Straight thrust on a dummy reinforced like a golem. Blade popped right out of your hands." Then he finally did look over. "So I'm asking you straight: we taking commissions?"

Nystin met his stare. "No. This is . . . Loch has enemies in high places. They want her down."

Hex pursed his lips in thought. "She actually dangerous?"

"Dangerous enough. She and her team dodged us twice now."

Hex snorted. "Means she's good, not dangerous." He lowered his voice. "We've got corpses rising and killing Republic soldiers on the Imperial border, sir. There's a necromancer out there who needs killing, and we should be the ones doing it. You tell me this is just politics, sir, and we're going to have a situation."

Nystin remembered the meeting with the Learned voyants, the expensive drinks and the dim candlelight. He remembered the knee slapping, the delighted laughter at the stories they'd asked him to tell. He remembered being told how expensive *yvkefer* armor and silver crossbow bolts were, and how the vote was going to be close. Those things were true enough to make up the weight on anything he shaded.

"It's not just politics, Hex. If she doesn't die, a lot of sons and daughters will."

Hex held his stare for a long moment.

Then, finally, the old knight nodded. "As you say, sir."

"We take her down at Jershel's Nest," Nystin said firmly, "and then we move our asses to the border and find that necromancer."

Hex nodded curtly, then limped back to where the rest of the knights were resting or training; Nystin leaned against the railing. When he was sure he was alone, he slid the message crystal from its case, snapped it in half, and let the pieces fall from the railing.

Loch went down the stairs slowly. The inn was small and quaint, a place for merchants to get a hot meal and rest rather than get rowdy and celebrate. Oil lamps glowed softly as she came down to the ground floor and into the common room, where merchants and traders ate while a harpist played something gentle and calm over by the fire.

"Back room," Kail said behind her, and Loch crossed to a closed door and turned the latch.

The room likely saw some gambling. The lights were lower, and members of her team sat around one large table with drinks in front of them—except for Ululenia—who lay half-curled in the corner of the room in her natural form, glowing faintly, flowers blooming around her.

". . . is more aware of the unintended consequences of my magic than I am," Hessler was saying, pointing at Icy with his free hand.

"Well, *I* might be." Tern sipped her fruity drink. Her shoulder was bandaged, and her arm was in a sling, but judging by the color in her cheeks, she was doing all right.

Hessler looked over at Tern, face taut. "I'm sorry."

"You said that already, baby. A lot. You don't have to impress anyone with your magic. You just—" Tern stopped as Loch stepped in.

"All right," Loch said. "Thank you for waiting for me to wake up. Kail tells me I owe some of you for the healing as well."

It was the least we could do, Little One, Ululenia said, and Desidora smiled and nodded as well, raising a fluted glass of white wine in Loch's direction.

Icy's tea sat unfinished in front of him, steeped until specks marred the bottom of the cup. Hessler looked like he hadn't slept in a few days, and Tern, for all her rosy flush, had lost some weight.

Still, there was her team, just about everyone in the world she let herself care about, except for Pyvic. And it was unfair of her to expect him here, anyway.

She'd planned to put it as a question, give them the option of an out. Icy might want to get back to the Empire if the war heated up, and most of them had family somewhere. But looking at them, Loch realized that that would hardly be fair. It smacked of the kind of manipulation her pretty baroness sister would do.

"So," she said, "this was a viable job when we had a target. Irrethelathlialann's back in the Elflands now, or near enough, and the book is with him."

"Yeah, since you threw it at him," Tern said, and sipped her fruity drink again.

"If you could avoid returning the stolen objects to their owners, the operation would go much more smoothly," Icy added.

"Noted," Loch said, shooting Icy a flat look. "What matters now is—"

"Our elven friend Ethel has passage booked into the Elflands tomorrow afternoon on a giant elven luxury treeship called . . ." Kail trailed off and picked up a mug of beer from the table. "Help?"

"No," said Tern. "You're the one who started calling the airship *Iofegemet.* That puts you in charge of all stupid names we encounter on this job."

"Wow, I really don't see how that follows at all."

The elven ship's name translates as 'the way the vixen's ears prick up when she catches her mate's scent as she approaches her burrow after a night devoid of good hunting.'

"Oh, well, that's much easier to say." Kail sipped his beer.

"We're not going to hit the ship," Loch said, stepping forward and putting her hands on the table.

"Of course we're not," Tern said, and held her glass out to Hessler. "Drink me."

"It'd be crazy to try to get all of us aboard," he agreed as he took the glass. "The treeship has living wards that set off alerts if anyone whose aura hasn't been altered with a guest frequency boards the vessel."

"Now, I can see the aura of the wards, but I can't alter anyone's auras to match." Desidora finished off the rest of her wine and held out her glass as Hessler went by. "While you're up? Thank you," she said as he took it from her. "The wards run from a central station deep in lower hold, so we'll need to get someone inside there to disable them at the source."

"That's after we figure out the tickets," Tern added. "Some kind of rare natural leaf with golden ink. I can copy the ink, but the leaves are going to be . . ." She trailed off as a pale green leaf shaped like a diamond fluttered slowly down to the table. "Oh. All right, then."

Nature magic. Ululenia shifted back into human form, her horn flaring as she smiled. "They are also printed with specific numbers, are they not?"

"Yeah, I doubt just scrawling 'Please Let Me Aboard' on a leaf will cut it." Kail sidestepped Hessler and went to the bar, then looked over his shoulder at Loch. "Red or white?"

"I believe I have her covered," came a voice from behind her, and she turned to see Pyvic holding a pair of wineglasses, one of them held up her way.

Loch stood up, blinking, and swallowed despite herself. She took the wineglass as Pyvic came over to stand beside her. "Thank you."

"Hey, don't thank us. We're charging all this to your room." Kail refilled his beer and shot her a grin.

"Good to know." Loch looked at the room, at her crew. "The ship leaves tomorrow? That doesn't give us a lot of time."

"Tomorrow *afternoon*," Kail said, waving absently. "Tern makes the ink tonight, someone hits the ticket office in the morning while you run a cat-bell on Ethel, then Tern writes everything during lunch."

"Wait, I don't get lunch?"

"I'll bring back something for you," Hessler said, and then winced as Tern kicked him in the shins.

"Well, as long as we've got a plan." Loch nodded and took a larger gulp of wine than was probably wise on an empty stomach. "Captain Pyvic can brief me on the specifics."

He smiled a little and followed as she left the room, passed through the bar, and stepped out onto the twilight.

She wiped her eyes then, since nobody but Pyvic was around. His arm came to rest around her shoulder, warm and smelling of leather and in all ways right, and she took a deep breath, then sighed.

"You've got a good team."

"Damn right I do," she said.

"Kail told you about the dead marching out of the Empire?"

"He did. Bet that's helping keep the peace."

"The talks ended yesterday. The Imperials deny raising an army of the dead and insist that the Republic caused them to rise by misusing ancient magic."

"That's convenient."

Pyvic grinned. Loch wasn't looking at him, but she could feel the muscles in his face move as she leaned against him.

"Share," he said.

"Kail said the dead came out of the water. Now, granted, I've never had an undead army at my command . . ." she started.

"Didn't Desidora raise a zombie for you one time?" Pyvic cut in.

"Isolated incident. We just needed his aura to crack a safe."

"Oh, *well*, then." Pyvic chuckled, and his arm tightened around her. More quietly, he added, "She's having trouble, you know? Trying to find her place without her powers."

"She figured out how to deal with death magic. I'm sure she'll figure out how to deal without it." Loch filed the concern away for later thought, though. "Anyway, I've never had an undead army at my command, beyond one *specific isolated incident*, but they're slow and clumsy. If I was going to surprise the Republic with them, I wouldn't march them through water on *my* side."

"You'd march them on land until you were close to the Republic border, and *then* march them underwater."

"Right. You'd catch the Republic with its pants down, instead of tipping off the scouts and starting an ugly fight on the border." Loch finished off the last of her wine. "So, frame-up?"

"Looks that way. No idea who's behind it, though."

Loch nodded. "Think we can still end it if we get the book?"

"I don't see anything else that will." Pyvic turned her around gently and gave her a cautious look. "Just don't get stabbed anymore."

"Kail said something very much like that," Loch said.

"Kail has sporadic but verifiable moments of genuine wisdom."

She uncrossed her arms and leaned in close, letting him enfold her in a circle of warmth. "Thanks for coming."

"Not a problem." He bent his head, and she moved to meet his kiss.

That was when the crossbow bolt cracked into the wall next to their heads.

Nystin signaled, and Rib smashed the door open.

Glass threw the smoke bag even as Rib dove in, crossbow coming up to cover the screaming patrons, and Nystin darted past them both, his own crossbow up and ready, strafing the stairwell with a shot ready. A serving maid at the top of the stairs froze, towels in her hand, and Nystin knew she wasn't the death priestess or the unicorn even as his finger pulled the trigger. It caught her cleanly in the chest, and she gasped, coughed, and went down.

Glass pounded past Nystin, covering even as Nystin dropped his crossbow and unslung his mace.

Rib was beside him, but stopped at the serving maid. "What—"

"Cultist," Nystin snapped. "Went for a knife." He darted past Rib, who was strong as an ox but had demonstrated some trouble dealing with the realities of war, and met Glass, who was ready by the door.

He kicked hard, got the sweet spot, and popped the cheap knob clean off the frame as the door snapped in. Glass moved in and fired at the bed.

Had Loch been in it, it would've been a perfect head shot. She wasn't in it.

Less than a minute had passed.

Nystin flung the drapes aside and glared down at the street, where Grid's team was covering any attempt at escape, and signaled failure.

Grid looked confused, then checked corners and flung back a signal of her own.

"Outside! Move!" Nystin shoved past the two recruits and ran for the stairs, mace and dagger both out now.

The serving maid was still on the ground at the top of the stairs. She reached for Nystin as he came her way. She was going to say something, and Nystin didn't have time for Rib or Glass to get confused.

His dagger came up, then came down.

A slim, tan-skinned hand caught his wrist.

"I do not believe she needs to be involved in this confrontation," said Loch's Imperial acrobat as the dagger twisted from Nystin's grip.

Nystin lunged forward, shoving the Imperial back, and lashed out with his mace. The Imperial ducked, spun, and slid under the blow, and then Nystin remembered the man's priorities and swung down at the fallen serving maid instead. The Imperial darted in and caught the blow mid-swing, and this time, Nystin smashed a fist into the man's jaw. He went down on top of the girl he'd tried to protect, and Nystin raised his mace again.

He heard the keening shriek of a bird of prey, but when he looked over, what he saw coming his way was a great white bear.

He felt the smashing impact, then the crash of the wall on his back, and then the shuddering shaking roll of the floor beneath him. The bear was closing to strike again, but then Glass stepped in, and his silver dagger slashed out, leaving a thin line of blood across the bear's paw.

The bear roared in pain and stumbled back as though burned. The air around it shifted, and suddenly it was a horse with a shimmering rainbow horn, collapsing to her knees by the stairs.

"Eat silver, bitch!" Glass shouted, and lunged in.

Then, just as suddenly, he jerked back, took two steps, and fell.

A crossbow bolt protruded from his visor.

"One-handed!" a woman yelled from downstairs.

Nystin lunged past the unicorn—past the serving girl and the Imperial and his own recruit—and down the stairs, to where a target had just fired and was hopefully unarmed. He didn't look back to see if Rib was coming.

Loch's alchemist woman stood in the smoke, her crossbow still raised, and as he came down the stairs, Nystin saw Grid rush in and come down hard with her mace, a blow that should have smashed the woman's skull open like an overripe fruit.

It passed through harmlessly, and Grid stumbled through the illusion, turned, and took a chair across the head from behind as Loch's Urujar lieutenant came out from under a table. Grid went down, and the Urujar grabbed the mace, turned, and blocked Nystin's blow before it could smash in his skull.

It still sent the man stumbling back, though, and that was all Nystin needed. He kicked the chair at the Urujar, then turned as the rest of Grid's people charged into the room.

Another sprouted a bolt between the eyes, and Nystin traced its path with speed from a hundred similar fights, saw the telltale gleam in the smoke that marked a cloaking field, slid his second and final silver dagger from its sheath at his wrist, and threw it.

A warhammer spun across the room and knocked the dagger from the air, and Nystin looked to see a woman in the robes of a love priestess still standing with her arm extended. "No."

Then Hex slammed her into the wall. "Repent, necromancer."

The woman hit hard, and her head rattled, eyes going vacant, but her arm still moved up to block Hex's blade as it came in at her throat. It was the warhammer, Nystin saw, already back in her grasp and protecting its necromancer mistress even after she fell. Hex stumbled back, slammed a kick into her midsection as the hammer blocked his high stab, and then screamed as a vial of something green splashed over him.

"Ever wanted to know what makes *yvkefer* melt?" a woman holding a crossbow said as she stepped out of the cloaking field where Nystin had thrown the dagger. "Maybe next time you come after the women in the dresses—" She broke off as another knight lunged at her, and a gangly robed man knocked her aside and hit the knight with a chair.

Nystin had caught it all as he moved through the room, seeing his men charge in, watching them fall, running the numbers, and above all looking for his target. She was nowhere in sight, and he broke out through the inn's front room, kicked open the door, and grabbed a mace from the fallen knight in the street in front of him.

"Stand down!" shouted a man holding a sword like he knew how to use it—military training, nothing fancy, but enough. There was blood on the blade. The knight on the ground was Scale, who had always been good against beasts but a little too slow against plain old people.

Behind the man was Nystin's target, Isafesira de Lochenville. She wasn't even holding a blade.

"On me!" Nystin shouted. "On me!"

He swung. The man with the sword was fast, but he wasn't wearing armor, and the blade skated along Nystin's reinforced banding, and then Nystin's mace smashed down, forcing the man back. He moved fast, eyes tracking everything around him, and that was when the face clicked for him.

"Captain Pyvic." Nystin spat the name. "Here to protect your convict, your criminal."

"I'd know if there was an order for her arrest," Pyvic said. There were two other knights on the ground around him, and while they weren't moving, Pyvic was trying to hide how he favored his right leg a little.

Loch herself just stood there, arms folded over the wound the report had said she'd taken.

"You've done good work, Justicar," Nystin said, "closed some cases, handled what needed handling. But you're soft."

His men burst out of the inn and into the street. There were only five of them left, but it would be enough.

"Do your men think this is a legal takedown?" Pyvic asked, and turned to them. "This is a hit! Your commander is carrying out an assassination against—"

Nystin moved. Pyvic caught it, but he was indeed favoring the leg a bit, and while he ducked away from Nystin's strike, he left his stance sloppy, and Nystin followed up fast with an ugly short swing that Pyvic had no choice but to block. The impact battered his blade and he staggered. As he did, one of Nystin's knights came in from behind with a pommel-strike to the back of Pyvic's skull, putting the justicar on the ground.

Nystin looked at Loch, still standing unarmed and unmoving.

"I surrender," she said.

"I don't care." Nystin stepped to one of the fallen knights and slid a dagger free from the man's hip.

"I'm sorry," she said. Nystin ignored it, flipping his dagger to an inverted grip as he came toward her. "I told you it would be hard," she said, "and you'd have to follow orders even when you disagreed, but I never thought it would be like this when I made you promise."

"When the hell did you tell me that?" Nystin asked, not stopping. They always talked, always asked questions to slow you down. The key was to keep going, no matter what they said.

Loch shook her head. "I wasn't talking to you."

Nystin heard the jangle of metal as someone hit the ground behind him.

He kept moving toward her as someone grunted and dropped to their knees, and then as someone hit the wall of the building across the street.

Nystin didn't stop. If he didn't look, they couldn't stop him.

"You think you're too good for the rules the rest of us live by?" he said, raising his dagger as he took the final steps. "You think you're above the law?"

"No." Loch met his stare. "But I'm not beneath it, either."

"Captain Nystin," said Rib from behind him, "I need you to stop."

Nystin swung.

A grip like a vise clamped down on his arm. The banded metal creaked, then crumpled, and as Nystin tried to turn, a great force slammed him to the ground. He bounced, fell, bounced again, and slid.

When his eyes worked again, he saw Rib coming toward him, helmet off.

"You always were too damn strong, Recruit Rybindaris." Nystin struggled back to his feet. The pain was savage, but he'd gone through worse. "What are you? Golem? Monster? Some new kind of undead?"

"I just wanted to help," Recruit Rybindaris said, and there were tears in his pale blue eyes as he said it. "But you care more about killing people than stopping innocent people from getting hurt."

"Grow up, boy." Nystin looked around. The other knights lay unmoving on the ground around him. "You joined the bad guys today, you know that? What you did right here is going to get sons and daughters killed."

"Dairy has saved more lives than you or I ever will," Loch said from behind Rybindaris, "and after he did that, he wanted to serve the Republic with honor and dignity." She smiled, and now, for the first time, Nystin saw the anger. "Guess you got *that* out of his system."

Nystin heard movement inside the inn, and he doubted it was more of his own men.

"You're a traitor, Rib, and you'll die a traitor," he growled.

Then he turned and ran as Loch's monsters and criminals poured out into the street.

The last thing he saw as he turned the corner was Rybindaris falling to his knees, crying.

Fifteen

So you joined the Knights of Gedesar," Hessler said to Dairy the next morning as he, Ululenia, and the young man walked into the ticket office for ships to the Elflands.

Dairy flushed. "I wanted to help people."

The ticket office was done in rich wood paneling and green carpets and curtains that made Hessler feel like he was inside a tree. That was probably the point. A dark-haired young human woman sat behind a counter that curved gently to meet the wall, smiling as they came inside.

"You saved the entire world from the Glimmering Folk, which would seem to meet any reasonable quota for altruistic good works," Hessler said, "and then you decided that you would *hunt us down* as your next big act?"

Rybindaris, or "Dairy", former Champion of Dawn who had fulfilled the prophecies by defeating the Champion of Dusk atop Heaven's Spire a few months ago, continued to flush. "But see, Mister Hessler, that wasn't really me. That was just the prophecy."

At the counter, Ululenia spoke to the ticket woman. "I wish to book passage to the Elflands, that my friends might see a land of true magic unfettered by the restrictions of mortals," she said, allowing her horn to shine brightly.

"Of course." The dark-haired woman at the counter apparently had experience dealing with fairy creatures. "Are your friends cleared for travel? As citizens of the Republic, they'll need a permit and written permission from the elven embassy to enter the Elflands."

"As the hare pats down the burrow with the first fall of snow, we have made all necessary preparations," Ululenia said, smiling and confident. "I shall purchase my ticket first."

"What do you mean it was just the prophecy?" Hessler asked, turning to Dairy and lowering his voice. "You're stronger than any normal person, you're immune to magic, and lucky things happen around you. You can't turn any of those things off."

"But all I did with that was fulfill the prophecy," Dairy said, sighing. "I didn't do anything that I decided to do on my own."

"Here you are," Ululenia said to the woman at the counter, passing over a small pouch of coins. "I understand if you must ensure that they are not enspelled."

The woman behind the counter smiled as she carefully poured the coins into a shallow golden bowl inset with detection crystals and runes. "I'm glad someone does. Last week we had an ogre who took it as an insult."

"That is not uncommon for ogres," Ululenia said, smiling, and the young woman laughed.

"So putting aside the fact that you think you can make future accomplishment immune to accusations of privilege just by going off the expected trail laid for you by the prophecy," Hessler said to Dairy, "what you decided to do on your own was *hunt us down*."

"Well, I'm immune to magic," Dairy said, "and I'm stronger than most people, like you said, so it didn't seem fair to join the normal army."

The young woman had the ticket out now and set it down on the counter, smiling at Ululenia. "I hope you enjoy your visit to the Elflands. I hear it's wonderful, though few humans ever get to see it."

"You have never been yourself?" Ululenia looked at the dark-haired woman and raised an eyebrow. "Ah, it seems there are *many* things you have never done." As the dark-haired woman blushed, Ululenia put a pale, slim finger on the ticket and slid it around the table in a little circle.

"At first, it was good," Dairy insisted. "We fought some daemons that had gotten loose. We killed a woman who was using magic to kill people. We even stopped a manticore that was terrorizing a village . . ."

"Two, please," Hessler said to the woman, "and I understand that there are restrictions of some kind on what we're allowed to bring with us?"

The woman, who was now chewing on a pen while looking at Ululenia, blinked, and then nodded and held out a piece of paper with a long list of banned items. When Hessler made no move to take it, she put it down on the table next to Ululenia's ticket.

"But then they talked about hunting Miss Loch," Dairy continued as he followed Hessler to the counter, "and a lot of what they said didn't sound right, but Miss Loch said that I had to do what they said, even if I disagreed with it, because that was part of being in the military, and anyway, I thought that once they arrested her, it would turn out that she was innocent, and everything would be all right."

Hessler gave Dairy a look. "And how did that work out for you, kid?"

Back at the counter, the shallow bowl filled with coins gave a soft but discordant chime, and everyone stopped.

"Oh," said Ululenia, looking over and still idly moving the ticket around in little circles on the table, "something disturbs it?"

The dark-haired woman looked at the bowl. "Yes, I'm afraid it does. These coins have been altered with illusion magic."

As the dark haired woman looked, Hessler hit the ticket and the travel restriction paper with the illusion that swapped them, then gave a big obvious flinch as Ululenia turned and glared at him. "You *swore* these were good!" she said, her horn crackling with energy even as her finger danced from the ticket that now looked like a travel restrictions paper to the travel restrictions paper that now looked like a ticket and continued to make little circles on the table.

"They were!" Hessler raised his hands in dismay. "I got them myself from that illusionist for purging a daemonic infestation from her tower!" He slapped his forehead. "The illusionist . . ."

"The illusionist with the low-cut gown you were admiring as she paid you?" Ululenia asked, and then schooled her face and her shining horn back to calmness as she looked at the dark-haired woman. "I apologize sincerely." She slid the false ticket across the desk, leaning forward a little to do so. "Although since my employer was fooled as the bird blinded by the wings of the butterfly, it seems I will be staying here longer than expected. If you wish to take the opportunity to . . . explore . . ."

The dark-haired woman blushed as she took the false ticket. "I, um, yes, perhaps that would be lovely." Ululenia smiled, then glared at Hessler and strode out of the office.

Hessler nodded to the woman. "She's very nice," he said, coughing, and grabbed the paper that currently appeared to be travel restrictions information. "I'll just take these to read while . . . sorry . . ." He hurried out after Ululenia, with Dairy in tow.

"I'm sorry I disappointed you," Dairy said to Hessler as the three of them crossed the street and headed back toward the inn.

"Were you part of the group that nearly killed Tern?"

"No," Dairy said, and sagged a little. "They had me doing unimportant things. I heard rumors that they were doing more, and that the things they were doing weren't nice, but no one ever said."

"They usually don't, kid." Hessler looked at Ululenia. "Anything you want to add, here?"

"Nope!" Ululenia said, not looking over. "Although I'm not sure why *he* had to come with us to the ticket office in the first place."

"I *wanted* to come along. I'm sorry if I disappointed you as well, Ululenia," Dairy said. "I think you're awfully nice, and whatever it is that, um, didn't make me want . . ."

"If you two want to bring the ticket back to Tern, I will see what the ticket seller is doing for lunch," Ululenia said.

"Are you really certain that you don't find Ululenia attractive?" Hessler asked. "Maybe it was first-time jitters. I mean, as far as I can tell, she is arrogant apple, babbling brook, creeping cat, all right, I'm stopping!" He glared at Ululenia. "There was no need to resort to cluttering up my mind."

"I disagree strongly." Ululenia's horn flared, and she headed back toward the office, her slim hips swaying in her white dress with every step.

"You're . . . you're *sure?*" Hessler said. "Because while I am by no means a paragon of masculine attitudes . . . you don't get many chances at something like that."

"I'm sure." Dairy looked at Ululenia, then Hessler.

"I thought you were with Tern, Mister Hessler."

"Well, yes, but I'm not *dead*."

Loch and Pyvic looked at the elven treeship at the docks at the edge of Jershel's Nest.

It was massive, its main deck high enough that a special ramp had been constructed to let people climb up to board. Great green sails lined with glowing, golden veins flared out from the trunks that served as its masts, angled to catch the wan morning sun, while workers both human and elven hung from long ropes, scouring the bark of the treeship's hull clean of all debris.

"They're sure it doesn't use daemons?" Loch asked.

"Strictly nature magic," Pyvic said. "You're going to have to do *something* about Jyelle-the-daemon wanting to kill you, though."

"Just as soon as I end this war."

"Fair enough." Pyvic chuckled and took her hand. For a moment, everything was all right.

"Reminds me of scrubbing the stones in the Cleaners," Loch said. "Hanging from the pipes, straining to reach the stones with those damn enchanted brooms, nothing but an ankle chain to catch you if you slip."

"Sounds exciting," Pyvic said.

"You were there. You should remember it."

"I was there for a couple of minutes," Pyvic said, "at the end of which, Archvoyant Silestin hit me with lightning until I lost consciousness. Pardon me if my memory's a bit hazy."

"Silestin, right. Speaking of assholes, how are the Knights of Gedesar?" Loch asked as the workers moved slowly down the hull. It looked like thick, clean bark from where she stood, with no knotholes or cuts visible. A network of roots extended like a gangplank to the great ramp, and passengers were already boarding.

"The survivors? Tern killed a couple of them."

"I'm sure she was aiming for their shoulder and tragically missed," Loch shrugged, "since she was shooting one-handed as a result of them trying to kill her earlier."

"That's my opinion as a justicar, yes. The girl Icy and Ululenia saved on the stairs corroborates your team's version of the events." Pyvic looked over. "Desidora also caved in a few skulls before she got taken down."

"Not unless she did it by hand," Loch said. "That would be her magical sentient warhammer acting under its own power. Anyone wants to bring charges against a magical sentient warhammer, I wish them luck."

"I don't think it'll come to that." Pyvic grinned. "Archvoyant Bertram confirmed that there was no call for the Knights of Gedesar to arrest you. This was illegal from the start."

"Be nice if we got their commander to lock that all down." Loch saw the familiar form coming off the main road to the docks, an elf wearing loose-fitting silks and walking with easy grace, smiling as he made his way through the crowd. "Anyway, it's time. Let's go."

"You all right to move?"

She was already moving, and she shot him a look over her shoulder as she pulled out of his grip. He sighed and jogged to catch up.

Irrethelathlialann had a large black raven riding on his shoulder. Loch had no idea where it had come from, but its beady eyes moved to track her as she came in behind the elf.

"Isafesira de Lochenville," the elf said without turning around. "You're refreshingly difficult to kill. Thank you for returning my book, by the way."

He had evidently thought she would stop as he called out her name, because he yelped as she clapped him on the shoulder and grabbed his waist. His raven squawked and flapped off and away as Loch leaned in close.

"You're going to give me that manuscript before anyone else gets killed," she hissed into his ear.

He shook her off and spun, his robes turning his whole body into a sheet billowing in the breeze. "Oh, Loch," he murmured as he moved smoothly into a combat stance, jostling a passing dockhand as he did, "you insult me. After I heard of your encounter with the Knights of Gedesar, did you really think I would keep the manuscript on my person? I sent it ahead. You have nothing, your clumsy, desperate attempt to pick my pocket notwithstanding."

Pyvic came in from the other side. "Irrethelathlialann, as a justicar, I have the authority to—"

"Oh, no, you do not." He didn't even look at Pyvic. "By now, you've found out that I represent the interests of the Dragon, and you've been troubled by your inability to find out anything else, but your superiors have told you in no uncertain terms that whatever happens to me unofficially, I am *not* to be touched."

Pyvic glared, then set himself between Irrethelathlialann and the ship. The raven fluttered back down and landed on the elf's shoulders, glaring at Loch and cleaning glossy black feathers under one wing.

"It has something to do with the ancients, doesn't it?" Loch saw the elf raise an eyebrow. "You told me as much on the train. You don't much care for them, do you?"

"Urujar," the elf said. "You know what it means in the language of the ancients?"

"I'm guessing you'd love to tell me," Loch said.

"You guess wrong." Irrethelathlialann turned away from her. "Farewell, Isafesira. This conversation has begun to bore me, so please trust that the manuscript will be better off with the Dragon than it will with you. Now, I believe I will be enjoying a morning breakfast at one of the finer local establishments, and then boarding that treeship and returning home. As you will under no condition receive a travel permit for the Elflands, I believe our business is concluded."

"Like hell it is," Loch said. The raven cocked its head at her as she came forward. "Before you angry apricot, buttery blueberry, crunchy carrot . . ." She broke off as the world started spinning.

Then Pyvic's hand was on her shoulder, keeping her steady. "It stops, or I draw," he said, "and your bird should know that I pocketed at least one silver dagger from last night's fight with the Knights of Gedesar."

Loch's vision cleared, and she saw, for the briefest moment, a pair of stag's antlers shining in all the colors of the rainbow atop the raven's head. Then it was gone, and the bird dipped its head and croaked a laugh.

"Good day, Justicars," Irrethelathlialann said without turning around. "I wish you luck in your war."

He strode off with his raven laughing on his shoulder.

Pyvic waited until the elf was up the gangplank before he let go of Loch's shoulder. "You all right?"

"Still slow." She grimaced and put a hand to her waist. "Probably good that nobody drew steel. Or silver."

Pyvic laughed. "Probably," he said. "Now, let's hope the rest of it goes as well."

Walking with the wide-legged gait of an airship sailor, Kail sauntered back into the alley as Loch finished her distraction with the elf.

"It worked?" Desidora asked, though in truth, it was a foolish question. The elf would have turned on Kail immediately had he suspected that the sailor jostling him was anything out of the ordinary.

"Like a charm." Kail grinned as he tossed the sailor's cap into a sack by the wall, along with a thin black scarf on which were sewn silver wings crossing a crescent moon—the symbol of Jairytnef as the patron those who traveled by magic. "Timed it just like you said. You saw all that in his aura?" In just a moment, he was just Kail again, no longer a sailor.

"Love priestess, remember?" Desidora smiled back. Elves were enough like humans to have auras, which meant any priestess of Tasheveth with the proper training could look at Irrethelathlialann's peculiar soul—in particular, looking at how it would react and where it would leave him unsuspecting. "I was planting love notes in people's pockets long before you and Loch ever recruited me. Speaking of which . . ." She turned to a young man, a blacksmith's apprentice judging by his sooty apron. "Go get a bun," she said.

The young man blinked. "Um . . ."

"The stall in the square. Say that you like them with honey." Desidora looked at his aura, and remembered the aura of the *other* young man back in the market stall. "If you could find a way to have your sleeves rolled up to show off your arms, it wouldn't hurt." As the blacksmith's apprentice stared at her in confusion, she waved a little. "Off you go."

Kail chuckled. "Must be good to be back to hooking up young lovers again."

"*Kutesosh gajair'is,*" Ghylspwr said at her side, and Desidora tapped his handle to hush him.

"Yes," she said instead. "The powers of Byn-Kodar were dangerous. I don't regret being myself again."

Kail headed back through the alley to a side street, and Desidora followed, the hem of her pale-green skirt kicking up leaves as she swished behind him. Even the smaller streets were clean in Jershel's Nest. It was likely because of the elves, just like Ajeveth was kept neat by the dwarves. It seemed it was only humans who let their streets get filthy.

Jershel's Nest had more elves and fairy creatures than anywhere else in the Republic, and its architecture had taken on some of their nature. The buildings were largely wooden, and half the city was in a state of repair of growth, with old structures torn down and new ones already raised in intricate scaffolding. There were more parks than in a normal city, some with intricate fountains at their center, others with stages for musicians.

This was still the Republic, though, so of course there was a puppeteer performing in the park they passed through now.

". . . continued losses to the undead army the Empire has sent across the border," the dragon called out somberly, "including a squad of Republic military artificers whose mission to reinforce the walls of the town of Kinsmark turned into a heroic sacrifice to buy townsfolk the chance to escape."

"Now, there's still some confusion," the griffon said haltingly, its wings drooping low, "as the Empire continues to deny responsibility for these attacks, a stance that quite frankly defies understanding at this point."

"I think we're past the point where we should be worrying about what the Empire thinks," the manticore said, flapping its own wings angrily and swishing its scorpion's tail. "Now is the time to send airships across the border and show the Imperial forces what happens to those who attack and kill innocent civilians."

"That would mean a declaration of all-out war upon the Empire," the dragon said, snorting fire at the manticore, but the griffon tugged on the dragon's tail.

"With respect, my colleague and I don't agree on much, but I think we can agree that declaration or no, we are already at war," the griffon said, raising its claws in warning as the dragon turned on it. "The question now is whether we are prepared to win it."

The dragon stepped back from the manticore and the griffon, both now turned against it, and then turned to the crowd. "Strong words," it called out. "What do you think, listeners? Come and make your voices heard! Tell the voyants on Heaven's Spire how the Republic should respond to these attacks by the Imperial undead. Remember, *it's your republic!*"

"*Stay informed!*" the crowd called back.

"Don't regret losing those powers at all?" Kail said, not looking over, as some of the people in the crowd left and others came forward to sign slips of paper urging the voyants to declare war.

"They weren't who I was," Desidora said, tightening her grip on Ghylspwr a little. "I did awful things. I *almost* did even more."

"Yeah, and you could stop that army of undead in its tracks like *that*." Kail snapped his fingers. "Yeah, your dress would go black, and you'd sprout skulls and crap everywhere, but still, better than a town full of dead artificers."

"Byn-Kodar's powers are only for works that demand a united response by the gods." Desidora looked at the crowd clustered around the puppeteer's stage. "Like it or not, this is the work of people. I can only meet that with the power of Tasheveth."

"You and Icy." Kail shook his head. "That's a great restriction, provided we all have magical warhammers to bail us out when crap gets real."

"*Besyn larveth'is!*" Ghylspwr said angrily from Desidora's hip.

"You think I don't wish I could just stop all this?" Desidora snapped. "You think this is a *choice* on my part? I'm not holding back because I swore an oath. I don't *have* those powers anymore!"

"You ask your goddess to give them back?" Kail turned to her, his voice low, hands fisted at his sides.

"She's not a moneylender, Kail," Desidora said, turning and glaring at his little head-cocked challenge.

Kail shook his head again. "I'll take that as a no, then."

"When I first received the mantle of Byn-Kodar, I wept and fasted and *prayed* for the gods to pick someone else, and it didn't do me any damned good. Why should she listen to me now?"

This time, he blinked. "That came out a little less devout than I'd expected from a priestess. Little crisis of faith, there?"

The man had always been a little more insightful than she gave him credit for. Desidora turned away, raking hair from her face. "I can still help the team. I read Irrethelath-lialann's aura."

"And you're also one of, like, two people who can say his name," Kail said from behind her. "That's gotta be good for something."

A small smile touched her lips at that. Occasionally insightful *and* occasionally witty. "I told you how he'd move, how he'd react. I gave you everything you needed to make your move."

"A move I've been doing since before I shaved." Kail's voice was gentle. It would have been so much easier if he'd been angry.

She turned, her eyes hot with tears she wasn't going to let fall. "I have to believe that love will find a way, here, Kail. I have to. I can help us. I can see the hearts of everyone on this team, save Ululenia and Dairy. I can see what they need, the holes in their lives that need a partner to fill them."

Kail smiled. It didn't reach his eyes. "I hope that helps, Diz. I really do. Still, it's a good thing you've got that *and* the hammer."

She shut her eyes. "You were supposed to ask me what I saw when I looked at you."

"Besides a guy you almost killed?" He laughed to himself, and she heard the sound of his footsteps receding.

When she opened her eyes, he was gone.

Tern glared at the diamond-shaped leaf pinned to the table in front of her. She had a magnifying-glass attachment on her spectacles, which made her glare a *lot* more impressive. She was pretty sure she could light the leaf on fire if she scowled hard enough.

"Serifs," she muttered, holding up a griffon-feather pen stained with golden ink. "Always with the gods-damned serifs."

The border had been easy. The watermark in the background had taken most of the morning, since it was done in a style meant to *look* like it was carefully hand-inked with a bunch of tiny cross-hatches but was actually done with a stamp, but Tern had gotten it done with just the right level of slightly blurry efficiency and then moved over to the illuminated crap in the margins while waiting for it to dry. She'd done the lion, the dragon, and the tiny little thing she thought might be a pixie but was at *least* a naked lady lounging on a leaf.

She had a passable ticket now, with the exception of the actual text.

"Serifs," she said again. "Screw me sideways. Serifs. All right, ink me."

She held out her pen with her good arm. Icy very carefully dabbed it with the golden ink she'd whipped up last night and then modified this morning once she'd gotten a look at the ticket, since apparently the people in Jershel's Nest had never heard of color coordination and put in way too much red, turning the ink into more of a bronze than a proper gold.

She adjusted her magnifying glass, looked at the ticket Hessler had stolen for her, then looked at her own blank leaf page and made the tiniest mark.

"Do you need assistance?" Icy asked.

"If you could not talk, move, or breathe for the next hour, that would be fantastic."

"The treeship leaves in a little more than two hours," Icy said.

"Thank you, Icy." Tern made another mark, squinted, and added the tiniest little flourish, since some genius had opted to use a printing press whose font included serifs, as though that was going to fool anyone into thinking the tickets were hand-printed. All it really did was make it a hell of a lot harder for her to fake them, which, yes, was probably the point, but still.

She made another line, waited, and then blew cautiously on the paper. "Okay, yeah, we can do this."

"In less than two hours?" Icy asked.

"*Thank* you, Icy."

The door to the room slid open, and Tern looked up, ready to glare death at whomever was bothering her right now.

"I'm sorry," said Dairy, blinking and trying hard to only look at the eye that didn't have the magnifying glass attachment on the spectacles. "I didn't realize—"

"No, no, fine, come in." Tern jabbed her pen in Icy's direction. "Ink me."

"I wanted to apologize," Dairy said, "for your arm, and . . . wait, if we have a real ticket, why do you need to make a . . . copy?"

"Forgery." Tern made a few careful lines. She was still working on the normal writing that appeared on every ticket. Things would get harder when she had to start making up numbers on her own. "It's called a forgery."

"Yes, ma'am."

"And we have to make one because the one you all stole isn't encoded with the aural signature that marks it as official," Tern said, still writing very, very carefully, "which means that when it's fed into the little reader at the top of the gangplank, it won't make the happy little chime that tells them to hit Loch with the guest aura that makes the ship like her. And to answer your next question," she added, pausing momentarily to blow on the leaf, "we can't just fake the aura on the real ticket, because they're deliberately constructed to be fragile with respect to magical tampering. Try to mess with one, and the leaf withers. Ululenia made this one for us, though, so she can slap the aura on it safely, assuming that she's neither still injured from the Knights of Gedesar slashing her with silver nor exhausted from you finally taking out your virginity on her."

"Um . . ." He stammered and blushed while Tern kept working, and then finally said, "No. She's fine. And we're not . . . I'm not . . . um."

"Got it. Ink me." Tern waited while Icy hit the tip again. "Hessler already yell at you about joining the Knights of Gedesar?"

"Yes, ma'am."

"Well, then, I don't see what I need to—*son of a bitch*, is that beveled?" Tern ran her fingers along the real ticket. "Damn it. Okay. Fine. Assholes." She looked up at Dairy. "Who the hell bevels a serifed font? I mean, seriously, it's bad enough that they serifed the title, but now they're just drawing attention to the whole—"

"I'm sorry you got shot," Dairy cut in. When Tern looked up, the kid had tears in his eyes. "I didn't want it to happen, but I didn't know how to stop it, and they seemed so sure, and I told myself . . ."

"You told yourself I wasn't really the woman you knew." Tern held out her pen. Icy dabbed it. She went back to writing. "Told yourself I was somebody else, right? A bad person, someone who deserved it, because this was how the rules said it worked, so you had to be missing something."

"How did you know?"

Tern finished the horrible, awful serifed title beveling. "I used to wear really pretty dresses. It was like a competition among the merchants' daughters to see who had the best, the most fashionable. One year, this utter bitch named Enella had me beat. She had a maid who could work pearls into the lacing with this little trick nobody else could manage, so they stood out just perfectly. She said something cutting at a dance when she and her friends had the pretty pearled lacing and I didn't, and, well, I didn't even *like* the dances, because I was smarter than most of the merchants' sons, but there was no way she was getting away with that, so I took steps." She looked over at the real ticket. "Okay, drop the first and last number, those are filler, you can tell by the offset spacing. That there at the end is the date, month first . . . location, then . . . time? No." She chewed her bottom lip, working at the numbers.

"What did you do?" Dairy asked.

"I spread a rumor that the pearls the maid used weren't clean and carried a nasty disease, then slipped something into Enella's drink to give her a rash. She and her friends were a laughingstock, and I got *all* the best dances for the rest of the season. Batch, purchase location, ticket number. All right." She'd have done better with a larger sample, but it was the best guess time allowed for. "And Enella's maid lost her job and went off to starve in the streets, and when my own maid told me, I went through everything you told yourself. She chose to play the game, she knew the consequences, she was probably a cruel person, since she served Enella, all of it." Tern whipped through the numbers with a sure and steady hand. "And then I admitted the truth to myself, and I dropped out of society life. Ink me."

"Oh," Dairy said as Icy wordlessly dabbed the pen. "The money from my first job went to the maid. She's a seamstress in a shop now. Doing fine." Tern looked up and smiled, her apple cheeks dimpling. "So, thank you for apologizing, thank you for not killing the girl at the top of the stairs after your captain shot her, and thank you for helping Loch when it mattered. Now figure out what happens *next*."

"Choosing to walk away from your culture's values is difficult," Icy added as Tern went back to work. "Once you realize that you cannot in good conscience follow the orders with which you were raised, you must find your own path."

"Sometimes that path has you siding with guys who turn out to be following bad orders." Tern traced a carefully edged line. "Sometimes it involves you having sex with Loch's sister, who turns out to be an assassin working for the bad guy."

"I do not believe it was absolutely necessary to bring up that example," Icy said.

"It made the kid feel better," Tern said.

Dairy stood back up and swallowed. "I . . . thank you. I don't know what I'm supposed to do now."

"Well, if you want to help, go tell Loch I'll be finished on time, so she can get everyone started on the rest of her brilliant plan to get onto the damn treeship, steal the damn book, and stop the damn war."

He nodded. "I'll help however I can," he said, and strode out. He'd already gotten taller since the last time Tern had seen him.

"Ink me."

Icy coughed. "You never told me about Enella and the maid."

"Oh, yeah, just made it up. Can't have a kid as strong as an ogre and immune to magic going around feeling self-destructive and desperate to redeem himself. That's a recipe for crap going wrong. Hey, ink me?"

Icy reached over and dabbed the pen. "Remind me not to underestimate you, Tern."

"Why the hell would I ever do that? Rest of you all have magic and talents and combat training to get by." Tern carefully moved onto another unfortunate series of serifs. "I've gotta rely on *skill*."

Sixteen

Archvoyant Bertram dipped a dry biscuit into his kahva, sighed, and put it down on the saucer while he read the report.

"Damn it, Cevirt," he said plaintively, tossing the paper to the voyant across the table, "I wasn't ready to retire quite yet."

The Urujar voyant sighed. "Neither was I, as it happens."

"Tell me the airships will be enough, then." Bertram bolted his kahva, wincing at the heat as it worked its way down to his gut.

"Enough to do punitive raids, certainly." Cevirt didn't look at the report. He didn't have to, as he'd written it late the evening before. "Enough to provoke a retaliation from the Empire."

"But not enough to stop that undead army from destroying half the towns along the border."

"Not nearly enough, no."

A display case on the far wall held an old suit of armor, heavy and decked out with crystals that glowed even after a hundred years. Archvoyant Silestin, Bertram's power-mad predecessor, had probably kept it around as a sign of power. In the few months since Bertram had come to lead the Republic, he'd looked at the damn thing as a warning.

"A ground war." Nervous, he grabbed the biscuit he hadn't wanted before and took a bite. It was cold and damp in his mouth, but he chewed mechanically and swallowed. "A godsdamned ground war."

"An offensive." Cevirt slid the report back across the table. "If you want to stop the undead, we cannot just station troops on the border and hope to contain them. We need to march them across the border and take the battle to them."

Bertram tossed the rest of his biscuit back onto the saucer. Crumbs dotted the table. "We barely won the last war, Cevirt."

"We *didn't* win the last war." Cevirt took a small sip of his own kahva. Bertram always had trouble reading Urujar faces—he was old, and there hadn't been many of the dark-skinned fellows around where he'd grown up—but it was obvious Cevirt hadn't slept any better than Bertram had himself. "We fought some ugly battles neither side really wanted, and then we signed a treaty and threw a parade."

Cevirt was, if anything, sugar-coating it. The Empire had had most of its airships tied up further north, and the Republic had been able to use its own air superiority to push the Imperial forces into a fight the Republic could win. If Republic troops marched in openly, the Imperial airships would be waiting, and then the only question would be which side was more willing to catch its own people with the flamecannons.

"If you don't have the nerve, say so," Cevirt snapped, and Bertram realized he'd fallen silent for too long. "We sent my niece out on a wild hope, and that was the only other option we had."

Bertram waved in apology. "Do you have the Skilled votes?"

"I've spent the last week putting knives to the throats of my four." Cevirt sat back, fingers clasped. "I've got two of them. If you can get three, that will take us to seven."

"I don't want to go to war on a simple majority, Cevirt."

"Then get more votes. Your party *wanted* to go to war, remember?" Cevirt's voice was calm, but his dark fingers were pressed together so tightly that the color had been leeched from the tips. "And if they protest, remind them that you all backed Silestin, and he's the reason we're here . . . and if *that* doesn't work, then tell them the Skilled will be running on defense next election, and if you want the puppeteers calling the Learned fat old men who'd rather hide on the Spire than fight for their country, we can make that happen."

Bertram felt the muscles at the back of his neck tense, and he leaned forward. "Now hold on just a minute."

Then he paused at a curious whining noise coming from behind him.

It was coming from the walls, Bertram thought, and then saw that the crystals in the old suit of armor were glowing an angry red. He raised a hand to point it out to Cevirt, but even as he did, the crystals crackled and popped cleanly from the armor and skittered across the ground to the doorway. With an angry little shudder, crystals spat from the walls as well, sending little puffs of plaster flying as they shot free.

The glowing red crystals formed a pile, and the pile moved, and Bertram's first thought was assassins. His second thought was, to his shame, *They're welcome to this damn job, then.*

But then the pile slid into a humanoid shape, and the crystals dimmed into earth tones and flesh tones and normal colors, until something stood before them that could, in dim light after a few too many drinks, be taken as a man.

"You wish to protect yourselves," it said. "I will show you how."

Irrethelathlialann made his way up the ramp toward the tree-ship that would take him home.

Skoreinis croaked on his shoulder, and his voice sounded in Irrethelathlialann's head. *You hate it so much, this outside world?*

"Clearly." He could block the creature from his head with a sufficient effort of will, but Skoreinis had always been, if not friendly, at least loyal as a fellow servant of the Dragon.

There is plenty of other work to do. Ask him to send some-one else.

Irrethelathlialann let out a breath through his nose. "Then I would be inflicting this world upon some other elf." His fingers played at the ring he wore, reassuring him of the comforting magic it carried.

And you do not think they could perform at your level. Skoreinis laughed in his mind, and a stag's antlers flickered momentarily atop the raven's head. *Such arrogance, elf.*

Irrethelathlialann chuckled along with him, unwilling to argue. The creature was rarely kind, but he was also rarely wrong. What mattered was that his job was done. *The Love Song of Eillenfiniel* would be safe with his master soon, and the humans could shed each other's blood to their hearts' content while the *real* war played out more quietly.

Down below, porters handled luggage while servants lashed down crates carrying supplies for the journey. The treeship's voyage was actually a cruise, complete with stops at beautiful sites all across the Elflands and a high-stakes *suf-gesuf* tournament available to all passengers. He would be leaving once they reached the Dragon's palace, however.

The human woman, Loch, had played well, and Irrethelathlialann smiled to himself as he reached the back of the line near the top of the ramp. Her plan at Ajeveth had been sound, and she had very nearly gotten away with the manuscript on the train.

You admire her?

"I *acknowledge* her." He lowered his voice to avoid disturbing an elven couple in front of him, clutching their bags nervously. This visit out of the Elflands had to have been trying for them.

Her last attempt to rifle your pockets was pathetic.

Irrethelathlialann frowned. It *had* been unlike her. He had not had the manuscript on him, of course, so that had never been a possibility. He had checked immediately to ensure that he still had his ticket as well. "Desperation, perhaps," he murmured, twirling the ring on his finger as he thought. The urge to activate its magic was quick and temporary. At this range, the elves in front of him might be affected, and that would be needlessly cruel.

"If you would present your ticket, we would be grateful," said a lovely elven woman with sapphires glittering on her cheeks. Irrethelathlialann favored her with a smile and passed the diamond-shaped leaf to her. "One plus a guest?"

"Indeed." Irrethelathlialann nodded, and on his shoulder, Skoreinis ducked his head as well, and said something in the elven woman's mind that made her laugh.

"Regretfully," she added, still smiling, "I remind all passengers boarding that crystal-based magic is forbidden in the Elflands."

"I hear your words and appreciate your courtesy," he said, bowing with a little grin that matched her own. The rule had been put in place for fairy creatures, and those few humans who were granted leave to visit. The idea that any elf would bring artifacts of such a nature into the Elflands was absurd.

"Pleasant voyage, carried upon winds of joy," she said, and Irrethelathlialann moved past her and up the gangplank.

The alarm sounded as he stepped onto the deck of the great treeship, and Irrethelathlialann looked around in confusion.

A pair of large elven guards in leaf-armor stepped toward him. "Your pardon, respected traveler, but it would be dangerous for us not to perform a brief inspection of your person, as our fragile ship is sensitive to even the most seemingly innocent magics."

They were already prodding him with wooden wands, and one of them chimed as it passed near his waist.

"That is of course only reasonable," Irrethelathlialann said through gritted teeth.

The guard reached into his pocket cautiously.

A moment later, he pulled out what had to be the ugliest contraption of fused-together crystals Irrethelathlialann had ever seen.

Perhaps she is less pathetic than I had believed, Skoreinis said.

"Well played, Isafesira." Irrethelathlialann smiled, let out a long breath, and prepared for a long and tedious visit to the enhanced security station.

The alarm went off on the treeship, and Loch kissed Pyvic long and hard.

"You're sure about this?" he asked as he pulled away.

"Positive. You're an awful thief."

"I'm a good scout," he shot back, clearly not sure whether to be offended.

"And I may need you for the rescue later. Keep Kail out of trouble, and do whatever you can to keep the war under control until I get the manuscript."

"Wait." Pyvic frowned. "Your job is to get a book, and mine is to stop a war?"

"This is what happens when you let me assign jobs." She squeezed his hand. "Stay alive."

"You, too." Pyvic turned to Dairy, who had been watching them with embarrassment. "Keep her safe."

"Yes, sir." Dairy gave a salute. He was wearing a normal shirt and riding pants now, but a few months of military service had apparently trained some things into him.

Loch watched Pyvic leave, sighed, and shook her head.

"What was that for?" Dairy asked.

"I'm not supposed to tell him I'll miss him. Considered bad luck among scouts." At Dairy's confused look, Loch smiled. "Superstition more than anything else, but you were with the Knights of Gedesar, and I'm sure they had their own odd bits. You ever try to sneak up behind someone, but they could sense you coming, even when you were certain you weren't making any noise?"

Dairy thought for a moment. "No, ma'am. Everyone always sees me."

"I suppose that makes sense for you, Champion of Dawn," Loch said, and Dairy blushed. "But for us normal people, that happens sometimes. Like we've all got a bit of Ululenia's ability to read minds, or Desidora's way of seeing people's auras. Something like that." Ahead of them, a crowd was forming at the base of the gangplank, as elves and fairy creatures (she assumed, though they mostly looked human) grumbled about the now-stalled boarding line. "Anyway, among the scouts, there's a superstition that if you miss someone, it's like your heart is reaching out to them wherever they are . . . and that if their heart hears your heart, it will reach back, and someone the scout is trying to sneak past could feel that movement even when the scout wasn't making any noise at all." She shook her head. "It's a little stupid when you try to explain it out loud. Most of the time, we just say that it's bad luck."

"No, I think I understand," Dairy said. "You're afraid that caring will make you weaker. That seems very sad."

"It's war, kid. It's pretty much built on sad."

"Miss Loch," Dairy asked, looking at the crowd, "are we going to join the people going on board now?"

"Not just yet," Loch said.

"All right." Dairy waited a moment, and when Loch remained silent, he added, "Can I ask why not?"

Then Tern was pressing through the crowd. "Excuse me, pardon me, *hey, chivalry, jerk!* Yeah, I see that look," she added, "try me, these things are steel-toed!" She reached Loch and produced a diamond-shaped leaf covered in gold-inked writing. "Edges," she said, passing it to Loch.

"Still wet?" Loch asked, taking it very carefully.

"Little bit."

"Should I—"

"Do *not* blow on it," Tern said, "unless you want to smear the elven goddess lady in the upper corner."

"Noted." Loch continued to hold the ticket very carefully by the edges.

"Also don't fold it, shake it, or . . . look at it too hard."

"You blew on it," Dairy said, and Tern glared at him. "I'm sorry!"

"You all would just pant all over it and mess up the ink," Tern growled. "I have an expert degree of precision when blowing."

"Please give Hessler my congratulations," Loch said, and had the satisfaction of watching Tern go red. "Now go get to the ship, and tell Desidora and Ululenia to be ready."

Tern stalked back off into the crowd boots-first, glaring at everyone. Loch smiled and held up the ticket to see it in the light. It was, as far as Loch could tell, very official looking.

"Shall we join the crowd now?" Dairy asked.

"Gradually," Loch said. "We don't want to be the last in line, but we need to give our guys time to get into position for the plan."

"Yes," said Dairy, after a moment's hesitation. "I don't think I actually heard what the plan was."

"I've got it written down," Loch said as they started to make their way through the crowd. "I'll show you once we're aboard."

"Oh. All right." Dairy fell in beside her. "You . . . you do miss him, though, right?"

"Wouldn't be human if I didn't, Dairy."

"So you're saying yes?"

"That would be bad luck."

Kail had the airship now semi-definitively known as *Iofegemet* ready for departure by the time the others arrived.

Desidora came alone—well, with her hammer, but that didn't exactly count. Pyvic showed up a few minutes after the alarm sounded, nodding to both of them and taking a spot at the railing while Kail tied down the lines and brought the control console online.

Icy, Tern, and Hessler came along soon after. Icy looked calm, while Tern was wiping bits of gold ink off her fingers.

"How'd it go?" Kail asked.

"Pretty sure I messed up the kerning," Tern said.

"I believe Tern did an admirable job, given her injury and the limited time available."

"How's your arm?" Hessler asked. "Do you need a chair?"

"I'm good," Tern said, swaying in place a little. "Maybe I won't throw up this time!"

"Works for me." Kail thumbed the master control crystal, and the panel hummed. "*Iofegemet*'s ready to go as soon as Ululenia gets here."

"Is she not here?" Icy asked, frowning. "I have not seen her since this morning."

With a flutter of white wings, a dove landed on the railing. *My apologies,* Ululenia said into everyone's mind. *I was delayed.*

"I hope you gave the matter the attention it needed," Hessler said, and then, as everyone on the deck except Desidora turned to look at him, he coughed. "I'm just saying, if you're going to . . . you should really ask her."

"We really shouldn't," Pyvic said.

"Although the fact that you care marks you as good boyfriend material," Tern said. Kail noticed that she was losing color again. "Okay, yes, chair, thank you."

"Everyone hold on." Kail lifted *Iofegemet* up, flashing the signals to people on the ground for a normal departure.

The deck swayed slightly. Tern clomped in her boots and determinedly refused to sit down.

Ahead, the afternoon sky was clear but cool, a perfect day for flying. Off to starboard, the treeship's alarm was still going strong. According to information Ululenia had scrounged up, it should keep going for a few more minutes like that, even if they destroyed or removed the crystals Kail had planted in the elf's pocket.

"Tern, seriously, sit down," Kail called over. "Turbulence in five, four, three . . ."

"Hessler *said* he was going to get me a chair!"

"I thought I was going to *take you to* a chair! Aren't most of them bolted to the deck?"

"And, oh no, turbulence," Kail said, and swung *Iofegemet* hard to starboard.

The deck pitched. Alarms went up on the ground below. Tern fell over with a thud and a curse.

Iofegemet swung out of its flight lane and veered dangerously close to the treeship.

"Oh, dear, what a terrible mistake on my part," Kail deadpanned.

"You *ass!*"

"Timed operation, Tern. You know how it goes." Kail looked over at Ululenia and Desidora "Ladies? Icy?"

Desidora spun Ghylspwr and nodded. Ululenia bobbed her head. Icy stepped into a kind of low, wide-legged crouch with his hands linked together at about knee-level. "We are ready."

He hauled back on the rudder, and *Iofegemet* jerked to a stop.

As she did, Desidora ran directly at Icy, swinging Ghylspwr in an arc off to one side as she did. The love priestess kicked into Icy's linked hands just as the deck jolted, flung her hammer up over her head, and flew across the space between the two ships.

A moment later, she went hammer-first through the hull of the treeship, with a little white bird trailing behind her.

"Subtle," Pyvic said, helping Tern up.

"Right on my bad arm, damn it!"

"You got hit in the chest, not the arm," Kail said without looking over. Alarm bells were ringing down below, and Kail started pushing crystals on the console. "Oh, yes, my, what a terrible mistake."

"And nobody is going to notice that Desidora just knocked a hole in the side of that ship?" Pyvic asked.

"Not if I had the sailwing positioned correctly to block their view from the ground." Kail pointed, then pressed some more buttons to send the right signals down to ground. "Yes, yes, terrible mistake, apologies to everyone, send all fines to the justicars . . ."

"And Ululenia will heal the ship's hull, so nobody aboard is aware of their arrival," Icy added.

Pyvic shrugged. "I'm not going to lie. I'm skeptical."

"This is probably the smoothest one of Loch's plans has ever gone," Kail said, right as the grappling hooks latched onto the railing.

Desidora felt the crash in the strange way that she felt things when Ghylspwr was guiding her. It wasn't that the splinters didn't touch her, but for just one moment, as they went through the hull, all of her was so much more solid than she usually was that nothing seemed to matter.

He pulled her into a roll and brought her up into an acrobatic pose that she would never have managed on her own, hammer over her head, one knee bent, the other leg flung out wide.

Desidora could not believe anyone would ever stand like that voluntarily. With a self-conscious adjustment of her skirts, she brought Ghylspwr down close by her side, so as not to scream to everyone who saw her that she was carrying a large warhammer, while still leaving him available to gently concuss anyone who got in her way.

They had been aiming for the passenger cabins, and as she looked around, she saw a bare room whose sloped wall was marked with sprouting beams and what looked like great leather tarps or sacks. It was lit only by yellow-green veins that pulsed along the wall, marking everything with harsh shadows.

"Not the passenger cabins," she said.

The air shimmered beside her. "No," Ululenia said, turning back to the impressive hole Ghylspwr had made in the hull. "The bladders."

"I . . . may need more context than that," Desidora said, "unless this is where everyone is supposed to go use the privy."

"Air bladders." Ululenia extended a slim white hand to the jagged edges of the hole, and Desidora saw the wood begin to glow. "Air is drawn in through the sails, funneled through the bladders, and then released from the roots at the stern to propel the ship forward."

"Do normal trees have bladders?" Desidora asked, peeking out the doorway. The hallway ahead was deserted, but with the senses of her goddess, she could feel an aura approaching.

"Normal trees do not fly," Ululenia said, and without looking, Desidora heard the hum of magic and the tiny crackle of wood beginning to grow. "The hare has heard the vixens approaching. Its ears are sharp, and it is ready to thump the ground with its feet."

"I'll take care of it." Desidora felt the guard approaching. He was elven, young, and nervous. His aura felt like excitement and longing, a dawning awareness that life on the treeship was not giving him the happiness he had hoped for, but home felt wrong as well. He had dreamed of sailing on smaller treeships, fighting wild fairy folk on the frontier and finding adventure, and he was not sure what to do.

Desidora reached around the corner and tapped him very lightly with Ghylspwr.

He went down bonelessly, and Desidora reached out with Ghylspwr's head and dragged the boy inside. "Ululenia, what's the most adventurous job a young man in the Elflands can reasonably find that has something to do with sailing treeships?"

Ululenia did not look back from where she worked, both hands now pressed to the wood. "The Blackwood Riggers sail small treeships through forest fires so that water druids can stop them from spreading."

"Thank you." Desidora leaned down close to the unconscious elf. "Blackwood Riggers," she whispered.

She had no idea whether it would take, but it was the most a love priestess could reasonably do in such a situation.

"How much longer?" she asked Ululenia.

"The flower blossoms when the seed is ready."

Desidora bit her lip. "All right. I'll get to the central security station and analyze the aura we need to mask our presence. I should have a reasonable picture by the time you're finished."

She made her way quietly down the hallway until she found stairs leading up. She sensed no auras upstairs and headed up to a deck that was brighter, lit by glowing stones set into neat little recesses in the wall that made it seem they had grown there. For all she knew, they had.

Doors along the walls were decorated with inlaid patterns of twining gold and green leaves, with numbers marking each door. "One floor off," Desidora muttered to Ghylspwr. "Kail did a passable job after all."

She noted the numbers, checked the mental map in her head, and then gave up and picked a direction at random. She was moving carefully down the hallway when the outside alarm finally shut off.

That meant they'd finished checking the horrifically sloppy crystals Hessler had concocted, which had indeed been strong enough to overload the security wards. They would now shut down the wards, wait a few moments, and power them back on.

If that happened without Desidora and Ululenia having the proper aural signature, that would be when everyone on the treeship would find out they were here.

With that in mind, she picked up the pace a bit, jogging down the hallway. A wealthy human woman in rich furs stepped out of one of the passenger rooms and stared at her imperiously. "The towels are completely unacceptable," she said, and then Desidora knocked her on the head with Ghylspwr, and she went down just like the elven sailor.

It took a few precious seconds to nudge the woman back inside, and Desidora couldn't help but notice the woman's aura as she did. "You have enough money," she whispered into the woman's ear. "See if the noble who loved to play with feathers is ready to settle down."

She found the door leading to the security center around the next corner, popped the lock off with a sharp rap from Ghylspwr, and stepped inside. A pair of elven security officers turned as she entered. Desidora knocked one of them on the head, then felt herself step to the side without really meaning to as Ghylspwr nudged her out of the way of the second guard's wooden blade. Ghylspwr caught the guard on the chin, and the guard staggered back, then went down as Desidora knocked him on the head as well.

"Stop spending time with people just because they're smart, and start spending time with people who make you happy," she whispered to the first one as she shoved her up against a wall. The second was actually in a happy relationship already, as far as Desidora could tell. "Looking good. Try cuddling more," she said, and then turned to the control console.

It looked a lot like one made from crystals, but everything was wood and roots and leaves instead. A shallow pool of water had roots and—Desidora thought—mushrooms, perhaps, growing in the bottom of it, all blinking or shining in a variety of colors.

Desidora let her eyes unfocus and concentrated on seeing the auras. As a death priestess, she could have affected them with a simple effort of will. Now, she could only see them, but if she could get an accurate picture of what the auras felt like and communicate that to Ululenia, then Ululenia could use her nature magic to give them something that would fool the wards for them.

"I believe this might actually work," she murmured, smiling as she looked at the auras.

Then one of them caught her eye.

"Oh," she said. "Oh, dear."

"Besyn larveth'is!" Ghylspwr agreed.

As he spoke, the alarms roared back to life.

This time, they included a harsh buzzing light that took Desidora by surprise, forcing her to shield her eyes. It was glaring red, almost too bright to look at.

When she forced her eyes open, she realized that the light was actually hundreds of tiny little red motes pouring from vents in the walls and ceiling.

The motes were all swarming around Ghylspwr.

"Hey, Kail, just fly the airship, Kail, I'll have the hard job standing in line with a fake ticket, Kail . . ." Kail hauled *Iofegemet* into a quick twist that made the hull creak as the grappling lines strained against it, then whipped the airship back the other way to free up a little slack. "Get them loose!"

Hessler strained at one of the hooks. "Is there a trick to—"

He broke off abruptly as a crossbow bolt chopped neatly through the line and sank into the hull.

"Nope," Tern said. "Reload me?"

Pyvic was sawing at one with a dagger, and grunted as the line finally snapped. "Little fast with the grappling cables here in Jershel's Nest, aren't they?"

"Yeah, they should have fired some warning flares or offered some guidance first." Alarms started going off again on the treeship off to starboard. They were a nice complement to the ones going off down on the ground. "Ululenia, the hell's going on over there?"

Across the gap, still standing in the now-somewhat-smaller hole in the hull, Ululenia gave Kail a helpless look. "As the bee swarming when the bear jostles—"

"Fine!" Kail moved on. "Justicar, anybody trying to climb up?"

Pyvic leaned over the railing. "Negative."

"Hey, Icy, you got any fancy oath against hurting ropes?"

"I do not." Icy stepped to the railing, rubbed his hands together a few times briskly, and then did *something*. One moment his hand was at his side, and the next, it was out by the railing, fingers pointing and thumb tucked in, and the grappling line had been cut neatly through with smoke coming off the edges.

"Marvelous. One line left. Anybody?"

"I've got it," Hessler said, and moved his hands through a complex incantation before thrusting them out at the last grappling hook.

A sizzling line of fire lashed out, burned through the rope . . . and set the railing on fire.

"Beautifully done, Hessler, no idea why everyone thinks you should just stick to illusions!" Kail called out. The lines were down, and *Iofegemet* was free. "All right, baby, I'll make sure the stupid wizard doesn't light you on fire again. Now, let's just lift the hell out of here and—"

"Kail!" At the sound of Desidora's voice, he looked back at the treeship, and saw the priestess standing by Ululenia, waving frantically.

"Little busy!" he yelled back.

"The ticket checker has a secondary security ward!" she shouted.

"What does that mean?" Kail shouted.

"Aural or procedural?" Tern shouted at the same time.

"Okay, yeah, talk to Tern instead!" Kail forced the controls back into a holding pattern, then grimaced as he saw another grappling hook come sailing over the railing. "Seriously?"

Pyvic starting hacking at the new line, pausing for a moment to look over the edge. "We've got an airship coming up portside!"

Tern and Desidora were yelling back and forth. Kail decided he'd leave them to it. "Hessler, that lighting-ships-on-fire-by-accident thing you just did? Think you can manage another one?"

"You did say that you wanted me to clear the grappling line," Hessler said, "and a small fire seemed preferable to—"

"Great! Tern, Desidora, how we doing?"

"We've figured out what we need to do!" Tern shouted, gesturing impatiently with her good arm while Hessler finished cocking the crossbow.

"Anything I should know?"

"Desidora can't know enough about security wards to do it. I'm going to have to go over."

"Over there? Really?" Kail looked at the gap between the ships, and then at Tern in her crafter's dress, one arm still bound with a sling. "I'll see what I can do."

The other airship came up beside them, and undead sailors leaped across to board *Iofegemet*.

"Are you here for the *suf-gesuf* tournament?" asked a well-dressed young man whose traveling clothes were marked with a noble's family heraldry.

"I've heard people talking about that," Loch said, trying to ignore the multiple alarms going off and the people on the ground below pointing up into the sky. "It sounds exciting." She put a little nobility into her own voice as well, and also pitched it up about an octave. The men usually liked that.

"It is. Only reason we've got so many of our kind on this treeship. Buy-in is two hundred plus twenty." He smiled, showing nice teeth. "I've done well for myself in a few tournaments near Ros-Oanki, so I thought I might try something a little larger. Baron Lechien, at your service."

"A baron! Oh, my." People down in the crowd below were still pointing, and Loch was almost positive she heard the ring of weapons clashing in the sky overhead. "I'm surprised the tournaments are still going on, what with all the trouble with the Empire," she said without looking up.

"I'm afraid I'm a bit out of touch with all that." Lechien chuckled. "Politics and I have an agreed not to bother each other."

"I'm glad that's working for you," Loch said, smiling at the wealthy young nobleman. "What was the buy-in, did you say?"

"Oh, here." Lechien handed her a paper. "Tournament rules, in case you're interested. See you on board." He smiled again and stepped forward, passing his ticket to the elf standing by a pedestal of polished wood.

"We wish you good afternoon," said an elven woman with blue stones set in her cheeks, smiling. "Welcome, and we hope you inform us if there is anything we may do to improve the spirit of your journey. If you have not traveled to the Elflands before, we inform you that all crystal-based magic is forbidden, and if you wish to leave any items behind, it is our privilege to provide storage lockers for you down at the ticket office."

Loch's father had told her how the elves spoke, and how to speak to them without giving offense. "Thank you," she said. "I left all my crystal devices at home."

"Your gesture is appreciated." The elven woman smiled and nodded. "You may present your ticket over there."

Loch nodded in return and moved ahead as the nobleman headed across the gangplank. Behind her, Dairy had been silent for the last little while.

"Something is happening up there," he said.

"Sure is."

"Do you know what's going on?"

"Not at the moment." She smiled at the elven man at the ticket pedestal. "One, plus a guest," she said, gesturing at Dairy, and passed her ticket over.

He placed it on the pedestal, and the pedestal glowed for a moment.

Then it gave an angry chirp.

Desidora watched the undead leap onto her friends' airship.

They were new, many of them freshly killed, and they moved without the jerky clumsiness that would have marked a wizard simply animating the corpses. Their auras were intact, horribly shackled to bodies that no longer wanted them with chains of dark magic.

"No," she whispered.

They swung weapons or bare fists. Some of them were human, while many more were dwarven. From the train wreck, she guessed, and the thought made her stomach twist with revulsion.

Pyvic and Kail were holding the deck, but there were more than a dozen undead warriors. Icy was guarding Tern and Hessler. Hessler had evidently convinced Icy that the undead were no longer living creatures, and Icy was driving the sad creatures back with great sweeping kicks.

"There!" Ululenia pointed through the small hole that was all that remained of the breach Ghylspwr had made in the hull. "Hunter Shenziencis and the bodyguard!"

And with that, Desidora knew who was responsible for the corpses rising from the dead to attack the Republic. The Imperial warrior cast no aura Desidora could see. He might have been masked, or he might have been other than human.

The Hunter should have had no aura at all, like the golems Desidora had fought before . . . and she did not have one of her own, it was true.

But the black chains that bound all the dead warriors ended in thin lines of pain that snaked back to her. She was not even fighting. She was directing the undead, flexing the evil magic that emanated from her to bend them to her will.

"Ululenia," she said, "you need Tern to get Loch aboard?"

The pale woman looked at her, horn flickering in fear. "Yes."

"I will fetch her for you."

Desidora swung Ghylspwr in a fast underhanded arc, took two steps, and leaped through the small hole just as she Ghylspwr pulled her forward.

The Imperial warrior held a magical ax, and he moved with grace and power that bespoke the same guidance Ghylspwr gave Desidora. He blocked Pyvic's swing, and Pyvic dove back desperately from a return strike that shattered his blade. As the Imperial warrior came forward, one of the zombies grabbed Pyvic by the arm, holding him in place.

"*Kutesosh gajair'is!*" the ax cried.

Desidora blasted through the corpse and caught the blow from the ax just behind Ghylspwr's head.

"I believe that's our line," she said, caving in another corpse's skull with a backhanded strike and then coming in low against the Imperial warrior. His ax knocked the blow aside, and he spun with the motion, coming around with a backhanded strike of his own.

Desidora slid under it with skill Ghylspwr had lent her, parrying high so that the ax only sliced through a single strand of auburn hair, and as she came back to her feet, Ghylspwr was already circling down, then up and around to come down with a great overhand strike.

The Imperial warrior blocked it.

That was just what Ghylspwr had hoped.

The Imperial warrior smashed down through the deck, the planks giving way to the force of Ghylspwr's mighty blow, and sank down to his armpits, legs dangling down in the hold below.

"Hey!" Kail yelled, even as he caved in an undead dwarf's skull. "Could you *not?*"

Desidora smashed through one zombie, then blasted aside another. Ahead of her, Icy leaped, kicked a zombie to the ground, twisted in midair, and somehow kicked a zombie's head off before landing. "Hessler assured me that they have no souls," he said as Desidora approached.

"Their spirits are being held in cruel bondage, prevented from reaching the afterlife—"

"Diz!" Kail shouted, kicking a zombie in the knee. "Don't complicate it for the man!"

"Yes, no souls!" Desidora passed Ghylspwr to Tern, who took it with her one good arm. "Here!"

"Why am I holding Ghylspwr?" Tern asked. "And did you see Arikayurichi, the Bringer of Order? He's like Ghylspwr, only Imperial, and I thought maybe they'd be friends, but—"

"Go!"

"What?"

"Ululenia can't do it without you!"

Tern looked at Ghylspwr. "Can you get me across even with me only having one useful arm, big guy?"

"Besyn larveth'is," said Ghylspwr, which sounded less than entirely confident about the matter.

"He won't have to," Hessler said, and took Ghylspwr from Tern. "Come on."

The rangy wizard wrapped one arm around Tern's waist, swung Ghylspwr up over his head, and started running.

"I shall clear you a path!" Icy called.

"But you're terrified of heights!" Tern shouted to Hessler as Icy threw one zombie into another zombie, giving them a brief open lane.

"Yes! Desperately!" he shouted back . . . and flung himself from the airship with Ghylspwr held high.

They crossed the gap together, the wizard and the alchemist, and arced smoothly through the hole in the hull that Ululenia had left open.

Desidora savored a brief smile. However she might feel about losing her old powers, she was a *very* good love priestess, and it was always good to see a match work out.

Then, from behind her, she heard a woman's voice say, "You were the death priestess, were you not? I can see it in your aura."

She turned to see Hunter Shenziencis coming forward, unhampered by the zombies around her. Pyvic and Kail were fighting for their lives across the deck, zombies flanking them both. She had lifted her visor, and her green make-up accentuated her smirk.

"A pity you have lost your powers," she said.

"If she is a Hunter, then she is a golem as well," Icy said, stepping between Desidora and Shenziencis, "which means that she has no soul, correct?" He had assumed a fighting stance.

Shenziencis smiled. *"Clear a path,"* she said, and Desidora felt the magic in the words even as Icy staggered to the side, a thousand tiny snarls of magic twining around him to bend him to the creature's will.

It was his words. The words he had spoken in her hearing contained tiny bits of his own aura, and somehow, with her own magic, Shenziencis flung the words back at him to command him.

Desidora wondered what *she* had said in the last minute or so, even as Ghylspwr appeared in her hand with a flare of magic. She lunged forward.

"You are held in cruel bondage," Shenziencis said, and Desidora staggered and stopped, her joints wracked with agony that locked her in place. "And I imagine you will taste *delicious.*"

"Okay, I need to get to whatever powers the ticket pedestals," Tern said, getting back to her feet. She was pale and staggering, and Ululenia touched her injured shoulder and sent a bit of healing her way. Ghylspwr, and to some extent Hessler, had sheltered her as best they could, but it was still more activity than was healthy for the girl.

"Oh, we made it." Hessler was still on the ground. "Thank you, Ghylspwr. I could clearly feel when our trajectory began to head downward, and I greatly appreciate your efforts to bring us the rest of the way."

"*Kun-kabynalti osu fuir'is,*" Ghylspwr said, and then flashed away, presumably back to where Desidora was fighting the undead.

"You're the best boyfriend ever," Tern said, swaying in place, "which is why I'm giving you a five-count to rest and recover. Then we go find the place that powers the pedestals. Ululenia, you get to the security center. When the power goes out, switch the . . . crap, what are these things, mushrooms? Switch the things we said to switch."

Ululenia sensed Tern's fear and pain and smiled, letting her horn shine brightly in the pale-green light of the room. "As the seasons pass, each blade of grass knows its place. Let us help my Little One aboard."

"Right. Four, five, up and at 'em, big guy."

"I didn't hear *three*," Hessler said, getting back to his feet shakily, followed by, "What are you doing in my pockets?"

"Crystals," Tern said. "Anything with crystals sets off the alarms, so . . ." She held up Hessler's message crystal, smiled, and tossed it out through the hole in the hull.

"I feel I should have been informed about that before I heroically volunteered to leap across the void with you in my arms," Hessler said.

"Remember: best boyfriend ever," Tern repeated, and tossed Hessler's attunable thaumaturgic capacitor out as well.

"The center that nourishes the pedestals is down the hallway." Ululenia pointed. "Hunt well."

Then, with a shimmer, she was a tiny white dove, flapping down the hallway in the other direction and up the stairs.

The treeship was completely unlike an airship. Ululenia had been on them before, and always came away in awe. Humans sought to master magic, with crystals and daemons bending to their will. The elves worked *with* magic instead, and the harmony touched her heart.

She felt the treeship's living trunk, the energy of life that dwelt in the walls, even the luminescent organs that lit up the hallway, all of it the magic of life.

It was like being back in the forest. Ululenia had not realized how much she had missed that feeling.

Or perhaps, she admitted, she was only feeling sentimental because she had lain with a virgin earlier in the morning and broadened the young woman's world a little.

She shimmered back into her human shape as she reached the security center. The elven guards lay unconscious in the corner where Desidora had left them, and the pool flickered in countless colors as it sent information from all over the ship.

She knew that Desidora could understand the energies here at an intellectual level. Ululenia, though, could feel them as a part of herself. She reached out, touched the console, and smiled. While she might not have been able to alter the system herself, any more than she could force a deer to grow an extra lung, she could certainly make the changes Tern asked.

She turned to close the door, and felt the other mind lunging at her even as she saw black wings framing shining stag's antlers in the hallway.

The elven man frowned and looked down at the ticket.

"Is there a problem?" Loch asked, smiling and not looking up at the sound of battle above.

"The pedestal seems to be having some difficulty reading your ticket," the elf said, frowning.

"That's odd," Loch said, and then gasped. "Oh, I may have spilled kahva on it this morning, but I thought I got it all off. Would that do it?"

The elf smiled, though it was a bit more guarded than it had been before. "Perhaps that is it. I will try it again."

"Whatever you feel best," Loch said, and started reading the rules for the *suf-gesuf* tournament.

"You are wiser than most," Shenziencis said as Desidora sank to her knees, teeth clenched to hold back a scream. "Few have even heard of the Hunters, and fewer still would recognize their armor."

"You . . . are no . . . Hunter," Desidora gasped. She could feel the words sliding into Shenziencis as she said them, knew it was dangerous to give the creature more power to use against her, but as it was, she was already helpless.

Her own aura was locked down, shackled with her own words flung back at her. Had she been a death priestess . . .

Shenziencis laughed. "Look at you. So desperate to return to the darkness that you once hated?" She stepped forward. "No, priestess, I am no Hunter. When a Hunter dared come to my domain, those I shared words with tore him apart, and I took what was left for myself." Her smile was cold and superior and not human in the slightest. "Its weapons have served me well against any of my cousins who dared get in my way."

"You are a fairy creature," Icy said, struggling to move forward.

"The Temple of Butterflies was not always home to the Empire's monks, priestess." She leaned over Desidora, and her jaw unhinged a great deal further than seemed possible as she said, "Every soul lost to the frigid waters of the Iceford was *mine*."

Through the pain, Desidora had a flash of realization. "You." She pushed the words out through gritted teeth. "Queen of the Cold River."

Shenziencis paused, and her gold-shaded eyes narrowed even as her great gaping mouth hung open. Deep in the throat, Desidora saw a light shining in the same color as Ululenia's horn. "You *have* learned a great deal," she said, the words distorted by her impossible jaw.

Then she frowned. "And where did your hammer go?"

Ghylspwr blasted into her from behind, the ancient magic cracking her Hunter's armor and sending her crashing to the ground.

Justicar Pyvic held the hammer in a two-handed grip and looked down at her.

"Say nothing," Desidora gasped, even as the pain that locked her in place suddenly vanished. "She eats words!"

He raised an eyebrow, shut his mouth, and stepped forward to smash Ghylspwr into Shenziencis again.

The Hunter's armor was cracked, straps hanging loose, and she hissed at Pyvic from the deck. "Will you strike me down as I lay helpless?"

For a moment, Desidora feared he would answer.

But Loch had chosen well. As much as she loved her witty rejoinders and clever banter, Isafesira de Lochenville had chosen for herself a man who knew when to let his actions speak.

The armor shattered under the next blow. Ringmail scattered across the deck, greaves and plates and buckles spraying in every direction.

From the wreckage, a serpent the size of a man—with a woman's face—darted away, leaving only a husk of empty armor.

Pyvic raised Ghylspwr, and then twisted against his will, his strike turning into a block as he caught the Imperial warrior's ax before it cut him down from behind. The effort sent him stumbling back nevertheless, and the Imperial warrior, splinters of wood still dropping from his shoulders, spun his ax as he stepped in to follow up.

"Ghylspwr!" Desidora cried, and in a flash, he was in her hands, and however fast the Imperial warrior was, it wasn't fast enough to turn that quickly.

"*Kutesosh gajair'is!*" Ghylspwr's blow smashed into his breastplate from behind—knocking him not down but *up*—and he sailed from the airship. He should have fallen to his death, but the ax wrenched the warrior's arm to the side, and he crashed instead into his own airship.

"Kail," Desidora called over, and threw Ghylspwr. "I believe it is time for us to leave."

"Fine with me!" Kail yelled. Ghylspwr blasted one of the zombies that was on top of him, then flared back into Desidora's hand. With the rest of the team relatively safe, he looked for the serpent-beast only to see zombies leaping back into their own airship with the thing that was Shenziencis in their arms.

She smashed in the skulls of the few remaining zombies on *Iofegemet*, covering her shuddering and shaking with grunts as she struck, and tried to forget the feeling of the dark coils wrapped around her aura.

And how once again, it had fallen to another to save her.

"That should do it," Tern said, stepping back from what she swore was some kind of fern covered in slime. The lights in the room flickered, then came back to normal. "Now, if Ululenia swapped the mushrooms or whatever the hell they are, Loch should be good to go."

"You're welcome, by the way," Hessler said, wiping his hands on his robes.

"Only had one arm," Tern said.

"A fact that is both compelling and convenient," Hessler said. "I suppose we should join up with Ululenia."

They headed back down the hallway. An elven guard headed their way, and Hessler covered them with a cloaking field until he was gone.

"You are very good at that," Tern said.

"Cloaking fields are more difficult than the layman really expects," Hessler said as they started walking again, "given that the caster has to decide whether to make the body of the target perfectly transparent—which gives more reliable cloaking, but also risks severe damage to the target if the spell goes awry—or create a bubble that projects an image of what a viewer would see if the object inside the bubble were not present, which is far more difficult, but . . ." He broke off. "I mean, thank you."

"You're welcome." She leaned against him, letting him take the lead for a little bit. "You don't need to do more than illusions to impress me."

"What about to save you?" Hessler asked. "My illusions nearly got you killed."

"Overloading the railway bindings and freeing the fire-daemon didn't help either," Tern said.

"So what?" Hessler asked, and she heard the pain in his voice. "I should just stick to the figments instead of trying anything *beyond* me?"

"I *like* the figments," Tern said, "and you were plenty useful. You could maybe worry less about impressing me and just keep doing what you were doing . . . which *was* impressing me."

He looked away, flushing. "I didn't say it was to impress you."

"You didn't have to. I am a sensitive and caring girlfriend."

They reached the stairs up to the passenger deck and started up.

Then the door opened quickly, and Ululenia stepped through and closed the door behind her. She was out of breath, her pale hair askew and her horn not shining. She held up a hand to stop them, and it was red and blistered.

"What's wrong?" Hessler asked.

Ululenia listened for a moment, looking at the closed door as though she could see something behind.

Then she turned and gave them a thin smile. "Nothing. Everything is going as planned."

Another elven guard was moving very casually into a position on Loch's left.

"Ma'am?" Dairy asked beside her.

"All within the parameters of the plan," she murmured.

"Perhaps one more time, then," the first elf said, "and then I am afraid that the situation will be outside my ability to help you. However, you may be assured that one of our other experts will ensure that your needs are met."

One of the other experts had just taken up a polite stance that ensured Loch would be blocked if she made a run for it.

"As you say," she said, and gestured for him to try again. He placed the ticket on the pedestal.

The pedestal blinked, went silent for a moment, and then finally chimed happily.

"Ah, good," Loch said, and swept past the elf with a smile.

"It is our hope that you enjoy your trip," he said, still seeming a little doubtful, as Loch crossed the gangplank with Dairy in tow and stepped onto the deck of the great treeship.

"Gawk for me," she murmured. "How are Kail and the others doing?"

"They're flying off," Dairy said. "The alarms are still going, though, and there's another airship. And part of the railing is on fire."

"As long as they're leaving, we're good."

"Is that part of the plan?" Dairy asked with a little edge in his voice that wouldn't have been there a few months ago.

"Right. I was going to show you the plan once we were aboard." She fished into her pocket and came out with a slip of paper. "Here you go." She passed it over.

Dairy unfolded the paper as Loch started walking. "Wait."

She took in the treeship. The deck was spacious and crowded even still. The wood was light underfoot and dark at the railings, shining as though it had been smoothed, though it gripped her feet like living bark with every step. Elves leaned at the railing, chatting happily, the crystals in their cheeks sparkling. Humans, some white, some Urujar, and a few even Imperial, looked at the treeship curiously while their servants carried the luggage aboard.

Fairy creatures walked the deck as well. A pixie fluttered past, her wings shining in all the colors of the rainbow, while a centaur, elven from the waist up and deer from the waist down, trotted after her, laughing, a crown of leaves glowing around his head.

"Ma'am. Loch." Dairy came up beside her. "All this says is 'Get in. Get book. Get out.'"

"I was unconscious this time yesterday," Loch said. "What did you expect?"

"I *expect* you to surrender," Princess Veiled Lightning said as she stepped out from around the corner and came at Loch, hands crackling with blue energy, "but I *hope* you fight."

Seventeen

Dairy," Loch said, "if you would?"

Dairy stepped into Veiled Lightning's path, and the Imperial princess reached out, the first two fingers of her hand straightened to a point that shone with radiant azure light.

She hit Dairy, and energy played around him, sputtered, and died out.

"I was pretty sure that qualified as magic," Loch said. "Where's your muscle?"

"Only pretty sure?" Dairy asked.

"My bodyguard and Attendant Shenziencis were covering your airship, on the chance that you would attempt to flee that way." Veiled Lightning tried to sidestep Dairy, then glared when he moved to block her again. "But I knew you would come here."

"Here's where the book is." Loch smiled. "Remember how I tried to surrender last time, and your idiot bodyguard came at me anyway and crashed the train and killed innocent people?"

Veiled Lightning glared. "You crashed the train yourself to escape him. At least have the honor to own your murders."

"Oh, right, you'd already gone down by that point. Is that what Gentle Thunder told you? I guess he guards you from unpleasant truths. Did he hide the fact that he and Shenziencis killed a justicar to find out I was at Ajeveth, or were you there for that one?" Loch took a quick glance at the crowd of humans and elves and fairy creatures starting to form around them. "Dairy, I'll need a moment."

With that, she stepped back, cut politely through the crowd, and walked briskly toward the treeship's main hall.

"Ma'am?"

"All part of the plan, Dairy," she called without looking back.

"I *saw* the plan!"

And then she heard the sound of punches flying and lightning crackling.

The crowd watched her walk through the great arched doorway but did nothing to stop her, though murmurs were moving around the deck. She guessed she had five minutes at most.

The main hall had windows running along its sides and a raised stage at the far end. The overhead chandeliers were formed from what looked like petrified sap, shining with the pale light of a fall afternoon. At night, guests who did not wish to dine in their cabins could come to the main hall for meals suited to human, elven, and fairy-creature appetites, after which the chairs and tables were removed to make room for drinks and dancing. Loch guessed that the *suf-gesuf* tournament would be held in here as well.

The bar was open at the moment, and those with strong livers or a fear of flying were already taking advantage of the unlimited service, which gave Loch enough of a crowd to lose the eyes.

Then, by the windows on the right, Loch saw Irrethelathlialann holding a wineglass and speaking to a massive, red-bearded man whose fine robes could not completely hide the muscles underneath. He looked human, but the ship carried both humans and very dangerous things that *looked* human, and Loch knew which group she'd put the red-bearded man in.

She stepped into a crowd of laughing human nobles, laughed along with them, and spotted Baron Lechien, the noble who'd been ahead of her in the line. "Hello again," she said, smiling and leaning in a little. "Signed up for the tournament already?"

"Just did, yes." He blinked, having already forgotten her, but Loch was smiling, so he went along with it. "And you?"

She put herself opposite the noble. The crowd outside was getting louder, and elven guards with wooden blades and leaf-armor were making their way to the door with the purposeful, no-eye-contact body language that all discreet guards who worked for wealthy people learned to cultivate. "I was considering signing up. Sounds more interesting than looking at a bunch of trees, and it's either that or listen to everyone complain about things going to hell with the Imperials." She looked at the wealthy Imperial man who'd been talking to the noble, shrugged with a bit more shoulder than usual, and smiled helplessly. "No offense."

"None taken." The Imperial man wore rose-colored spectacles that matched his flowing silk robe, and he smiled genially while staring at Loch's chest. "Who knows what foolishness our two countries will put themselves through before returning to the beneficial friendship we all want?"

"Exactly." Loch leaned against Lechien a little. "Where do I sign up? Might as well spend the family inheritance *somehow* on this trip."

Lechien put his hand on the small of her back while the Imperial man pointed down the hall toward the stage. "Right down there."

"Great!" She smiled, looked past him, and saw Irrethelathlialann staring directly at her. He stepped away from the large red-bearded man he was talking to and gestured to one of the guards who was passing by. "Oh, crap. Really, he can't just let it go?" As the Imperial man and Lechien looked at her in confusion, she sighed. "The elf over there, the rich one with the green cheeks? He's been bothering me ever since my family did business with him last year. You know how it is—don't want to cause offense, but he refuses to take the hint that I'm more interested in . . ." She looked over at Lechien and lowered her lashes a little. ". . . men."

"Well, I wouldn't worry about that," Baron Lechien said, puffing out his chest a bit. The Imperial man chuckled.

"I think I'll go sign up," Loch said, easing herself from Lechien's arm with a smile. "Hope to run into you both later."

Somewhere, her sister was laughing. Loch wanted a long hot bath.

She strutted through the main hall, shoulders and hips tossing off the scent of money and power with every step.

Behind her, Irrethelathlialann called, "Well, fancy meeting—" and then broke off.

"I think the lady would rather be left alone," Baron Lechien said, and Loch heard the sound of robes swishing and boots stomping manfully.

She kept going.

Behind her and to the left, a window shattered, and people shouted in surprise as someone hit the ground. "Sorry!" Dairy cried, and Loch nodded to herself without looking up.

"Isafesira!" came the yell from by the window, and Loch spared a single glance to look around like everyone else was doing to see who this Isafesira person was and what trouble she might have gotten herself into. In the corner of her vision, elven guards were coming in from side doors on both sides.

She reached the main stage, ignored the stairs, and vaulted up with an effort that made her wounded side pull a little. The pretty elven woman behind the signup table looked at her with polite surprise.

"I'd like to sign up for the tournament," she said, and as the elven woman opened her mouth, Loch unbuckled her belt and dropped her sword on the table. "This is the Nine-Ringed Dragon, legendary sword of the Empire. I believe it should cover the buy-in. Agreed?"

"Ah—"

The elven guards were coming up the stairs, although some of them had moved to stop Veiled Lightning, judging by the sound of electricity crackling in the main hall and people yelling in surprise. "The sword is genuine. I swear it. If you later believe its worth to be less than the buy-in, you may ask me to cover the difference, but I will be greatly offended if you refuse this, and it will adversely affect my enjoyment of my trip, now do we have an agreement and where do I sign?"

The elven woman stammered, and finally, as the guards reached the stage, produced a page and a pen. "Well, then, I suppose—"

"That's a yes." Loch grabbed the pen and wrote her name just as half a dozen swords pressed gently into her back.

"We are not technically in the Elflands yet," Irrethelath-lialann said coldly from behind her, "so it would probably break some kind of law to kill you."

Loch turned around extremely slowly. "Probably," she said, smiling. "So what do you intend to do, then?"

Irrethelathlialann stepped past the elven guards until his face was just inches from Loch's. "I can think of *nothing* worse for you," he murmured, "than to see you ejected from this treeship and tossed back into that little town, watching help-lessly as I leave and your pathetic country goes off to war."

Loch blinked. "That *does* sound bad."

She very slowly lifted a hand and showed Irrethelathlial-ann the card in it.

"It also violates rule seven, that no member of the tourna-ment be denied admission once payment has been accepted until such time as he-slash-she has dropped out, or the tour-nament is complete."

The elven woman at the table behind Loch squeaked.

Irrethelathlialann closed his eyes and pressed his lips together, and Loch smiled.

"See you at the table."

Captain Thelenea of the treeship whose name Loch had never quite figured out was a tall elven woman whose crystals glit-tered like angry diamonds in her age-lined cheeks. Her skin was darker than many of the elves Loch had seen, closer to olive green than the mint or emerald she saw on most of them. She wore a long black coat and trousers rather than the robes most elves favored, and the sword that hung at her waist was most definitely metal and not wood.

"Am I to understand," she said, standing with her arms behind her back while Loch sat flanked by a pair of guards, "that you wish to participate in the *suf-gesuf* tournament despite having boarded my ship illegally?"

"The rules say that the tournament is open to anyone on the ship," Loch said. "It specifies nothing about having to purchase a ticket."

Irrethelathlialann stalked across the room, his robes flaring. "You think you can game the system, Isafesira? You're in *my* homeland now."

"Oh, we crossed the border? Glad to hear it." Loch grinned. "Too late to dump me back in port." As Irrethelathlialann shook his head, Loch's grin faded. "Stings a bit when it's *your* country's rules being sidestepped, doesn't it?"

Captain Thelenea raised a gloved hand in Loch's direction. "I'll refund the buy-in, pay for your passage back to Republic territory, drop the trespassing and fraud charges, and give you a discount on your next *legally purchased* ticket."

"You can keep the buy-in," Loch said, "and forget about the discount—if you have Ethel here return the elven manuscript he stole. It's the only reason I'm here."

Irrethelathlialann laughed. "You have committed an act of war against the Elflands—"

"And *you* are the reason that act of war against the Elflands is on *my ship*," Captain Thelenea cut him off, "a fact you neglected to warn me about when you took advantage of my hospitality."

Irrethelathlialann smiled thinly. "I was on the Dragon's business, Captain. Is it your wish to get in the way of that business?"

The silence hung between the two elves for a long moment.

"She plays," Captain Thelenea finally said, and Irrethe-lathlialann shook his head and turned away with a snarl. "The sword is good for two hundred plus twenty, so she starts with eleven thousand." She turned and gave Loch a hard smile. "Anyone confident enough to bluff her way onto a ship to enter a tournament *must* be a professional, and I'm permitted to place bounties on professionals. Five thousand to whoever knocks her out," she said, and smiled at Irrethelathlialann. "At which point, Ambassador, she's all yours to dump off in the Republic."

"You're making a mistake, Captain," he said, the stones in his cheeks glittering balefully.

Captain Thelenea kept smiling, one hand on her sword. "And hopefully you will remember the kind of mistakes I tend to make next time you consider bringing trouble onto my ship."

Irrethelathlialann stalked out the door and slammed it behind him without replying. The captain waved to the guards flanking Loch, and they bowed and left as well, shutting the door much more quietly.

"I regret causing you difficulty," Loch said, giving a small seated bow.

"No, you don't." Captain Thelenea gave Loch a flat-eyed look.

Loch tried not to smile. "I am pained at the necessity, then?"

Captain Thelenea sighed. "For your sake, Urujar, I hope you either play well enough to win or poorly enough to lose before Irrethelathlialann tires of my rules." She fixed Loch with a look. "I recommend caution."

"It is appreciated."

"You are welcome to enjoy a complimentary cabin on the passenger deck. It should be large enough for you, your

servant, and any other servants my crew might have mistak-
enly missed during check-in . . . since they came in through
the hole in the side of my ship." Captain Thelenea picked up
the card with the tournament rules on it, twirled it through
her fingers, and then flicked it away so quickly that the card
stuck in the wall, quivering. "Now, it is my solemn hope that
you feel free to get the hell out of my quarters."

Loch got the hell out of her quarters.

"So the good news," said Kail to nobody in particular, "is that
we know who made all the zombies."

He was piloting the now significantly damaged *Iofegemet*
toward Heaven's Spire. With luck, a good headwind, and no
further disintegration of the main deck, they could reach the
floating capital city soon.

Icy and Pyvic were doing what they could to repair the
shattered deck and burned railing, while Desidora leaned
against a non-burned section of railing looking moody and
contemplative.

"I don't suppose we know what she is, exactly?" Kail
added.

"Naga," Desidora said without looking back from the
railing. "Very powerful. Most of their magic is tied to the
voice."

"Didn't figure it was tied to her arms, what with her being
a snake and all." Kail took a reading and adjusted course
slightly. "So we kill her, we stop the zombies, right? No more
war with the Empire, everybody calms down."

"Just like they calmed down after Heaven's Spire scorched
several acres of farmland with a blast of fire from the sky?"

Pyvic asked, pulling a plank into place and then rolling his eyes as Icy drove a nail into the plank with the palm of his hand to secure it.

"We were unable to locate a hammer," Icy said by way of explanation, driving another nail in, "except Ghylspwr, who was somewhat insulted by the suggestion that he be used to drive in nails, and yes, I concur with your assessment. The Republic will continue its offensive, and the Empire, if indeed it had no hand in these attacks, will defend itself from perceived aggression."

"Why do you say *if*?" Pyvic grabbed another plank.

Icy was silent for a moment as he drove another nail into place. Finally, he looked over at Desidora. "Are my concerns groundless?"

"No." She still didn't look back.

Kail looked from Icy to Desidora, and then at Pyvic, who shrugged. "Care to share?"

"The body is composed of energy centers," Desidora said, "called chakras. There are . . . well, the exact number depends upon how you classify them—"

"Seven," said Icy.

"Of course, that is the commonly agreed-upon number, plus some ancillary energy centers that may or may not—"

"Or simply seven," said Icy, "since I have been meditating since the age of five and am well-versed in chakras." He turned to Kail. "Fairy creatures are tied to one of the chakras in ways that may or may not be evident. Ululenia manifests her abilities through the brow, or third-eye, chakra." He touched his forehead. "Shenziencis manifests hers through the throat chakra."

"That fits with her using people's words against them," Pyvic said. "What's the problem?"

"The chakras at the top or base of the spine tend to radiate outward," Desidora said, "while those closer to the middle of the body stay closer. It makes sense for Ululenia to be able to affect minds at a distance, since her magic manifests through the brow."

Kail nodded slowly as he got it. "But those undead attacks have been happening over at the border while naga-lady has been out here attacking us."

"We know she's involved somehow." Pyvic stood up, dusting sawdust from his knees as he did. "I'm inclined to take her down first and try to determine how she increased her effective control range later."

"Assuming that whatever extends her power does not also make it impossible for us to take her down." Desidora's voice held a hint of bitterness. "If I were—"

"Does Tasheveth ever get tired of your 'If I were still a death priestess' thing?" Kail asked. "I'm just asking for her. The rest of us are great with it."

"Kail." Pyvic gave him a look. "Uncalled for."

"I'm sorry," Desidora said after a long, quiet moment. "I'm sorry I hurt you. I'm sorry I let Silestin hurt you. I should have seen that he was using the *lapiscaela* to bind the souls of prisoners in the Cleaners. I should have read it in your aura and broken the binding upon you before Silestin ever used it." She turned to him, then, and her voice caught. "But I didn't. I missed it."

"Lo and behold," Kail said, "being a death priestess doesn't magically solve everything."

She blinked, forced a smile, and looked away. "Then I guess it's a good thing I have the hammer."

Icy coughed. "The one piece of information we do have regarding Shenziencis is that she has served as attendant at the Temple of Butterflies for as long as anyone can remember. If she was the Queen of the Cold River, then her presence at the temple may predate the Empire."

"The temple is older than the Empire itself?" Pyvic asked, and Icy nodded.

"Like Heaven's Spire, it was left behind by the ancients."

"Speaking of Heaven's Spire," Kail said, checking his control console for the third time, "we may have a situation."

Pyvic looked over. "What's wrong with Heaven's Spire?"

"I'll let you know," said Kail, gesturing out at the empty sky ahead of them, "as soon as we find it."

The cabin that Captain Thelenea had provided was a spacious multi-roomed suite with a full bar. Loch imagined that somewhere, Kail was seething with jealousy and not knowing why.

"We were just lucky Ululenia was able to give us the auras," Tern said. She was sitting in an overstuffed chair that seemed to be made from living wood and a lot of very expensive moss, stirring a bright-pink drink with her straw. "The plan got thrown a bit with us here instead of Desidora."

"Have you seen the plan?" Dairy asked. He sat on the edge of the bed, drinking milk. Loch supposed that some things didn't change.

"I was given to understand that it included a number of contingencies," Hessler said from behind Tern, and Dairy looked at him, then at Loch, and laughed despite himself.

"We're good until either the tournament ends . . . or I do." Loch took a sip of an elven white wine that was a little too sweet for her, closer to a dessert wine than she liked, but apparently one couldn't get a good red in the Elflands for love or money. "The tournament starts tomorrow, and as long as it's running, there'll be a crowd in the main hall. That gives the rest of you plenty of time to hit Irrethelathlialann's room before I run out of chips."

"How can you be certain he has it in his room," Ululenia asked, "instead of in the captain's safe?" She lounged on the massive bed, twirling a flower through her fingers, drinking nothing for a change.

"The captain and our elf aren't on the best of terms, apparently." Loch sipped the too-sweet wine again. "She's not happy that he brought trouble onto her ship, and I don't see her agreeing to store more trouble in the ship's safe."

"That's a little weak," Ululenia said.

"So are the drinks, but this is the only way we get them," Loch said, and raised her wineglass. "If it's not in the room, we look at the safe, but the room's easier."

Ululenia didn't look happy, but she nodded nevertheless.

"How are you going to keep yourself in the tournament?" Tern asked, and everyone looked at her. She pointed at Loch with a straw. "Hey, *I* didn't sign up for a tournament with a five-thousand-chip bounty on my head. I assume you can take the idle rich, no problem, but some of these players are here *just* for this tournament, as it's one of the biggest ones they do this year. They're professionals!"

"You can't cheat," Ululenia said, still twirling the flower through her fingers with her eyes closed. "Half the people playing will be fairy creatures. The main hall will have wards in place to prevent anyone from reading a player's mind, and I imagine they'll have illusion magic locked down as well."

"I've played a few hands of *suf-gesuf* in my time," Loch said. "I'll stay alive until you have the book."

"What about me?" Dairy asked, finishing the last of his milk and setting the glass down hard on the table.

"What *about* you, kid?" Hessler asked after an awkward moment of silence.

"I can't open locks or break wards. I can't pick pockets. I don't even lie very well." Dairy balled one hand into a fist, glaring at the floor. "I defeated Bi'ul, so the world is safe. There's no more prophecy anymore, so why am I even *here*?"

Loch looked at Ululenia, but the unicorn was suspiciously silent. Hessler didn't jump in, either.

"You're here because you wanted to be on our side," Loch finally said. "Don't worry. We'll find something for you to do."

Dairy swallowed. "Because you feel sorry for me?"

"Because you're one of us," Tern said, and Loch saw her elbow Hessler with her good arm. "For now, you're getting Loch drinks during the tournament. Nobody gambles well when they're thirsty."

Loch raised her glass of too-sweet wine to Tern, then finished it off. "That'll do for a start."

Eighteen

LADIES, GENTLEMEN, AND BEINGS TO WHOM GENDER CLASSIFICATIONS do not apply," Captain Thelenea said from the main stage, "it is my pleasure to welcome you to the Elflands Classic *Suf-Gesuf* Tournament. Play begins in five minutes. Anyone not ready to play at that time will forfeit their place in the tournament." She glanced through the crowd at Loch as she said it, and Loch cracked a smile and nodded slightly.

"You look very nice, ma'am," said Dairy.

"Thank you." The treeship staff had helpfully provided a change of clothes for Loch. Evidently the sword was worth enough for them to feel guilty taking it as the buy-in. She'd changed into a simple white blouse with loose flowing sleeves, and a burgundy skirt slit high enough to let her walk comfortably. "I thought I might stand out less this way than if I were wearing riding leathers."

Dairy coughed. "You're not going to, ah, tear parts of your clothes off again, like you did at the Archvoyant's ball, are you?"

Loch smirked. "I'll try to avoid it." Most of the players wore hats or spectacles, anything that would hide their expressions. "Where are we at?"

"Right over here, ma'am," Dairy said, gesturing, and Loch made her way to one of the many round tables that filled the main hall. They were lined with thin moss instead of felt, and the chairs were made from thin green wood that flexed oddly when she sat down.

"Isafesira de Lochenville?" The dealer was narrow-faced even for an elf, and one of the crystals in his cheek had been cut out, leaving a thin scar. The other glowed angry red.

"That's me." Loch smiled.

The dealer didn't. He slid over a stack of chips as other players sat down at the table. "We crossed over into the Elflands, which means we're playing by elven rules." He looked around the table, glaring at everyone about equally. "For those unfamiliar with the system, that means that a flush is not a valid hand, but a concordance is, and holds a similar rank, just above a straight and below four of a kind. That would be four numbered cards, one from each suit, with different numbers showing, plus a single face card that must come from one of your two hidden cards. We also do not recognize a full house as you do when playing by Republic or Imperial rules, counting it only as three of a kind. Does anyone have any questions so far?"

Loch looked at the other players. One was an elven woman whose face was obscured by a feathered half-mask. Her hair was cropped short, as though she'd seen military service. Next to her was a fat dwarf wearing an enormous floppy hat. Next to *him* was the Imperial man she'd flirted with earlier, still wearing his smoked spectacles, and next to him was Baron Lechien, her noble defender.

The last seat was empty.

The dealer glared at them all for a moment, letting the silence drag out, and then continued. "Four shared cards, two open, two hidden. Three rounds of betting, once after the first two shared and the redraw, then on the third shared, and finally on the fourth. The maximum raise is listed here." He jabbed a thin, ash-stained finger at a board by his seat at the table. "It increases along with the minimum ante every half hour. We play with a half-hour break every two hours, until few enough players remain that we can form a finals table. Now, and for the last time, any questions?"

Princess Veiled Lightning slid into the last empty seat. "My apologies for my tardiness," she said, flashing them all a thin smile.

"You are of course forgiven," the dealer said sourly, and shoved the chips her way.

"Glad you could make it," Loch said.

Veiled Lightning glanced over. "You play games while innocent people die on both sides of this fight."

Loch raised an eyebrow. "Says the woman who just sat down to join us."

"I heard about your bounty. I thought I might earn a little money as long as I am here."

"Earning money must be a nice change for you, princess. Earn enough, and they might let you buy back the Nine-Ringed Dragon. I had to use it for collateral."

Little bits of moss peeled away from the table under Veiled Lightning's fingernails. "You—"

"If you two ladies are finished," the dealer growled, "perhaps we might all play a hand or two of *suf-gesuf*."

"I was just waiting for you to deal. Dairy?" Loch slid a chip into the center of the table with everyone else. "I do believe I'm going to need something stronger than wine."

Tern peeked around the corner and looked down the luxury-deck hallway. "Clear."

"Unless they are invisible or shapeshifted into something small you are overlooking," Ululenia said from behind her.

Tern looked over her shoulder and glared. *"Probably clear."*

"The tournament has started," Hessler said. "I doubt we'll have a better opportunity."

Tern stepped out around the corner and walked down the hallway with as much confidence as she could muster. The carpet looked like grass but felt more like thick, spongy moss beneath her feet. It damped the impact of her boots on the ground, which was unfortunate, because she felt like a little confidence-stomping could have made her feel better right then.

She reached the door to the elf's room. It was locked with a more sophisticated version of the lock on their own suite, something analogous to crystal magic but based on the plant magic they used instead. It was built to respond to a leaf-key they'd been given.

"This'd be a lot easier if the elves would just use crystals like the rest of us," she muttered. "Cloak me."

"I don't think they can," Hessler said, throwing the cloak up around Tern. "Loch said something about it back in Jershel's Nest. The elf seemed to imply that his people specifically avoided crystal-based magic in favor of such ungainly and unpredictable—"

"The magic of nature is not unpredictable," Ululenia cut in. "It is simply less abrasive. Magic based on crystals emits an aura that elves and my kind can both feel. For those like me, it feels like kinship, since we sprang forth from such magic. For the elves, however, it is an overwhelming noise that affects how they think."

"That sounds creepy," Tern said, using a tiny knife to test the edges of the lock. "Could you have maybe softened that with a metaphor about trees or flowers or something?"

"As the wolf cannot think when dropped into a vat of perfume," Ululenia said dryly.

"Okay, close enough. Oh, ew. Most locks don't spit sap all over my picks."

"I suppose that explains why they're so reclusive," Hessler said, lowering his voice as an elven servant came around the corner. Everyone stayed still until the servant opened a door down the hall and went inside. "In any good-sized city, there are enough crystal artifacts to affect how they think."

"What do you think that's like?" Tern rubbed a bit of sap off her pick, then slid it in. She felt the edge of *something* that was probably the bit that reacted to the leaf-key, and while the specifics were completely alien to her, there were only so many ways to keep a door closed. "Is it like being really drunk, or like chewing some of the berries they tell you not to chew in gardening classes?"

The others were silent behind her.

"Gardening classes?" Hessler finally said.

"Mother thought that if I had something to do with my hands, I might be less interested in mixing chemicals and picking locks. And speaking of the former, I'm about done trying this thing." She produced a vial from one sleeve and small case of powder from one of her many dress pockets.

"You're going to want to back up a bit. The smoke really stings your eyes."

"You realize they'll know that someone broke into the elf's suite," Hessler said.

"That was probably a given as soon as the lock started oozing sap," Tern said, and sprinkled a bit of the powder into the vial. She sealed the vial, shook it, and reached into another pocket for a pair of tongs. Using her good arm, she put the vial in the tongs, and then held it to the lock. "Knock, knock."

The lock hissed and crackled and blackened as the acid ate through the vial, then it. In a few moments, that whole section of door was a smoking mess. Tern grinned. "No lock I can't beat."

"You ate through the lock with acid," Hessler said.

"I probably would've gone for picking it had I not been still weak from being shot in the chest with a crossbow bolt because *somebody* gave them aiming support."

"And the acid absolutely counts as a win," Hessler added.

"Glad to hear it." Tern kicked the door open.

"I'm so pleased you could join us," said a very large red-bearded man in a chair in the middle of the room, fingers steepled, as elves on either side of the door drew swords.

Captain Nystin got off the airship in Ros-Oanki with nothing left.

His men were either dead or in custody. The new recruits would be explaining to a team of justicars that this had all been part of a covert operation. The veterans would be sitting silently, waiting for a release order that would never come.

Nystin had served the Republic for a good quarter of a century. He'd killed his share of daemons and worse. He'd fought wars that earned no medals and would appear in no history books, all to ensure the safety of his country. And just like that, Isafesira de Lochenville had taken it all from him.

He vanished into the crowd in the docks, a stolen cloak covering the wool shirt whose stains marked it too clearly as having been worn under armor. He had ditched the armor but kept his crystal-tipped mace and silver daggers. They could be traced, but he'd lived too long to go without some way to defend himself.

The puppeteers had a show running near the ticket office, and a larger crowd than normal had gathered around the stage. They looked angry.

"The important thing is that everyone keeps doing their part," the manticore insisted, flapping his wings indignantly.

"Obviously, we aren't going to win this war if we panic and stop trusting our government," the griffon added.

"Where's Heaven's Spire?" someone in the crowd shouted. Nystin stopped walking and looked over casually.

"Well, a general doesn't explain his every move to the privates," the griffon said, stammering a little, "and I think wherever the capital city has moved to, it's acting for the good of the Republic."

"They're running away!" came a yell from the crowd.

"Bring back the Spire!"

"Stand and fight!"

"Enough!" the dragon roared, sending a little ball of flame rolling out and startling the crowd into silence. "Heaven's Spire has deviated from its normal route, yes. We have no new information at this time about where it is located, or why the Voyancy has decided to move the city."

Nystin started walking again, eyes down, shoulders hunched. The crowd was yelling more loudly. The puppeteer would be lucky to get out of there alive.

If the Spire was gone, that would make things harder. He had go-bags dropped all across the Republic, but he had assumed that it was still worth a trip to the Spire to make one last case for himself.

Loch was in the Elflands. He had no way to get to her.

He figured he might know where she'd be going, though, and that was the next best thing.

He walked the dock at a casual, ground-eating pace, eyes wandering to the registry and listed destination of each airship. When he found a small cargo ship heading close to the Imperial border, he passed it, ducked back into an alley between two hangars, and waited.

Workers loaded the cargo ship and started boarding. Nystin was getting ready to make his move when a coach pulled up. An armored and helmeted man got out. Like Nystin, he wore a cloak that obscured his armor, but the helmet was golden and had a great dragon face.

Just like the Imperials, Nystin figured. Too proud of their armor to toss it.

The muscle headed to the airship and began what looked like a negotiation with the captain. Nystin ambled across the docks, casual and forgettable, and slipped into the coach.

"Don't move," he said to the Imperial woman sitting on the bench across from him. His dagger was out as he slid the door closed. "Stop. Make one sound, and I'll kill you before your guard arrives." She looked like she'd been sleeping, and was bundled in blankets that hid most of her, leaving only her delicate face visible. She looked at him wide-eyed as he continued. "Now listen carefully. You're getting onto this airship, and you're going to see to it that I come with you. If your guard gets any ideas, I kill you. If you try to escape, I kill you. If you do anything stupid at all, I kill you." He smiled, letting the hardness show in his eyes. "None of that means I *want* to kill you. You let me get onto that ship, you play along like I'm your guest, and nobody has to get hurt." His dagger was up, the silver catching the light to throw the glint into her eyes. That always made it scarier. "You hear me?"

"I hear you," the Imperial woman said, and then a green-scaled tail slid from the blanket to coil around his wrist. "*Don't move.*"

"You're certain?" Kail asked for the third time. He had *Iofegemet* sailing at full speed already, but he had never liked flying blind, least of all when magic was involved, even *more* least of all when he was *literally* flying.

"Heaven's Spire casts magic like the sun casts light," Desidora said. She was standing at the railing, staring off into what looked to Kail like empty space. Her auburn hair swayed as she looked back and forth. "It's bright enough that most people who can see auras learn to tune it out, so as to be able to see anything else, but if I squint and focus, the wake is just barely visible." She held up an arm. "A little more that way."

Kail eased *Iofegemet* a bit to port, squinting off into empty space as though he'd be able to see auras if he just tried hard enough. Then he gave up and played with the airship's controls a little, on the off chance that any of the diagnostic functions could pick up the trail. So far, both options worked equally well, in that neither had done anything worth a damn.

"*Besyn larveth'is,*" Ghylspwr said reassuringly, and Kail looked up at Desidora to see what the hammer was saying to her, only to realize that she was still looking over the railing, and the hammer was, in as much as Kail could tell, pointed at him.

"Yeah, we're all good," he said, and looked back down at his console.

"We're not," Desidora said, not turning back around. "A tiny bit to starboard, please."

Kail edged *Iofegemet* over. "You're supposed to say 'right', so that I can correct you irately like a good airship captain."

"You need to do something to feel strong again," she said quietly, "after having your soul trapped by Silestin, you need *something* that makes you remember who you are, something nobody else can touch." She looked back at him. "That's what I see when I look at you with the eyes of a love priestess." Her eyes shone with unshed tears. "And I can't give you that, because I'm part of the thing that hurt you."

"Thanks, Diz. That helps a ton." Kail kept working at the console.

"*Kun-kabynalti osu fuir'is,*" Ghylspwr chided.

"Hey, big guy, you can spit out those three lines as often as you like. You already did your big deal for your people, helping Dairy stop the Glimmering Folk and saving the world and everything." Kail pointed. "You get to hit crap with no cares in the world and make Diz look good in fights. The rest of us are just trying to get by."

"*Kutesosh gajair'is!*"

"No, it's all right." Desidora patted the hammer and gave Kail a harder look. "It must seem awfully easy to have your destiny already fulfilled, looking at it from your side. Did you ever think about what it's like afterward?" She turned all the way around, leaning back against the railing, her casual stance a deliberate challenge. "Knowing that you had one reason to live this life, and now that reason is done? Dairy feels it, now that his time as the Champion of Dawn is done. Ghylspwr feels it. *I* feel it. There's no reason for us to be here anymore."

"I've got two countries full of scared people who say otherwise." Kail smiled. "That's why Dairy has you two beat, even though he screwed up with the Knights of Gedesar. The kid never knew he had a destiny, so he just did the best he could. Same as Loch, same as me. And yeah." He patted the console. "Maybe I started training with airships as a way to regain control. Maybe I've got some work left to do. But I'm working on it while saving the Republic with no fancy destiny or godly powers or any of that. Sit back and take notes if you like. Or better yet? Help." He pointed at Ghylspwr. "Not because you've got some big magical destiny, but because it's what needs doing."

Desidora swallowed. "A bit to port."

Kail nudged *Iofegemet* over. "Thanks."

"I think I know where Heaven's Spire went," Pyvic said, headed over from where he and Icy had been charting their course on a map. "I initially thought they'd be trying to pull the city back somewhere safer, further from the fighting."

"But they are not," said Icy, holding up the map so that Kail could see.

"You guys wrote all over my map!" Kail said, followed shortly by, "Why in Gedesar's name would they take Heaven's Spire to the Temple of Butterflies?"

"Good question." Pyvic grimaced, then looked at Desidora. "Sister, the only thing we know about Shenziencis is that she has lived at the Temple of Butterflies for centuries. Could the temple be tied into her power?"

"If the temple is a legacy of the ancients," she said slowly, "then yes."

Kail grunted. "And if the four of us—"

"*Besyn larveth'is!*"

"Sorry, if the *five* of us can figure it out, it stands to reason somebody up on the Spire could as well." Kail nodded slowly. "So they're going to fly Heaven's Spire over to the temple and threaten to send down the giant beam of fire."

"It stands to reason." Pyvic nodded. "The Imperials are already worried enough about it to go to war. Might as well make use of it."

"So they will make a show of force, hoping my people will back down," Icy said. "But since my people are not in fact responsible for the attacks, the bluff will fail."

"We had better *hope* it's just a bluff," Desidora said. Everyone looked at her. "You all saw what Heaven's Spire did to the ground below."

"Well, yeah." Kail shrugged. "But the Temple of Butterflies is kind of an ugly temple, anyway. No offense, Icy."

"None taken."

"No," Desidora said, "you don't understand. The Temple of Butterflies is an artifact of the ancients, just like Heaven's Spire. If we're right, it has enough magical strength to augment the naga's power and let her control a massive army of the dead from halfway across the Republic."

"So you're thinking it might be hard to attack?" Kail asked.

"I'm thinking," Desidora said, "that attacking it with *another* artifact of the ancients might blow up a good chunk of both the Republic *and* the Empire."

Loch played *suf-gesuf* as her father had taught her, getting out of bad hands with minimal losses and staying in enough of them to keep her chips up. Her luck was less than great, but good enough that she was ahead of the ever-increasing minimum ante.

The dwarf in the enormous hat came in too aggressively, staying in bad hands longer than he should have. He busted within the first hour and left swearing that the game was rigged. The elf in the feathered half-mask was holding back, her chips slowly dwindling as she folded each turn rather than take a risk on an uncertain hand. Loch figured she'd be out in a few more hours.

Veiled Lightning's stack of chips was the largest at the table, and she looked over at Loch with a little smirk as the dealer flipped out the cards for the next hand. "I will stand on my cards and raise two hundred." She looked at her hidden cards as Loch did the same. The flop showed a pair of eights, and Veiled Lightning had another eight in her open cards. By her smile, she was sitting on a fourth.

"Not for me," Lechien said, sighing and tossing his cards away.

"I am interested in seeing what the young lady has," said the Imperial, smiling affably from behind his spectacles and pushing a few chips forward.

"Draw one and one," Loch said, pushing forward a hidden card and an open one, along with the chips to keep her in the hand.

"Two for the Urujar." The dealer flicked two cards her way, flipping one of them open. "Possible straight, depending on what she's got hidden. Ranger?" He looked to the elven woman in the feathered mask, who shook her head. "The ranger folds."

"I will raise," Veiled Lightning said, tossing in more chips.

"Hmm." The Imperial hemmed and hawed for a moment, then checked as well.

"The Imperial evidently has something exciting that isn't showing for the rest of us," the dealer said, then looked at Loch. "Urujar?"

"Two," Loch said, "and two more."

Veiled Lightning slid her chips into the pot. "You don't think I have the fourth eight."

"Nobody thinks you have the fourth eight," Loch said. "But by all means, call me."

Veiled Lightning glared, and then shook her head sharply at the dealer.

"The princess folds," he said. "Imperial?" The Imperial wiped his face and dropped his cards as well. "Hand goes to the Urujar. We'll take a half-hour break, now. If you aren't back in thirty, you forfeit." The dealer gathered the cards in and shuffled them quickly enough that his fingers blurred.

Loch stood, stretching out tight muscles in the back of her neck. Dairy hurried to her side.

"Ma'am?"

"Drink," she said, heading for the bar, "and report."

"Nothing yet from Tern and the others," Dairy said, pushing a drink of dwarven whiskey into her hands. "How did you know she didn't have the last eight?"

"Because I was sitting on it myself. That wasn't about winning." Loch bolted the whiskey, winced, and handed Dairy the empty glass. "If it'd been about winning, I'd've drawn it out a bit more and lured her into raising."

"What was it about, then?" Dairy asked.

"It was about the Imperial." Loch saw Baron Lechien standing by the bar, playing with a cocktail sword while sipping a fruity drink Tern would have liked. "Give me a minute, Dairy."

Lechien lifted his fruity drink in a toast as Loch came over. "You've had a good run so far."

"As have you," Loch said, smiling. It was a professional smile this time, not a flirty one. "You're only a bit behind the princess at our table."

"Yes." Lechien sipped his drink. "About that."

"Noticed, did you?"

"Hard not to." Lechien glared. "I've sat across the table from Benevolent Dawn a hundred times. He has never chased a hand that badly, and if he had some stratagem, he would have seen it through rather than folding."

"He's been feeding the princess," Loch said. "Staying in on hands to put chips in her lap."

"I told you before that politics and I generally agree to leave each other alone," Lechien said, and shook his head, "but word around the ship is that you are here for more than a game, as is she."

"The Republic and the Empire are hurtling toward war." Loch lowered her voice. "If I stay in long enough, I can stop that from happening."

"Benevolent Dawn has apparently chosen his side." Lechien grimaced. "And it gets a lot more expensive after this break."

Loch nodded. "You have a suggestion?"

Lechien swallowed, looked around, and then downed the rest of his drink. "All right. I can eat a tournament loss, if need be. Next time I draw a possible four of a kind, I'll tap twice. It'll *actually* just be three. You'll be able to beat it with a straight or a concordance. If you can get either of those, tap twice back, and I'll go all in."

"You're doing a service to the Republic," Loch said gravely, and Lechien grinned and shook his head.

"All I wanted was a good game of cards with a pretty girl." He turned away from her and signaled to the bartender for another.

Loch sidestepped the crowd and went into the hallway leading to the head. The treeship had better plumbing than most Republic cities, and everything apparently got recycled and used to help power the ship. Loch tried not to think about it.

She turned a corner, and that was when something slammed into her head.

Loch hit the grass-carpeted floor hard, arms shielding her instinctively, and curled up to catch the kick that followed on the elbows.

"Do you believe she will remain unconscious for a full half-hour?" an elven voice asked.

"She has proven durable even by human standards," Irrethelathlialann replied. "I would appreciate it if she were placed somewhere where she was unlikely to escape until the allotted time had passed."

A hand came down, curling into a fist in Loch's hair, while another hooked under her armpit. "As you wish."

Loch slammed the heel of her palm up and shattered the nose of the elf holding her. As he stumbled back, she kicked and caught someone else in the leg.

"The worst part about being injured," she said, coming back to her feet, "is the first fight after. You're always thinking, 'Am I really back? Did it heal right?'"

There were three of them, plus Irrethelathlialann, though he stood back by the corner. One was already lunging in, and she kicked, caught him in the gut, then put him down with a right hook. "It's not until the first time you get hit again that you really know for sure," she added, stomping on the back of his knee and dropping an elbow onto the base of his skull.

The last elf crashed into her, and she hit the wall hard, got a knee up, and took a shot across the cheek as she shoved him back. The one whose nose she'd broken caught her with a kick to the gut, not far from where she'd been stabbed, and it felt tight, but not too tight, and she grinned, caught the leg, leaned in, and popped her palm down hard just under the kneecap. He squealed and went down, holding his leg.

"So what I really want to say . . ." She got her arms up in a guard as the other elf came in high, caught him with a low body shot, slammed him back into the far wall, and then reached up and tore one of the crystals from his cheeks. "Is *thank you* for getting me past that first fight."

She tossed the crystal to the ground as the elf slid to a seated position, keening and clutching his face, and looked at Irrethelathlialann. "You must think I'm *really* good at *sufgesuf* to be this worried."

His hand went to the ruby-red blade at his waist. "You're a savage, Lochenville, the worst of the breed of a race of savages. The ancients bred us for magic, and we carry the scars of that even today. But you?" He sneered. "You were bred for brute labor."

"Shame you didn't think of that before you tried to use brute force to stop me." She looked at the elves on the ground. "You could've brought better fighters."

Irrethelathlialann opened his mouth to reply, then glanced back out into the main hall and blinked. He slid back, his hand leaving the blade at his waist.

Captain Thelenea came around the corner with a pair of her guards with her. She looked at Irrethelathlialann, then at the three elves on the ground, most of them still rocking back and forth and making little noises to themselves, and then finally at Loch.

"Does anyone have anything they wish to report?" she asked.

Irrethelathlialann didn't say anything.

Loch smiled.

"I suspect that if I did wish to report anything, I'd be taken to your cabin to fill out that report, wouldn't I?" she asked, and caught Irrethelathlialann's glare. "And that would take more than a half-hour, which would mean I'd forfeit my place in the tournament, which would in turn mean that you'd have to kick my ass off the ship."

Thelenea pursed her lips. "That is indeed how matters would likely proceed."

"Then no, thank you." Loch coughed and rolled out one shoulder. "I have nothing I wish to report."

"Then perhaps I will make a report," Irrethelathlialann said, stepping forward with his gaze steady on Loch, "stating that this Urujar woman assaulted my three friends, a vicious and all-too-human attack—"

"If that would work, you'd have spoken first," Loch said, waving at him absently. "Thelenea, if he files a report, do I have to come answer charges immediately, or are they deferred until after the tournament?"

"Our social laws dictate—"

"After the tournament," the captain said, giving Loch a small smile.

"Well, then." Loch nodded to each of them. "If you'll excuse me, I'm going to hit the head."

She turned her back on both of them and walked into the head, a large room with a number of individual stalls, and mirrors and sinks by the door.

Princess Veiled Lightning stood by the sink, staring at her wordlessly.

Her braids hung looser in the front than Loch had seen before. She'd removed the crystals at the tips, Loch realized, when she boarded the ship. Her little necklace hung over her brow, making it look like she was glaring, but the expression on her face was in fact carefully neutral.

"You want to take a shot?" Loch asked. "I've still got about twenty minutes to get back to the table."

Energy crackled at Veiled Lightning's fingertips. "I could take you in two."

"Like you've taken me all the past times." Loch shook her head. "No bodyguard, no . . . whatever Shenziencis is, and no chance that my surrender would actually stop the Republic and the Empire from getting a lot of people killed, now that your side is sending undead to attack my towns."

"My side?" Veiled Lightning glared. "Your own Republic has sent the undead into *my* Empire. You *dare* spout your lies!"

Loch stepped to the sink and turned it on. As she washed her hands, she looked up into the mirror at Veiled Lightning, who stood behind her, electricity snaking around both hands now. "Do your parents even know you're out here trying to take me in?"

The question seemed to catch Veiled Lightning by surprise. Loch heard her catch her breath, trying to form an answer.

"I'm guessing they don't," Loch went on. "I'm guessing you went off because you saw trouble brewing and people hemming and hawing and politicking, and you decided that *someone* had to go do what was right. You snuck off on your own to show them how to get things *done*." She scrubbed her hands. "Only it wasn't really on your own, was it? Not with an attendant and a bodyguard and a magical ax. You come all the way to the Republic, all the way to the Elflands, and you still wonder whether you're just coasting on things your family did."

"Your family's title bought your rank in the Republic's army, *Captain*," Veiled Lightning said behind her.

"Yes, it did. I went a long way before finding out that you can't outrun the privilege you grow up with. All you can do is try to use it well, to honor the people who work in the fields so you don't have to."

"That's what I'm doing," Veiled Lightning said slowly, "and I swear to you, I will do everything in my power to end this war . . . once you are in custody."

Her hand stabbed forward, lightning snapping from her fingers.

Loch spun and flung a spray of water from the sink. Veiled Lightning sidestepped it, face twisting into a smirk that vanished as Loch's knuckles sank into her kidneys. She stumbled, the magic fading from her hands, and Loch feinted low, then drilled a straight punch clean into her chest. "Takes a peaceful, harmonious mind to get that magic going, doesn't it? I try not to rely on any fighting style that doesn't work when I'm pissed off."

Veiled Lightning glared death at Loch and lunged in, her fists blurring with a series of strikes that battered Loch's guard until a high spinning kick broke through it and cracked across Loch's jaw.

Loch's fist caught Veiled Lightning's ribs. Loch's elbow caught her forehead. Loch's foot caught her knee.

Nose bloody and face flushed, Veiled Lightning spun and leaped with a high kick that might well have taken Loch's head off.

Loch caught her, pivoted, and hurled her into the mirror over the sink.

Princess Veiled Lightning hit the ground, moved like she was going to get up, and then slumped back down.

Loch flexed her jaw as she walked into one of the stalls. She was going to need a drink with ice in it later.

She sat, did her business, and indulged in a few deep breaths.

Then she heard the sound of heavy booted feet clopping on the bathroom floor.

The underside of the stall had about a foot of clearance, so Loch could see the booted feet come in, walk past the shattered glass of the mirror, and stride down the length of the bathroom to stop before her stall.

"Isafesira de Lochenville," came a deep and not entirely human voice, "we need to talk."

Nineteen

THE BOOTED FEET BELONGED TO THE LARGE, RED-BEARDED MAN Loch had seen talking to Irrethelathlialann earlier.

He stepped aside politely as Loch came out of the stall. He was a head taller than she was, and up close, his fine elven robes hung over a broad body of corded muscle and sinew. He had a prominent, oft-broken nose, a beard that could have hidden several daggers and a set of lock picks, and laugh lines around his eyes.

"You're the Dragon," Loch said, and went over to wash her hands.

"Mister Dragon, if you prefer," he said with a smile that made his mustache twist up.

"Are you *actually* a dragon?" Loch asked.

"That's a more complex question than our time together allows for," Mister Dragon said. Faster than Loch had believed possible, he was by her side . . . holding out a hand towel.

She took it and dried her hands. "True. I should be getting back to the table shortly."

Mister Dragon chuckled, and his chest glowed for a moment, bright enough to be visible even through the robes. "You're impressive, Lochenville. Not impressive enough to get my book, but impressive."

"The book has to do with the ancients," Loch said, tossing the hand towel aside. "I figured out that much. And your elf told me a little about the ancients as well."

"About how they bred the elves to service their crystals?" Mister Dragon nodded. "All true. Exposure to it heightens their mental acuity, but it more or less turns off their souls. I'm part of the group that keeps the Elflands free of crystal-based magic. Lotion?"

Loch blinked, then realized Mister Dragon was holding out a small bottle of scented liquid. "What's that for?"

"We're fairly high up. The air gets dry." Mister Dragon shrugged and put the bottle aside. "Suit yourself."

"So the elves were bred by the ancients—"

"The dwarves, too. Miners and crafters, for the most part, and then later as soldiers when the ancients needed people to fight the new arrivals."

"The Glimmering Folk."

Mister Dragon smiled. "The ancients weren't very happy with the Glimmering Folk. After all, the ancients were ruling this land quite comfortably. They had humans and elves and dwarves to serve them, and their golems to hunt down any fairy creatures who formed when their magic got too carried away . . . and then the Glimmering Folk came and ruined everything." He stepped away from Loch and knelt down beside Veiled Lightning, who still lay on the floor. "The ancients locked themselves and the Glimmering Folk out of this world, so that nobody could rule it, but the gods—who like to keep things *interesting*—didn't see fit to just leave things that way."

He laid a hand on Veiled Lightning, and it began to glow with a soft but steady energy. Veiled Lightning shuddered, and then curled up and coughed.

"You're talking about the prophecies," Loch said. "The Champions of Dawn and Dusk."

Mister Dragon smiled. "See? Right there in front of you. You'll recall that the ancients left instructions with their golems to kill the Champion of Dawn if they ever found him. They *really* didn't want to risk letting the Glimmering Folk back in. But." He stood, walked over to the sink, and washed his hands carefully. "You took care of that for them, didn't you?"

Loch swallowed. "I helped the Champion of Dawn defeat the Glimmering Folk."

"Indeed." Mister Dragon toweled off his hands. "And now the Glimmering Folk are no longer a threat, which means that there's no reason for the ancients to stay off in . . . wherever it is they are right now. You and your gullible friends helpfully got rid of the only thing keeping the ancients out of our world. Lotion?" he asked again.

Loch passed it over. Mister Dragon squeezed out a small ball of creamy liquid and rubbed his hands briskly.

"So they're going to come back." Loch caught Mister Dragon's smile again, the little approving nod.

"They are. Back to a world that has humans and dwarves and elves and even fairy creatures taking care of themselves just fine without the ancients there to rule them." Mister Dragon stared at her directly. "How do you think they're going to take that?"

Loch took a very small step back. "I've got a hammer with the soul of an ancient in my team. They can't all be bad."

"They never are." Mister Dragon smiled. "I've traveled the Republic, you know. I love your puppeteers, how they share the news in such an excited fashion. The manticore and the griffon, always arguing, getting people to pick a side. Truth is, though, they're both just lions with a bit of fancy costuming, a simplistic option presented for small minds, while the real matters of your country are dealt with far overhead, away from prying eyes. I think the Glimmering Folk and the ancients are not wholly dissimilar."

"Don't forget the dragon who keeps the manticore and the griffon in line," Loch said, and Mister Dragon rolled his eyes and snorted. "So can you breathe a little fire and keep the ancients from coming back?"

He shrugged. "I'm not sure that's even an option, Lochenville. But that manuscript carries the impressions of the elf who sang the first song, and in the middle of all the bits about flowers and springtime, there's a reference to when the ancients are supposed to return. And *that* is why everyone who knows anything is after that book, from me to the Empire to that damned Queen of the Cold River."

Loch shut her eyes for a long moment. "It's a warning."

"Several of your servants accidentally walked into my suite, by the way," Mister Dragon said. "Ah, not even a wince. You have some hope in this tournament yet."

"I am certain it was a mistake on their part," Loch said politely, "and I would appreciate it if they were released into my care."

"And then?" Mister Dragon asked.

She tried a smile and said, "I still need the manuscript."

Mister Dragon chuckled again, a deep grumbling laugh that rolled across Loch's belly. "What you *need* is a way to stop the Empire and the Republic from killing each other. The city of Heaven's Spire is on course to raze the Temple of Butterflies, and unbeknownst to most people on both sides, the resulting explosion is going to level both of your countries. My elf would rather just let your people drown in each other's blood, since that might make it more likely that the ancients take you first. I have to say, I'm on the fence, myself. I have no great interest in your people dying, but . . ." He smiled, showing very white teeth. "They do seem intent on going to war."

Loch looked down at Veiled Lightning, who was slowly coming up to a seated position.

"What do you say," Loch asked, "to a wager?"

Kail sighted Heaven's Spire just after sunset, a glittering star low on the horizon.

"Hey, Diz," he called up to the railing, and Desidora looked back and smiled. The setting sun was behind Kail, and the light cast a golden halo across Desidora's face, lighting up her auburn hair with lines of fire. "Not bad for a love priestess with no real skills."

"*Kutesosh gajair'is,*" Ghylspwr shot back as Desidora laughed.

"You too, big guy." Kail grinned.

Pyvic had his message crystal out. "I've had no luck getting a message through so far. Maybe line of sight will be a bit kinder." He thumbed the crystal until it glowed. "Captain Pyvic to any available justicar. Requesting an updated status report on what Heaven's Spire is doing and requesting assistance upon docking." He let go, frowned, and then raised an eyebrow. "Well, it's away, at least."

"I'll be in range of the docks in a few minutes," Kail said. "I can try signaling them as well."

They drew slowly closer to the city as twilight edged slowly toward darkness. Heaven's Spire shone with glittering radiance all across the top of the great disc that formed it, shops and streetlamps and palaces all glowing with their own magical radiance.

Finally, when *Iofegemet* was close enough for Kail to make out the lighting pattern on the rim of Heaven's Spire, he said, "All right, we're closest to the transportation docks. Let me see if they're interested in letting us aboard."

"Wait." Pyvic held up his message crystal, then held it to his ear. "I've got a reply."

"From your people?" Desidora asked.

"Apparently. Golem voice. They must have transcribed it." Pyvic squinted, listening. "They're telling us to come in high and maintain altitude. They'll open a gap in the barrier."

Kail pursed his lips. "That seems a lot more complicated than necessary."

"What barrier are they referring to?" Icy asked.

"A bubble of magic encircling Heaven's Spire," Desidora said, "save by the docks. It keeps the air from leaking out and maintains the temperature."

"Well, it'll be faster to land at the archvoyant's palace and get some answers from Bertram than to come over all the way from the docks," Pyvic said.

Kail tapped his console and brought *Iofegemet* up. "How far out from the Temple of Butterflies are we?"

"A few hours, at this speed," Icy said.

"Well, faster sounds good, then." Kail saw a crystal flashing amber and flicked it. "Crap."

Pyvic looked over. "Problem?"

"We went to war with the Empire before I actually got my piloting license," Kail said, "so I'm not *entirely* certain what that means, but it has something to do with magical energy readings on our projected course."

"Can you determine whether the barrier has been lowered?" Icy asked.

"Oh, probably, if I pressed a bunch of these crystals in the right combination."

Pyvic glanced at his message crystal. "That's odd." He thumbed it. "I've got another message."

Desidora was squinting ahead. "The barrier is still up," she said. "I can sense the magic. And it's hard to tell at this range, but I think—"

"Come in silent, the city is in lockdown." Pyvic looked at Kail. "Dive, please."

The first blasts of fire streaked toward them moments later.

"As heists go," Loch said, "I've seen better."

Tern and Hessler sat shamefacedly on the bed. Both looked bedraggled, and several of Tern's pockets were inside out.

"They were *kinda* waiting for us," Tern said.

"Given that your main job was to create the distraction and lure everyone away from their rooms," Hessler added, "I fail to see how us walking into a trap is anyone's fault but yours."

"*You* walked into a trap," said Ululenia from the chair. She was drinking brandy now, one pale leg kicked out and resting on the bed. "*Some* of us turned into a bird and escaped."

"And thanks for the solidarity, there," Tern added. "You could have *tried* your mind-thing on them, or turned into a bear, or—"

"Gotten killed by the Dragon," Ululenia finished, swirling her brandy, "who is, in fact, a dragon."

Hessler sighed. "I had really hoped that was a metaphor."

"What kind of powers does he have?" Tern asked. "You do minds, that satyr who worked for Silestin did sex, I guess, and Shenziencis controls voices, or the dead, or . . . both?"

"A dragon is a force of raw, unmitigated power," said Ululenia. "In his true form, he could tear this ship apart, and then set the kindling ablaze with his flaming breath."

"Wow," said Dairy, sipping his milk. "That sounds . . ."

"Like we should avoid a frontal assault," Hessler finished.

"I have a plan," Loch said, and everyone turned to glare at her. "Really, this time. And no frontal assaults. Mister Dragon let you go upon my assurance that you wouldn't bother him. You've got a new job."

Ululenia raised an eyebrow. "Go on."

Loch gave them an optimistic smile. "How much do you know about treeship security?"

"Wards at fifty percent!" Kail shouted as flame battered the great balloon over his head, and then, as another blast of fire roared at them, this time at the deck, "Crap, everyone down!"

"*Kun-kabynalti osu fuir'is!*" Ghylspwr shouted, and Desidora reached out from the railing and swung.

Light blazed, and Kail shielded his eyes. When it cleared, Desidora stood, slightly scorched but none the worse for wear, atop the smoking railing.

"Ow," she said, and toppled over backwards. Icy dove forward and caught her.

"Diving!" Kail said, in case anyone was curious, and pushed *Iofegemet* down hard. "Forward full!"

"The flamecannons won't be able to shoot straight down," Pyvic said quickly. "If you get us under the city, we should be safe!"

"Not counting the giant blast of lightning it can shoot down at us?" Kail winced as another blast of flame roared out and splashed across the balloon overhead. "Wards at twenty percent!"

"Can you go any faster?" Pyvic asked.

"Yes, I'm just choosing to go this speed because your mother likes it when I take my time!" Another blast roared out, and the balloon groaned as the wind-daemon inside it stretched and strained the canvas. "Wards are down, by the way!"

He looked up past the balloon to where Heaven's Spire was a great coin that blotted out most of the night sky overhead. The *lapiscaela* that kept the city floating during the day had gone dark, but he could still see glimpses of violet as crystals here and there glinted in the twilight.

They were going to make it. Kail pulled *Iofegemet* up to cut off the angle of fire further and bring the ship up under the barrier so they could dock.

One last blast spat out from above and hissed behind the balloon, past Kail's field of view.

"Did it miss?" Icy asked, and then the blast hit the balloon.

"You had to ask!" Kail shouted.

It didn't sound like the splashing spray of fire sloshing against magical barriers. This was the crackling burn of flames hitting the canvas, and while the canvas was treated to be fireproof in the event of just this sort of thing happening, few things in the world were *actually* fireproof when you got them hot enough.

"Byn-kodar's hell," Kail muttered, "no offense, Diz."

"None taken."

"Did it breach?" Pyvic asked.

Kail looked at the console. "Not yet. It's burning, though. We've got a minute or two, tops." Pyvic opened his mouth, and Kail waved. "And no, I can't get us up to the Spire in that time, and no, I can't land us in that time, and no, the life balloons got wrecked when we lost half of *Iofegemet* fighting the naga and her ax-swinging boyfriend. I'm sorry. I've got nothing."

"What if we extinguish the fire?" Icy asked.

"Sure," Kail said, "except that they hit the top of the balloon, which is a bit out of reach."

Icy rolled out his arms. "Then perhaps someone could prepare me some damp rags," he said politely, "so that I may stop the war with my little acrobatic tricks."

"Oh, you were just *itching* to throw that one back in my face." Kail pulled *Iofegemet* into a level ascent while Pyvic and Desidora scrambled to get the rags. "You know your way around the rigging?"

Icy sank into a low stretch. "I will, shortly," he said, shifting his weight from one leg to the other.

"There's not a lot to hold onto up on top."

"A lesser man," Icy said, "would find a way to reference your mother in response to that sentence." Pyvic and Desidora passed him a handful of wet rags, and he tucked them into his robes. "Continue docking, smoothly if possible."

He took three steps, vaulted to the railing, leaped *from* the railing, caught a line in one hand, and pulled himself into another flying leap that, as he somersaulted in midair, let him loop one leg around a line hanging from the underside of the balloon.

He swung once, pulled himself upright, and proceeded to climb through the rigging, upside-down, along the underside of the balloon. In moments, he was out of sight.

"Just *imagine* if he would just man up and hit people," Kail muttered. "All right, everyone hold tight. We're coming up under the Spire. Perimeter alarm is telling me we lose containment in about thirty."

"But Icy can stop it," Desidora said.

"Icy can buy us a bit more time," Kail said. "Once the wind-daemon on the other side of that canvas gets a taste of freedom, though, there's not a whole lot that can stop it. Remember when that one got loose on our way up last time?"

"I remember Tern shooting me with a knockout dart," Pyvic said.

"I'll mix that in if we have time." Kail checked their course. "Getting a few more alerts, just so you know. Probably not a bad idea to start holding onto things."

Overhead, the canvas groaned, and something deep inside it rumbled.

A line back near the stern snapped from the balloon and fluttered down, still smoldering.

"*Kun-kabynalti osu fuir'is,*" Ghylspwr said quietly.

"Perimeter alarm's saying the fire is out." Kail kept the ascent going. The ship lifted slowly past the *lapiscaela,* the great violet crystals nestled snugly in the grids that held them in place during the night.

The canvas groaned again, and the balloon bulged as something inside it swam, pressing against the barrier.

"Kail?" Desidora looked at the balloon in alarm. "I can feel the daemon."

"Yeah, it's . . ." Kail looked at his console as the *lapiscaela* slid down below them. "It's poking for holes."

The canvas tore, the sound of fabric ripping unmistakable as they all waited silently.

"Well, no sense going in gentle now." Kail pulled *Iofegemet* into a full ascent, and the ship shrieked. "Everybody hang on!"

The ship lurched up, alarms going off all over the place, and Kail looked at the mirror-walled edge of Heaven's Spire floating a few yards off the bow while his ship slowly came apart overhead.

"We're going to make it," Desidora said.

"No." Kail swallowed, balling his fists on the console. "Daemon's got a seam. It's about to start working its way out. Ships can't ascend when the daemon stops obeying commands and starts breaking free."

They'd been so damn close.

"Come on." Pyvic yanked on Kail's arm. "We can still jump."

The canvas overhead tore again, and Kail heard the sound of something breaking out.

And then an inhuman roar that still somehow carried the very understandable sound of pain.

Iofegemet kept ascending.

"All right." Kail stepped away from his console, which was going black and dead on him anyway. "Happy to be wrong."

"You weren't," Desidora said, looking up with a strange little smile.

The flat and sterile open yard of Heaven's Spire's transport docks gleamed overhead, and still *Iofegemet* rose, as the daemon roared overhead.

And then they were level, and Kail took a running jump, covered the yards, and landed in a clumsy roll, banging his shin and ankle as he slid to a stop, with Pyvic beside him and Desidora coming to a gentle landing from a hammer-assisted leap.

Kail's ship was already falling again, and now Kail could see why it had kept ascending for the few extra seconds that had brought them high enough.

A great clawed tentacle protruded from a scorched tear in the balloon, back near the rear.

Icy Fist had the tentacle in a joint lock.

He'd wrapped one of the lines around it, and was standing atop it, like a trick rider on the back of a prancing show horse, if the show horse had been growing claws and shrieking with inhuman fury while Icy hauled it back and forth.

"Icy!" Desidora yelled, and the daemon tore free, the rest of its shapeless mass splitting the canvas open and sliding out like the yolk of a rotten egg.

Icy leaped, landed on the remains of the balloon, took two steps on the fluttering canvas, and somehow leaped again.

He fell short by a good dozen meters, still reaching.

"Besyn larveth'is!"

A shining warhammer spun through the air, arced over the side of the docks, and sailed down out of sight.

Desidora extended her hand, shut her eyes, and winced.

With a flash of light, Ghylspwr appeared in her grasp, Icy Fist clinging to the handle.

In a flash of gold and pale-green robes, two humans and a warhammer crashed to the ground.

"Nice catch," Kail said, moving forward with Pyvic to help them up.

"I was motivated," Icy said. He waved Pyvic's hand away. "I am afraid that because Ghylspwr's teleportation carries momentum across, and I had fallen some distance before I caught him . . ."

Kail looked down and saw that Icy's leg was twisted at an entirely unnatural angle. "Oh."

"Can you take care of yourself?" Pyvic asked, pulling Desidora back to her feet.

"I can at least begin treatment of my injuries," Icy replied. He reached out, took hold of his leg, and twisted it sharply. The leg made a cracking crunching popping noise as it snapped back to something more like a normal angle.

"Holy . . ." Kail shook his head. "I wish *I* knew some monk trick to snap broken bones back into place without it hurting."

Icy smiled faintly. "So do I."

Kail swallowed. "Hey. Nice job with the daemon."

"A restraining hold is not quite harm," Icy said, and then winced. "I would appreciate it if you left now so that I am free to allow myself undignified expressions of pain."

Kail looked over at his ship as it fell back down toward the ground below, the wind-daemon a blob of tentacles floating off behind it.

"Justicar Pyvic, Sister Desidora?" he said. "Let's go stop a war."

Loch returned to her seat with two minutes to spare, sent Dairy to freshen her drink, smiled at the other players, and played *suf-gesuf* like her life depended on it.

The elf in the feathered mask went all in on three of a kind and lost to Benevolent Dawn, the Imperial man with the spectacles, about an hour later. He himself lost the last of his chips an hour after that, just before their next break, and tipped the dealer politely after praising everyone else for their excellent play. Loch, sitting behind a shrinking pile of chips, looked at the large stack in front of Veiled Lightning, who was smiling despite the bruises on her face.

"Any word?" Loch asked Dairy as he led her to the bar at the next break.

"None yet, ma'am. Tern said that they were going to double-check this time before doing anything."

"I'd assumed they did that *last* time. Silly me."

"Ma'am," Dairy said, and then broke off awkwardly, still little more than a boy for all the hardening that a few months of military training had given him.

"What is it, Dairy?"

"I'm sorry." He flushed. "It's not important right now."

"I'm in danger of falling below the ante in the next round," Loch said. "Distract me with something frivolous."

"I'm worried about Ululenia," Dairy said.

"Ah."

"She seems . . ."

"Yes, she does." Loch signaled to the bartender, and he passed her a glass. She downed it in one gulp, then signaled for another. "And there's not a damned thing for you to do about it."

"Ma'am? You know we—"

"Didn't do anything, did you? That was how she put it." Loch looked over, and Dairy nodded, now beet-red and looking at his shoes. "You weren't interested. That's the end of the story."

"But she—"

"Dairy." She reached over and took his arm, and he looked up, eyes wide and sad as only the eyes of someone trying to figure out how to be older than they are can be. "You don't have to have sex with anyone just because they want to. She's allowed to be grumpy that you weren't into it, but that's not your problem, unless you're an ass about it, and I don't think you've been an ass about it."

Dairy let out a long breath. "Thank you, Miss Loch."

"Do you mind me asking why not, though?" Loch asked. "She's kind, she's pretty, she can purify bodies of water with her horn . . ."

"I don't know," Dairy said. "I *thought* I was interested, I *did*. I wasn't trying to lie to her, but I . . . I think that I was more, um . . . excited?"

"Sure, close enough." Loch grinned, which made Dairy smile back and relax a little.

"More *excited* about the *idea* of doing it, I think, than I was about actually doing it. Ululenia is very pretty, but . . ." Dairy shook his head. "I need something else."

"Nicely done," Loch said, and raised her empty glass in a toast.

"For what?"

"Figuring that out a lot earlier than most people." Loch left her glass on the bar and took the next one the bartender offered. She carried it back to the table rather than bolting it. "Pass me word when they're good."

Baron Lechien was stretching beside his seat. "Most of the other tables have gone out. It's down to the three of us, plus a few at another table."

"You've had a good run so far," Loch said, looking at his stack of chips, which was bit larger than hers.

"Decent." He glanced at the dealer, who was shuffling and ignoring them. "No possible four yet."

"We're good?"

"Better than." He looked over at the stack of chips by Veiled Lightning's seat. "Don't forget. A straight or a concordance."

Loch raised her glass in a toast to him as well.

Veiled Lightning returned a few minutes later, face a little puffy and newly made up, and caught the dealer's eye. "Is there any point in waiting, if we are all prepared to continue?"

"I suppose not," the dealer said, eyeing her stonily. "I welcome you to continue playing at your leisure."

The minimum ante grew faster. Loch sat out a couple of hands where she caught nothing worthwhile.

The next hand came out. "Pair of fives for the table," the dealer said, moving to deal out the open and hidden cards for each player. "Nothing showing for the Urujar. A third five for the Baron, plus whatever he's got facing the moss, and a distant summer's dream of a straight for the princess. Princess, the betting starts with you."

"I will raise one thousand," Veiled Lightning said, taking a sip of iced wine.

Loch flicked a glance at Lechien, who tapped his cards. She checked her hidden cards, then tapped back. "I'll see that," she said, and flicked her two open cards back to the dealer before sliding chips across the table.

"As will I." Lechien traded in a hidden card, nodded.

The dealer grunted and tossed out another shared card. "Seven of crystals, lending a little credence to the princess's claim of a straight, and gives the Urujar two pair with her shiny new seven of wands, or decent odds at a concordance. Princess?"

Veiled Lightning looked at Loch, then the chips. "Check."

Loch caught a tiny nod from Lechien. "I'll raise another thousand."

"See that and raise two," Lechien said.

The dealer raised an eyebrow. "Princess?"

Veiled Lightning grimaced. "No, thank you."

"I'll see that," Loch said, sliding in a sizable portion of her remaining chips.

The dealer dealt the last shared card. "Nothing helpful for anyone except the Urujar, who might in fact have what she requires for a concordance. Urujar?"

Loch looked at Baron Lechien. "Check."

"Raise," he said, sliding the rest of his chips in.

"All in." Loch slid the rest of her chips in as well.

"I suppose you have the concordance, then," the dealer said, "and you must be quite certain this young man has only three of a kind."

"Sadly," Lechien said, shaking his head, "I actually *do* have four fives."

"Really?" Loch gave him a hard smile. "I was absolutely *certain* you only had three."

"That's a common mistake for those who care more about politics than about a good game of *suf-gesuf*," he said, reaching for the chips.

"Fortunately," Loch added, turning over her cards, "four sevens still beats it."

Baron Lechien froze, swallowed, started to speak, laughed, and then swallowed again. "Well played," he said, and pushed his chair back, shaking his head. "I believe I'll go get a drink."

Loch looked over at Veiled Lightning. "Down to you and me, then, Princess?"

"The other table's down to two as well," the dealer said. "They were just waiting until it was down to four, so we could play the final hands."

An elven woman whose skin was a dark forest green came over and sat down across from Loch, the pink crystals in her cheeks shining as she smiled at Loch. "It has been a pleasure to watch you play," she said, smiling behind golden spectacles as a servant brought her chips over.

"Yes," said Irrethelathlialann, sitting down next to her and giving Loch a glittering smile. "And I imagine it will be an even greater pleasure to play *with* you."

Twenty

HEAVEN'S SPIRE CROSSED THE BORDER INTO IMPERIAL TERRITORY a few hours after sundown.

Still an hour north of the Iceford and the Temple of Butterflies, the great floating city's passage took it over an Imperial garrison that was posted atop a hill along the border.

Garrison Commander Seventh Tiger had been sent word of what to expect. Heaven's Spire traveled quickly, but not as quickly as the magic in message crystals. Spies in Ros-Oanki had seen the city depart and sent a warning along with a probable flight path. Tiger had spent most of the day checking and rechecking the flamecannons mounted on the walls and committing to memory the procedure needed to activate the head-sized sphere of crystal that had been delivered to his garrison some weeks earlier.

Seventh Tiger had a wife back on his family estate, and more children than he had ever expected to have. He had fought the Republic during the war with honor and distinction, and had put down his sword gladly when the order came. His personal opinion—shared only with his wife when they lay together in a bed that smelled of orange blossoms and sweat—was that the flamecannons and tools of the ancients were unnatural.

"We are as children playing with our fathers' swords," he had said, and she had sighed and kissed him along his collarbone until he forgot.

As the Republic capital city came into view, a dark silhouette against a starlit sky, Garrison Commander Seventh Tiger placed the crystal sphere atop the battlement, giving it a clear line of sight, and placed his hand upon it. He brought a small ruby wand over it, circled the sphere three times, and then rapped the crystal sharply.

The sphere lit up with a brilliant glow, and a pulsing light flared out in all directions. Blinking hard, Seventh Tiger watched as the shimmering light blossomed like an exploding firework.

The wave of energy passed over Heaven's Spire, and Seventh Tiger caught his breath.

A moment later, the violet crystals along the underside of the city flickered to life.

Seventh Tiger let out an explosive breath. Part of his heart was pleased, because there was always pleasure in watching a plan succeed, even if it was a plan passed down by political toadies Seventh Tiger disliked intensely. Part of his heart was saddened, because what would come next would kill every Republic citizen in the floating city, and while he had no choice in the matter, he still took no pleasure in it. And still another part of his heart was angry, because the plan's success meant that he had been correct. They *were* as children playing with their fathers' swords.

The Imperial experts had gambled. They had not explained this to Seventh Tiger, of course, as they considered him nothing more than a simple soldier, but Seventh Tiger had learned to read more than was written in the letters he received from his superiors, and from his wife as well.

The Republic nobles knew that their city could kill, and they had enough skill to break it from its long-automated course and send it toward the Empire. But if the signal came to Heaven's Spire that it was approaching a port city, the Imperial experts had reasoned, then the Republic city would return to its automated orders. It would halt in its path and assume a docking procedure, lowering its defenses to ensure that no harm came to the friendly city beneath it.

In the sky overhead, Heaven's Spire shuddered to a halt, the great crystals along its underside flaring with sudden light as the city lowered its defenses in response to the crystal sphere's docking invitation.

Which was all the invitation Seventh Tiger needed himself.

"All flamecannons, fire at will!" Seventh Tiger called out to his men.

The wall erupted with blazing light, orange and red searing the night sky as jets of flame spat up to sear the underside of the enemy city. The great violet crystals caught the fire, and even at a great distance, Seventh Tiger saw blossoms of red among the glowing violet as the magical energies mixed.

"Sir," his lieutenant called over, "sun or dragon?"

The sun's burning rays could shine all day, while a dragon's fire burned even hotter, but for a shorter time. "Dragon!" he called back. "Keep them firing until the cannons fail." It was wasteful, and he would lose cannons and possibly men for it, but his orders had been clear. His lieutenant, a woman who had served under him faithfully for more than a decade, read it all in his expression and simply nodded.

The underside of Heaven's Spire glowed cherry-red as the flamecannons spat fire at the magical crystals that held the city aloft, and the battlements of Seventh Tiger's garrison shone in the blood-red light as though they were being treated to a second sunset.

The reports Seventh Tiger had read had been clear and concise. In the aftermath of Heaven's Spire discharging its weapon months ago, the crystals on the underside of the city had taken on a magical charge due to some accident or infighting among the Republic nobles. A simple magical charge had destabilized the crystals to such a degree that had visiting elven dignitaries not solved the problem, the entire city would have shaken itself from the sky.

There were no elven dignitaries here to save the Republic city tonight.

Garrison Commander Seventh Tiger looked away as the city of Heaven's Spire glowed even more brightly. There were those among his soldiers who would cheer when the crystals finally shattered and the city fell, and he did not wish to know who they were. He would mourn the dead civilians in the silence of his heart, since it would show disobedience to do so aloud, and he would pray that historians never chose to write down the name of the man who had brought down Heaven's Spire.

"Commander!" his lieutenant shouted, and Seventh Tiger looked over at her frightened face.

It was only then that he looked up at the city.

Though the flamecannons still spat fire up into the starlit sky, the underside of the city had gone jet black. The sudden darkness was blinding after the brilliant red light of moments ago.

"Keep firing!" he called to his men. "Do not relent!"

He blinked, cursing himself as a fool for opening both eyes to the glare and losing what night vision he had, and tried to will the afterimages away from the night sky before him. It seemed to him that the crystals beneath Heaven's Spire were glowing again, violet, as they had before. Or perhaps they were lighter this time, closer to a pale blue, or even . . .

When the crystals blazed white and his men called out in alarm and shielded their eyes, Garrison Commander Seventh Tiger nodded.

The light of a thousand suns blossomed in the sky overhead.

Someone had taught the children how to swing that sword, Seven Tiger thought, and wished his own children well as the blazing radiance thundered down upon his garrison.

Captain Nystin stood at the railing, his hands gripping the wood hard enough to bruise the flesh of his palms.

He had tried to jump earlier. Shenziencis hadn't liked that.

His thoughts were still his own, and as he watched the light blossom in the sky off to the north, he realized what it signified almost immediately.

Shenziencis did as well. "Heaven's Spire is not far from my temple," she said, lips curling sweetly into a smile. She rested in a perfectly circular coil on the deck, her human head twisted to watch the flare of magic in the distance. Corpses had brought her food and drink from time to time as they had traveled. A glowing gem was set into the golden human flesh at the throat, just above the start of the glossy emerald scales. The gem shone in all the colors of the rainbow. When Nystin found his freedom, he would go for the gem first.

"Wasteful action," the Imperial whose name Nystin didn't know said. He didn't move from the control console where he had stood for the past several hours, making the minute adjustments necessary to keep the airship on course. "The grounding arc requires several hours between uses."

Shenziencis chuckled. "So you are not infallible after all. Rest easy, ancient. I believe your plan can accommodate a delay of a few hours."

The man didn't move. He wasn't controlled like Nystin was—the naga deferred to him—but his body language was too stiff. Maybe he was a golem under all that armor. Maybe he was something even worse than the naga, some kind of daemon riding that poor corpse or a necromancer speaking through the body while he himself was huddled safe in a crypt somewhere.

"What was your plan?" the man asked, and Shenziencis flinched, a little twitch of her tail that Nystin filed away for later.

"I thought the political tension would give me a chance to recover the elven manuscript," she said. "I was able to read it once, long ago, but I have grown more adept in the centuries since. I thought that if I could recover it, I could uncover more clearly the time of your people's return to this world."

"And prevent it," the man said.

Shenziencis flinched again. "I wish only to live. I hoped that I might serve you well, and in learning when you would grace this world with your presence again—"

"Stop." The man's voice suggested that he would have raised a hand to calm her, but he remained stock still. The corpses walking the deck had formed around Shenziencis, poised to defend her. "You were a worthy adversary, Queen of the Cold River. Do not demean yourself by lying."

Shenziencis glared, though the corpses around her shuffled back to their normal positions. Nystin tried to move. The muscles of his back and stomach strained, but his arms and legs remained locked. Still, she was weaker when distracted. Another note to file away.

"Of *course* I wished to prevent it," the naga said, rising up on her coils to face the man. "I was born from the magic that leaked out of the Temple of Butterflies. Over centuries of careful, patient work, I grew from the legendary guardian of an old ancient ruin into an oracle whose wisdom was sought by the Emperor himself. I had servants who would fight and die at my command, even *without* my magic to use their words upon them! I had a *life!*" The gem at her throat blazed. "And then one of *your* Hunter golems attacked my temple. It called me a waste of magic, an accident that had no business existing." Her coils twisted and twined, hypnotic in their agitation. "It took hundreds of my servants, the living *and* the dead, to break your golem, and when it was done, even as *it* died, *my* life was over." Her face twisted into something monstrous inhuman as she snarled. "The Queen of the Cold River faded to a distant memory, so that no golems would come hunting for her. The oracle respected across the empire was replaced by a simple *attendant*, and everything I had worked for, I cast away to *hide*."

"You used the Hunter golem's body," the man said.

"It seemed appropriate. I am a wasteful error of your magic, after all." Shenziencis smiled venomously. "Why should I not steal a body to hide in as well?" The coils beneath her head twisted in an approximation of a shrug. "I wished to live, and I have had centuries to learn patience, to be less than I seem. I suspect you have learned much the same, Arikayurichi."

"*Iry kahyur'isti*," the man said. "That was my original . . . *name* is the wrong word, but my purpose."

"'*We will rule,*'" Shenziencis said. "And the Imperials who spoke the language of the ancients heard, and thought only that you spoke of them."

"The Bringer of Order," the man said, "to a world lost to chaos, and waste, and other distasteful things . . . like you." At his words, Shenziencis narrowed her eyes. "You *are* leakage from our magic, an inefficient waste of resources. Your magic twists the words of the living and the bodies of the dead." The man raised his ax, and turned the head to face her, and Shenziencis flinched, the corpses around her coming to readiness again. "But that does not invalidate your right to exist."

"Meaning?" Shenziencis did not take her eyes off the ax. Not the man, Nystin noted, but the ax. They were at the corner of his vision, and he had not been given leave to turn, but he could still make it out.

"When we return, adjustments will be necessary on both sides," the man said, lowering his ax to his side. "When we deployed the Hunter golems, we never imagined the complexity creatures such as you could attain. Serve me honestly, and I will see to it that you live . . . and, if you wish, the other creatures like you—provided they are willing to serve."

Shenziencis went still. She raised an eyebrow at the man. "Is this part of your plan? You wish to comfort me so that I do not see my death coming, when Heaven's Spire reaches the Temple of Butterflies?"

The man chuckled at that. "The blast will destroy much of the Empire and the Republic," he said. "The human deaths it will cause are necessary for my people to return. Yours is not. Be at peace, Queen of the Cold River."

And while Nystin doubted Shenziencis fully believed him, he could feel that some part of her *was* at peace, surprised and touched. She had spent centuries believing that the people responsible for the magic that created her thought her a monster whose existence was a monstrosity. Now, for the first time, she felt that she belonged.

In some part of whatever the naga had instead of a heart, something small and tender blossomed.

Nystin knew this because, for one moment, he felt the control slip.

He had practiced the maneuver for the past several hours. His right hand went to the dagger at his boot, even as he pivoted and kicked off the railing with his other leg, stiff muscles wobbly but still strong enough.

She turned, and her mouth opened, and Nystin slammed a backhand across her face, the shock of impact enough to stop the words that would lock his muscles. He hooked fingers under her nose and wrenched her head back, baring her throat and the glowing rainbow gem. He brought the silver dagger down on the source of the fairy creature's power.

The haft of a magical ax cracked across his wrist, and the silver dagger fell to the deck.

"Your resolve is admirable," it said, and Nystin realized that the voice was coming from the ax itself even as emerald coils wrapped around him, "but she is mine, now. She will live."

"*Stop*," the naga hissed, and Nystin froze, his muscles cramping at the shock.

"You are mine as well," the ax said to Nystin, "so you will *also* live."

Shenziencis glared at Nystin, then looked to the ax and nodded shortly.

"Although," the ax added, "after what she does to you, that may not be to your advantage."

Shenziencis smiled.

The blasts of fire from the ground below hadn't gone unnoticed on Heaven's Spire, and when the great surge of blinding light had blasted down from the city to destroy the Imperial garrison below, the people of Heaven's Spire had taken to the streets.

Groups of wealthy merchants and lesser nobility packed the well-lit shopping plazas, chanting and waving signs. Glowlamps were torn from their casings and used as makeshift torches, waved to lead the crowd from the markets to the temples, and then from the temples to the palaces.

Everyone in the city that night was shouting, fighting, demanding answers.

This made it somewhat difficult for Captain Pyvic to get to the archvoyant's palace.

"Justicar business!" he bellowed, pushing through the crowd elbow-first. "One side!" A big red-faced man shoved into him, and he shoved back, clearing a few more feet for himself.

"War's gonna be over by the time we get there!" Kail shouted from behind him.

"Thank you, Kail!" Pyvic saw a man in the crowd pull a knife, shoved forward, and punched the man behind the ear. The man went down in the crowd. "A shame you never wanted to join the justicars, with that keen deductive int—" He broke off as another wave of people crashed into him.

Then the ground heaved beneath his feet as a massive boom sent everyone to their knees.

Desidora raised Ghylspwr back into the air dramatically, the only person still standing. "I am a priestess of the gods and a wielder of a weapon of the ancients," she cried, "and I cannot save you until you *get out of my way!*"

"*Besyn larveth'is!*" Ghylspwr boomed over her head, and then slammed back down.

Every window on the block shattered, and glowlamps popped and went dark as the ground sang like a beaten drum. The crowd fell back, and Desidora raised Ghylspwr again, looked down the street, and started walking.

Pyvic and Kail fell in behind her as the crowd parted.

"I liked how you neglected to say *who* you were a priestess of," Kail said.

"Shut up, Kail." Desidora had Ghylspwr raised before her, and the street had miraculously cleared before them.

"Because with the hammer, I'd've been thinking at *least* Esa-jolar. Maybe even Io-fergajar . . . except that you're wearing a dress."

"Shut *up*, Kail."

"I didn't see *you* clearing a path," Pyvic said to Kail.

"You think I'm being sarcastic? That was some great lying there! It wouldn't even have set off a verifier ward! I wish Icy were here to learn from this!"

"Sadly, he broke his leg saving us after you got your airship destroyed," Pyvic said without missing a beat.

"That hurts, Justicar. That wounds me."

"Yes, Pyvic, show some respect," Desidora added. "Her name was *Iofegemet.*"

Pyvic stifled a laugh, and then they turned the corner, and the archvoyant's palace stood before them. The great front lawn was lit by golden glowlamps, and hedges trimmed to look like dragons and manticores loomed large in the shadows. A great fountain spat streams of water that were bolstered with illusory light to create a falling display in all the colors of the rainbow.

It all sat safe behind high walls and wrought-iron gates protected with warding magic.

"How did all of you break into the palace last time?" Pyvic asked as they approached the front gate.

"Tern used a grappling line," Desidora said. "Ululenia turned into a fish and swam up through the water pipes."

"I think Icy just held his breath," Kail added.

"I'm not sure we have time for any of those options at the moment," Pyvic said.

"I agree." Desidora had not stopped walking toward the gate, which sat closed and locked, doubtlessly secured by warding magic. "Ghylspwr?"

"Kutesosh gajair'is!"

Her blow blasted the gate clean off its hinges. It flew across the lawn, took the head off a marble statue of a peasant girl, and smashed into the fountain.

"Direct approach it is," Kail said as warding alarms began shrieking all across the lawn. Guards poured out of the great palace itself, the faster human versions and the slower but much larger security golems behind them.

"I am Justicar Captain Pyvic, here on a matter of Republic security!" he shouted, throwing his shoulders back and stepping past Desidora as guards raced toward them, silhouettes against the brilliant glow of the palace behind them. "The entire city of Heaven's Spire is in immediate danger!"

"Of course it is," came a familiar voice from one of the guards, "which is why the justicars have been here the entire time."

"Justicar Derenky." Pyvic nodded, squinting into the darkness as Derenky came forward, smirking. "Report."

"Report?" Derenky laughed as guards closed in around Pyvic and the others. "We're at war, *Captain*, and some of us had to stay here and deal with matters of Republic security instead of chasing our girlfriend the *thief* into the Elflands."

"If Heaven's Spire uses its energy blast on the Temple of Butterflies," Desidora said, "the resulting explosion will destroy a quarter of the Empire and a third of the Republic."

Pyvic had the exquisite satisfaction of watching Derenky actually shut his damn mouth.

"The temple's an old artifact of the ancients, too," he said into the sudden silence around them. "You know how dangerous it can be to bang artifacts of the ancients against each other." He raised his voice, picking out the justicars among the palace guards by posture and stance, since most of them were still just silhouettes. "The whole thing is a setup by someone who wants both nations to destroy each other. I picked up that information while chasing my girlfriend the thief into the Elflands." He smiled at Derenky, showing some teeth. Another justicar stepped out of the shadows into the light, and Pyvic nodded at the heavyset female form. "Jyrre?"

"Captain." She nodded, her dark face pinched but calm. "I think I know where the weapon's being controlled."

"What?" Derenky shouted.

"Archvoyant Bertram ordered us to stay quiet about it, but I saw something in the rear garden." She grimaced. "It's a large column of crystal they had brought in special not long ago. We haven't been allowed near it."

"What are you talking about?" Derenky said. "I've been out back. I haven't seen a damned thing!"

"Damn it, Derenky!" Jyrre glared. "Everyone knows you want the captain's job. Are you going to risk the life of the Republic for it?"

The guards and the other justicars were silent. The security golems, finally catching up, clanked to a halt and surveyed the crowd, evidently waiting for orders.

"Show me," Pyvic said to Jyrre, and she nodded and started up one of the garden paths. Pyvic fell into step beside her, with guards and golems following. "And I'll need a spare blade."

"Misplaced your last one?" Derenky asked, as one of the palace guard handed Pyvic a fresh blade.

"Yes, Derenky. That's precisely how it happened. Well deduced. Who controls the golems?"

"We do," Derenky answered. "Archvoyant Bertram gave me direct control when he brought the justicars in to provide additional security to the palace."

"Good." Pyvic looked at the palace, sheathed in light from the glowlamps on the walls. They were approaching a lit courtyard surrounded by marble statues. "Any other additions to palace security?"

"Military units," Jyrre said. "Haven't been able to get anything out of them."

"The Knights of Gedesar," Derenky said, smiling at Jyrre. "If you look carefully at their armor, you'd have noted the blacked-out insignia . . . and the fact that it's *yvkefer*-alloy armor would also be a clue for any competent justicar."

"Sorry," Jyrre said tightly. "Suppose I've been a little distracted with the war on." She gestured ahead, past the courtyard. "Should be just through here, Captain."

"What, the ambush?" Pyvic asked, and stopped.

So did everyone else.

"Captain?" Jyrre asked.

"The ambush," Pyvic said, "that you're going to lead me into with the Knights of Gedesar." He smiled at Jyrre. "You've always been smarter than Derenky, Justicar, and you've got more experience with fairy-creature crimes than anyone else on the squad. There's no way he'd make them while you missed them, unless you were lying because you're their inside source."

"Those guys always *were* a little too good at tracking us down," Kail said.

Jyrre stepped back slowly. "Captain . . ."

"Tell me something, Derenky," Pyvic said, "do you want my job?"

Derenky smiled thinly. "Desperately, sir."

"Would you like it right now, right in the middle of this political nightmare?"

"All things considered," Derenky said, "I'd just as soon wait for you to trip up and then have you shuffled aside."

"Right." Pyvic drew his blade. "I don't see you trying to feed me to the flamecannons. You're a political animal."

"Which is why he would come straight from the justicar station to the kahva-shop," Desidora said, "to embarrass you by making you appear distracted from your job."

"While Jyrre," Pyvic finished, "who according to *everyone* left before he did, somehow arrived after him. Tell me, Justicar, who did you meet along the way?"

"Them," Jyrre said, and jerked a thumb back toward the statues. "Fire!"

The crossbow bolts came hissing out of the darkness.

"Down!" Pyvic yelled, even as guards fell with bolts in their throats. Kail was already rolling, and Desidora stood where she was, Ghylspwr spinning before her to knock bolts aside. "Derenky! Get those golems moving!"

"I'm trying!" Derenky yelled from the ground behind Desidora. "The control crystal isn't activating! They should be—"

"*Kutesosh gajair'is!*" Ghylspwr yelled, and Pyvic looked over.

The golems were indeed coming online, he saw.

One of them reached out, grabbed the control crystal from Derenky's hand, and crushed it.

"I recommend that you decelerate," the golem said to Archvoyant Bertram. "Since you insisted on unnecessarily destroying the garrison, you will be unable to activate the grounding arc for several hours. The Knights of Gedesar have encountered criminals who wish to disrupt the plan. Steps will need to be taken."

Archvoyant Bertram stood in a hub of crystals in the center of a cavern deep in the heart of the Archvoyant's palace. It was massive, the ceiling lost in the darkness that shrouded most of the room. In half the chamber, the floor was marked regularly with inlaid runes shaped from faintly glowing crystals. In the other half, the floor was missing entirely, leaving a great chasm that presumably led to the underside of the city below.

"It was hardly unnecessary," Bertram said, glaring at the golem. "When my predecessor's schemes fell through, he ended up fighting among the *lapiscaela*. One stray blast of lightning from his ring destabilized the entire city. I would prefer we not lose the capital city of the Republic to a dozen Imperial soldiers with flamecannons."

The golem looked at Bertram. It was unnerving. The thing's eyes were like stained glass diamonds, bright blue where the whites would be on a person, with glossy black chips of obsidian in place of pupils. Bertram couldn't tell whether the thing actually *saw* out of them or used magical senses and just moved the eyes around to try to make Bertram feel more comfortable. Neither option made Bertram happy.

"The *lapiscaela* were destabilized because you lack the knowledge to adjust their energy-modulation parameters," it finally said. "I altered the parameters to render the attacks from the flamecannons ineffective."

"Then those people at the garrison didn't die because of me," Bertram shot back, glaring. "They died because you didn't bother to share information."

"I'm sure that's a great comfort to them," Cevirt said from where he sat in a folding chair about midway between the control crystals and the chasm.

"Is there a problem, Voyant Cevirt?" Bertram asked. His last meal was roiling around in his stomach like a glowing coal, and he would have happily killed for a cup of kahva.

"How many people are at the Temple of Butterflies?" Cevirt asked.

"Do you mean living people, or corpses sent to attack the Republic?"

Cevirt glared at him. "I *mean* that we've just demonstrated to the Empire that we can wipe any city off the face of the earth. Do you really think we need to use the weapon again?"

"Damn it, Cevirt!" Bertram pointed angrily at him. "You sat in my office and chewed me out for not being willing to wage war! Don't get gutless on me now that we have the means to win!"

"It's a precedent, Archvoyant." Cevirt stood and came forward, leaning over the console. "At the border, it was self-defense after that garrison fired first. At the Temple of Butterflies, it will be an offensive strike to secure an objective."

Bertram looked up at the man he'd played politics with for more than twenty years. Cevirt didn't look much better than Bertram felt. His eyes were sunken and bloodshot, and his hands were shaking. "What do you want me to do, Cevirt? Let them fire first?"

"I want you to think, Bertram." Cevirt gave him a rictus grin and shook his head. "I know we're doing the right thing. I know we're saving lives. But who gets voted in after you? And after them? Do you trust some nobleman's son to do the same soul-searching and deliberation you've done, after he grew up hearing the stories about Heaven's Spire blasting all its enemies? I mean . . ." He waved at the chasm off to one side. "What is *he* going to use it against? Ogres causing trouble in the deep forests? Elves refusing to work with our lapitects? Some idiot peasants in a village protesting the latest taxes?"

Bertram swallowed. "Give me something else, Cevirt. What do you propose?"

"I . . . the airships sometimes dropped leaflets in a town before doing a raid." Cevirt looked down and shrugged. "Maybe if we—"

A liquid thump made Bertram look up in time to see Cevirt hit the ground, limp but not dead, at least as far as Bertram could see.

"The existing solution is the only reasonable way to save your people," the golem said, turning its shining diamond eyes to Bertram. "The grounding arc is already being prepared. It cannot be stopped now."

Bertram met its unnatural gaze directly. He'd faced down enough enemies in his time to know that looking at Cevirt would be a sign of weakness. "You just told me that we needed time to prepare for another blast. We should use that time to ensure that this is the proper solution."

"It is," the golem said, its stare not moving.

Bertram smiled. "I agree, of course. You believe Cevirt's plan to drop leaflets would warn the enemy of our intentions unwisely?"

"Yes."

"Fair enough. If you will remind me how to alter the course of the city, I will decelerate us and plot a course for the Imperial capital." Bertram smiled reassuringly. As he spoke, his right thumb squeezed a hidden stud on a ring on his middle finger, priming it to fire. The ring had a short range and only a few charges, but the golem still clicked and clacked when it walked. It couldn't be held together *that* tightly. "A strike against the heart of the Empire will demonstrate our superiority more than the destruction of a minor temple."

"No," the golem said.

As pain like Bertram had never believed possible shot through his body, the golem leaned forward until its diamond eyes were just inches from his face.

"We will continue on this course."

Twenty-One

Loch TOOK A FEW EARLY HANDS, GOT COCKY, GOT BURNED, AND then quickly realized that Irrethelathlialann had been studying her style. He raised hard, baited her into throwing money at a bad hand, and had her down back below where they'd started inside the first hour.

"I expected humans to be better," he said, raking a pile of chips toward him as the dealer shuffled. "But since your fighting style is mostly muscle, I suppose it stands to reason that you would suffer in any of the more complex forms of communication."

The dealer flipped cards at all of them, the motions so practiced that every card landed perfectly placed. "Flop shows dueling queens, which is entirely appropriate at this table. Mistress Helianthia, the first bet is yours."

The elven woman with the dark green skin smiled behind her golden spectacles. "I will take one hidden and stand."

"Helianthia," said Irrethelathlialann, "your scent-songs are a beauty and a marvel, and I would one day give my greatest understanding of beauty to play against you with the grace you deserve." He tossed an open card to the dealer. "Sadly, I am bound to defeat this human, who shares none of your countless virtues. Raise four hundred."

"Fold." Veiled Lightning lowered her cards in disgust.

"I see four," Loch said, "and raise two more."

"I appreciate you making this faster for all of us," Irrethelathlialann said.

"I will remain in long enough to at least see my new card," Helianthia said, still smiling, and slid her chips in.

"You do know that I have those queens as well," Irrethelathlialann asked Loch, seeming concerned, as he saw her raise.

"Oh, you have *those* ones, yes."

"It's just that you have a two and a seven showing, and neither of them are even the same *suit*, not that that would help you, since the flush isn't recognized in the Elflands."

"Whereas the king and the nine you've got over there really help you out a ton." Loch smiled.

The dealer flicked out the third open card. "Seven. At least two pair for the Urujar."

"At least." Irrethelathlialann fidgeted with his ring, studying his cards. "Raised two, discarded one, no discards from the Imperial, Helianthia discard one and had an ace and knave showing . . ." He slid another two hundred into the pot. Loch matched it.

"I believe my curiosity has been satisfied," Helianthia said, and folded.

The dealer flicked out the last open card. "Three. No good unless one of you was aiming to draw for a concordance."

"Check." Irrethelathlialann lowered his cards. "Unless the Urujar is more confident?"

Loch slid another hundred into the pot. "A little more."

Irrethelathlialann matched it. "You have the third queen."

"And you have the fourth," Loch said, turning over her hidden cards.

"Ah, no, I'm afraid Helianthia had the fourth," Irrethelathlialann said, "which was why she stayed in long enough to see that I was serious." He turned over his hidden cards. "Knave and ten. In the Elflands, we refer to this as a straight."

He smiled and raked in the chips.

"Please, try not to run out of chips until my luck improves," Veiled Lightning said beside Loch. "I would greatly love to kick you out myself."

Loch ignored her and looked at Dairy, who came over with another drink. "Any chance I could get something special from the bartender?"

"I'll ask," Dairy said, "but it might not be ready yet."

Loch sighed, smiled, and threw in her chips for the next hand.

Tern peeked around the corner, saw an elven guard coming, popped back, and then decided to hell with it and stepped out.

"I beg your pardon," the guard said as he saw them, "but this level is intended for crew members onlurrrrrk." He fell over with a sleep dart in his shoulder.

"I take it we're eschewing subtlety at this point, then?" Hessler asked.

"Ululenia said Loch's flailing. You mind finding a place to stow him?" Tern asked, not pausing. The stupid elf carpet on the stupid elf treeship pulled at her feet.

"Well, I had assumed that someone should, since I doubt we'll avoid detection with him lying in the middle of . . . I'll just catch up, then."

Tern's shoulder was hurting, which was part of the healing process, and she'd gotten tied up by elves and a very big man who was quite possibly a dragon, which wasn't part of the healing process. The original plan of "steal the book while Loch stalled" had been replaced by "hope Loch wins the tournament against seasoned professionals," and large tournaments had a nasty habit of making it significantly difficult to cheat.

Not impossible, though.

She reached the door, glanced up and down the hallway, tried briefly to pick the lock, and then just broke the door in with a few well-placed kicks from her steel-toed boots.

The room inside was an ancillary security pod, which in practical terms meant that it was a cramped, dark little room with strange pod-like growths on the walls and a security guard sitting in front of a pool with the glowing mushrooms in it.

He was already on his feet as Tern stepped in, since she'd had to kick the door a few times, but he hadn't drawn his blade, likely because nobody in their right mind would just burst into the room.

Tern shot *him* with a sleep dart as well, and he looked at her in hurt confusion before slumping to the ground.

"Oh, yeah," she said, nudging him aside. "No more elf crap. No more poems, no more names with too many vowels, no more inability to use imperatives." She pulled a vial from one pocket, unstoppered it, and upended a dose of thick green liquid into the pool. "We're finishing this bad-boy human-style."

As the pool began to bubble and froth, Tern looked up at Hessler, who stood in the doorway staring at her wordlessly.

"Problem?" she asked.

Hessler scratched at the back of his neck. "I'm a little embarrassed about how attractive you were right then."

"Good boyfriend." Tern grinned and held up her hand drill. "Get to work on the wall."

They worked for a moment in silence. Tern added a few more reagents to the pool.

Then she began swearing.

"Problem?" Hessler asked. He'd made a decent hole in the wall and was working with some green vines that had been threaded inside it.

"You could say that." Tern gestured at the pool. "It's locked."

"*How* locked?"

"Locked enough that I can maybe do the wards, but the navigation is totally off limits." Tern banged the pool. "Either Diz or Ululenia missed something, or they upped the security. I can't do it."

Hessler's hands came down gently on her shoulders. "It's all right."

"It's *not* all right!" Tern spun around and glared up at him. "How the hell is this *all right*? The whole plan hinged on getting hold of navigation, and now we're screwed, and the Republic and the Empire go to war because I can't access anything more secure than their damn scrying pods!"

Hessler blinked. "They have scrying pods?"

"Of course they do. We're probably on one of them right now." Tern looked up at a little glowing blossom in the corner of the room. "Hey, security guys, here we are. Sorry, just trying to stop a war . . . but we can't." Her shoulder ached, and she was still too tired to be up and running around like this. "If Diz were here, or Ululenia wasn't tapped . . ."

"No." Hessler's hands came back down on her shoulders again, and he pulled her in. "They aren't here, but we are. A brilliant, well-trained, beautiful—"

"One-armed," Tern added.

"—one-armed alchemist . . ." Hessler lifted her chin up. "And an illusionist."

He smiled in a way that made Tern's stomach flip over and added, "Now, if you could show me to those scrying pods?"

The Temple of Butterflies was a frenzy of activity, glowlamps blazing atop the pools in the great courtyard and all along the walls. The tiny squares of jade set into the courtyard's marble flagstones blazed with their own light, sending a hum of energy through the air and making the golden sand quiver in the training squares. Runes on the vases along the walls pulsed steadily, and the vivid green bushes shone with the same magical heartbeat, their warm radiance spreading with each pulse along the walls.

Imperial soldiers manned the walls, ready at the flame-cannons. They diligently checked all directions, in the event that the approach of Heaven's Spire was a ruse to cover an attack from some other approach. A fortune in charms were spent every hour, shattered bits of crystal crunching under-foot as the men on the walls magically enhanced their night vision and ability to sense the presence of invisible foes.

In the inner sanctum at the top of the stairs, monks in golden robes moved through the building with perfect deliberation. Here, a pair of young students adjusted the position of the great bronze gong under the supervision of an old man who stood with his head cocked and his eyes closed, listening. There, a woman of middle years paced the hall, pausing every so often to whisk a bit of dust from the runes on the walls with a velvet-tipped wand.

In the innermost sanctum, two distinguished figures waited.

General Jade Blossom was a square-jawed woman of perhaps fifty. Her armor was enameled black and inlaid with jade, ruby, and opal into the shape of a twining dragon. Her hair was cut short, with no attempt made to hide the streaks of white at her temples. She stood with her arms clasped behind her, looking at the glossy black table in the center of the room, and the gong decorated with a great butterfly that stood behind it.

First Listener Sparrow was an ancient man whose golden robes were decorated with crimson butterflies at the wrists and collar. He wore a crimson skullcap as well. The wings on his wasp-bodied face were a pair of smoked-glass spectacles whose magic compensated for the blindness that had fallen upon him decades ago. He knelt before the glossy black table, his fingers tracing the contours of the golden bowls and crystal glasses set upon it.

"Less than an hour," Sparrow said, and Blossom let out something between a grunt and a sigh and shifted in place. "Its energies are still not sufficient to attack again, but the city maintains its present speed."

"Perhaps they think we cannot hurt them." Blossom turned as if to pace, then checked herself. The old monk had asked that she remain still.

"If the interplay of energies at the garrison is accurate, they are correct in that assumption," Sparrow said, running a finger along the lip of a vase and raising a thin, spectral tone. "Our flamecannons will do nothing."

"This temple is supposed to be indestructible," Blossom growled. Her knuckles popped as she clenched one fist.

"Against anything less than the wrath of the ancients personified, it is," Sparrow said, and then paused to look at the water in the golden bowl. The surface rippled as though a single pebble had broken its stillness. "An airship approaches from Republic space."

"So it *is* a distraction." Blossom stepped toward the door. "Threaten us with the city, then land troops to seize the temple rather than destroying it."

"No." Sparrow reached out to the bowl, then grimaced and removed his spectacles. His eyes were pale milky blue, unfocused and wet as he touched the bowl as though caressing a lover for the first time. "This is no enemy. Attendant Shenziencis returns." His shoulders slumped in relaxation. "We are saved, General."

Blossom stepped outside and barked the order for the flamecannons to stand down. Under the foolishly ostentatious armor that offered protection only from the barbed wit of nobles and the condescending stares of old monks, she was sweating and hungry.

Ten minutes later, Attendant Shenziencis swept up the steps and into the inner sanctum, with Princess Veiled Lightning's personal bodyguard Gentle Thunder at her side. Shenziencis wore simple green robes rather than the ringmail Blossom had seen her wear on formal occasions, showing nothing of her body save her face as she moved into the room with liquid grace. Gentle Thunder's armor was battered and chipped, and he moved with a hint of stiffness Blossom only noticed from years of watching the movements of men who lived by making others die.

"Attendant." Sparrow dropped to a bow. "We await your words."

"You have already begun the preparations," she said, looking at the vases on the table, and something under her robe moved that Blossom could not quite place, something that seemed like the instinctual reaching of a hand, but placed wrong. "Your work is beyond reproach, Sparrow."

"What of the princess?" Blossom asked, because someone had to, and Gentle Thunder turned to her and bowed.

"She is dead," he said, and Sparrow gasped. "Slain by the Republic's assassins while she met with them in secret talks to negotiate a peace treaty."

General Jade Blossom had expected no less when Thunder had walked in without her. Still, her gut clenched, and her bones suddenly felt the four hours of sleep she had gotten in the last three days. Veiled Lightning had been intelligent, skilled, and tougher than most nobles ever learned to be. Had she fought a few battles in the world outside the palace walls, she might have grown into a remarkable Empress. "Then why are you here, Thunder?"

"Veil ordered me to return Shenziencis safely here," Gentle Thunder said grimly. "It was her last request. When our work here is done, I will embrace the blade."

Blossom was tired, and Thunder's voice seemed to echo faintly inside his helmet, giving his words a tinny buzz that set her teeth on edge. "And what is our work, then? We have no means of stopping Heaven's Spire from destroying this temple."

"Untrue," Gentle Thunder said, and stepped past Sparrow where he bowed. "The city approaches, and it will not fall to flamecannons. However, in our meetings with the Republic nobles, we learned of a weakness that may still bring it to earth." He turned to Shenziencis. "Attendant, you will complete preparations as we discussed?"

"I would be honored," Shenziencis said, bowing, and though Blossom was exhausted, something in it still nagged at her, whether it was the respect the temple master was showing a simple bodyguard or just the way the woman moved as she inclined her head. "It will be as you have said."

"General," said Thunder, turning to Blossom. "I go now to carry out the final wishes of my mistress. I beg of you, trust Attendant Shenziencis as you would our own Veiled Lightning, for she carries our last hope of survival against the barbarians of the Republic."

Blossom raised an eyebrow, about to ask what exactly *that* was supposed to tell her as far as useful information, but then Gentle Thunder brought up his magical ax, the Bringer of Order, and swung it at the gong on the wall.

"Besyn larveth'is!" the ax cried as it struck, and instead of the great noise that Blossom was already flinching against, the room was bathed in brilliant light.

Gentle Thunder and his magical ax were silhouetted against that light, flickering, and when it dimmed, he was gone.

General Jade Blossom looked at Attendant Shenziencis and First Listener Sparrow. "Well, then," she said. "How the hell do you expect us to get through this crap alive?"

When the *suf-gesuf* game reached the next break, Irrethelathlialann was up and Helianthia, the elven woman with the forest-green skin and the golden spectacles, was about even, along with Veiled Lightning.

Loch, of course, was down.

She didn't take a chance on leaving the main hall this time. There were guards by the doorways, and only in a perfect world would all of them be loyal to the ship's captain. She went to the bar instead, where Dairy was waiting for her.

"Water?" she asked, looking at the wooden cup he held out in her direction.

"You told me to cut you off after two, ma'am."

"That sounds like a terrible thing for Past Me to have said." Loch drank the water anyway. "Any word on getting that special?"

"Nothing yet. I'll let you know as soon as I hear anything."

"Or she will." Loch looked up as Ululenia entered the room.

Everyone looked up as Ululenia entered the room.

The unicorn's natural shape was a horse with a shining rainbow horn of energy, of course, but her normal human shape was a slim, fresh-faced woman with ash-blond hair and a simple white dress.

Tonight, she had taken the form of an elf, her skin pale jade and her cheeks lit with opals that shimmered with their own rainbow light. Her hair remained ash-white, but she had pulled it up into a complex coiling knot that left little curls free to dangle at the side of her face, glittering where they caught the light. Her dress was a strapless white satin sheath with coils of jade twining around her curves in ways that drew the eye.

"Seriously, nothing?" Loch asked Dairy. "Because I'm a few years out of date on virginity—and I don't usually go for women—but even I'm a *little* tempted there."

"Sorry."

"Hey, what did I say? No apologies." Loch glanced at Ululenia again. "I'm *mystified*, but no apologies."

"Delicious." The voice came from beside Loch, and she turned to see Irrethelathlialann looking at Ululenia as she came their way, his gaze smoldering. "Is there any chance you could introduce me?"

"Trade you for the book?" Loch asked.

"Sadly, no longer within my purview, as it now resides with my employer."

"Mister Dragon. Yes. We talked. He seems nice." Loch cocked her head, appeared to give it some thought. "Big."

Irrethelathlialann smiled. "I heard about your wager. Do you truly believe that you can win?"

"I believe people are dying, and it's going to be more unless I win."

"Not people," Irrethelathlialann said, smiling. "Humans. Key difference, you see."

"You hate us that much?" Everyone turned to see Veiled Lightning, a drink in hand, standing nearby. "What have we done to earn such disgust as a species in its entirety?"

"What have you done?" He looked at her, and then at Loch, and finally at Ululenia again as she approached. His voice was incredulous, bordering on outraged. "Humans. You litter this world with the magic of the ancients, using carelessly an energy that burns the very souls of others. You spread across the land like locusts, finding any excuse to kill or cut down any life that stands between you and your presumed domination. And even amongst yourselves . . ." He jerked his chin at Loch. "You make war upon your neighbors for the color of their skin, even as your own country reviles you for the color of yours. Whatever humans once were, you have been broken by your beloved ancients, as surely as my people cannot bear crystals and the dwarves slot themselves into three perfect castes. I cannot hate such madness." He smiled and shook his head. "I can only pity it."

Ululenia had been listening with the others. As Irrethelathlialann finished, she extended a hand. "You are cruel . . . but attractive. A pity we did not meet earlier in your life."

"A pity indeed." The elf took her hand, raised it to his lips, and held it there for longer than was absolutely necessary. "Perhaps when your current engagement is finished . . ."

"I have made no commitments." Ululenia bowed, the gems in her cheeks flashing as she caught the elf's eye, and added, "I enjoy flexibility."

"Ululenia!" Dairy looked at her in shock.

She cut him with a look as she drew back her hand from the elf. "Was there something you wanted, Dairy?" He stammered awkwardly for a moment, and she let him, before finally saying, "I did not think so."

"Where's your big black bird?" Loch asked Irrethelathlialann. "Don't you want him around to protect you in case someone tries to read your mind?"

"I'm certain we're all far too civilized for that," Irrethelathlialann said, still smiling.

"And the wards would make it impossible, regardless," Ululenia added.

Veiled Lightning shook her head angrily. "I am pleased that you all find this so amusing."

"She doesn't, usually," Dairy said. "We're trying to stop the war."

"Fascinating. So was I."

"Humans." Irrethelathlialann looked over at Ululenia. "So hard for them to see past differences in the skin to see the truth that lies underneath, is it not?"

Ululenia shrugged one shoulder in a way that accentuated the pale jade skin from her neck down past her collarbone. "Are you interested in what lies underneath?"

"We are ready to begin the next round," came the call from the table, and everyone looked at each other.

Loch slugged the water, handed the cup back to Dairy. "Let me know."

"Yes, ma'am."

She followed the others back to the table. Helianthia was already seated, a drink in one hand, and she looked at them all with curiosity evident even behind her golden spectacles. No one said anything.

The dealer flipped out the cards. Loch took a hand with an obvious trio of nines. Helianthia went in hard against Irrethelathlialann on the next hand but came out with knaves and eights against what turned out to be three fours. Veiled Lightning caught two good hands in a row.

The next hand showed nothing helpful in the flop. Veiled Lightning had what would have been a good start to a flush if the Elflands recognized a flush as a valid hand, which did nothing for her right now. Loch had the start of a possible straight, while Helianthia sat on a pair of tens.

Irrethelathlialann had what looked like garbage. It took Loch a second to remember why he was raising instead of bowing out.

"A concordance?" she asked. "Really?" As Veiled Lightning folded, Loch checked, redrawing a hidden card. Helianthia did the same.

"If you doubt me," he said, "you are more than welcome to offer me more money."

"It's funny," Loch said to Helianthia, "growing up in the Republic, we don't have the concordance, and it feels unfamiliar. I don't quite have the feel for how to guess my odds, the way I would if I were trying to decide whether to hope for an inside straight, or guess whether you had a third ten in your hidden cards."

"Gauging the odds of a concordance *is* difficult," Helianthia agreed, "more a dance than a march, given how many factors are beyond control. The simplest question to start is to see how many face cards you have seen this hand, since Irrethelathlialann's hidden cards must include one, unless he is bluffing."

"Veil had a queen." Loch ticked it off on a finger. "Irrethelathlialann himself has a knave, as do I, and there's a king in the flop." She looked at her hidden cards. "At times like this, I wish I could somehow run the math in my mind, just see all the numbers spread out before me, telling me my odds of picking up this straight and whether he really does have that concordance."

The dealer flipped the next card out. "A seven, giving the Dragon's servant a pair, if he does not, in fact, have a face card hiding before him. No help for the Urujar or the poet."

"It must be tricky, trying to guess whether you're going to see more than just that pair," Loch said to Irrethelathlialann as he raised. "On the off chance you don't have a face card, that is."

"Oh, it's easier for some than others," he murmured, and clasped his hands thoughtfully.

A moment later, he blinked and looked at his bare fingers.

A laugh came from the crowd, and Irrethelathlialann turned to see Ululenia smiling. She leaned over to give him a bow, and as she did, a ring dangled from a thin golden chain on her neck, sparkling in the light.

Irrethelathlialann burst out laughing. "Oh, nicely done!"

"When you played with it, your mannerisms changed," Loch said. "That little clasp of the hands was you activating the ring, tossing out just enough magic from whatever crystal you've got hidden inside it to sharpen your mind."

Helianthia's dark face had gone the sickly color of old lettuce. "No elf would deaden his soul in such a fashion."

"No *poet* would deaden his soul in such a fashion," Irrethelathlialann corrected, still laughing. "Sometimes, out in the real world, it helps to be able to run the numbers a little." He shook his head, grinning at Loch with the crystals in his cheeks glittering merrily. "Oh, you are a rare treasure. I had that ring warded to avoid alarms and everything."

"I imagine that was expensive," Loch said. "Speaking of which, I raise six thousand."

"Check." Helianthia shoved her chips into the pot. Her hand was shaking.

"The only problem with putting your faith in the lovely little unicorn in the low-cut dress, Isafesira, is that you assume I needed the ring to beat you." Irrethelathlialann pointed at Loch. "No straight. You're hoping to draw inside, but you won't, because Veiled Lightning had one of the eights you needed, and I discarded another." He shifted to Helianthia. "You're sitting on three, hoping for four, but even you know it won't happen." He sat back. "I can read your body language. I can read this one-stoned dealer's movements as he shuffles. I can read the odds, even without the very expensive ring I'll be peeling slowly from the unicorn's lovely body later . . . among other things." He slid his chips in. "Check. Next card is either a five or three. I raise twenty thousand."

The dealer flipped out the three of crystals as the last shared card. "One-stoned is a bit offensive."

Loch folded, smiling tightly. Helianthia did the same.

"Ma'am," Dairy said beside her as Irrethelathlialann raked in his chips, "you don't look very good."

"I'm fine, Dairy," she said in a low voice, not looking over.

Dairy coughed. "Would you like a drink?"

Loch looked over then. Dairy held a shotglass on a napkin with a pale pink liquid inside.

"Yes, Dairy. Yes, I would."

Loch took it, raised it, downed it, and handed it back to him. It tasted sweeter than she liked and stronger than she needed, buzzing in her mouth and burning in her throat as it went down.

And something in it crackled and hummed as well, and a moment later, Loch's ears popped.

And a voice in her head said, *As the vixen covers her tracks, so have Tern and Hessler masked my voice to you, Little One. Whenever you are ready, we may show this elf how one actually cheats at cards.*

The good news where security golems were concerned was that they were fairly slow. As long as Pyvic kept running, the golems were in no danger of catching them.

The bad news where security golems were concerned was that even Desidora and her magical hammer hadn't been able to do much more than knock them a few steps backward.

So they ran through the night, bolts hissing behind them and metal feet clanking. The glowlamps inside the gates had flickered and died a few moments after their fight had started, and Pyvic had lost track of time, concentrating only on staying alive and having somewhere to keep running to. They were in the western hedge garden now, which wasn't quite a maze, but offered enough cover to buy them some time.

"Suggestions?" In the darkness, the whole palace had burned like a brand, but now *all* the glowlamps were starting to dim.

"We cannot survive against both the Knights of Gedesar and the golems," Icy said. "Any guards not loyal to the enemy are likely dead."

"The mausoleum," Desidora said between breaths. "There's an entrance that should give us a way inside. Tern, Hessler, and I used it when we broke in last time."

"All right. We're all dead anyway if we don't get inside, so the mausoleum's as good a place as any." Pyvic looked over at Kail, who was scanning the hedges with a scout's ready eyes. "Can you pick the lock?"

"*Besyn larveth'is!*"

"Good point," Pyvic said, nodding to Ghylspwr. "At this point, we can probably just break the door down and be fine."

"I *could* pick the lock, though," Kail muttered.

"We all believe you," Desidora said.

"*Kutesosh gajair'is.*"

"Well, most of us, anyway." Desidora had recovered enough to breathe normally. She nodded and set off through the hedges with Pyvic and the rest in tow.

They passed the stately mausoleum and reached a small servant's entrance shortly after, sneaking through the hedges as far as they could and then finally dashing across a short stretch of lawn. By the time they neared the door, the glowlamps were almost entirely dead.

"I'm guessing that isn't good," Kail said as the lamp by the door failed altogether.

"They must be drawing power to prepare for the next blast," Desidora said.

"Or you sabotaged them," came the calm voice from behind them, and Pyvic turned.

Jyrre stood with a half-dozen Knights of Gedesar at the edge of the nearest hedge. Her normal blade was gone, tossed aside in favor of one of the crystal-tipped maces that the knights favored. Pyvic gave the knights a quick glance. Most of them had chunks torn from their armor, bands battered and hanging loose.

"No crossbows?" Kail asked. "I mean, not that I'm complaining, since you probably would've opened fire instead of coming up to talk with us . . ."

"They lost them," Pyvic said, "when it turned out that the golems weren't on their side, either."

"They are controlled by the unseen player," Icy said, "the one who wishes for the Republic and the Empire to destroy one another."

Pyvic nodded. "So, the question now is whether the Knights of Gedesar want to save the Republic." He looked at them, young men and women for the most part, only a few his own age. "Ladies and gentlemen?"

"You've got a lot of nerve, *Captain*." Jyrre sneered. "You want to act like you're playing some big game the rest of us don't understand, all the while working with a *death priestess*—"

"She's not a death priestess anymore," Kail tossed off.

"And monsters," Jyrre went on, as if he hadn't spoken, "and criminals. You were a damned fine justicar until you let them corrupt you. Now you'd rather play in the shadows than carry out the law you swore to uphold. I grew up on the frontier, Captain. I learned the hard way that you don't go into that darkness. You don't cross that line. And when others do, even people you respect . . ." She brought up the hand she'd had down by her side and stared at Pyvic down the length of a bolt. "And we didn't lose *all* our crossbows."

"Captain!" The cry made all of them turn, and then Justicar Derenky tackled Jyrre and crashed to the turf.

Pyvic went in fast, Kail at his side. He stabbed at one knight's face, and as the man blocked, Kail tackled him at the knees. Pyvic stabbed down through the visor, deep enough to be sure, and then spun and kicked another knight in the knee as he raised his mace over Kail.

Off to the side, Desidora smashed one knight to the ground with a blow that tore a furrow in the ground, then blocked a blow from another.

"Thought these guys were tough." Kail slammed a stolen mace into the helmet of the knight who'd dropped to one knee. "What's the matter, guys? Did I leave your mothers too tired to make you breakfast this morning?"

Pyvic ducked back from a blow that would have caved in his skull, lunged in, and trapped the knight's arms. "I *assume* the golems left them tired."

"Hell, we're *all* tired." Kail smashed his own mace into the back of the knight's helmet before he could free himself. "Difference between a knight and a scout?" He turned as Desidora smashed a second knight to the turf, then blocked a blow from the third.

Kail's mace flew end over end and smashed into the third knight's legs from behind.

As the knight dropped to his knees, Pyvic took two running steps and slashed through ringmail to open the man's throat. "Tired just makes a scout fight dirtier," he called back, and went for Jyrre.

She had a knife in Derenky's ribs, though the blond justicar had gotten a few blows of his own in and wasn't finished yet. Pyvic hauled her off of him and put his blade to her throat as she turned.

"You backed the wrong side," he said. "You got good people killed doing it, and I don't have time to arrest you right now. If I were what you thought I was, it'd be *really* easy for me to slit your throat. But I'm not. Ghylspwr? Unconscious, please."

Her eyes narrowed. "You bastard," she snapped, one hand coming up so that he wouldn't notice the one going to her waist. "If you think—"

"Shut up, Jyrre." He grabbed her wrist with his free hand, twisted it into a lock, and put her on her knees. "And if you wake up before I get back, I suggest you turn yourself in peacefully, because you and I both know I'll find you, and if it's heat of battle next time, I can cut you down and sleep like a baby."

"*Kun-kabynalti osu fuir'is,*" Ghylspwr said in Desidora's hands, and rapped Jyrre sharply on the head. The justicar dropped without another word.

"Thank you. Derenky, any chance you're going to die and leave me in peace?"

"Sadly, sir," Derenky said, holding the blade in his stomach, "I still very much want your job."

"Noted." Pyvic looked at Desidora. "If you were the control mechanism for a giant energy weapon, where would you be?"

It was Kail who answered. "The big room with the runes on the floor. It controlled all the security for the archvoyant's palace. You remember, Diz?"

"Being possessed by the power of death didn't affect my memory," Desidora said, grinning. "I can get us there."

She smashed open the door with a single blow from Ghylspwr and took off down the hallway.

"Possessed by the spirit of death?" Pyvic asked, falling into step with Kail as the two of them jogged after Desidora.

"Yeah, she was dead for a bit, and when she came out of it, she was pretty pissed off."

"That when whatever happened to you two happened to you two?"

"More or less," Kail said, and didn't elaborate. "Later I got possessed and took out her and Tern. That wasn't good, either."

Pyvic shook his head and kept running.

Desidora's memory was sound, and she led them to a narrow hallway not far from the grand ballroom, where a previously blank section of wall had slid open to reveal a darkened doorway.

"I believe you guessed correctly," Desidora said. "Shall we?"

Pyvic nodded, and they went in, weapons raised.

The room was lit primarily by the floor, where runes glowed in a flickering pattern, shifting through the rainbow with no two the same color at any given moment. Half the floor ended in a great chasm that presumably led to the underside of the city, although Pyvic suspected that the rules of nature in this room might be a bit looser than usual.

Archvoyant Bertram sat at a hub of crystals. A figure stood before him that was much more human than the great stomping piles of metal out in the gardens, but much less human than anyone else in the room. It turned as they came in, and its eyes shone blue. "You have come."

"Ghylspwr, please hit it," Pyvic said, not altering his stride, "and continue to do so every time it tries to put itself back together. Archvoyant Bertram, I'm guessing the golem has *not* informed you that using the weapon on the Temple of Butterflies will destroy half the Republic?"

Bertram didn't respond, didn't even look up from the console.

Desidora and Ghylspwr smashed into the golem, who seemed too surprised to resist. Kail had his mace raised and was looking off into the darkness of the chasm. "Last time, there were spectral . . . ghosts? Spirit golems? I don't know. They came out of the chasm. If someone's using the golems, they might show up again."

"Noted. Archvoyant, please. I know you didn't want this war, and no matter how far you've gone, it's not too late to . . ." Pyvic trailed off as he reached the control console and looked down.

The crystals on the control console had sprouted dozens of little spurs, a forest of needle-thin spikes that extended from their base into Archvoyant Bertram's fingers. They glowed in an oscillating pattern that matched the runes on the floor, and Pyvic realized with sick fascination that he could see them glowing under the skin of the man's hands and arms.

The archvoyant didn't move his head to look at him, but his eyes flicked ever so faintly up to Pyvic. Words whispered from under the man's slow and wheezing breaths. "Help . . . me."

The whites of his eyes were glowing as well.

"Desidora? Ghylspwr?" Pyvic looked over to where they stood over the slowly reforming pile of crystals. "I may need you to do some very careful smashing."

"*Besyn lar—*"

The chasm flared with crackling radiance, and then it went dark, so dark that it was as though the darkness itself were a shade of light, bathing the room in a blackness so complete that even the afterimages were wiped from Pyvic's eyes.

When that darkness faded, a tall man in Imperial armor stood at the edge of the chasm. It was the bodyguard Pyvic had fought on Kail's airship, the one with the magical ax.

"The groundside amplifier has been prepared," he said, "but I would prefer not to risk waiting for a normal recharge. Continue recalibrating the matrix for a forced burn."

The golem, still reforming, started to say something, and Desidora hit it again. The Imperial man seemed to notice them for the first time.

Kail was already ambling toward the man, likely considering options regarding the man's mother. "Diz, I'm guessing *forced burn* is something we should worry about."

"I believe he intends to deliberately unbalance the energies that maintain all of Heaven's Spire," she said, and after hitting the pile of golem-crystals one more time for good measure, she moved in the Imperial man's direction, Ghylspwr already spinning. "It would generate an incredible amount of energy, but there's a very good chance it would also flash-fry every living thing in the city."

"Correct." The Imperial man raised his ax into a guard.

"You're willing to kill everyone here?" Pyvic asked. "Even your own people?"

The Imperial bodyguard lifted his free hand to his helmet and pulled up the visor, and Pyvic looked at what now only vaguely resembled a face.

The ceiling burst into shimmering red radiance as thousands of crystals fell free, falling to the floor between the Imperial man, or rather, the ax animating the obviously dead body of the Imperial man, and them. They landed in a pile of glowing red and rose in the form of a dozen armored golems wielding great jagged spikes of black crystal.

"I am Arikayurichi, the Bringer of Order, and *my people* are waiting to return to this world," said the ax. "Does it look like I care what happens to a few sacks of skin along the way?"

Twenty-Two

THREE HANDS LATER, ULULENIA'S VOICE ECHOED QUIETLY IN Loch's mind. *The elf scratches at the ground for scraps. The Imperial holds only two pair, while the poet carries three nines.*

Loch, sitting on one hidden knave, one open knave, and a knave in the shared cards, nodded ever so slightly.

"I shall raise twenty thousand," Irrethelathlialann said.

"On that?" Veiled Lightning said, looking down at the pair of sixes she had showing. "I think not. Call."

"I'm in." Loch slid most of the rest of her chips in.

"As am I," said Helianthia, and did the same.

The dealer pursed his lips and flipped out the next shared card. "Seven of palms, no help there."

Irrethelathlialann shrugged. "Check."

Veiled Lightning raised an eyebrow. "I thought you could see all the cards. You bragged about it quite explicitly. Raise thirty thousand." She slid most of her chips in.

Loch looked at her stack. "I seem to be a little shy."

"I would accuse you of many things, Isafesira," Veiled Lightning said, smiling, "but shyness is not among them."

Loch slid the last of her chips into the pot. "All in. And if you win, I will use my own funds to purchase the Nine-Ringed Dragon back from the elves and return it to you."

"I am not entirely certain that is legal, given how short you are," the dealer said.

"I beg your pardon," Veiled Lightning interrupted him, and turned to Loch. "Before . . . you said that you ran away to join the Republic's army."

Loch nodded. "Yes."

Veiled Lightning frowned. "Why did you tell me that? Was that your way of warning me off? If I acted like you had, I would end up a criminal, disgracing my family's name?"

Loch laughed. It was a laugh with some hurt in it—dead parents and a sister who'd gone wrong in a lot of ways would do that—but it was a laugh nevertheless. "Honestly, Princess, it probably should have been . . . but no." She nodded across the table. "I told you that out of respect. I get what you're trying to do."

Veiled Lightning smiled. "Is there any chance you'd be willing to surrender, then?"

Loch smiled back. "I didn't say you were right. When this is over, win or lose, check your bodyguard's story."

"I may do that. You may even question him yourself, as you will be there with me in chains." Veiled Lightning turned to the dealer. "I accept her offer as covering the difference."

"I call as well," Helianthia said, pushing her chips into the pot.

"Fold." Irrethelathlialann lowered his cards, still smiling.

"Problem?" Loch asked him.

"Even I cannot simply make the cards I need appear on demand," he said. "But this was an easy way to take most of you out of the action. Fewer spots at the table, you see."

The dealer flipped out the last shared card, a nine of swords. Loch's smile froze.

"Rather than complicate this further," Veiled Lightning said, "I will check."

Loch smiled, nodded, and looked from her to Helianthia, the elven poet now sitting on *four* nines.

She looked back at Loch, her face inscrutable behind the golden spectacles. "You answered a question from the Imperial princess. Would you be willing to answer one from me?"

Loch looked at her. "Of course."

Helianthia smiled, the expression genuinely warm without giving away anything. "Do you truly believe that you can best Irrethelathlialann?"

"I do," Loch said.

Irrethelathlialann shook his head, his nose twitching in silent laughter.

"In that case," Helianthia said, "I fold."

"You *what?*" Irrethelathlialann shot from his seat. "You're sitting on—"

"Dealer," Helianthia said, "am I within my rights to fold?"

"You are," the dealer said solemnly.

"Then I do."

"You would endanger the Elflands!" Irrethelathlialann pointed at her with a shaking finger.

"Dealer," Loch said, "how long is Ethel allowed to be out of his seat before he's considered to be forfeiting his place at the table?"

Irrethelathlialann sat down abruptly, glaring at her, his face flushed deep green and the crystals in his cheeks sparkling. He turned back to Helianthia. "You made a foolish mistake and a wise enemy this day, poet. Remember it well."

The room went silent. Several people gasped.

The elves do not use the imperative, Ululenia said in Loch's mind. *It is considered unspeakably offensive.*

"You have either been too long outside our borders," Helianthia said evenly, "or you have let your crystal trinkets steal your soul one time too many." She pulled her spectacles from her face, and Loch saw that her eyes shone with tears. "You have forgotten who you are, and you speak to me as a master to a slave. I unspeak you." She stood from the table and turned to Loch. "I hope that you play well," she said, and cut through the crowd.

"The poet folds. Imperial and Urujar, I give you the last card." The dealer flipped it out. "Nothing there. If you are ready to show your cards?"

"How do you intend to pay for the Nine-Ringed Dragon?" Veiled Lightning asked, turning over her cards.

"With my winnings, presumably." Loch showed her hidden cards and watched as Veiled Lightning's face went slack.

She recovered quickly, though, swallowed with a jerky nod, and left the table without another word.

Irrethelathlialann smiled at Loch. "Well, you outplayed her, at least. Helianthia you got out of pity."

"I thought I got her thanks to that mouth of yours," Loch said, pulling the chips her way.

The dealer took what was left from Veiled Lightning and Helianthia's stacks. "Since neither of the ladies had enough to make the initial ante, their chips enter the pot general. Dragon's man, Urujar—if you are ready?"

He flipped out the cards. "Seven of swords and three of palms showing for the Dragon, six and nine of crystals for the Urujar. The flop shows seven of crystals and king of wands. Urujar, the first bet is yours."

Irrethelathlialann looked at his hidden cards and smiled, and Ululenia's voice whispered in Loch's head. *As the hunting cat flares her fur to make herself large to her rivals, the elf intends to bluff a concordance. For now, he holds only a pair of sevens.*

Loch looked at her hidden cards. Eight of crystals, king of palms. "No trades. Let's start with ten thousand."

"Isafesira de Lochenville, you'll need to do more than that to get my attention. See ten and raise fifty."

"Call."

The dealer nodded and flipped out the next shared card. "Two of wands."

"Check." Loch put her cards down.

"Oh, *that* isn't the straight you were hoping for," Irrethelathlialann said, grinning. "Raise another fifty."

He still holds only the pair of sevens, Ululenia said.

"Right. Call. Something funny?" she added as the elf chuckled.

"I'll tell you in a moment," he said.

The dealer flipped out the fourth and final shared card. "Four of crystals."

"Oh, dear." Irrethelathlialann clucked his tongue. "*That doesn't make a straight very likely for you at all.*"

"About as likely as your concordance," Loch said. "Raise fifty."

"See that," he shot back, "and raise . . ." He looked down at his chips. "I'll tell you what. You seem very confident. I *could* take most of your chips now, and then spend two or three more hands whittling you down to an embarrassing final defeat . . ." He leaned forward. "But that would delay taking you into custody and removing you to what is soon to be the war-wracked wasteland of your country. So what would you say to this?" He slid the entirety of his chips across the table. "One hand."

He is certain you will flinch, Little One.

"Works for me," Loch said, and slid all of her own chips into match him.

"Boldly played," Irrethelathlialann said, glancing over at the dealer. "You were far more challenging than most humans I've ever encountered . . . Little One."

Loch went very still.

"Oh, that's right." Irrethelathlialann snapped his fingers. "I said I'd tell you what I found so funny. You see, do you remember when you asked me where my fairy-creature friend went? Skoreinis? He's quite gifted as both a mind reader *and* a shapeshifter. Much like your unicorn." He smiled over at Ululenia. "In fact, almost *exactly* like your unicorn."

Ululenia smiled back, sauntered over to the table, and sat down on Irrethelathlialann's leg.

Loch looked from him to her. "Where is Ululenia?"

"Like the little white deer when the ravens are done feasting," the thing that looked like Ululenia said, "I think it's fair to say that there's a bit of her inside all of us." She smiled sweetly. "Some of us more than others."

Dairy broke out of the crowd, fists raised, and instantly, a pair of ruby-red blades were crossed before him. "I'll kill you!"

"You're welcome to try, boy," Irrethelathlialann said, and nuzzled the neck of woman on his lap as he flipped over his cards. "Concordance. Although my *three* sevens would still handily beat the pair of kings you hold, I believe."

He reached out to sweep the chips in.

Loch's hand closed on his wrist.

"I haven't shown my hidden cards yet."

He raised an eyebrow. "Oh, my mistake." He shook his hand from her grasp and drew it back, then gestured for her to proceed.

"Dealer," Loch said, "as I recall, your exact words when I sat down at this table were, 'We crossed over into the Elflands, which means we're playing by elven rules.' Is that correct?"

"It is, ma'am." He raised an eyebrow. "You going anywhere in particular with this? I don't like the soulless bastard any more than you do, but he does appear to have won."

"By your wording, then, we are only playing by elven rules because we are in the Elflands." Loch looked to the crowd. "Is Captain Thelenea present? Is there any chance that she could do me the enormous favor of confirming the current position of this ship?"

Irrethelathlialann froze. "You're bluffing."

Captain Thelenea cut through the crowd. "Urujar, if you have done something to my ship . . ."

"I apologize sincerely for the unfortunate necessity," Loch said.

The elven woman cut her a look, then murmured into what looked like a pea-pod curled around her wrist.

Irrethelathlialann shook his head. "This tournament was started under elven rules, which means—"

"Absolutely nothing," Loch said, drawing the card upon which the tournament rules were printed. "And in the absence of that, we have only what the dealer said, which clearly says elven territory, elven rules. And by inference—and if you want to take back the crystal ring around my unicorn's throat to think this over more carefully, you are more than welcome to do so—if we *aren't* in elven territory, then we *aren't* playing by elven rules."

"Someone has evidently tampered with security and navigation," Captain Thelenea said coldly, drawing her blade. "The former to allow covert mindspeaking, presumably to cheat at cards, and the latter to place an illusion over our course heading. My helmsman has evidently been accidentally steering us a few degrees off for the past hour or so to compensate for drift that was not actually present except on the helm display, and we crossed into Imperial airspace several minutes ago."

"You don't say." Loch grinned. The plan had been to actually turn the ship, not fake it with an illusion, but it appeared to have worked nevertheless.

Irrethelathlialann looked from Loch to the captain to the woman sitting in his lap. "But you can't . . . Skoreinis, you would have—"

"Skoreinis was a mighty warrior," Ululenia said as she stood, "and a part of him lives on inside all of us." She smiled down at Irrethelathlialann. "Some more than others."

Dairy took a very small step backward.

"I still have three kings," Irrethelathlialann said, staring at Loch's hidden cards on the table. "And you never got that straight."

"Correct." Loch turned over her hidden cards. "I believe that here in human lands, we refer to what I have as a flush. That's just a bit higher."

"You cheating . . ."

"Winner." Loch pulled the chips in, even as Captain Thelenea brought her blade to Loch's throat. She ignored it. Paying attention to the sword at her throat would cause complications she didn't need right now. "The word you're looking for is *winner*, Ethel."

A very large, very solid hand clapped down on Irrethelathlialann's shoulder, and the elf looked up at the tall red-bearded man who had—despite all logic to the contrary—approached without Loch noticing.

Mister Dragon looked at her, and she *definitely* noticed him now. There might have been no one else in the room, for all the weight of his attention. It made him seem very big, and Loch very small.

"I believe we had a wager," she said.

Mister Dragon smiled, showing clean white teeth.

"I would appreciate a moment of privacy with our winner," he said to no one in particular, and though he did not raise his voice in any perceptible way, the words seemed to hum in the floorboards and the wood of the table.

The blade at Loch's throat slid away. Irrethelathlialann slid from his seat and left without a word, and Mister Dragon sat down, still smiling at Loch.

"In celebration of a successful tournament," Captain Thelenea called out to the room, "we are pleased to serve drinks on the outside deck. We welcome your immediate presence."

The room cleared out immediately. The elves and fairy creatures left as though the place was on fire, while the humans trailed out when it became clear that the captain was serious.

The captain herself was the last to leave. "You messed with my ship, Isafesira de Lochenville. I will not forget that."

"Sincere apologies, Captain," Loch said without breaking eye contact with Mister Dragon.

Mister Dragon shook his head, the corners of his eyes crinkling from the smile. "People and their toys. So much anger over . . ." He broke off and looked over Loch's shoulder, and in a mild voice that this time made the very air tremble, said, "I *did* request a moment of privacy."

"I appreciate that, sir," said Dairy from behind Loch, "but I answer to Captain Loch, not you."

Mister Dragon blinked.

Loch started counting in her mind, with the apology to come at five.

At a bit past four, Mister Dragon pursed his lips and said, "And what is it you do for Captain Loch, young man, that is so important that you would stand against my wishes?"

Dairy coughed. "Right now, sir, I mainly fetch drinks."

Mister Dragon looked at Loch curiously, his lips twitching as though hiding a smile, and then slid his gaze over to Dairy again. "I see that the man at the bar has gone and left us. Tell me, young man . . . if I asked very nicely, would you fetch *me* something to drink?"

"I . . ." It was actually possible to *feel* Dairy blushing. "That would depend on what you were in the mood for, sir."

"Hmm." Mister Dragon actually *did* smile now.

"So," Loch said, and managed not to flinch as the weight of Mister Dragon's stare settled back on her like red-hot lead, "I won the tournament."

Mister Dragon's gaze did not lighten. "You cheated, Lochenville."

"More effectively than your elf, Veiled Lightning, or the rest, yes. Hence me winning. But," Loch added as the table creaked beneath Mister Dragon's fingers, "that's a very negative way of thinking about it."

Mister Dragon raised a hand and stroked his beard. "And the positive way of thinking about it would be?"

"Now that I've won the tournament," Loch said, "I'd very much like to get to the Temple of Butterflies before it explodes and takes half the Republic with it. Anyone who could get us there quickly would enjoy the pleasure of my company . . . along with my associate, Rybindaris, former Champion of Dawn."

Mister Dragon's eyes widened, and he leaned forward a little and smiled over Loch's shoulder in delight. *"Really."*

Loch looked over and saw Dairy blushing and trying to figure out what to do with his hands. Since she'd just spent several hours playing cards, she had a pretty good sense of when to play a good hand.

"Dairy, would you mind getting Mister Dragon a drink? I suspect he'd enjoy something strong and virgin."

When a lock needed picking or someone needed to be distracted with fast words and a good, solid line about their mothers, Kail knew it was his time to shine.

A heavily armored Imperial guy with a magical ax who subsequently turned out to be a severely defaced corpse being controlled *by* the magical ax, along with a dozen or so crystal golems? Not one of those times.

"Diz! Ghyl! You're the muscle!" he shouted, bringing his mace up in a two-handed grip and smashing the nearest golem, which crumbled into ruby-red fragments . . . that immediately started to pull themselves back together. "Pyvic and I have your back!"

"We do?" Pyvic yelled, taking a golem's head off with a backhanded swing.

"Ideally!"

Desidora lunged forward, Ghylspwr raised. "I bear a weapon that carries the soul of your king!" she yelled.

"Kun-kabynalti osu fuir'is!"

For one moment, Kail thought it might work, even as he smashed another golem back into crystals.

Then Arikayurichi said, "Good for you, priestess," and slashed forward with a lightning-fast blow that knocked Desidora back even as Ghylspwr flipped up to block it. "I shall kill you most *respectfully.*"

A golem behind Desidora reached out with jagged black arms, and Pyvic lopped them off, then chopped the creature down the middle, just as Desidora lunged back at the dead man and the ax with a blow that connected hard enough to make every crystal in the chamber ring like a bell.

Kail smashed another golem, ducked, drove a mace through the kneecap of one that was coming in on Desidora's flank, and danced away, eyes flicking across the room for something, *anything*, that could be useful.

For all the damage they were dealing, the golems had them surrounded, while Desidora and the dead man traded blows that echoed around the whole chamber. Off by the control console, Archvoyant Bertram was still frozen in place. By the chasm, Kail saw a fallen form he hadn't noticed before: Urujar skin and voyant robes.

"Pyvic, you hold! I'm going scouting!" Kail blocked a black blade with the head of his mace, shattering the crystal, then dove through the enemy lines.

"Expect anything useful to come out of that?" Pyvic yelled behind him.

"Ideally!" Kail rolled, came up with an uppercut that would have hurt a lot more if the golem in question had been anatomically correct, and body-checked the golem off the edge of the chasm.

He spun, saw that he was free for a moment, and turned to the man on the ground. "Voyant Cevirt? Cevirt!"

The little man blinked, groaning. "Man made of crystals . . ."

"Yeah, we're a ways past that." Kail looked over his shoulder, saw a golem coming at him, turned, and smashed the thing's blade.

It barreled into him heedlessly, caught him with a shoulder, and put him on the ground.

Kail came up with an awkward swing that the already-reforming blade knocked aside. The golem lashed out with a kick that caught Kail in the ribs, and as the room went dark and the air left his lungs, Kail saw the golem raise its black blade.

Then, with a snapping hiss that made Kail's ears pop, the golem fell apart into a pile of dark cracked crystal.

Voyant Cevirt grinned weakly and sank back to the floor. A wand of pale-blue crystal tinkled as it rolled from his hand. "Lightning. Thought it might work. You should . . ."

He went limp.

Kail grabbed the wand, rolled to his feet, pointed at an oncoming golem, and activated it. The wand flashed, lightning arced in a sizzle of blue light between him and the golem, and another pile of dull and broken crystal sank to the floor.

"Hey, You-really-are-itchy, or whatever your name is!" he yelled, striding back into battle with mace in one hand and wand in the other. "Anybody ever tell you it's rude to hit a lady?" He blasted another golem, spun, and smashed one away, just on the off chance that the wand had a limited number of charges. "See, when your mother and I do it, we have safe words! Hers is *fuller*, but let me tell you, she is a full-tang kind of lady, if you know what I mean!"

Arikayurichi actually shifted in the dead man's grip, turning toward Kail just a fraction.

It was enough for Desidora to sidestep one blow, and she got Ghylspwr up to knock a fast reverse-swing high.

Then she slammed Ghylspwr hilt-first against the dead man's ribs.

The dead man stumbled, then spun into a backhanded blow that Desidora caught at the last second, staggering backward against the shock.

Her back foot came down on empty air as she slipped at the edge of the chasm, and with a short cry, she dropped to her knees.

It gave Kail the shot he needed. "Diz, I've got it!"

The dead man lunged in, Arikayurichi raised for a massive overhand blow.

Kail fired.

Lightning snapped, hissed, and sizzled around the dead man and the weapon of the ancients.

It did nothing.

The blow fell.

Ghylspwr rose.

The noise shattered every golem in the room and sent Kail to his knees, fumbling blindly, yelling with a voice he couldn't even hear for a few seconds. The floor beneath him showed cracks, and that seemed important to him somehow as he scrambled for purchase.

When he could see again clearly, he saw that the cracks led to the edge of the chasm.

The chasm had grown a few feet wider, the last little bit shattered off. Near the edge, Ghylspwr lay alone on the floor.

The dead man and his ax turned to Kail. "Have you, little Urujar? Have you got it?"

"Ideally." Kail got back to his feet, mace and wand still in hand, and ran forward to his death.

Loch had flown on airships, on treeships, and once on a magical crystal that had been in a state of freefall until the sun's rays had activated its levitation magic.

The Dragon trumped all of them.

She clung to shimmering rainbow spines atop a great muscled back of red scales that flickered gold with each flap of the dragon's blazing wings. The wind whipped around them in a constant dull roar, and Loch could see the mountains pass by below them as they blazed a comet's trail across the night sky.

"I was worried you had turned evil!" Hessler was yelling, hanging from one of the spines tighter than was necessary.

You worry too much, Ululenia said into all of their minds. She soared in the Dragon's wake, a ghostly pale shape in the night. She had chosen what looked to Loch like a white raven, although she had a spot on her flank she hadn't had before.

"She told me what happened with the elf's creature, and she agreed to let him think that he'd killed her and taken his place," Loch said, and met Hessler's aggrieved stare. "Did I forget to mention that?"

"You did, yes."

"So, what happened to overriding the treeship's navigation with a magical pulse of energy?" she asked.

Hessler coughed. "Well, I saw no need to use a hammer when a scalpel would suffice."

"Just to be clear," Tern said, "he could *absolutely* have used a hammer if it had been necessary. I was very impressed."

Veiled Lightning, standing with perfect balance while the rest of them clung to the spines, shook her head with disdain. "I respected you as a master criminal, a worthy adversary," she called over the wind. "It is *greatly* disappointing to find out how much of it was just luck!"

"Why is she even here?" Tern asked, and then followed it immediately with, "Not that I'm complaining, Princess—still a *huge* fan."

"She needed a ride." Loch grinned. "Hopefully she helps us end this war."

Technically, came a voice from all around them, ***Skoreinis was my creature, not the elf's.***

Hessler visibly winced.

Do you deny me right of self-protection as a free-willed individual? Ululenia asked.

I do not. The muscles of the great blazing wings seemed to strain for a moment, a tiny hitch in the rhythm. ***Nor do I envy you the price.***

"Price?" Hessler asked.

"So is this like a normal outfit for you, Princess, or is this something you'd wear specially for traveling?" Tern asked.

Loch sighed and looked up to the base of the neck, where Dairy rode alone. "How are you doing up there, Dairy?"

Dairy turned back to look at her. In the light of the Dragon's glowing wings, his face was flushed and smiling. "I can feel the muscles in his back bunch up and then release between my legs every time he flaps his wings, ma'am!"

"That was a little more than I needed, kid, but good for you." Loch tossed him a salute, then slapped the Dragon on the side. "You will be kind."

I will be an absolute gentleman. The voice rang just as loudly, but felt confined to Loch's head this time.

"There!" Veiled Lightning called, pointing. "The temple!"

Squinting down past gray peaks speckled white with glittering snow, Loch saw the golden glowing butterfly shape of the temple nestled at the top of a mountain pass. Not far from it, a speck of glowing violet light hung in the air. "And that would be Heaven's Spire."

"Where to first?" Tern called. "I assume we want to stop the voyants from activating the crystals and blasting the temple."

Silhouetted against the night sky, Loch could make out the glowing crystals on the underside of the city. They weren't supposed to glow at night. "Tern, Hessler, can you tell me anything about the *lapiscaela*?"

"They're not supposed to glow at night!" Tern called back.

"This was your team of master criminals?" Veiled Lightning shouted again.

"Cut her some slack, Princess. She's your biggest fan."

"Something is charging them," Hessler called over, "likely in preparation to fire. That can't be safe for anyone in the city, though."

"Well, then, I'm assuming Desidora is already there trying to stop it. I need you and Tern at the temple in case there's a way to shut it down on your end. Princess?"

Veiled Lightning glared. "I would rather not let you out of my sight at the moment, thank you."

"Good to see you learning." Loch patted the Dragon's flank. "You get all that?"

I did. I will bring you and whoever wishes to accompany you as far as I can into the city of the ancients, then carry the rest to the temple.

"Appreciate it. As far as you can?"

The city's wards do not react well to beings of my size. Do you really believe you can stop this, Lochenville?

Loch opened her mouth to answer, then winced as something on the underside of Heaven's Spire exploded and fell down toward the ground below, a silhouette that could have been a person, lost almost immediately in the night.

"I believe," she said, "that you could maybe flap a bit faster."

Desidora felt the shock of impact, the rush of wind and darkness . . .

. . . And then a soft springy bounce as she sank deep into red satin sheets.

She blinked.

The room was intimate, with room only for a great bed and a few small tables where scented candles rested in pink and orange crystal bowls, casting intimate light across the chamber. A bottle of sparkling white wine sat in a bucket of ice on another table, and a silver platter held a fluted glass, already full, next to a bowl of strawberries and a dish of brown sugar.

"So," said the woman at the foot of the bed, lifting a glass of her own, "how do *you* think the job is going so far?"

Desidora pushed herself up to a seated position, her hands sliding on the satin. "Goddess."

"Sister." The woman at the foot of the bed smiled. It was a friendly smile, playful and flirtatious without implying anything serious—which was good, because the woman at the foot of the bed looked exactly like Desidora herself, from the auburn hair and sun-kissed skin to the ever-so-slightly crooked nose and the arch of her eyebrows.

"Is this . . . am I dead?"

"Not yet." Tasheveth, goddess of love, looked up at the ceiling, where candlelit shadows danced. "The magic of the hammer shielded you as you got blasted through the foundation of the city, and you are now falling from Heaven's Spire to your death below."

"And . . . you're speaking to me in my mind?" Desidora guessed. "I'm going to snap out of it when this is over and find that just a moment has passed?"

The goddess laughed. It was Desidora's laugh, only a bit less inhibited, and Desidora didn't think of herself as that inhibited in the first place. "I'm afraid mortal minds can only think so quickly. Time is passing at about normal speed. Don't worry, though. You were a ways up there." She gestured at the glass on the platter. "Drink?"

Desidora's fingers hurt. She looked down and realized that she was clenching the satin sheets hard enough to bleach her fingernails white. "So I'm going to die."

"I'd say that's up to you, Sister." Tasheveth hopped up onto the bed and settled back next to Desidora, sighing as she eased back into the pillows.

Desidora could feel the warmth of her goddess lying next to her. She rolled over to look into eyes that matched her own, only half-lidded with relaxed amusement. "Are you going to give me the power of Byn-kodar again?"

Tasheveth looked over, still smiling. A little curl of auburn hair dangled over her face. "No. Have you tried the strawberries?"

Desidora shut her eyes against the angry heat that made them sting. "Why not?"

"Why not, indeed? Do you know how hard it is to make someone imagine the taste of fresh strawberries?" Tasheveth inhaled deeply. "Everyone thinks they're sweet, but you need to get the right amount of tartness, or else they're just wet candy, and the texture is all wrong for candy."

Desidora pushed herself from the bed and stalked away, arms wrapped tight around herself. "Do I have to beg, Goddess? Do I have to plead for you to bestow the curse upon me again?"

Something bounced off the back of her head. Desidora flinched, turned, and saw a strawberry land on the other side of the bed.

"When you received the powers of *Byn-kodar'isti kuru'ur*," Tasheveth said, rising from the bed, "you prayed for me, begging for the gods to choose someone else, and I told you that it had to be you, that no one else could take that power." She flicked strawberry juice from her fingers and sipped her wine. "I may have been less than entirely forthcoming about that."

Desidora blinked. "You *lied* to your own priestess?"

Tasheveth blinked right back at her. "Hello, I'm Tasheveth, goddess of *love*, and you are?" As Desidora turned away angrily, Tasheveth kept going. "Of *course* I lied! How many times have you lied to bolster a young woman's confidence or shaded the truth to put a couple on the path back to reconciliation?" Her voice softened. "The world is a big place, and it's got a lot of sharp edges for people to hurt themselves. It *needs* someone who will cheat a little bit to give the little people a chance. It needs trickery and sneakiness, and not for profit or to prove how smart you are, like Gedesar, but because you want people to end up *happy*. That's what I am. That's what you are." Her hand—the same slender fingers as Desidora's own—came down gently on Desidora's shoulder. "That's why you were chosen."

"Because I can lie?" Desidora shook her head.

"Imagine us giving that power to a warrior-priest of Io-fergajar, or a stern champion of Ael-meseth." Tasheveth pulled gently, turning Desidora back, and her voice went hard. "Imagine the trail of bodies they would have left as they finally got the chance they had always wanted to bathe themselves in the blood of their enemies, all sanctified by the gods themselves. Imagine them tearing the souls from innocent bystanders, grim but determined, always telling themselves it was for the *greater good*, that they were the ones chosen to make the hard decisions no one else could stomach." She nodded as Desidora flinched. "You don't have to imagine. You've read the histories. Now . . . tell me that you think we should've given that power to one of them."

Desidora shut her eyes again, blinking back the tears. "I don't."

"Tell me that you think it'd be better off with them than with a trickster priestess who would use it reluctantly and put it away as soon as she could."

"I don't."

"Tell me," Tasheveth said quietly, "that you see a way to save lives and restore peace, but that you don't want it."

Desidora opened her eyes and stared into her own face.

"I do," she said. "I'm sorry, Goddess. I didn't *want* to want it, but—"

"That's why we chose you, my love." Tasheveth reached out, took Desidora by the shoulders, and kissed her gently on the forehead. "Because you'd lock it away inside yourself far more tightly than we ever could have . . ."

". . . until I needed it again." Desidora smiled, and now it was Tasheveth whose eyes shone with tears. "I'll miss you."

Her goddess wiped her nose and forced a smile. "Damn it, Diz, I worked really hard on the strawberries."

The night wind tore at her pale-green skirts and her auburn hair. The mountains rushed past her in a blur.

Desidora let the power come.

She landed in a crouch at the stairs leading up to the Temple of Butterflies, shattered stone blasting out like smoke around her. Her raven-black skirts and hair billowed out around her in a phantom wind, and her alabaster skin glowed like the moon.

She rose, and looked upon the horde of zombies that roared and gurgled and lurched toward her.

"Bitch, *please*," said Desidora, priestess of Byn-kodar, and with a wave of her hand, tore away the magic that locked unwilling spirits into decaying flesh.

She walked through the dead up the stairs to the Temple of Butterflies, and no force of man or god stood in her way.

Twenty-Three

WARDS FLARED, MAGIC CRACKLED ALONG THE DRAGON'S SCALES, and Loch rolled as she landed on the lawn outside the Archvoyant's palace.

When she came to her feet, Veiled Lightning was beside her, brushing off her dress, while Ululenia, Tern, Hessler, and Dairy rode off into the night.

"Right," Loch said. "Let's see if we can find the control room."

"Find?" Veiled Lightning asked.

"Yeah, the room I'm guessing we want is the main control . . . place. When we hit Silestin, I was in a completely different part of the palace."

A muscle by Veiled Lightning's jaw twitched. "So how do you expect to *find* this room before your city destroys my temple, then?"

"Fortunately, my people often leave me these subtle little clues," Loch said, gesturing at the smashed-open door leading inside. "Shall we?"

A few minutes later, Loch burst through the doorway and into the control chamber.

Voyant Cevirt lay unconscious on the crazily glowing floor near the chasm, while Archvoyant Bertram sat rigid in the center of a ring of control crystals. Piles of debris littered the ground, marking what looked like dead golems.

Pyvic, wielding Ghylspwr, fell to the floor, grunting, as Loch came in. A badly mangled corpse wearing Gentle Thunder's armor stood over him, a shining magical ax in its hands.

"Sorry I'm late," Loch said, and the corpse turned to her.

"Thunder." Veiled Lightning's voice was choked, and she stepped past Loch toward the corpse and the ax.

"Veil." It sounded like Gentle Thunder's voice, but Loch wasn't sure the corpse's ruined face even had a mouth anymore. "Veil, I'm sorry. The Republic soldiers did this to me. Arikayurichi is keeping me alive as long as he can." The ax slammed down, and Pyvic, still on his knees, caught the blow inches from his face with Ghylspwr's haft.

"He's lying," Loch said, even as Veiled Lightning kept going forward. "Listen to me! We're on the same side!" She moved in as Veiled Lightning stood over Pyvic, who knelt defenseless, Ghylspwr locked against Arikayurichi. "When did he last lift his visor?" Veiled Lightning raised a fist that crackled with blue energy. "When did he—"

The blow slammed into Gentle Thunder, sending blue sparks shooting across his armor and knocking him back.

"Shut up, Isafesira." Veiled Lightning did not look at Loch as she helped Pyvic to his feet. "I may be a fool, but even I can learn."

"The ax wants Heaven's Spire to destroy the Temple of Butterflies," Pyvic said, bringing Ghylspwr back up to a guard. "The firing mechanism is tied to the control console over there. It's trying to destroy the Republic and the Empire."

"Trying?" The corpse, now even more mangled, rose back to its feet, the ax moving in a deadly spin. "The groundside amplifier is ready, and the matrix is calibrated for a forced burn. This city is a few minutes away from optimal firing position. I believe I have surpassed *trying*."

"*Kun-kabynalti osu fuir'is!*" Ghylspwr yelled, and Pyvic lunged forward, hammer flashing. The ax blocked, swung, and lunged in to slam Pyvic back.

He was still on his feet, which was all that mattered, and Loch started circling toward Archvoyant Bertram at the console. "Princess!" Loch called, and tossed the Nine-Ringed Dragon to her. "Buy me a minute."

Veiled Lightning slashed high, spun her blade in an intricate pattern, and then slashed down, tearing into the corpse's leg.

As the corpse staggered, its guard down, Pyvic swung, and his blow caved in the corpse's skull.

He didn't bring Ghylspwr back fast enough to block the counterstrike.

He shouldn't have had to. Very few fighting styles trained a warrior in how to defend himself from a man whose skull he'd just caved in. The haft of the magical ax slammed into Pyvic's temple, and he went down hard, rolled, and went limp.

Veiled Lightning screamed and lunged. Her blade cut through armor, and her free hand hissed with lightning that shot blue sparks across the corpse's armor.

"I cared for you as much as he did," Arikayurichi said, and let Veiled Lightning's blade catch in his torso. The ax snapped out, catching the princess with the haft and slamming her against the wall hard. "I take no pleasure from your death, Veil."

Veiled Lightning grunted and staggered back to her feet, pain etched across her face. "Do not call me by that name."

"I'm sorry," the ax said again as he moved in, shouldering Veiled Lightning into the wall. This time, she hit the ground limp. "You're good servants, all of you. Centuries of waiting and watching have made it easy for me to be bitter, but this isn't your fault. You and the elves and the dwarves, you were made to serve, and when most of my people left, you had to fend for yourselves. But once we return to set things right . . ."

A scream of absolute agony cut the ax off, and the corpse turned to the control console.

Archvoyant Bertram sank to the floor, fingers bleeding, curled up and shaking uncontrollably, with bits of crystal still jutting from his skin.

Loch picked up Ghylspwr, tested his weight, and turned to the ax. "Sorry, I was too busy messing up your plan to really pay attention. You mind repeating that?"

They both charged each other.

The monks poured from the gates of the Temple of Butterflies. Golden robes shining in the warding lights on the walls, they came down the stairs, a line of corded muscle and disciplined power.

Desidora lifted one hand and clenched her fist, and the monks stumbled, hands clutching weakly at their chests.

"I could draw the life from every last one of you," she said, voice colder than the river that flowed below. "It would be within my power, within my *rights*."

Her pale fingers curled into claws, and the monks fell to their knees, their energy of their very souls wrung free from their bodies, coalescing in a swirling sphere of light between Desidora's fingers.

She let them writhe as she ascended the stairs, her jet-black skirt trailing behind her and her silver-trimmed heels clicking on each step. She reached the top of the steps, the energy still clutched in her grasp. Her fingernails were black with tiny silver skulls painted on them.

She looked back down the stairs at the dying monks and the river rushing below.

"But I would regret that later," she said in a voice that, while still cold, was controlled.

She flung the ball of swirling light at the temple gate, and it exploded inward as soldiers shouted and drew blades. She spared a glance back down the steps, saw that the monks were weak but alive, and nodded to herself.

She walked into the temple courtyard.

Soldiers charged her, and she tugged on the fabric of their souls until they fell, helpless. She heard shouting behind her, turned, and saw men on the wall trying to aim a flamecannon down at her.

She gestured, twisted its own energy back upon it, and it exploded with a wave of raw magical power that left the guards unconscious on the ground.

In the sky overhead, Heaven's Spire shone like a great violet moon.

Desidora opened herself to the magical aura of the area. Even those blind to magic would feel it humming across their skin, and to one who had once served Tasheveth, it was like hearing every instrument performing in a perfect symphony. Heaven's Spire crackled, ready to spit down fire again, and the Temple of Butterflies would catch that energy, magnify it a hundredfold, and blot the life out of the land for hundreds of miles.

It was simple, it was elegant, and it was very nearly ready. Desidora followed the path of the energy to the inner sanctum up above the courtyard and walked up the stairs, ignoring the men gasping and retching behind her. The life-energy she had taken from them danced through her fingers. But they would survive.

"Shenziencis!" she called out as she reached the top of the stairs. "Queen of the Cold River! You would destroy two countries in your selfish pride! In the name of the gods, I charge you now, *surrender or die!*"

The door to the inner sanctum swung open, and Shenziencis was there, her coils bearing her up to a tall man's height. Her scales were glossy, forest green that shone like emeralds in the courtyard light.

"I have already surrendered to a force more powerful than you," she called back, sneering. *"You are held in cruel bondage."*

Desidora felt the magic coalesce around her, twisted it away, and drew it into the sphere light that danced between her fingers, the prize of life she had claimed from the fools below. "So be it." She shaped the energy in her grasp to a bolt and flung it at Shenziencis with deadly accuracy.

An old man in golden robes and a crimson skullcap stepped into the path of the bolt. It ripped into him, leaving a scorched and jagged hole as he dropped to the ground.

Shenziencis did not even look down at the man who had died for her. "Kill."

An armored Imperial woman leaped through the doorway, swinging a halberd as long as Desidora was tall.

Desidora dove back, ducked, saw the shackles of magical power binding the woman, and shattered them with a thought. The woman collapsed, gasping, and Desidora turned to the Shenziencis, smiling coldly.

A crossbow bolt hissed through the doorway and slammed into Desidora's chest, and a cloud of choking gas wreathed her body as it hit. The shock sent her staggering back, coughing and blind, and the bolt clattered on the ground as she kept breathing the gas all around her. Then her foot came down on empty space instead of solid ground for the second time tonight, and she was falling, trying to pull the magic around her to cushion the fall as she had done before. But something was wrong. She couldn't catch her breath. The magic wouldn't come.

She hit the sand hard, and could only watch as dazedly—silhouetted against the violet energy of Heaven's Spire—a man with a crossbow came for her.

"Powdered *yvkefer*-pouch on the head of the bolt," he called as he came down the steps. "I imagine you're having a hard time summoning that death magic right about now." Halfway down the steps, he jumped down into the sand, landing in a clean roll. "Captain Nystin, Knights of Gedesar."

Desidora coughed, trying to catch her breath. She couldn't even see the shackles that bound him, couldn't reach the magic that would let her break them. The powder in her lungs blocked her from doing any more than shakily raising one hand.

The man was still a silhouette in her vision, black against the light from Heaven's Spire, which seemed even brighter now than it had been moments ago.

"I know what you're thinking," Nystin said, tossing the crossbow to the sand. "Push through it, work through the pain, and you can break her control over me." He drew a thick-bladed dagger. "Bad news for you, death priestess. Right now, that snaky bitch isn't doing a damned thing to control me. She could've ordered me to do this, and I'd have done it clumsily, like some cut-rate flunky, but she knows me well enough by now to know the things I'd be happy to do of my own free will."

Desidora coughed again and rolled onto her side, scrabbling for purchase on the sand.

"All you monsters," Nystin said, shifting the dagger so that he held it point down as he approached, "you fairy creatures and necromancers and death priests. You think you own this world because you've got power the rest of us don't. But a little silver, a little *yvkefer*, and all your fancy tricks go away. And then what are you?"

"A *love* priestess," gasped Desidora, and flung sand into Nystin's face. He stumbled back, clawing at his eyes, and Desidora lunged from the sand pit to where a fallen soldier lay unconscious, his sword next to him. "And we cheat." She grabbed it, turned, and swung it two-handed as Nystin stumbled toward her.

She had carried Ghylspwr for months, and every time she had swung him, his magic had guided her. Priests of Tasheveth went through no formal combat training, and Desidora could count the number of times she'd swung a nonmagical weapon on one hand.

Her swing was slow and clumsy, but it was a swing nevertheless, and Nystin leaped backward. The light from Heaven's Spire blazed bright enough to bathe the courtyard in violet, and up above, Desidora could hear a high-pitched whistling.

Nystin feinted, then slashed at her throat, and Desidora's block left her off balance. His leg snapped into her ankle, and she fell and landed hard on the stone of the courtyard.

Nystin raised his dagger, his face a pale violet in the radiance coming down from above.

Then he glanced up overhead, squinted, and then flinched.

A bone-shaking impact rattled the courtyard, spraying sand from the pits and water from the fountains and causing intricate glowing runes to overload and blow out in the walls.

Desidora looked to the middle of the courtyard, where one of the giant purple crystals that normally clung to the underside of Heaven's Spire lay amid a spiderweb of cracks on the ground, glowing fitfully. It lurched back into the air, bobbed for a moment, and then fell back down into a sandpit as its glow died altogether.

"Sorry that took so long, Diz," Kail said, pushing himself back to his feet shakily. "Had to get a ride."

"You rode a *lapiscaelum* down from Heaven's Spire?" Nystin growled, coming back to his feet with his dagger ready. "For what? Your death priestess?"

Desidora hit him hard on the back of the head with the pommel of her sword, and he went down hard.

She looked at Kail, who was swaying a bit. "He had a point, though."

"Ah, I've ridden one before. S'how Loch and I escaped the Cleaners."

"That wasn't what I meant."

He shrugged.

Desidora looked to where the great purple crystal lay in the sand, confused. "They don't levitate at night."

"Yeah. I got a lightning wand." Kail held up a blackened and dead length of crystal. "Figured if I hit the *lapiscaelum* with enough energy, it'd probably turn on enough to slow down the fall."

"Probably?" Desidora asked. When he didn't answer, she added, "And what gave you any idea I had survived that fall in the first place?"

"Nothing." Kail stumbled, and Desidora caught him before he fell. "But I figured the gods hadn't given you up just yet. And if there's a chance you're alive, no matter how small, I'm coming every time. Anything that wants to kill you comes through me first."

He was heavier than he looked, but Desidora held him upright. "Kail—"

"How charming," came a voice from the stairs. "*Fall.*"

Kail dropped to the ground, pulling himself from Desidora's arms and sending her staggering.

Attendant Shenziencis slid into the courtyard. Her neck flared with a hood that shadowed her human head, and her coils caught the blazing light of Heaven's Spire overhead. "I detest fighting my opponents myself. *Up.*" Kail hauled himself to his feet, and the jewel at Shenziencis's throat shone with blazing rainbow glory. "Fortunately, I do not have to."

Desidora reached for her magic, but the *yvkefer* in her lungs still blocked it. "Kail . . ."

"*Kill,*" said Shenziencis, and Kail staggered forward.

Desidora had dropped her sword. She turned and lunged for it, knowing she wouldn't make it in time . . .

But she did.

She came up with the sword in hand, looked back, and saw Shenziencis looking as surprised as Desidora felt.

"Mind charm," Kail said in a very low voice. He had one hand on the back of the naga's head, just above the hood. The other held Nystin's silver dagger, which was lodged in the jewel at Shenziencis's throat. "Grabbed it from one of the Knights of Gedesar."

He pulled the knife free. Attendant Shenziencis had turned gray, and the jewel at her throat was black and dead. "*Nobody* screws with my mind. Ever. Again." Kail stepped back, and Shenziencis fell to the ground, her body crumbling slowly to dust. "It ain't much, but it's *mine*. It's mine." His voice broke, and he dropped to his knees. "It's mine."

Desidora put her arms around him as the shaking started.

She was still holding him when the Dragon, carrying her friends, landed in the courtyard.

Loch swung Ghylspwr, leaned into the clash with Arikayurichi, and then dove back as the ax turned its corpse-wielder's stumble into a spin that brought it back at her head in a vicious backhand.

"Do you think you can stop me, Urujar?" Arikayurichi called, spinning as the corpse lumbered toward her again. "Do you think pulling your archvoyant out of my lattice is anything other than a mild inconvenience?"

He swung. Loch knocked it high, slid under, took out the corpse's kneecap, and blocked a backhanded strike inches from her face. "Well, since you brought it up, I'm guessing it slows down your big plan *some*," she said, shoving it back. "Thanks for letting me know."

"You were bred to serve, Urujar," Arikayurichi said, and Loch could hear the sneer in its voice. "You belong in the fields, tilling the soil to grow crops for the more important servants."

It lunged in, and Loch blocked one blow, slapped aside another, and then rolled away from its furious onslaught.

"Oh, no," she called back, "not *racism*. How will I ever keep my feelings in check from *that*?" She laughed, spinning Ghylspwr into a guard. "But by all means, come and get me, big guy."

"*Kun-kabynalti osu fuir'is!*" Ghylspwr added.

"As you wish." Arikayurichi came in with a great overhand blow, so large that the wind-up left the corpse's entire body unguarded for one critical moment.

She was *supposed* to take the shot, hit the body with a great blow.

She feinted, shifted her weight, and chopped *up* instead, catching the corpse's arms just past the elbow. The blow wrenched Arikayurichi from the corpse's dead fingers, and it clattered to the brightly flashing floor along with Ghylspwr, who was torn from Loch's grasp by the move.

Against a living opponent, such a move would have been foolish—ignoring an easy strike to the head or chest in favor of a disarming attack that left Loch unarmed within easy reach of her otherwise unharmed opponent was a great way to get yourself killed.

The corpse slumped against her shoulder, and then slowly slid back and fell to the ground.

"No!" Arikayurichi shouted, twitching on the floor. "You cannot stop us!"

"Looks suspiciously like I can." Loch looked to Ghylspwr, who lay not far away on the ground. "All right. What's our next step, Ghyl?"

"*Kutesosh gajair'is,*" Ghylspwr said urgently.

"The console, I'm guessing?"

"*Kutesosh gajair'is!*"

"Taking that as a yes." Loch hurried over to where Archvoyant Bertram had been held. The entire floor vibrated beneath her feet now, runes blazing as bright as the sun, and the crystals at the control console blazed in every color of the rainbow. "All right? What do I do? Smash something, press something?"

"*Kutesosh gajair'is,*" Ghylspwr said again, and Loch saw one of the crystals, the bright red of blood, flaring even brighter than the rest.

"The red one?" She pointed. "Push that one?"

"*Kutesosh gajair'is!*"

"Got it." Loch leaned against the console, for a moment, breathing hard. "Just be a moment. Side's not quite ready for this much fighting yet. Hey, Arikayurichi, what did you mean by 'us'?"

"*Besyn larveth'is?*" Ghylspwr asked in alarm.

Arikayurichi laughed. "My golems and I," it said. "The plan I put into motion with them will destroy your Republic, and that old hammer does not have enough wits left to tell you how to stop my plans."

"Sure he does." Loch looked over at Ghylspwr. "He just did, clear as day. I'm supposed to hit that red crystal, right?"

"*Kutesosh gajair'is!*" Ghylspwr said urgently.

"No!" Arikayurichi shouted. "You must not!"

Loch waited until the echoes of both shouts died. The chamber was lit brighter than day now, and in the ceiling, she could see the craters where golems had been formed from the crystals in the ceiling.

"If they were your golems the whole time," Loch said quietly, "why did they come after my people in the library, long before you ever came to Heaven's Spire? I can buy that they could keep running on their own once someone started them, but it had to be someone *up here*."

"Foolish Urujar," said Arikayurichi, "my automated wards—"

"If they were your golems the whole time," Loch said, "why didn't you use them to stop me from getting the manuscript when you fought me on the rooftops in Ajeveth? Or on the dwarven train?"

"You are unworthy of the magic required to—"

"If they were your golems the whole time," Loch said, "why did the golems have orders to let Desidora live?"

The ax was silent.

"Because you cared about her," Loch said, and she was no longer speaking to Arikayurichi. "You care about all of us, which is why you made the golems spare her. It's why Pyvic over there is unconscious but alive, why you saved my people every time they were in danger, even as you tripped up the plan every now and then to slow them down. It's why Arikayurichi came in high and let me disarm it. Because you asked it to be merciful. What's the phrase you use for that?"

"*Kun-kabynalti osu fuir'is*," Ghylspwr said quietly.

The runes on the floor were no longer shining in different colors. They were all a uniform blazing white now. The shaking was growing worse, rattling the room enough that Loch had to hold onto the edge of the crystal console for balance. She kept her hands far from anything that looked like it did anything.

"Most people just think of you as Desidora's magical hammer, Ghyl," Loch said. "They forget you were . . . still are . . . an ancient. A person. You've got your own mind. Your own people. And you'd do anything for them."

"*Besyn larveth'is,*" Ghylspwr said, his voice low and sad. "And because most people just think of you as something that gives the death priestess a little hitting power, they'd never in a million years expect you to be part of a two-man con." The chamber shuddered as something deep in the heart of Heaven's Spire began to hum, and Loch caught her balance, looking at the weapons on the floor. "One to fulfill the prophecy and take down the Glimmering Folk, and the other to clear the way so the rest of your people could return."

"You should have let me cut her down and be done with it," Arikayurichi said.

"*Kun-kabynalti osu fuir'is.*"

"Yes, but for her mind and your pity, we'd have the arch-voyant back in the lattice and the forced burn already underway." The ax twitched on the ground again. "For whatever it's worth, Urujar, well done."

"On the train." It was Veiled Lightning's voice. Loch looked over and saw her crawling over to where Gentle Thunder's corpse lay. "Isafesira was ready to surrender. You made Thunder attack."

"It's always easier when they get a little old and a little slow," Arikayurichi said. "A warrior in his prime would never tolerate a weapon that wanted to move on its own. But a warrior getting on in years but still too proud to step down? A warrior who wanted to impress the girl he'd watched over since she was a child? He practically begged me to take control."

Veiled Lightning touched Gentle Thunder's body. "He never had to impress me," she said quietly.

"Pity you didn't tell him that when you were alive," Arikayurichi said, chuckling. "What about you, Urujar? What tipped you off?"

Loch swallowed. "One of my enemies asked me if I knew where the word 'Urujar' came from. I asked my wizard. Turns out, it comes from *euru*, which means 'happy', and *jair*, which means 'work'." She smiled. "Happy workers, in the language of the ancients. It's funny. That's what the Old Kingdom nobles used to call their slaves."

The chamber shook again, and both Ghylspwr and Arikayurichi slid on the floor.

"It wasn't like that," the ax said. "You were barely even people."

"The Old Kingdom nobles used to say that, too."

"We were taking care of you."

Loch gave Arikayurichi a hard smile. "Thanks, awfully."

As the floor bucked hard, Loch caught her balance again. Veiled Lightning fell back as well.

"I'm sorry, but we're running short on time," said the ax, shifting the last few inches into Gentle Thunder's dead hand. "Nothing personal."

The corpse rose to its feet.

Veiled Lightning stepped between it and Loch, shaking and weak. "It is absolutely personal."

Arikayurichi swung, and Veiled Lightning moved, flowing like water *past* the ax-head and pivoting, and then the Nine-Ringed Dragon came up in a perfect arc.

Arikayurichi flew through the air and into the chasm, still in the grip of a hand severed cleanly just past the wrist.

"Thunder taught me that move, you bastard," Veiled Lightning said, and fell to her knees.

Loch looked down at Ghylspwr. "So, what about you? Any last plan to distract me and then cut me down?"

"*Kun-kabynalti—*"

"Don't." She chopped the air with her palm. "Don't tell me you were trying to save lives. Don't tell me it was for the greater good. You picked your side. You helped your friend get Heaven's Spire ready to blow up half the Republic."

She turned and walked back to the console.

"I have no idea what happens if I don't let this energy out," she said, "but I doubt it'll be worse than what you wanted me to do."

"*Besyn larveth'is?*"

"Now we wait."

Dairy stood by Mister Dragon, now in his still-very-large human form, and looked up at Heaven's Spire overhead. The underside of the city was now a brilliant white, shining like the sun on an overcast day. Every crystal in the courtyard of the Temple of Butterflies hummed with a faint crackling energy.

"Is there anything we can do?" he asked Mister Dragon.

Mister Dragon smiled gently. "Your alchemist, your illusionist, and your death priestess are doing all they can down here. If there is any way for them to stop the Temple of Butterflies from amplifying the blast, they will find it." He looked up at the city, one hand shielding his eyes.

He smelled *very* good.

"What about you, sir?" Dairy asked. "You know more about this magic than most."

Mister Dragon shook his head. "I am not a creature of subtlety, my young man. I believe you will find that out yourself, if you are willing." He grinned, and Dairy's stomach went a little funny, but not in a bad way. "I could tear this temple apart, if I wished, but for all we know, that would cause the very explosion we were trying to prevent."

"Then why wait?" came a dry voice, and Dairy looked over to see Ululenia sauntering over. She was a woman again, and her dress was white, but it had a mark on the hip that wasn't normally there. "You and your young man should get a room."

Mister Dragon shot her a look, and Ululenia shot him one back. Dairy didn't know what it all meant.

He did know that Ululenia was his friend, though.

"I'll just be a moment," Dairy said, and pulled away from Mister Dragon. The large man nodded gravely, then went back to watching Heaven's Spire overhead.

Ululenia raised an eyebrow as he approached. *I do not need your pity, Dairy. You made your feelings clear, and I am pleased you have found happiness.*

"What price?" Dairy asked.

Ululenia blinked.

"I don't know what you mean," she said aloud.

"You talked about a price when we were riding Mister Dragon. You never said what it was." Dairy pointed at your hip. "And now you have a black mask with antlers on it on your dress, and you're not as kind as you used to be."

"We all change, Dairy." Ululenia smiled. "After all, didn't you join the Knights of Gedesar?"

It was meant to hurt him, and a younger Dairy would have flinched from it.

"You still haven't told me what the price is," he said firmly, "and I'm worried. I would still like to be your friend, even if I don't sleep with you."

She blinked again, and then she looked away, grimacing.

Then she reached out a hand. *Here,* she said.

Dairy felt it wash over him all at once.

Skoreinis lunged in, antlers blazing with his aura, and Ululenia's horn blazed in response. They clashed, and they were talons and hooves, claws and tusks, all at once, shining in the little room as they struck. It was magical as much as physical, arrogant apples and buttery blueberries washing across both of their minds as they sought to bring the other low.

Then Ululenia fell, and Skoreinis stood over her, and he laughed. "You fight well for one unblooded, unicorn, but you were overmatched from the start."

"I know," said Ululenia, and drew the silver dagger that the Knights of Gedesar had used on her from the pocket of her dress. It burned, even through the leather she had wrapped around the hilt, and her hand blistered.

As did Skoreinis's flesh as it sank into his chest.

He stammered, and then he was silent, and then he laughed.

And then his magic fell into bits of light, and the bits of light fell into Ululenia.

Dairy stepped back, blinking and shaking his head.

"He is inside me now," Ululenia said. "His anger, his cruelty, all of it. I am still me, but . . ."

"You're growing up," Dairy said. "It makes you different, but you don't have to let it make you evil. It's hard, sometimes, and you'll make mistakes, but you'll be all right."

Ululenia smiled and shut her eyes. "Damn you, Dairy," she said, looking away and wiping her face. "You could have just ignored it, like the rest."

"I care about you, Ululenia. You're my friend." He took her hand again. "If you still want to be, that is."

"As the wolf cub nosing at his mother's flank, only to flinch back when he sees her muzzle, you . . ." She pulled him in and held him tightly for a moment. "Thank you," she whispered, and her cheeks were wet.

Heaven's Spire flared a brilliant purple-white, so bright that everyone in the courtyard had to look away, and a wave of energy flashed out in all directions.

Dairy felt it wash over him, tingling like a spray of cool water.

Then it passed, and the courtyard was dark again.

Dairy looked up at Heaven's Spire, and saw that it hung in the sky, safely dark again.

Ululenia let him go, and smiled, her pale skin glowing in the now-dark sky. "Go slay your dragon, Rybindaris."

Dairy smiled a little nervously and turned to Mister Dragon, who was looking at Heaven's Spire as well, pleased and apparently unworried.

"Well, then," Mister Dragon said, letting out a long and happy sigh, "my young man and I will need a room."

When the complete and utter blackness of the room gave way to the faint glimmer of runes on the floor again, Loch saw that Ghylspwr was no longer on the floor.

Archvoyant Bertram stood, his eyes glassy and blank, with Ghylspwr held in a careful two-handed grip. He looked at Loch for a long moment.

Then, without a word, he stepped off the edge of the chasm and plunged into the darkness below.

"What happened?" Veiled Lightning asked groggily. The last moments had flung them all around the room like rag dolls.

"Looks like we're not exploding," Loch said.

Pyvic groaned, as did Cevirt on the far side of the room.

"What now, then?" Veiled Lightning asked.

Loch let out a long breath and got back to her feet. "Now we put things right."

Epilogue

As the sun rose on the Temple of Butterflies, Loch stood in the courtyard next to Pyvic, looking up to where Veiled Lightning and General Jade Blossom stood at the top of the steps.

"This is a mistake," Pyvic said very quietly.

"Could be," Loch admitted, "but not as big as it'd be if we waited for the diplomats to come down. We make the deal now, them and us, and the diplomats will at least have to work within whatever we come up with."

"So we stole an airship—"

"—commandeered—"

"—just because you're afraid of the diplomats screwing this up."

Loch looked over at him, leaned in, and kissed him gently. "Yes."

He hugged her once, then let go as she stepped back. "All right. You beat her at cards. I assume you know whether she'll be willing to take the elven manuscript in return for ceasing hostilities."

Loch took a breath, looked up the stairs at Veiled Lightning and the general, and started walking, with Pyvic at her side.

"You know I cheated to beat her at cards, right?" she asked without moving her lips.

"Then I guess you'd better cheat now, too," Pyvic said quietly, and Loch smiled back at him and hoped that all he saw in her face was the stress of preparing for negotiation.

The others were around as well. As concerns turned from technical to diplomatic, Desidora was investigating the runes and crystals running through the Temple of Butterflies, while Mister Dragon stood beside a flushed but *very* happy-looking Dairy, watching the proceedings with interest. Tern and Hessler, who had helped commandeer the airship, were checking the walls for any damage. Imperial guards watched them all nervously, with Icy Fist acting as mediator.

As Loch and Pyvic reached the top of the steps, General Jade Blossom stepped forward. "You enter the presence of Imperial Princess Veiled Lightning, Gift of Heaven and heir to the Empire."

Veiled Lightning had had a bath and a change of outfits since last night, which was more than Loch had gotten. Her dress was once again deep lavender cut with violet. The Nine-Ringed Dragon rode at her hip.

"Your Highness." Loch bowed. "General."

"The last time you entered this temple," General Blossom said, "you desecrated the inner sanctum and assaulted the princess."

"To be fair," Loch said without missing a beat, "she kind of brought that upon herself."

General Jade Blossom's mouth moved in what someone with more observational ability than political savvy would have suggested was an attempt to hide a smile. "And the time before *that*, you led a scouting unit that attacked this temple."

"Only because some brilliant Imperial military strategist decided to park her troops in the middle of said temple without admitting it," Loch said.

This time, it was Veiled Lightning hiding a smile.

"Next time, I will make sure to send a polite letter your way," General Jade Blossom said. "Your crimes against the Empire are facts known to all."

"Nevertheless," Veiled Lightning said, raising an arm to check General Blossom, "our two great nations have both suffered losses from this scourge of undead. The Empire has no wish for more death to follow so quickly."

"Provided," General Blossom added, speaking right over Veiled Lightning's raised arm, "that it can be assured that Heaven's Spire will not be used as a weapon again."

"Granted," Loch said. "The *lapiscaelum* that fell to the ground last night, we offer to you freely, that you might study its magic, lest you be concerned about us violating our agreement and wish to develop defenses against just such an attack in the future."

The courtyard went silent and still for a moment.

"We already *had* that," General Jade Blossom said after a moment.

"And now we're letting you keep it," Pyvic said, smiling cheerfully.

"While your generous offer goes far in healing the harm done to both nations," Veiled Lightning said dryly, "we cannot be satisfied with that alone. As a gesture of faith and friendship between our two nations, I remind you of several Imperial treasures taken illegally from our borders. I believe there is one in particular, an elven manuscript, whose return would show all the assembled that this is the dawn of peace between our two nations. Can you give us that manuscript, Isafesira de Lochenville?"

Loch looked over at Pyvic, let out a long breath, and stepped forward to the two Imperial women, her hand going to her belt.

"No," she said.

"What?" Pyvic barked behind her.

"What?" Veiled Lightning barked in front of her.

Loch drew her knife from her belt and passed it to General Blossom. "I cannot give you what I have already given away, and while I don't know that the elves are the rightful owners, what with passing the dwarves a fake, they've got a better claim to it than I do."

"Loch!" Pyvic snapped. *"What the hell are you doing?"*

"Good question," Veiled Lightning said, her stare never leaving Loch.

"I believe the original peace agreement between the Empire and Heaven's Spire hinged upon me surrendering myself into Imperial custody," Loch said, "to answer charges of turning Heaven's Spire into a weapon and committing hostile acts. I stand ready to . . ."

Loch trailed off at a sudden poke at her back.

She turned. "Damn it, Pyvic, this was the only . . ."

Then she looked down and saw the bolt, its barbed head protruding dead center from her chest.

"Oh," she said, and fell.

Nystin lifted the crossbow in triumph as Isafesira de Lochenville dropped to the ground.

He'd waited all night.

The other Imperial guards had thought he'd been with the Republic group, and he'd stayed out of sight of anyone who could have recognized him, biding his time. He had no armor and no weapons. Attacking an Imperial guard would have yielded something, but the risk had been too great. After days locked into the service of that *thing*, Nystin wasn't at his best. His hands were shaking, clenching and unclenching all by themselves, and he found himself giggling and twitching when he didn't pay attention to things.

None of that mattered, though, because he had *known* that when they'd all gathered in the courtyard, he'd have a chance. He'd *known* that the little alchemist would get excited about the flamecannons and leave her crossbow resting on the battlements where anyone could just go pick it up.

And he'd *known* he'd get one last chance at Loch.

They all pooled around the woman now, just like the blood pooled around her. As the Imperial guards wrenched the crossbow from his grasp and drove him to the ground with fists and the butts of their weapons, Nystin kept his eyes fixed upon her.

Justicar Pyvic, traitor to his own, stepped away, pale and shaking, and looked at Nystin with murder in his eyes. The death priestess dashed out from the inner sanctum, her face deadly pale, and when she reached the crowd, it parted for her, all save the Imperial princess, who knelt by Loch.

"She is dead," Veiled Lightning said, her voice ringing clearly through the courtyard.

Nystin began to laugh. One of the guards hit him. Off at the edge of his vision, the mousy little alchemist picked up her crossbow and looked at Nystin, her eyes huge behind her spectacles.

"Do you think you need to tell me that?" the death priestess asked, and even from where she stood across the courtyard, Nystin felt the chill in the air. The runes on the walls slid into the shape of skulls and gargoyles. "She died in Imperial custody."

"You will receive reparations," Veiled Lightning snapped, and stood, wiping the blood from her hands. "Unless you wish to destroy the peace she was willing to surrender herself for."

The death priestess paused.

"Diz," said Loch's little Urujar lieutenant from the doorway of the inner sanctum.

The walls slid back into their normal shapes, and the death priestess shook her head. "I will see her body preserved for a proper burial at her family's estate."

Justicar Pyvic dropped to his knees then, and the death priestess put her hand on his shoulder, and Nystin laughed until the darkness overtook him once and for all.

"Repairs are currently underway," the griffon said to the crowd gathered around the puppet stage. "Interim Archvoyant Cevirt anticipates that all parts of Heaven's Spire should have light and water again by the end of the day."

"Damage is reportedly light," the dragon added, "and temples of all faiths have invited any citizen suffering from injuries to request help. If you find anyone who is unable to reach a temple themselves, please contact the justicars or go to the temples directly, and help will be dispatched."

The manticore, looking very subdued, was the last to speak. "We still have no sign of Archvoyant Bertram, who is presumed dead after the attack that damaged Heaven's

Spire and nearly sparked a full-out war with the Empire." He turned to the dragon and added, "Although really, when you consider the attacks by the undead—"

"That's enough!" the griffon yelled. "I was against escalating hostilities this entire time, and seeing that this may have been the work of independent organizations trying to provoke a fight between our two great nations simply shows that—"

The dragon snorted out a tiny puff of flame, and both of the other puppets went silent.

"We ask that everyone keep watch closely," the dragon said, looking out into the crowd, "as we continue to investigate. Remember, it's your republic."

"Stay informed!" the crowd shouted back.

At the edge of the crowd, an elf in a heavy green cloak rubbed a ring on one hand and smiled thoughtfully. Perhaps the humans would change this time.

Stranger things had happened.

Acknowledgments

No work this large can be written on its own. My thanks go out to my alpha readers, all of whom provided excellent feedback when I was floundering around the idea of writing my very first sequel: Jennifer Whitson, Christina Grenhart, Susan Peterman, Ritzy Foxx, and Matthew Breen. David Hale Smith, my agent, and David Pomerico, my editor, made the clunky parts significantly less clunky, and were very kind about giving me the time and suggestions to make this something I was proud of. Greg Rucka managed to keep me alive in multiplayer sessions while *also* getting me comfortable with managing the emotional contract one makes with the reader in a sequel with returning characters.

I would also like to thank David Gaider, Cori May, and my wife, Karin, all of whom I owe drinks for the good lines I stole from them.

Many others helped with location checking, internal consistency, and all the other fun and exciting things that happen when you come back to the world for a second time.

Finally, I would also like to thank the readers who cared about what happened to Loch and her gang enough to give them another shot.

Thanks, all. I couldn't have done this without all of you.

Post-Script

"*And clear!*" Icy Fist shouted from somewhere.

Loch felt the worst pain in her life, a surge of power all through her body that wrenched her upright.

"Easy," Pyvic said, holding her as she shook and shivered for a moment. He pulled her shirt closed. "Easy, there. I missed you."

"Bad luck," Loch mumbled. They were in the woods, all of them gathered in a small clearing. Loch smelled evergreen trees and fresh water and ice that came from mountains. Woods not far from the Temple of Butterflies.

"Welcome back to the living," Desidora said, her hair a few shades darker than normal.

"You . . ." Loch coughed. "You . . . what?"

Desidora's hair eased back to its normal auburn. "Slowed your heart down to basically nothing. You were, for all intents and purposes, dead."

"I was able to shock your heart into starting again," Icy said, rubbing his hands briskly. "It is an interesting technique. I am pleased that I remembered it correctly."

"When was the last time you had to do that?" Tern asked.

"Oh, never. But I read about it perhaps a dozen years ago."

"Well. Glad it worked, then."

"I got *shot*," Loch said, staring down at her chest.

"Pff." Tern lifted her crossbow. "You got shot with a stage-craft bolt. Reinforced paper tip strong enough to carry it in flight, but the head crumples on impact, leaving just these tiny barbs that stick to make it look good. I added a little sleep dust from my knockout darts to put you down."

"It was sticking out of the *front* of my *chest*," Loch said.

Hessler coughed.

"*Best illusionist boyfriend ever*," Tern added, wrapping her arm around him.

"Nystin actually only hit you in the shoulder," Hessler added. "I had to make it look good."

"And it did look good," Veiled Lightning said as she stepped into the clearing. "Had I not known you employed a wide range of thieves and cheats in your gang, I would never have suspected."

"You knew?" Pyvic asked.

"I also knew she had three knaves," Veiled Lightning said, "but *I* wasn't going to beat the elf, and she seemed to know what she was doing."

"Really? But . . ." Loch pulled her shirt closed and looked up at Veiled Lightning, trying to get her mind working again. She pushed herself up, and Pyvic helped her to her feet. "*I* didn't know. About this. I didn't . . ." She turned to Pyvic. "You *let them* let Nystin shoot me?"

Pyvic shrugged. "My part of the plan was to shout, '*What the hell are you doing?*' if you tried something noble and self-sacrificial instead of giving the manuscript over. Tern said she'd take care of the rest."

Loch looked at Tern.

"I *may* have gone through your bags as we were getting ready to ride the Dragon," she said. "Speaking of which, how are you this morning, Dairy?"

"Just fine, ma'am," Dairy said, grinning from ear to ear. Ululenia harrumphed.

"Good. Anyway, you didn't have the book, so I told the others that there was a chance you were going to do something stupid, and we all agreed that we'd stop you if that proved to be the case."

Loch looked back at Pyvic. "Trying to keep the Republic and the Empire from war is *stupid?*"

"*I* said noble and self-sacrificial," he said.

"Drink some juice," Icy said. "You need to elevate your body's energies again."

"Why? For prison?" Loch gestured at Veiled Lightning.

"Oh, please," the princess said, waving absently. "You being dead takes care of everything. As far as the Empire is concerned, you're one troublesome political prisoner erased. We have the *lapiscaelum*, so there's a good chance that we can actually calm down and stop agitating for war now, as long as your side does the same."

"The Republic just lost a proud patriot who was preparing to surrender herself to bring about peace," Pyvic said. "If the voyants can't work with that, I'll get us some new ones who can."

"So . . ." Loch looked around at all of them slowly. "You all had a plan to take me down?"

"You'd do the same for us," Tern said with absolute sincerity, and Loch found herself smiling.

"Damn right I would." She put her arm around Pyvic. "So, since you all appear to be a bit ahead of me on this, what's the plan?"

Desidora's face went slightly pale. "Ghylspwr is still missing. I have a number of very firm questions for him." Kail put his arm around her, and her skin went rosy again. "And I could use some help. It might be dangerous."

"I was tired of being a lapitect, anyway," Hessler said. "This sounds much closer to stealing. Also, Desidora and I have ideas on how to ward you against detection from the daemon carrying Jyelle's memories and emotional impulses." He paused. "I understand that it's natural to think that it actually *is* Jyelle, but—"

"I'm just happy we're presumably stealing something besides the damn book this time," Tern added.

"Speaking of which . . ." Dairy coughed. "Mister Dragon has offered to share any information he finds while studying the manuscript."

"I'll keep an ear to the ground up on Heaven's Spire," Pyvic said, and nodded to Veiled Lightning. "We're willing to share information if you are."

The princess smiled. "I'll see what I can do."

"I'll probably need a sword," Loch added.

"Don't push it." Veiled Lightning sauntered back through the trees, turning to call over her shoulder, "I'll be in touch."

"I should go, too," Pyvic said. "The rest have already left their positions, but they're expecting me back up on Heaven's Spire to help with repairs."

"You all left your positions in a single afternoon?" Loch asked.

Tern coughed.

"It's been a week," Dairy said.

Loch shut her eyes. "You killed me for a *week*?"

"It had to look good!" Tern shouted.

"It looked wonderful," Hessler said. "That was my job."

Tern glared at him. "How did *I* know the princess was going to go for it?"

"In any case," Loch said, "I believe we have some ancients to locate and thwart."

She looked at Pyvic, who smiled sadly.

"Don't say it," he said.

"You did."

"You were dead."

"For a week, apparently."

He kissed her, and she held him long enough for his warmth to seep in.

Then she let him leave the clearing and go back to the job, which she knew was where he needed to be to give them the best chance of success.

Still, though.

"I'll miss you," she said, very, very quietly.

Then she turned to her gang, who stood waiting for her expectantly.

"All right, then," she said. "Let's get to work."

About the Author

Baos Photography, 2010

Patrick Weekes was born in the San Francisco Bay Area and attended Stanford University, where he received both a BA and an MA in English literature.

In 2005, Patrick joined BioWare's writing team in Alberta, Canada. Since then, he's worked on all three games in the Mass Effect trilogy, where he helped write characters like Mordin, Tali, and Samantha Traynor. He is now working with the Dragon Age team on the third game in the critically acclaimed series. He has written tie-in fiction for both series, including Tali's issue in Dark Horse Comics' Mass Effect: Homeworlds series and *Dragon Age: Masked Empire*.

Patrick lives in Edmonton with his wife, Karin, his two Lego-and-video-game-obsessed sons, and (currently) nine rescued animals. In his spare time, he takes on unrealistic Lego-building projects, practices Kenpo Karate, and embarrasses himself in video games.

Made in the USA
Monee, IL
15 April 2024

56612552R10298